DEAR FRIENDS

DEAR FRIENDS

Tom McHale

DOUBLEDAY & COMPANY, INC.
GARDEN CITY, NEW YORK
1982

To my family and especially to *Marie*

ISBN: 0-385-03503-9
Library of Congress Catalog Card Number 79-8566

Copyright © 1982 by Tom McHale
ALL RIGHTS RESERVED
PRINTED IN THE UNITED STATES OF AMERICA
FIRST EDITION

Contents

PART I

The Suicide
on the
River Charles

CHAPTER 1

Postmortem
on Manfredi

Later, in February of that memorable winter, when the numb-
ness of his mind receded and Sutherland wondered if he would
ever have a reason to laugh again in life, he began to think
about Manfredi. But which Manfredi? Manfredi, demented,
who had rushed back from Italy in the grip of a powerful
dream to recapture a lost American past that had rendered
them all dazed, then frightened, then finally pitying?

Or Manfredi of the pious peasant ethic, caught and floun-
dering confused in the maelstrom of his own moral nature? A
shared maelstrom that had dragged Sutherland down with him
into a netherworld of hit men and death threats and elusive
game playing with the police—a place in which no up-and-
coming Boston civil-liberties lawyer ought ever to be seen lurking.

Or Manfredi the malevolent who had retreated with a dark
passion into the Italian North End and terrorized them with
whispered threats of retribution and stalked Sutherland's pregnant wife through Back Bay streets and parks? Or Manfredi—
the old Manfredi—of the vast loving-kindness and the endless
generous giving who had been condemned to death by a tribu-
nal of teary-eyed judges? There were many Manfredis. A
different one for everyone who knew him, it seemed. For

Sutherland's purposes, when it came to fixing the reality of his Manfredi Occhapenti, the only certainty that occurred to him was that Manfredi had unwittingly signed his own death warrant that afternoon two days before Christmas when he touched down on American soil on the daily Alitalia flight from Rome.

Sutherland's pity was bottomless when he thought of the reason for Manfredi's return.

CHAPTER 2

The
Christmas Blizzard

The plane, winging out of the east, had beaten the storm to Boston.

It snowed everywhere in New England that night: the front had come west from the Rockies, clogging, then closing, the long straight ribbons of the midwestern turnpikes in its progress. Now it was stalled in a wide band that stretched from the middle of New York state out into the Atlantic. The apologetic meteorologist on the 11 P.M. news predicted the snow would continue until well into the next afternoon, then bade his wife go to bed and not wait up for him.

Sutherland hoped his son would not decide to be born this night. On impulse he left his chair to draw back the curtain and stare out into the howling swirl that obliterated much of the familiar Boston landscape. Fourteen stories below, Storrow Drive was empty but for the lights of two plows receding slowly downtown. Beyond, on the Esplanade between the drive and the River Charles, the gooseneck arc lamps danced in the wind and the pools of light they gave off hopscotched across the snow.

Across the Charles in Cambridge the lights of the M.I.T. complex were a vague blur, and the realization that the lights were so near, yet almost invisible, heightened his anxiety about the baby's impending arrival. Sutherland, who was born of New Hampshire farmers and had long since chosen this as his favorite season, decided he would gladly forgo the winter carnival spirit of his heart for a hot, sticky night in July. Otherwise, he saw himself delivering his own son in the rear seat of the snowbound car. That image sent a tremor through him: Childbirth was mystery enough without being compounded by ravaging nature. And this promised son would be his firstborn.

He drew the curtain closed, flicked off the television in the midst of the weatherman's recap, mounted the stairs to their bedroom and slid naked beneath the covers beside Jane. She stirred slightly as he settled himself and he winced with the thought he had awakened her. But she slept on after a moment of ragged snoring, nine months pregnant, seven months married, her body naked and heaving slightly, the mound of his son in her belly heaving with the rest of her. He watched her, an unworried part of him as content with the sight of her as with anything he could remember in life. Then he kissed her softly good night. This woman is heaven-sent, he thought for perhaps—what?—the millionth time? since she launched what had to be Boston's most unorthodox chase after a husband.

"You blew it, James. I'm awake," she announced with a yawn. "I was covertly watching to see what you'd do. I can read the perspiration and terror in your expectant father's face." She pulled herself up against the headboard of the bed and fixed him with her special look of mock contempt. "You're a real late-twentieth-century Yankee lawyer, aren't you? Brainwashed by the American Medical Association, victim of that same bunch of quacks you're always dragging into court to blow holes in the prosecution's argument. Tsk! Tsk! All babies aren't born in hospitals, you know. What do you think Eskimo women do during a little inclement weather? Fly down to Seattle on their Blue Cross plan?"

He whistled his exasperation, staring blank-eyed at the ceiling. "This isn't a little inclement weather, Janie my love. It's a major blizzard. And I don't know anything about delivering babies in the backseats of cars."

He rose on one elbow, petitioning her with his left hand outstretched as he would a trial jury: "What if I bungled it and was responsible for the death of my own son? How do you think I'd feel?"

"Not nearly as bad as if your own son came out a daughter instead. Remember husband, I've been warning you for months to temper that childlike happiness of yours. Thirty-six isn't the tenderest of ages any longer. A cavalier type that's known his share of the bitter and the sweet the way you have shouldn't be putting all his eggs in one Greek Easter basket when one of the best pediatricians in town told me we're going to have a girl."

Then she began to laugh. It was her most effortless joke these days. An old aproned waiter in their favorite Greek restaurant had gravely taken down all their known genealogy and disappeared into the kitchen to work his computations. In fifteen minutes he emerged, bearing plates of cold souvlaki but smiling broadly with the announcement that theirs was to be a male offspring. Sutherland, effusive with thanks at hearing precisely what he wanted to hear, had tipped the man generously. Jane thought he had just been diddled and dismissed the waiter's prediction with a wave of her hand. It troubled Sutherland that she bore his child so casually, had no particular preference as to its sex.

"Constantinos the owner says that guy bats right-handed better than ninety per cent of the time," he reminded her for perhaps the hundredth time. He knew he was pleading. She was silent a moment, then exhaled a long sigh, audible above the rattling bedroom window.

"James, I have some bad news for you, I'm afraid. Remember how you got so anxious waiting for the old guy's verdict that you had to get up and go for a pee?"

"I remember going to the men's room. Yes. I'd drunk a lot of wine."

"Well, while you were gone, all the waiters, cooks, pot wallopers and baklava bakers were laughing and leering through the kitchen door window at me like the old guy had just figured out I was going to give birth to a gnu or something even more bestial. I didn't have the heart to tell you then. We're a funny Greek joke. Night, love."

"We're never going back to that place, Jane," he assured her. But there was no response. She was lying prone again and fell back to sleep while he determinedly rekindled his belief in his unborn son. Before he slept, Sutherland's last thought was to wonder if it was also snowing in Rome. When the darkness descended, he was picturing the great piazza in the curved arms of the colonnade before St. Peter's. A gentle snow fell and for once there were no tourists. Only the fiacre horses, their bent backs covered with woolen blankets, and two separate clusters of shawl-covered nuns, shuffling slowly toward the basilica. Manfredi stood there also, dragging on a Gauloise, his lips framed by his eternal half-bemused smile. A woman stood beside him, her arm through the crook of his arm, but from as far away as Boston, Sutherland could not tell if the woman was Manfredi's wife. Yet there was no reason to suspect she was not, because for all Manfredi's infernal attractiveness to women, he was scrupulously faithful to his wives. In any case the woman's identity was of minimal concern to Sutherland right now; more than anything he puzzled over the intrusion— for the last two months running—of Manfredi Occhapenti into his final waking thoughts.

CHAPTER 3

The Midlife Wakefulness

Sutherland came alive to complete wakefulness at 4 A.M. as he had each morning for the past two or three years. He wondered if this was the midlife crisis. At first he had fought against the wakefulness with doses of scotch or pills, cursing the robbery of his precious sleep. Older men, senior partners in the two law firms he had belonged to before he had finally settled on private practice, had predicted the wakefulness. They were family men in their late forties with careers secured at last who had begun casting an appraising eye about the junior echelon of their fiefdom at the onset of their time of patronage. In at least two instances that gaze had fallen upon Sutherland.

Now when he thought of those two men and their wives and his own amused, even contemptuous, response to the solicitude they had shown, Sutherland could only wince with loathing at the memory of how the old Sutherland had been. These early mornings he found himself often recalling his past, if only because it made the present seem that much more gratifying. Back then his would-be patrons were lavishing free advice on a bona fide cutthroat opportunist: a Harvard Law degree from hardscrabble farm roots who stalked the Boston landscape in impudent pursuit of reputation, money, a surfeit of power and a glittering vacuous ornament of a wife that was the numbingly beautiful Edith, Jane's predecessor. Taking stock at one point along the way, he realized he had acquired very nearly everything he had set his sights on at the beginning of his career and marriage, and had acquired also into the bargain a yoke of inexplicable misery that accompanied him everywhere. Later he would be forced to see his life for what he had actually made of it: a hollow, resounding, beautifully packaged interior, that he had neglected to provision with the proper emotional goods. Once recognized, disturbing glimpses of his own mortality began turning up in the kaleidoscope of his confusion in the early darkness: persistently, his bright lawyer's mind came up with totally defensible propositions for the joys of suicide.

Lord, the tinselly self-delusion of those days! All that gathering of accouterments and contacts and club memberships to bolster the isinglass framework of what purported to be a successful marriage. In the end, when the framework collapsed and the marriage was done and he and Edith had gone their separate, embittered ways, the scales finally fell from his eyes. Alas for the things he had not understood. . . . The stunning realization that for years the erstwhile cuckolder had been cuckolded all along came to him during one of his 4 A.M. awakenings. (It had come to him in other ways too: friends, he found, were ever so sagacious about having spotted the structural weaknesses once it was too late to do anything about them.)

These days, however, the early-morning advent of the unassailable law of his body was different. There was no morbidity now, no scotch and no pills, and he took advantage of the dependable forty minutes or so afforded him until he would ease back into sleep to do the clearest thinking of his day. The hulks of problems crumbled to mounds of discernible building blocks that Sutherland's mind rearranged with swift dexterity into solutions. Balky trial cases came suddenly to him with machine-tool precision. But these days, after all, Sutherland was happier than he had ever thought possible in life, and certainly thinking more clearly. In consequence, everything—the ease of his profession, the peace of his mind, his delirious expectancy of the birth of his son when he had always sworn he never meant to father a child—all went along with the package.

He felt it was all the gift of Jane, that happiness. She had once been Jane Winters Occhapenti, for six years the first wife of Manfredi Occhapenti, whom Sutherland's blurred sleepy vision had earlier left standing before St. Peter's in a snowstorm. Happily for all concerned, the trade-offs had not been complete in the aftermath of Sutherland's and Jane's nearly simultaneous divorces. Edith had not gone to Manfredi. Edith had gone to nobody so far (though not for a lack of trying), despite all her money and her glacial beauty (that other men had kept professing to find attractive as long as she was married to Sutherland), because nobody seemed to want her. Before he left the country for Italy, Manfredi had married a Greek beauty from Chicopee, New Hampshire, named Marlena Avgerinos, who absorbed the news of the return to Rome effortlessly since she hated the New England winters anyhow.

Sutherland slid out of bed, threw on a robe, and walked across the room through the thick carpeting to stare out at the storm through the open slit of curtain covering the wide expanse of floor-to-ceiling glass that looked out on the Charles.

The windows no longer rattled in their frames. The snow still fell heavily, but now there was no wind and the visibility was improved. Directly across from their apartment was the tallest building of the M.I.T. campus on Memorial Drive, and squinting through the storm Sutherland could just discern its pattern of lights left illuminated for the Christmas-season nights—an enormous Latin cross that was eleven stories tall. The perfect cheerless tribute of that teeming race of scientists on the opposite bank of the river to the Savior's birth amused him for a long moment until he remembered that this very day, December 24, was his own birthday and he was thirty-seven years old.

The realization was hardly convulsing. Not anything like his feeling that he had just crossed the River Styx when he turned thirty in the midst of his marriage to Edith. Then he never expected to make fifty. Wished never to make fifty, perhaps: he could never quite decide. Socially prominent, Edith had given him a surprise birthday party, peopled by the waxy desiccated older couples she favored whom Sutherland always joked could snub the surprise reveler in Poe's "Masque of the Red Death"

into leaving the ball. Fitfully depressed, getting drunk and con-
tentious the way no consort to a very rich wife ever should,
Sutherland left, went into the kitchen locker for two bottles of
champagne and climbed the steps of Edith's great Beacon Hill
house to the unheated attic for a little revelry on his own. For
good measure he stopped along the way in their bedroom to
fetch a bottle of sleeping pills from Edith's medicine chest.

There, where nails punctured the roof, he drew an old
braided rug about his shoulders for warmth, sat down on a
trunk, opened the champagne, popped half a bottle of pills,
and made out his will. He left everything except his Lhamborghini and his beach house, to his parents, two garrulous old
people who farmed granite up in New Hampshire on the
shores of Winnipesaukee near Laconia, admonishing them to
use the money to at least spruce up the place a bit since he
conceded they meant to draw their last breaths there. (They
clung to the land like peasants of legend. Since leaving law
school Sutherland had tried repeatedly to buy them out and
set them up someplace down in Florida where there was a
colony of Granite Staters, but they would have none of it.
Each hard-fought winter seemed to increase their resolve to
stay.)

The Lhamborghini he left to his girlfriend Maureen, with
fondness and affection. His only condition was a hopeful
request that she go once each year for five years on the anniver-
sary of his death to his favorite bar in Cambridge that he had
patronized steadily during his undergraduate and law school
days at Harvard and have a commemorative drink with George
McKitrick, the owner. George was probably Sutherland's best
friend and had lent him money uncomplainingly whenever
Sutherland was broke during those years at school.

But Sutherland had no doubt his request would be honored.
Maureen loved him though he did not love her back and that
once yearly trip to George's Place would assume the sacred
tones of a pilgrimage. She would be there if it meant flying in
from Bangkok for a single day and George would be there with
her and together they would have many more than one drink.
The thought of leaving behind two people he actually liked
presiding at a ceremony over his memory warmed him some-

how despite the twenty-degree chill of Edith's attic. If anything, he had too few friends to leave behind. Women were
sexual objects or otherwise uninteresting to him; most men
simply did not trust him. Anyhow, sweet Maureen and good,
kind George. Drink up, friends.

His beach house on the Cape he left to his sister Elaine.
Elaine who taught skiing in Colorado and licked her wounds
after her tempestuous and awful marriage to wife-beater Ste-
phen Clark Turner III.

Two summers before, after a despairing midnight phone call
from his sister, Sutherland had hopped a plane to Colorado
and walked in on the two of them unannounced when Ste-
phen Clark Turner III was practicing his handiwork on Elaine.
Like a good older brother should, Sutherland wound up and
broke his brother-in-law's nose with a roundhouse right. Predictably enough, Turner, who did not fight men, did not fight
back. He did not press charges either. Sutherland and Elaine
went scouting for a good local lawyer the same day and the
thing was concluded before the snows flew. Well, Lainey,
here's your consolation prize, Sutherland decided. Property
taxes and upkeep are minimal, so use the place instead of
selling it and move back East where you can keep an eye on
Mother and Dad. Find yourself a new husband, a New
Englander this time, and have those kids you always wanted.
Good-bye, Elaine.

That done, Elaine provided for, Sutherland felt not a little
warm and satisfied about that one, too.

He left detailed instructions about where and how he was to
be buried on the farm in New Hampshire.

Then he lay down and tried to die of exposure.

But after a while he realized it was no good. He was not yet
drunk enough to pass out and was only shivering agitatedly
from the cold instead. So he sat up, and as he finished the bottle of champagne and the rest of the pills, he wrote a thoughtful letter to his parents, forgiving them for everything they had
done to him as a child.

That done, the champagne drained to the dregs, he lay
down this time to die in earnest.

CHAPTER 4

McGivern

When he awoke, it was in response to the deft sharp kicks of Miss McGivern's shoe. An old Irishwoman, the housekeeper was Edith's only real friend and had worked for Edith's parents before her. She was mean as the dickens as far as Sutherland was concerned, and as loyal to Edith as a slave. (It was a natural progress from another life: She had once belonged to a now-defunct order of Catholic nuns called the Slaves of the Immaculate Conception. Once the order was disbanded, she looked elsewhere for a renewal of her vows and settled on a young virginal girl named Edith Watkins.) Now she wore her little old lady's black woolen winter coat against the chill of the attic. Her head was wrapped in a shawl that covered her face as well, except for the slit through which the two beady McGivern eyes glared down at him. With resignation he understood that he was not going to be allowed to die. In the rule book of McGivern's voracious Catholicism, suicide was a grave mortal sin.

"Well, Sutherland, what are you up to?" she rasped at him.

"If you must know, McGivern, I'm trying to die."

"Suicide, is it?"

"Yes." His teeth were chattering now and he shook uncontrollably in the cold that had dropped at least ten degrees since he had first entered the chosen death place. He raised a hand to study it carefully for frostbite and McGivern kicked him fiercely on his right kneecap.

"You traitor bastard, you! Poor Edith downstairs beside herself with worry callin' all over Boston tryin' to find out where you got yourself to. . . . It's damn ungrateful, that's what it is, after everything she's given you. And walkin' out on that nice party she threw when you were the guest of honor to boot. I never heard of such a thing!"

"McGivern," he warned her stonily, despite the chattering of his teeth, "don't kick me again. Hear? And it wasn't a nice party. It was a goddamn bore. Those friends of Edith comprise a tribe so remote it hasn't even been discovered yet. And she hasn't given me anything! Just a lot of clothes and cars and endless boring Lindholm trips to places like Antarctica and the Sahal in perfectly natural fraternity with people twice our age. . . . To say nothing of the rest of it, McGivern! Do you hear me, you old crone? To say nothing of the depressive stoop of my shoulders at thirty that wasn't there when I married Edith at twenty-five. And all the body heat I've expended trying to melt my way into the polar icecap of our marriage bed. . . . I've got a girlfriend, McGivern!" he told her defiantly, sitting up and deciding to save his hands from amputation by shoving them into his armpits for warming. "I've got a girlfriend! What do you think about that?"

"We know that, Sutherland," McGivern told him somewhat pityingly. "Her name is Maureen. We've known about her for over two years now. We also know about the pickup truck you keep hidden in your old man's barn up there in New Hampshire, the one you use for galavantin' all over the bush throwin' beer cans out the window. And we know about the house on the beach at the Cape that nobody else is supposed to know about, and them fishin' trips up to Gaspé with your friend Frazier when you buy all them nice salmon that you bring home from the Indians because you're too busy frolickin' with them ladies from Montreal to throw a line in the water . . ."

"What else do you know, McGivern?"

"I know everything, Sutherland."

"What, McGivern?"

She slid her hands almost imperceptibly down her cheeks and the woolen shawl covering most of her face slid imperceptibly behind them, revealing the beady dark eyes squinting almost closed above the flushed ridges of puffy old-lady cheeks. Her religious training, which Sutherland always supposed had little to do with the intellect, had prepared her to ferret out the secrets of the hearts of children. Over the years she had refined her talents somewhat on Edith and was pretty good with drunks.

Neither Edith nor her slave McGivern knew about Vogelmeister, though, Sutherland was quite certain. Vogelmeister was Sutherland's shrink, the salvation of his sanity (until now, of course; he would have some explaining to do to Vogelmeister, especially if they hauled him to Mass General to pump all the pills and booze out of his stomach) and the salvation of his career as well. In desperation some two years before he had rushed to Vogelmeister for help when something dire became apparent from the knuckle-whitening clench of his hand on the arm of his chair. The anger that he habitually turned inward upon himself at home, where he lived with Edith and McGivern, he frequently turned outward in the offices, where he could barely resist the temptation to throw some of the firm's prized clients through a twelfth-floor plate-glass window.

Vogelmeister, salvator, he understood everything. He joyed in wresting the minds of borderline psychotics back from the brink of the abyss. You paid for it, of course, but Vogelmeister dispensed bountiful cure. Secrecy was the patient's absolute prerogative, and adaptability was Volgelmeister's special forte —even to presiding over the lightening of Sutherland's heart in Sutherland's secret beach house when that was for a time the only place Sutherland thought he could really let his hair down. No, they did not know about Vogelmeister.

"Come on, McGivern," he smirked at her. "Tell me what you know."

"I'm savin' that knowledge for later, Sutherland, when I can use it to best advantage."

"There won't be a later, McGivern. You don't know the dark secret of Sutherland's heart and you won't ever find it out. After a time you'll die and go to your Catholic hell and burn in the awful fires because you'll draw your last breath full of curiosity instead of being full of contrition and reap the reward your catechism promises. You're twice doomed to failure, McGivern. Oh, how I pity you."

He pulled himself to his feet, wobbly from the pills and the booze, intending to make his way downstairs and phone Vogelmeister. But McGivern was on him in a flash, grasping at the lapels of his tux and shaking him like a straw doll. "What? What?" she screamed. "I want to know what you know that I don't! I want to know that dark secret of your heart!"

He shook with convulsive laughter in her face, thinking of his also burdened brother, Dimmesdale the clergyman in Hawthorne's *Scarlet Letter*, and wondered what the sainted shrink Vogelmeister might have done for him. Sutherland tried shoving her off, but she thrust him rudely to the floor, knocking the wind right out of him. Uncanny strength in an old lady. She was on top of him now, her breath that smelled endlessly of tea and stale cauliflower flooding into his face as she pounded on one of the studs of his shirtfront with the stubby heel of her little shoe. The stud thudded painfully into his chest, but Sutherland could not keep from laughing despite himself.

"Catherine! Dear Catherine, is he hurting you?"

It was Edith. She stood at the top of the stairs, her gloved left hand clutching the railing, her right hand grasping tentatively about her heart in one of her classic frail gestures—like the shy averting of her eyes or the raising of a fully extended hand to her throat to disguise the progress of a swallow down her thin, arched neck—that had attracted Sutherland to her in the first place. She wore her long hooded Russian sable cape though the hood lay back and her hair seemed unaccountably wet.

Her hair that was long and dark and hung curtain-straight to the level of her shoulders framed a thin white face of impossibly perfect bones. Despite wanting to die to get away from her, Sutherland still had to admit his wife was an extraordinarily beautiful woman. Even in the fifth year of a miserable mute marriage he still loved being seen with her.

In public places in Boston or New York, in restaurants or at the Symphony or the ballet, Sutherland basked in the animosity directed at him by other men for being with her.

When she had gone shopping in New York and found the sable cape the furrier tried to return her check, propositioned her instead with the cape if only he could have one full page of her wearing it in a *New Yorker* advertisement. She declined, of course, and the daunted furrier had to settle for the check after all.

In a four-star Paris restaurant a well-known American mobster had intercepted their bill and would hear no arguments. At the end, when they left, he stood angelic and reformed as an altar boy and kissed her hand with studied European eloquence. Weeks after when she read he had been bumped off by a rival mob she shook her head sadly in remembrance and Sutherland supposed that the earth that held the cavalier mobster's remains might even have trembled a little in joyful gratitude. The occasions were astonishing in number. Even Sutherland, who hated her, was susceptible to the pernicious aura she dispelled. He invariably had the fast flashy cars he savored repainted in the dark aristocratic tones of her special coloring. He made certain she would look right in them: Italian racing red was not an Edith color.

McGivern had gotten off him and stood wriggling her foot back into her bludgeon shoe. On the floor Sutherland had stopped laughing. It did not seem right to laugh around Edith.

"Edith, dearest," McGivern crooned, "your hair is wet."

"Oh, it's begun snowing, Catherine. The Mortons stayed behind when they saw I was upset after the others left the party. We walked over to the Common for a little air. We met a policeman on horseback and talked with him awhile. He was very nice. But what's happening here? Why is James lying on the floor?"

"Oh, that? He was tryin' to kill himself, the poor fool. . . . But Edith, you won't believe! He's kept something from us! He has a secret!"

The gloved hand that gripped the railing tightened its grip perceptibly; the one that tentatively fingered the area of her heart grabbed a handful of the rich sable. She approached, looking startled.

"Not the woman, Catherine?"

"No."

"The pickup truck?"

"No."

"The Gaspé trips?"

"No, not that either, Edith."

"The beach house?"

"No. It's something else."

"What is it, James? It's your duty as a husband to tell me. You can tell Edith."

He stared up at her blankly: how had he married this woman?

"I have no intention of telling you anything, Edith. And I want a divorce. Pronto!" The revolt was on: fuck her. He was getting out and taking his Lhamborghini with him. He pulled himself woozily to his feet. He would make his way downstairs, first phone Yellow Cab to send by a taxi, then alert Mass General that he would be by momentarily to have his stomach pumped. Lastly, he would contact Vogelmeister's answering service to tell the shrink where he might be found.

"A divorce is out of the question, James," Edith told him stonily. "Where are you going?"

"Downstairs to call a cab to take me to Mass General to have my stomach pumped."

"But why?"

"Because as far as I can recollect it contains about a quart of scotch, sixty sleeping pills, two magnums of champagne and a single cracker spread with caviar. That's a pretty fair reason, I'd say—"

"My God, Sutherland, you are a wild man," McGivern judged, shaking her head in wonderment. "Here, at least let me help you down the stairs or you'll be spendin' a couple weeks in traction as well."

He was suspicious of her solicitude, but he let himself be helped. Once downstairs she sat him down on a deep cushioned sofa where he began dozing almost immediately while she went to phone the cab and Mass General Hospital. When he awoke, he was a patient in a private room in Linwood, a plush sanitarium on a secluded reservation somewhere out near Wellesley, a place where, if he remembered correctly, some of the very best families sent their alcoholic members to dry out. They kept him there a week and a nurse of the McGivern variety was stationed outside the door twenty-four hours a day. There was no question of trying to get a phone call out to Vogelmeister.

During that week he reread the French realists he had enjoyed so much during his undergraduate days at Harvard. Otherwise there was nothing to sustain him but his secret. Each day sleek, lovely Edith came to visit him with the battleship McGivern hovering protectively nearby as ever. Each day they asked him to tell them his secret. Each day he smiled his best enigmatic smile and said nothing. But when they left his eyes misted over at the thought of how he loved his mad, fatherly psychiatrist Vogelmeister, to whom he had rushed in desperation some two years before when he felt himself to be hurtling out of control down a rickety track that could only be a dead end at a blank wall. Vogelmeister had shown him how to apply the brakes and begin the slow return. There was still a way to go, though.

His thoughts traveled back to the present, where he still stood at the window, gazing out at the white maelstrom of the blizzard, and found himself uttering a silent prayer. His prayer was that tonight was truly not the baby's time as Jane had assured him. An accident such as skidding off the road on the way to the hospital and losing the baby would spell real disaster to all his future plans.

CHAPTER 5

Edith at
First Christmas:
Christmas Eve

Two plows, perhaps the ones he had seen beating their way downtown hours before, moved now in the opposite direction up the drive toward Brighton and Watertown, the scrape of their blades on the asphalt loud and grating. Moments after they disappeared, the blurred flashings of their yellow warning lights turning a sudden sharp bend, a man materialized on the Esplanade below.

He had come from nowhere, it seemed, a startling apparition who must have stepped into the glow of the arc lamps from behind the trunk of a tree. Sutherland searched for footprints to convince himself of the man's reality and felt relief when he spied them—a long, lurching series of steps coming upriver from the direction of the Longfellow Bridge through what was now more than a foot of snow. He looked about for a dog, but there was none to be seen, and Sutherland gave in to an obvious perplexity: what the hell are you doing out there on the riverbank in the middle of a blizzard at four-fifteen in the morning? He was about to add "You dumb bastard" in a throwaway judgment, but then changed his mind after a minute of closer scrutiny.

The man was an unkempt and disheveled apparition, his long shaggy hair matted and wet from melting snow, his stooped shoulders clad in an overcoat many sizes too large for him. There was no way of knowing his age from that distance. Sutherland guessed he was a homeless derelict—one of the sad, broken men that he often saw sleeping on benches when he ran along the river early on summer mornings. Dependable warm-weather fixtures, fueled on cheap wine, they departed for unknown indoor places after the night of the first frost. But this one, perhaps for some private reason, had chosen not to join mid-October's migration.

Directly opposite the apartment building the apparition stood stock-still now, staring upward, Sutherland imagined, exactly at the level of their penthouse bedroom. It was as if he knew somehow that Sutherland, many stories above him, half hidden behind a curtain in an unlighted room on a moonless night, was there watching him. Uncanny telepathy, if such a thing were possible, given the hour, the darkness, the elements, the distance and not least of all the fact that their apartment sat astride a modern innocuous building that shared the river frontage with perhaps ten or twelve others nearly identical. Why mine? Why me? Sutherland was puzzled, almost giving way to an absurd self-protective gesture such as pulling the open notch of curtain entirely closed. But the man abruptly turned and struggled off upriver without a backward glance. In another minute he was gone from sight and just as quickly chased from Sutherland's mind except for a vague prayer that he not die of exposure this night. Edith returned to his thoughts. She was going to make a holiday visit. This was something he had not anticipated. He didn't like her appearing in the first year of his new marriage.

He disliked thinking of Edith, but sighed resignedly at the certainty that like the ghost of Christmas past she would probably show up at this time of year to haunt the joy of his new start in life. Vogelmeister had called this shot though Sutherland at first had been unwilling to believe him. It was simply not possible to banish someone from memory with the wave of a hand when that someone had taken out a ten-year ironclad lease on your emotions.

Christmas had been her special season, the time of year she withdrew briefly into her house from the regimen of the Boston social calendar in the closeted company of her bought husband Sutherland and her slavish companion McGivern. To wreak havoc, not to celebrate. The first year of their marriage there had been no warning of the fireworks that were to go off on Christmas morning. She went disarmingly into the holiday. The night before there had been tender toasts, then a quiet informal dinner before a crackling fire with McGivern, who always ate with them when there were no guests, and whom Sutherland had not yet come to despise.

All three laughed and joked over Sutherland's and Edith's curious courtship, passing lightly over Sutherland's father Archibald (who embarrassed Sutherland) (whom Edith despised) (who had actually pinched ex-nun McGivern's ass at the tented wedding reception and sent her toppling into a just-refilled silver punch bowl).

Later, after McGivern had set the stage for them to be quietly alone, she departed in a battery of patronizing winks intended to suggest, Sutherland supposed, that this was the best of all possible nights for them to put that much vaunted youthful concupiscence to the test. Neither needed much prompting, Sutherland remembered. They dimmed the lights and stoked the fire, put on the elemental soft, undistracting music and made ecstatic love on a fur rug while the glow of flames flickered over their bodies. That night, for the first time ever, Edith was like a tigress in the sack, as if she were somehow bent on besting invisible rivals. Sutherland's notion of a frightened young wife (though actually she was two years older than he) needing to be made familiar and trusting in her new husband was completely dispelled by her passion. Afterward she slept while he watched the flames across the milky-white curves of her body, an indissoluble smile on his face from thinking that her towering reserve had finally been broken, that all sexual encounters in their thus far tentative and groping marriage would ever afterward be this satisfying.

He should have known better. It was just an odd night out, a once-a-year fluke. The duenna McGivern even gave verbal testimony to the fact, though at the time Sutherland had not understood her meaning. Hearing a creak in the ancient parquet floor he turned and looked up to see the beady-eyed housekeeper regarding them from the darkness just beyond the feathering edges of the fire's illumination. Her sudden presence startled him to modesty at first and he rushed to cover his sex with a sweater cast off on the floor beside him, wondering at the same time how long this ghostly intrusion had been standing there: clad in a floor-length white nightgown and brilliantine black robe with a kind of white skullcap tied beneath her chin, she reminded him of a Dominican prioress from an earlier century come to check on the princess's bedchamber. He resisted the urge to laugh at her anomaly until he remembered she was not supposed to be there at all.

"What is it, Miss McGivern? What do you want? How long have you been standing there?"

"Long enough to see that you know how to do what a good man is supposed to do, Mr. Sutherland."

Then he did laugh: "How kind of you, Miss McGivern. You're just the most invaluable helper any young couple getting started in life ever had."

But she rushed on, oblivious to his judgment: "She needed that, poor dear. Her mother, the wicked bitch, at least knew what she was about when she picked you for Edith."

Now he did not laugh: "She didn't pick me, Miss McGivern. She introduced us. Edith and I chose each other."

Edith began to snore. McGivern began to cackle: "A lot you know about things, Sutherland."

"What do you mean, McGivern?" After he had said it, he realized they had just closed the door on formalities. Except before guests or Edith he would never be addressed as "Mr. Sutherland" again.

"I said, what do you mean by that statement. McGivern?"

"You don't need to know, Sutherland. Just do your duty 'n' things'll work out fine."

He threw aside the sweater and leaped to his feet to stand before her, stark naked with his hands planted on his hips. She was not intimidated; a flickering smile of approval crossed her face as her eyes traveled his body.

"Duty?" he hissed at her in a low whisper so Edith would not awaken. "You work here, McGivern! Not me! This is my house!"

"Is it, Sutherland?" she hissed right back. "Well, you waltz on down to the lawyers one of these fine days 'n' see if you can find your name on the deed. In the meantime let's get dear Edith up to a proper bed before the poor thing catches her death of cold."

McGivern started forward toward the naked form, but Sutherland took a firm grip on her fleshy arm: "Go to bed, McGivern. I'll take care of my wife. Even if it is my duty, I'd intended to do it anyhow."

She sighed heavily, lowering her eyes: "Sutherland, I didn't come here to be your enemy. It's just that you've got to understand. . . . Edith is—well, she's such a curious—a different— well, a frightened child, if you understand my meanin'. . . . Oh what's the use? I don't have the education to explain it to you. Your mother-in-law, that whore Miz Watkins, said you was adaptable. . . . I just hope you're adaptable enough, lad."

"Of course I'm adaptable, McGivern. Why wouldn't I be?"

"We'll see, Sutherland," she sighed heavily again. "You haven't been through a tomorrow yet. It'll be a real eye-opener for you, I expect, your first tomorrow."

"What's tomorrow?"

"Christmas for everybody else. For us, it's gonna be somethin' else again. Here, take your wife 'n' carry her upstairs. I'll lead the way with this candle so we won't have to turn on the lights 'n' wake poor Edith."

Sutherland considered his adaptableness as McGivern produced a candle from the pocket of her robe and lit it from the fireplace. Then he shrugged his compliance, covered Edith with the ends of the fur rug and lifted her in his arms, follow-

ing after McGivern and her flickering candle through the darkness toward the spiral staircase. Poor Edith snored on without
interruption.

This is all very Arthurian, Sutherland thought, barely resist-
ing the urge to laugh as he watched their grotesque, enormous
shadows mounting the stairwell at some ritual pace: the ancient prioress leading the stark-naked knight who bore the
sleeping (snoring) princess in his arms upward to the safety of
their tower bedchamber (later: dungeon).

What a strange place it is we live in, Sutherland remembered thinking just before he fell asleep later that night. Again,
he had yet to learn.

CHAPTER 6

Edith at First Christmas: Christmas Day

The next morning on waking Sutherland was deceived into thinking that the universal Christmas promise of peace and love and hope had left its mark on his doorpost despite McGivern's grim forebodings of the night before. He awoke about eight-thirty in the dull gray morning to the stomach-churning odors of roasting turkey wafting upstairs from the kitchen. Edith still lay beside him, her face angelic in a rarely seen peaceful sleep. (By day it had the masklike composure of flawless marble; by night, sleeping, demons often invaded her and the mask writhed and twisted and cries and whimpers escaped her lips.) Sutherland thought he loved her very much at that moment, saw the future unwind before him in a stack of perfect abstractions: perfect wife, children, status and affluence —Sutherland, the complete professional Bostonian. The sight of the first of his nine Christmas Lhamborghinis in the drive below was the icing on his many-tiered cake. His heart leaped and his nostrils flared as he surveyed the gleaming Burgundy-brown wheeled weapon for the highway wars. And what had he done to earn it? Not much of anything, he absolutely gloried in thinking.

He might have known better. Nothing for nothing in this life.

Sutherland dressed while Edith slept. He went downstairs to join McGivern in the kitchen for a light breakfast of toast and coffee. She had just returned from Christmas mass and was happy with that purer happiness that visits to churches always brought her—purer because the only other happiness Sutherland ever credited her with usually derived from somebody else's misfortune. Her mass, its prayers and its sacrament had also apparently obliterated any memory of their confrontation of the night before. He was addressed as Mr. Sutherland once again. She pecked his cheek and wished him a Merry Christmas as he produced a box from behind his back that contained his gift to her of an Irish-wool shawl. In turn she proudly presented him with a conservative striped tie that he suspected Edith had helped her choose since it was pure silk and not polyester. In another minute he sat sipping coffee at the large center-island zinc-top work table and laughed at McGivern's pirouetting as she tried to catch sight of herself wearing the shawl in the stainless steel of the kitchen sink.

"Do we have a surprise houseguest I don't know about, McGivern, or did somebody park that gorgeous Lhamborghini in our driveway so it wouldn't be whacked by a plow out on the street?"

He used the brogue on her. Today she was in the mood for more.

"Oh, now what do you think, Mr. Sutherland? It was brought by Santa himself."

Just then Santa came softly through the kitchen door, wearing a full-length robe over her nightgown, stunningly beautiful and, more pleasing still to Sutherland—looking more assured and self-possessed than at any time he had ever seen her.

"Merry Christmas, James. Merry Christmas, Catherine dear."

"Merry Christmas, Edith," they both chorused, McGivern pirouetting once more in her gift shawl for Edith's benefit while Sutherland shook his head in pretended disbelief at the generosity of his wife: "Why did you spend all that money on me, Edith?"

"Because quite simply I love you, James." She came up to him then, her breath smelling sweetly of one of the mouth washes that infested her dressing room along with the facial creams, perfumes and the rest, and kissed him passionately on the lips, so heedless of the duenna McGivern that Sutherland was unexpectedly embarrassed.

"Let's go look at your present, James," Edith invited, leading him out of the kitchen and through the house to the side entry and outdoors where a light wind blew the inch or so of powdery new snow about in swirls. She wore no shoes, and despite his admonition, she followed him raptly about the Lhamborghini's glittering flanks as he brushed the light dusting of flakes from the windows and peered in at the upholstery and instrument panel.

"Do you like it, James?" she asked. There was no apprehension in her voice. She stood barefoot in the brick driveway with the wind flopping at the light robe whose drawstring had come undone, the look of her face perfectly certain he had no recourse but to like it.

"What can I say, Edith? I'm so overwhelmed I can't describe my feelings."

He came up to her, intending again to wrap her in his arms, but she made for the open door of the house where McGivern stood dangling the Lhamborghini's keys.

"Let's take her out 'n' spin some wheels and wake up the fuckin' Christmas dead, Jimbo!"

She stood now with her hands planted firmly on her hips, tapping one bare foot impatiently in the snow. Her nostrils were flared and her eyes flashing and Sutherland suspected the demonic Christmas McGivern had hinted at the night before was upon them. He flashed a glance at the old housekeeper and saw that a grim look like dread had come into her eyes.

"Oh, Jesus, Mary 'n' Joseph, Mr. Sutherland! It's begun 'n' it's only nine-thirty in the mornin' this year! Don't let her drive the car! Promise me that!"

"I promise," Sutherland mumbled back, so astounded at the transformation in Edith that it was long moments before the scattered ends of a thought forming in his mind were able to group themselves. In all the time he had known her, he had never heard a coarse word pass Edith's lips.

"Edith, I don't like hearing that kind of language from you. It's not you."

"Too fuckin' bad, Jimbo. Today's Christmas and Edith is always raunchy on Christmas. Now let's get this mother movin' outta this driveway 'n' shock the shit outta some pious churchgoers!"

She pattered around the nose of the car to the passenger door and Sutherland found himself pleading with McGivern: "What do I do?"

But the housekeeper only beseeched heaven in response. "Oh, saints preserve them! The roads is icy 'n' the salt trucks ain't been out yet!"

They tore out of the driveway in a roar of throaty muffler in the Christmas-morning quiet, ran slithering on the icy cobbles through Louisburg Square, then off the Hill and down Beacon Street. Edith planted her wet feet on the opulent dashboard, and shoved a tape from a stack of about ten wrapped in a bright red Christmas ribbon into the tape deck. Janis Joplin began howling against the sacredness of the day in quadraphonic sound. Then the booze came out of the glove compartment and Sutherland could only groan, "Edith, for God sakes, it's too early for that stuff—"

"Fuck it! Drinkin' time is only arbitrary shit anyhow. Want a hit on this, James?"

"No."

"Suit yourself," she shrugged. The pint bottle had no label. When she opened it, he puzzled for a long moment at the smell that flooded the car then he knew it: "That's corn liquor. Where'd you get that stuff?"

"You forget, Jimbo, that our summer digs were next to that tumbledown farm you grew up on. It wasn't hard to come by after I turned a few tricks for one of the local shitkickers."

He turned to stare at her while she took a deep swig of the

white lightning, then wiped her mouth with the back of her hand after a great lip-smacking sigh. Just like a Granite State woodsman.

"Who was the guy, Edith?"

"What guy?"

"The shitkicker who was balling you."

"Never mind, Jimbo. He's long since died and gone away. . . ." She grew reflective when she said it, an unexpected mournful pause in her boisterous holiday celebration. He watched her a moment too long, his mind a battleground of jealousy of and sadness for her, until he suddenly had to hit the brakes hard at Arlington Street to avoid the center-island traffic light. That reflex threw them into a skid around the corner of the Public Gardens and they slithered across Arlington, neatly missing a parked pickup in Sutherland's thirty-thousand-dollar Christmas present. He gulped air to calm himself as he gained control of the Lhamborghini again and in time felt the knuckle-whitening clench of his hands on the wheel relax. They moved ahead placidly now and stopped without a skid for a light before the Ritz Carlton.

Sutherland turned to the Christmas Day aberration of his wife and spoke above the steady throb of the engine and Janis Joplin's howl: "There are things I thought I knew about your past, Edith, that I evidently don't—"

"And won't," she pronounced evenly, taking another long hit on the white lightning while she continued stomping her feet on the dash in time to the music. She had raised her robe and nightdress so that her long sleek legs were bare and when she turned to see the doorman at the Ritz eyeing them with perplexity, she held up the bottle and flexed one of her legs in invitation. She even slid a lace-embroidered garter up her leg from a formerly unseen place high on her thigh to complete the package. The doorman was not amused. Sutherland shook his head miserably and could only groan. He wanted to go home. The light changed and he eased the car forward toward Boylston Street, glad to be away from the Ritz. The tires gripped firmly on the icy street. Edith seemed disappointed at their progress, then angered.

"C'mon James, goddamn it, hit it! Christmas is supposed to be fun, remember?"

"Hey, Edith, love of my life, Christmas is supposed to be a quiet family time. Remember?"

"Not when you're spendin' Christmas with Edith, Jamie," she warned in a low voice full of menace, then deftly reached her bare leg over the low console and smashed her foot down hard on top of his that nudged at the accelerator.

The pedal hit the floor and the car shot forward, whipping onto Boylston Street and glancing off the low curb of the center island. He grabbed her leg and flung it back over the console: "Knock it off, goddamn you, Edith! What the hell are you trying to do, kill us? We could have flipped right over that island and landed this boat upside down on the roof. How would you feel about that?"

She thought a long moment: "Differently, I suppose. I mean, you'd be looking up at the instruments and the gearshift and the pedals and the steering wheel and all that shit. It'd take a little gettin' used to, wouldn't it, James?"

He stared at her, growing steadily more afraid that Edith was at last wriggling out of her cocoon, but evolving into something far less serendipitous than a fragile and lovely butterfly. He turned down the Christmas-morning Janis Joplin, but Edith turned it up again. She winked at him, a devilish look on her face inviting him to continue playing this child's game. He did, then she did. They were stalled out in the middle of Boylston Street, occasional curious cars moving slowly past them, until a police cruiser sidled up beside them.

"What's wrong, mac?" one cop demanded after rolling down his window. The sight of the cop instantly restored the trappings of propriety. In a rush he remembered he was in Boston and thought of law school, the future, his wife of fabled beauty (who now concentrated on frowsing up her hair like her closet-kept heroine Janis, and thus, blessedly, kept the bottle clamped between her knees where the cops could not see it), his allowance and their fine house and lied easily. "We're just flooded, Officer. That's all."

"Put on your warning lights and wait a few minutes, then try it."

"Thank you, Officer. Merry Christmas."

"Merry Christmas to you and the lady," the cop wished them, staring at long-legged Edith, who was apparently satisfied now that her hair was frowsy and tangled enough and had gone back to stomping at the dashboard to the accompaniment of the music. The police exchanged a shrug, then cruised off slowly up Boylston toward the Common. Sutherland took another deep breath to bring his near-panic under control, then got out of the car to check for damage while Edith returned to polishing off her bottle.

About twelve spokes of the right rear wheel were neatly snapped in two from the impact and the wheel was canted inward, nearly touching the housing at the top. He returned inside and exhaled a long sigh: "I'm afraid the joyriding is over, Edith darling. We're just about minus one wheel. We'll have to take it home very slowly."

"Oh, shit, Jimbo! You mean no more slippin' 'n' slidin'?"

"Exactly. The calm repose of Christmas is about to begin, Edith." He flicked off the tape deck decisively. "We're going back."

"Good." She brightened at the notion unexpectedly. But she had her reason: "This bottle's dead, Jimbo. Edith needs a refill." Then she touched a finger to the automatic window control and when it opened she flung out the dead bottle, which landed on the street but did not break, instead went slithering across the road under a parked car.

Sutherland started the car, moving it gingerly forward and feeling immediately the wobble in the right rear wheel.

"I don't want you to have anything else to drink, Edith, until just before Christmas dinner. Miss McGivern is fixing a wonderful turkey for us. She'll be very disappointed if you pass out before we sit down to table."

"No she won't, Jimbo. McGivern's been around a long time 'n' seen much. I always celebrate Christmas this way. I start about ten A.M. and conclude . . . when the conclusion comes. . . ." She spoke the last part through a shrill laughter, reveling in some private hysterical joke. Then she surged on: "I love Christmas, don't you, Jimbo? I love my way of celebrating it. That's why last year—well, I didn't think you were up to the level of Edith's festivities. I mean, you weren't Edith's husband yet. You might not have been so tolerant—"

He decided to seize control of the day here, recalling at the same time that she was emphatic he spend Christmas with his own family the year before: "What could you possibly do that I would think was intolerable, Edith? Janis Joplin and a pint of moonshine on Christmas morning is a bit of a letdown, and so is a mangled rear wheel on a Lhamborghini. But basically you're just too refined to do anything really intolerable, Edith darling." But then he added as an afterthought: "Don't do anything silly. . . ."

"Wait and see," she promised.

Then they were lurching back up Beacon Hill, the rear wheel pinging as if it were going to shear off the hub at any instant when Sutherland reached over reassuringly to pat the soft disheveled hair of his rich, beautiful wife. She responded by biting his hand as he swung the car into their driveway, keeping it clamped between her teeth until he saw drops of blood start to flow. Janis Joplin of minutes before was no competition for Sutherland howling in pain. Edith released his hand only when he stopped the car at the end of the driveway, where she bounded out the door and into the house while he looked after her with pain and amazement.

Thus began the first act of the first of the nine Christmases of the Lhamborghini.

CHAPTER 7

Edith at First Christmas: The Madness Contract

Act two began in as much time as it took McGivern, unbidden, to sally forth with a jug of moonshine from some unknowable place in the house that Sutherland was never to find in nine years of marriage. When he tried to put a stop to McGivern's delivery, the housekeeper actually pleaded with him: "Oh, Mr. Sutherland, don't be angry. It's just one day off in Edith's perfect, chaste and virtuous year. You've got to understand! It'll all be over by late this afternoon. . . ."

In response Sutherland grew analytical and decided to let the day's events play themselves out. There was something to be learned here among the Regency furnishings of their formal living room visited by incongruous intruders this Christmas Day. Discordant rock music in the season of sweet-voiced chorales and Edith, frowsy-haired and disheveled in her nightdress and robe, slumped in a chair before a blazing Yule log, slamming down the mean, awful firewater from the jug with her index finger crooked through the handle like a ridge runner. Sutherland sat opposite her and simply watched, looking for something—perhaps the key to the door that would unlock the remote, desperate parts of his wife.

In time, after nearly a half hour of drinking and staring reflectively into the flames crackling in the fireplace, Edith broke silence. But not before she glared at him for the first time ever as if she were appraising an adversary, a look he had never thought possible in shy, submissive Edith. Her words were slurred when she spoke: "Everybody needs a day off, Jimbo. This is the one day of the year I take mine. Wanna fight, turkey?"

"No, Edith, I just want you to pretend you're enjoying Christmas, if this is the way you have to do it."

She took another swig of the moonshine and a neat, precisely aimed stream erupted from between her teeth and began spattering his face and stinging his eyes. He could barely resist the temptation to stand up and smash her. McGivern, observing covertly from the corner of the room where she pretended to be occupied, came rushing toward him with a dustcloth that she shoved into his face to blot it dry. The dust made him sneeze instead. Blindly reaching out to push off the housekeeper, he snarled at her: "Get off me, you old bat!"

Then he looked up at her glowering over him with a heretofore unseen look that rivaled the one Edith had favored him with not a minute before.

"Don't even think about it, Sutherland! Not for one split instant!"

"About what?"

"About punishing Edith."

"I don't hit women," he told her bluntly.

"No, we didn't think you did. That's why you was chosen. A proper man'd make a punchin' bag outta poor, dear Edith on a day like today."

He scrutinized her for a long thoughtful moment, knowing unmistakably now that an enemy had surfaced, but not able to know then that she would be around for the next nine years to try alternately bullying him and challenging his masculinity in her terms of interpretation. She had brought a grim old Irish sickness to the environs of their marriage, he decided. Deep down she believed in the absolute servility of women.

"I take it, McGivern, that there are rules here? That the best is yet to come?"

She winked at him: "Now you've got it, Sutherland. Just keep remindin' yourself that the fever lasts but one day."

"What's next, then?"

"Christmas dinner. She symbolically destroys it."

It came to him in that moment that Edith, the animate Edith, had somehow slipped away in the midst of their exchange. She had become inanimate now though she sat easily within range of hearing and they viewed her as objectively as a percolating lab experiment. McGivern came closer and began whispering in his ear.

"It's that part, the destruction, I mean, that makes me cringe a bit at Edith's purposes. I mean, I always have to set the table with enough food for ten people—just think of the poor derelicts 'n' homeless children what could use it—'n' all that cookin' takes hours 'n' hours 'n' for what? To litter the dinin' room floor . . . to plaster the walls . . ." She looked around and shook her head gravely: "Things won't look the same after three this afternoon, I'll tell you, Sutherland. So prepare yourself. A lot will be broken, rugs 'n' furniture'll have to be sent out for cleanin' 'n' retouchin'. . . . The family portraits will all go out with the trash . . . strange, how she always goes after them ancestors of hers . . . 'n' the turkey . . . !"

"What happens to it, McGivern?" She had put her hand on his shoulder, supposing they were coconspirators evidently, her whispering voice coming very close to his face. He promptly removed the hand, encouraged the rest of her to move a distance away. He knew better than to participate in court intrigues with the likes of McGivern.

"What happens to the turkey, McGivern?"

A cold formality replaced her breathless conspiracy.

"I'd grab my drumstick as fast as I could, Sutherland, if I was you. Because the turkey goes into the fireplace 'n' gets itself immolated. A burnt offerin' is what it becomes."

"Is one privileged to know to whom the offering is proffered?"

"To the demon in Edith. Edith's Christmas demon."

He frowned his skepticism while she nodded her head in certainty at him. Her face was at once sagacious and convinced of what she spoke. He doubted any doctor had ever been consulted about Edith's Christmas demon. It derived, he supposed, from some chipped surface of Edith's psyche that was compliantly nurtured by the superstitious fatalism of McGivern's lowbrow religiosity. Edith evidently had a perfect right to her demon.

As they watched Edith grew sleepy and the jug abruptly slipped from her grip and toppled to the floor, spilling onto the magnificent Bokhara for a few long moments until McGivern snatched it upright and took it away to its hiding place. She returned in a few minutes more with a knitted coverlet and placed it over the shoulders of Edith who snored like a loud and ragged engine.

"Oh, Sutherland, it's gonna be an awful one this year!" McGivern pronounced. She drew her arms about herself as if for protection. "She hasn't snored this loud since her last year of boarding school when the terrible older man who introduced her to the patcheen went 'n' jilted her."

"What terrible man?" He was not a jealous or defending husband. Merely curious to know about this gap in Edith's past that was another missing part of the suddenly emerging puzzle about her.

"I can't tell you," she said emphatically. "I won't be responsible for any bloodshed by revealin' what I know."

He looked at her somewhat pityingly: "Don't be so dramatic, McGivern. Everybody has a past. Some of it's unsavory and some of it hurts. Do you actually think I'd go out and crucify the guy?"

"Any red-blooded husband would. That is, if he had a whit of manliness in him."

"You know something, McGivern? You are a pretty fucked-up lady yourself."

"I'm a good Catholic, Sutherland!" she rasped at him. "I always have been."

Sutherland sighed. The target she had unwittingly presented him was far too easy. He stood up and headed for the sane island of his study to phone Christmas greetings to his parents, calling to McGivern to rouse him again when the action resumed.

In the study, as he dialed the farm in New Hampshire, preparing to be comforted by the sounds of familiar voices, it occurred to him for the first time since his June wedding to Edith that he was lonely in his marriage. The child of the man within him wanted desperately to tell his two aged parents about the madness already set in motion downstairs. To spew it all out to someone who would see it from a Sutherland vantage point. But he knew he would not. They would have no sympathy for him.

His parents cared little for Edith, the girl next door. Worse, they despised his motive for marrying her. They were historically short on commiseration, these granite farmers, when a fool had been warned about the swamp ahead and plunged in anyhow. As he spoke with them he forced his voice to be emphatically merry, especially before he rang off. He pointedly neglected to tell them about his beautiful new Lhamborghini, and Edith was away at a church service and of course sent her best wishes. He might have sobbed for how rotten he felt.

With his sister Elaine in Colorado he was even more cautious. He got through to Aspen on the first try and had half the effort of seeming happy instantly relieved when her new house turned out to be full of laughing ski-bum revelers all of whom got on the phone one after another to wish him season's greetings. Just as well, too: their numbers, their boisterousness, voided Elaine's chance to go for Edith's jugular on the year's holiest day. Lord God, the savagery women reserved for each other! Elaine, though she loved him (revered-older-brother syndrome), would never forgive him his marriage to Edith. Edith in turn pretended Elaine simply did not exist.

On the night before his wedding his sister had actually dragged him away from a raucous bachelor party and urged him to flee in the night, before the morrow's event was consummated. She saw his future with Edith as a slough of misery. He saw it otherwise, despite some very calculated considerations, and chided her gently for being such a bleak visionary. She ended by weeping in frustration and flailing his chest with ineffectual fists. He left her whimpering softly beside the barn as he returned to his parents' house to erase the confrontation from his memory.

Now as he replaced the receiver in its cradle after bidding fond good-byes to his sister and brother-in-law of two years, Turner III, he was more determined than ever to prove Elaine's grim prophecy wrong. He forbade himself to feel sorry for himself. To his mind Edith's irrational Christmas Day self-abuse was the first instance of any real trouble in their marriage. Until then they had even managed to skim over the settling-in squabbles. So he would observe the afternoon's follow-up event that McGivern foretold, learn from it whatever there was to learn and find the means to make certain this was Edith's last Christmas in withdrawal. There would be children in the not too distant future, he anticipated; children could not be privy to a thing like this.

And one last item of business, he decided fiercely as he left the study to find his parka, intending to change the Lhamborghini's wounded wheel: McGivern had to go. He could not suffer that pernicious blob of hypocritical pieties with her slavish allegiance to Edith muddying up the waters of his marriage. In a flash of humor that set him to chuckling on the way out of the house, he even chose the day of her departure. For her, Ash Wednesday would be the cruelest day.

* * *

McGivern summoned him for Christmas dinner. Edith, already seated and waiting, looked just plain ghastly. As he took his place at the opposite end of the table she seemed suddenly an unaccountable distance away until it occurred to him that extra leaves had to have been added to accommodate the welter of dishes that would be required.

In moments more they began arriving, heaping bowls of a New England family Christmas dinner, borne with humble downcast eyes to the table by McGivern, who, instead of her maid's uniform, wore a simple black dress with lace collar and a cameo brooch for the event. It was all good elemental food made for streaking and staining: cranberry sauce, turnips, mounds of mashed potatoes (though they never ate potatoes), succotash, stuffings, wild rice and gravies, cauliflower and cream sauce, onions and cream sauce, peas and cream sauce, broccoli and cream sauce, carrots and cream sauce, red beets steaming and red beets pickled. . . . Sutherland, staring at the disheveled apparition of his wife, thought of little children in Roxbury perhaps sitting down to a Christmas dinner of Big Macs and french fries at McDonald's and at least had to give McGivern credit for her twinge of conscience. What an awesome waste this was all going to be.

Lastly, the turkey. Or two of them, to be precise. A twenty-pounder for Edith's immolation that was put directly on the table, and a smaller bird—perhaps less than ten pounds and intended for the two spectators—that McGivern carried to the sideboard, along with lesser portions of every vegetable that graced the table. The sprawl of foodstuffs that separated Sutherland from his wife were evidently for Edith's use alone. The housekeeper invited Sutherland to carve the sideboard turkey, but he declined, asking instead for several slices of white meat and a few small portions of anything else she recommended. She obliged him with turkey, a mountain of mashed potatoes with a crater lake of gravy in the middle, a scoop of succotash and a wedge of cranberry sauce. Her presentation was two-handed and suppliant, like her eyes beseeching his to remain calm and play by the rules. To her own place close to Sutherland at the table she carried a plate that contained only a drumstick and a mound of mashed potatoes.

Christmas dinner began.

Sutherland said grace and wished for peace in Vietnam.

McGivern responded with a pious "Amen." Edith weighed in with her own private judgment: "Shit on Christmas and Vietnam, too!" Then, in less than thirty seconds Edith had drained her crystal wineglass and thrown it against the wall between two of her ancestors' portraits where it shattered into tinkling slivers that rained down on the floor. A smile like vengeance being contemplated overcame her face, then she frowned as if she were trying to remember something flitting beyond the moonshine fog, and when she did apparently she turned to McGivern and commanded harshly: "Put on the Christmas music, you stupid old cow!"

"Yes, Edith, I'm sorry. I forgot. Forgive me, Edith, please," McGivern whined. She left her place and padded off to the library, where Sutherland heard her inserting a cassette into the stereo, then sighed resignedly when the Christmas music burst forth loud and clear and turned out to be Mussorgsky's "Pictures at an Exhibition." Edith swam dramatically into the current of sound and McGivern came back to the table at a trot: "C'mon, Sutherland, grab your plate 'n' let's clear out! The rage is just arrived!"

He believed her. They left the room, carrying cutlery, napkins and their plates of steaming food. Sutherland took the wine bottle and two glasses. McGivern went halfway up the hallway's spiral staircase and took a seat to watch Edith battle her ancestors through the open dining room door. Sutherland sat beside her, balancing his plate on his knees, thinking it was somehow not unlike witnessing a dinner theater production of *Marat/Sade*. McGivern watched delightedly and ate with relish, stopping between mouthfuls to exclaim: "Did you see that, Sutherland? Did you see how she clobbered her great-aunt Zenobia?"

"I always thought Zenobia was a very beautiful woman," Sutherland mourned. "It may be Edith's house, but it still seems criminal to permit a grown child on a tantrum to ruin a fine old portrait."

"Don't worry, Sutherland. Zenobia, Alfred, Theodore, Patience and all the others is reproductions, which is somethin' you'd know if you had any kind of an eye for paintin's. The

originals are all safely packed away up in the attic. I have to
remember to phone Donati in the spring 'n' tell him to come
for the originals."

"Who's Donati?"

"The hack who does the reproductions. You don't think
there's anybody alive who could restore them paintin's on the
wall in there after Edith gets done with 'em, do you?"

He supposed not. They continued watching Edith at her war
games with accompanying sound track. Crystal glasses and
Wedgwood plates flew one after another at the portraits. Then
drunken Edith lurched across the room from the table to the
walls carrying the bowls of creamed vegetables one at a time
and hurling them point-blank at her ancestors like a vaudeville
pie in the face. She muttered invectives all the while, garbled
for the most part except for the decipherable howl of the victim's name mounted on a brass plate at the base of the frame.
For no apparent reason she switched her tactic and threw the
gravy boat from the table, pitching it at great-grandfather
Theodore, though it missed and hit the wall between Theodore and Patience, spattering the contents in a wide arc.

"Don't worry, Sutherland," McGivern assured him, "the
wallpaper's washable. I had to see to that years ago."

In time the last thing left on the table was Edith's private
turkey. She seized it by the legs and went after her mother
with a vicious hatred, egged on by McGivern, who called down
from the staircase, "Let her have it, Edith darlin'! Slaughter
the miserable bitch!"

But Edith needed little encouragement. She flailed the turkey repeatedly at the portrait until the canvas ripped and the
frame fell clattering to the floor. Sutherland emitted a low
whistle.

"What's she getting even for, McGivern? Is that a fair question?"

"What indeed? All those Christmases past, that's what.
When her parents was always away in Bermuda or someplace
like that 'n' there was no one at home but the lonely two of us
in a big house with nobody in the family ever botherin' to call
us 'n' wish us a nice holiday. . . ."

"Why doesn't the turkey break apart?"

"Because it's wired together," she answered matter-of-factly through a spoonful of mashed potatoes. "Besides being rock-hard since I just brought it from the deep freeze. I cooked it two days ago. That's why it looks like it's just come out of the oven."

He only grunted in response. The preparation mechanics of Edith's Christmas purging were almost as fascinating as the purging itself. And what a purging at that! No wine-drunk, playful Greeks in a taverna smashing dishes in this house. Edith was content with nothing less than to charge right into the Watkinses' inner sanctum and destroy the family icons as well.

When she grew tired of bludgeoning her mother on the floor, she put down the board-stiff turkey on the edge of the carpeting and staggered and slipped through the mess she had made back to the table and her chair, where she sat down and wept bottomlessly onto her crossed arms. Sutherland began to rise from his perch, meaning to tell her it was all over now and put her to bed. But McGivern stayed him with a firm grip on his arm: "It's not over yet, Sutherland. Soon, but not yet. Her father is always last."

"Why him? He was a rather decent old guy, I thought." It did not seem necessary to add that he had died but four short months ago.

"He was a pig!" McGivern snarled. "He was a callous, indifferent son of a bitch who never cared a whit about my darling Edith. He never gave her anything!"

Sutherland looked about the house with its rich paneling and moldings and rugs and furniture and valuable paintings that he was certain by now were not going to suffer the same fate as Mother Watkins, the dining-room wallpaper and wain-scoting and the reproduction ancestor portraits. McGivern seemed to read his thoughts.

"All that isn't everything, Sutherland. Mark my words, it isn't everything at all. . . ."

In retrospect, Sutherland considered, it would turn out to be the wisest thing McGivern had ever said within his hearing.

He picked at the last slivers of his dry white turkey as Edith apparently approached climax. She sat up abruptly, then sprang from her chair and whipped the cloth from the table, spilling the last of the plates and dishes and two silver candlesticks to the floor. Then she went after her father with the carving knife from the sideboard, hacking and slashing at him until he too fell to the floor, his canvas-backed image in tatters, the frame's molding spewing apart at one corner. Lastly she retrieved the turkey from the floor, held it high above her head, her lips moving in some unknowable priestesslike incantation, before she hurled the frozen Christmas sacrifice into the fireplace, where it began to sputter and crackle almost instantly in the flames. Then she simply languished on the floor, falling crumpled and shrunken-looking into the mess of cream sauces and vegetables and began immediately to snore.

"It's over," McGivern exhaled a long sigh. "I'll just go in a little while and get the comforter to cover her. She'll sleep it off 'n' tomorrow she'll be good as new 'n' ready to be your faithful, lovin' wife for another year."

Sutherland blinked at the notion, his mind unable to focus on anything but the blur of seasons in between until the next Christmas pageant. He thought of his children once again: what of them? How many seasons to obliterate from their young minds the fact that their mother was a closet hoyden who took a fit every Christmas? That Christmas was a feast for punishing the defenseless dead? This had to cease if the union was to continue no matter what the fringe benefits.

"Next Christmas won't be like this, McGivern," he told her tonelessly.

"Wanna bet?"

"I'm putting my foot down. There'll be children in time. Do you think I want my children to see their mother acting like this?"

There was no sneer on her face now. Only a kind of pity for him: "If there are ever children here for Christmas, Sutherland, you'll have to rent them somewhere. You won't have children by Edith. She's not able to conceive, you poor thing."

"But—but—McGivern, we talked about it before we married. We often talked about it. She never said anything about being unable to have children. She wanted them badly—"

"Did she? Well, she wanted a husband even worse, Sutherland, to appease them awful parents of hers 'n' make sure her inheritance came through. She would've told him anything he wanted to hear. Edith can't have your kiddies because she had a hysterectomy when she was sixteen years old in boardin' school. The awful man who taught her to like the moonshine whiskey 'n' jilted her gave her a massive dose of the clap for good measure, you see. . . ."

She went on eating, but distractedly now avoiding the shock in his eyes, staring over the slow munching movement of her cheeks at prostrate and snoring Edith. No children. Abruptly Sutherland sailed his plate and the last of the food it contained over the staircase railing and against the nearest wall.

"Tsk! Tsk! You might make a better husband yet than we thought, Sutherland. However, that wallpaper ain't washable. It'll leave a stain."

He shrugged as he stood up: "It's not my house. Let's just call that flash of anger my contribution to Christmas. So that I won't forget what a fun holiday it was. So full of good news."

She smiled weakly, looking in on Edith and the carnage of the dining room: "Dearest Jesus, Sutherland, how could you ever forget? And mind you, despite my prediction, this just turned out to be a middlin' Christmas after all. . . ."

But it was over nonetheless. He left McGivern picking at the last of her mashed potatoes and strode off down the hallway to a closet for his parka. He exited the house, uncertain where he was going except that every impulse willed it had to be somewhere off the Hill. He found himself on Charles Street walking beneath tinkling holiday-light decorations toward the Longfellow Bridge and then decided he would head for Harvard Square.

He began to cross the bridge, pausing briefly in the bitter wind that came whipping up the Charles to turn and look back at the city. The antique bastion of Beacon Hill with the golden dome of the State House at its summit welled up before the towers of the financial district and the new high-rises near the waterfront. The Hill seemed suddenly a very foreign place to him. The elegant house peopled by the handsome Lhamborghini-driving couple and their slavish Irish housekeeper was no longer a lazy man's triumph. It was a trap instead. He had inadvertently willed himself into a high-class ghetto that for him was now as much a place of confinement as if all the exits were chained shut at night.

An immense self-loathing filled him and he did nothing to try to mollify it. Those Watkinses! They had sized him up correctly all right, then gone out and bought themselves a horse and not even a stud horse at that. Children: they had been an important part of his many-faceted dream of his perfect marriage. Then he snorted, shaking his head at the incredible naïveté he had brought to that marriage. All things considered, what were those children of the dream anyhow? No real objects of a passionate desire. No matter how hard he tried to conceive of them they never jelled into any more distinct forms than necessarily handsome and necessarily well-mannered blurred images. Stage props for the brilliant patina of a life Sutherland decided he was going to project to Boston and to the world. He laughed openly now: scratch one prop then. If people abounded who thought he was all that marvelously adaptable, surely he could find something to substitute for children.

The bridge began to rumble as a subway train emerged from the tunnel at the Cambridge end and passed slowly before him toward the Charles Street station. In the first car, except for the motorman in his cubicle, there was but a single young couple entwined about the shaft of a pole and each other, their joined and kissing faces smiling broadly at the pleasure. The sight of them made him jealous and angry and he wished he had a rock in hand to hurl at the passing train. But in moments more when the train was gone, the anger dissolved to a wretched burden of self-pity that he carried the whole distance through Cambridge along Broadway toward the back entrance of Harvard Yard. He passed the brightly lit wooden-frame houses of the Cambridge Portuguese and Hispanics. Music and laughter often sounded out of the houses to the street.

When he reached the Yard he went in through the Quincy Street gate. It seemed ages since he had been there, starting law school. Ages since he had squired the lovely Edith along these paths to one of their invariably cheap movie dates. He walked slowly past the statue of John Harvard seated immutably in his chair, then turned back on an impulse to stand looking upward at the chiseled face. The wind blew cold and raw, rattling the stiffened branches of naked trees, and the light snow had begun falling again.

Sutherland raised his arms to the founder and beseeched out loud: "Why me? Why did it have to end this way when I'm only twenty-six? I must have been the poorest kid who ever went through this fucking place. . . ." But the founder did not respond and when Sutherland turned about on hearing a sudden noise behind him, he saw that he was not alone in Harvard Yard on Christmas Day. Three foreign students—two African males so bundled against the cold that only the whites of their eyes were visible through layered wrappings of scarf, and an Indian woman who wore the light flowing sari covered by a heavy cloak, and only thin sandals on her feet—stared steadfastly at this American with his arms raised to the educator-god in an attitude of prayer. Sutherland hauled down the arms and jammed his hands sheepishly into the pockets of his parka. Then a witless laughter burst out of him that he could do nothing to control and he called out to them exuberantly: "Merry Christmas! Merry Christmas to you all!"

"Merry Christmas!" they rejoined. Then, unprompted, the Indian woman added: "We have just come from the traditional American Christmas dinner at Bickford's cafeteria. It was most enjoyable. . . ."

At Bickford's, he thought as the notion drained the smile from his face. With the transients, the lonely, the uninvited foreigners, the ones without family to go home to . . . while in Edith's house food and drink enough to welcome ten or fifteen of them littered and smeared the walls and floors!

"I wish I could have joined you," he told them mutely as he moved away, turning once to wave as they wished him a Merry Christmas yet another time. And if Edith tries the same stunt next year when I get finished reasoning with her, then I probably will join you. And be much the happier for it.

He left the Yard and started the trek back toward Boston. As he walked along, the recollection that he had completely forgotten to give Edith her Christmas present prompted a vengeful and somehow self-sustaining pleasure in him. Years later when he would learn a greater humanity and Jane had helped draw off his anger over the wasted years with Edith, he would often remember that he had not even thought to pity Edith the cruel loss of her fertility one little bit. The fact was that when she spoke eagerly of wanting those children, she really had meant it.

* * *

That night Edith slept in another bedroom. In the morning she came to him early, completely and magically restored, the frailty, the timidity, properly reinstated. He eyed her gravely as she removed her nightgown and climbed into bed beside him.

"Please hold me, James," she begged.

"I don't want you ever to do that again, Edith."

"I won't," she promised. "Not until next Christmas. It's not too much to ask. Just once a year." She stared at him earnestly and repeated the refrain he was to hear endlessly in the future: "James, everybody deserves just one day off."

"That was some day off, Edith. A real housewrecking. I think you ought to see a shrink."

She burrowed more closely against him: "A psychiatrist? No, James, we can't have that. People would find out. There'd be talk. I'd be embarrassed to go places if people were to find out."

"There's liable to be even more talk if somebody comes knocking on the door to this place some Christmas Day and finds out what's going on inside."

"They won't," she assured him in her special voice that never failed to convince him he had married the loneliest person he had ever met. "Nobody ever comes to visit Edith on Christmas. Christmas is the only day of the year I'm"—she searched for the word—"that I'm compromising—"

"I want a signed, notarized contract on that, Edith. I want it today."

"You'll have it, James."

"Good." Then: "Edith, McGivern told me we aren't going to have a family. She told me about the hysterectomy."

"I'm sorry, James. I'm sorry you had to find out that way. It was a terrible thing to keep from you. I was afraid I was going to lose you. But I'll make it up to you in other ways. Believe me I will."

He stifled a yawn: the money, he supposed. The amenities that came with the job of husbanding Edith Watkins Sutherland. On impulse he rose naked from the bed, went to the window and drew the curtain to peer out into the driveway.

"James . . . the neighbors! They might see you!"

"I want to see my Lhamborghini, Edith."

Outside the sun shone brightly, reflecting brilliant facets from the Lhamborghini's flanks. The tire with the splayed wheel spokes had evidently been taken away earlier that morning and an undamaged spare rested against the front bumper. Order restored, then. It was to be the same downstairs when they later went into the dining room for breakfast. This year's ancestor portraits were already hanging in place and the entire room looked as if the carnage of yesterday had simply been carried off like a portable movie set and replaced with the original. McGivern the day after Christmas was the same servile housekeeper as she had been the day before and Sutherland was Mr. Sutherland again.

After breakfast Sutherland drew up his contract with Edith, stating in effect that she had license to wreck the dining room of her own house on Christmas Day in exchange for a promise of reasonably good conduct for the remainder of the year. Then they went out and found a notary, a fat, balding man who puffed unhurriedly on a reeking cigar. The notary seemed baffled by the contract but he witnessed it anyhow, refusing to charge them his customary three-dollar fee and assuring them that the pleasure had been all his. Even as they left the office he was already dialing someone to tell them about what Sutherland would later refer to as the Madness Contract.

At dinner that evening Edith smiled lovingly across the table at him as she sipped her coffee: "James, do you know what? I'm going to give you a new Lhamborghini every Christmas from now on."

"That's wonderful, Edith," he smiled in return. "Really wonderful."

Looking back, he knew that the problem was he really meant it at the time. And with three hundred and sixty-four days of perfect behavior ahead of him, he decided he would manage to survive the forthcoming Christmas of the Lhamborghini. He made it for eight more. That was when he decided on a model change. He fell uncalculatingly in love with Jane Winters Occhapenti. At thirty-five years of age, it was a profound, profound surprise.

CHAPTER 8

Jane at First Christmas: Prinz Rupert's Attack

The apparition, lurching as before, reappeared as suddenly on the Esplanade as he had the first time. Again he seemed to come from nowhere. The sight of him brought Sutherland's mind back to a sudden sharp focus—away from the mellow pity he felt these days of his new marriage toward sick, lovely Edith, and the realization that major events always seemed to swim into his life at Christmastime. He drew back the curtain now to watch the derelict's progress northward toward the Longfellow Bridge, retracing his own footsteps measure for measure, but in the opposite direction.

Sutherland froze in the same self-protective instinct he had felt before. Once again the man stopped and gazed up in the direction of the windows of their apartment. He even moved a little sideways to put himself unmistakably opposite their building. Sutherland chided himself for giving way to such a paranoid notion, chuckling as he thought: It's me of all the citizenry of Boston that this guy is trying to communicate with only if he waves, lunkhead. . . .

But the apparition was apparently not trying to communicate with the expectant father, Sutherland. In the next instant he turned abruptly and began again his northward lurch through the snow, disappearing into the blizzard's whiteout. Sutherland wished him survival until dawn.

Edith returned to his mind again as he wondered who was going to get a Lhamborghini this Christmas. He also wondered who was going to do the ancestor-portrait reproductions this year since old Donati, the hack artist, had died sometime during last July. For himself there was a positive mirth in these considerations finally: thank God to see the humor of it now, when for nine years running he had seen only the madness, made worse by the fact that he had willingly abetted it, shrugged it off as just another clause in the marriage contract.

Curious, Sutherland thought, how no two women can mean the same thing to a man or enter a man's life in the identical fashion. Edith had flown in on the wings of a conspiracy, clutched tightly in the talons of her mother's fierce determination to set her up with a husband. She was a hapless burrowing creature delivered to his nest with a bankbook clamped between her teeth.

In the beginning he had loved her frailty and seen himself as her protector. In the case of Jane, on the other hand, it was her strength and aggression he learned to love. No shy conquest there. She had actually come charging into his life with an attack dog. It was two days before the Christmas of the Lhamborghini and her sudden appearance in Edith's mansion already tense with anticipation of the holiday housewrecking really sent Edith into the Christmas spirit. A whole day early, in fact.

He smiled at the memory. From where he stood he could see the very place that Jane had begun their courtship, the place where the German shepherd had brought him down while he was running along, deep in thought. His mind had been preoccupied with unraveling problems and steeling itself for the ordeal of Christmas when he caught sight of the vague black blur rushing at him from the right. In another moment he was on his hands and knees trying to crawl his way to escape across the slush-covered hardness of the winter lawn between the Esplanade pathways as the dog's owner screamed for it to stop.

The dog, for its own reasons, seemed intent on pulling his sweat pants from him. He looked back beyond the pearly glint of moonlight on his bare white buttocks to see the shepherd straining in the opposite direction to yank the elastic ankle clasp of the sweat pants over the heels of his track shoes. He saw the dog's owner advancing at a run across the slush, a woman wearing tall boots and a belted overcoat. Her head was covered by a scarf. She had been calling out commands in German all the way.

"Prinz Rupert!"

She grabbed at the dog's collar and hauled it backward with one deft heave: "Give that guy his pants back, you dumb mutherfuckin' dog!"

Sutherland leaped to his feet, outraged, though not quite totally outraged. He was still afraid of Prinz Rupert.

"Why don't you teach your damn dog to heel, lady?"

"Oh, I'm so sorry! I'm so very sorry! I just don't know what got into him. He's never done anything like this before . . ."

She was not German as he had assumed. And she was not sorry either. The tone of her voice told as much, to say nothing of the laughter in her eyes. As he stood there clad now in the sweat-suit top, a jockstrap and his track shoes with the sweat socks pulled down over the heels, he realized he also knew who she was—the about-to-be-ex-wife of his client Manfredi Occhapenti.

"Hello, Mrs. Occhapenti," he greeted her. "Rather balmy weather for this time of year, isn't it? Otherwise I'd be freezing my ass off right now, seeing how it's completely bared to the elements."

"You have a gorgeous ass, Mr. Sutherland. Very tight and firm and athletic. Exactly as I'd imagined it during all those lengthy and totally unnecessary depositions in your office. Lord knows there wasn't much else to think about during all that nonsense . . ."

How much had he skinned this one for? He squinted, trying to remember. A total of four depositions even though the last two were, indeed, totally unnecessary. Around eight thousand bucks if his memory served him correctly. She, like Edith, had all the money and was paying all the legal fees. In many ways, he had thought from the onset, his and Manfredi Occhapenti's situations had been analogous. They were both brothers after a fashion. It was one of the reasons he had taken the handsome Italian on as a client, then set about trying to shatter the ground rules of the complacent divorce agreement Occhapenti had already reached with his wife.

"Are you accusing me of unethical practices, Mrs. Occhapenti?"

"Yes." Her answer was unexpectedly matter-of-fact, but cheerful, he thought. Confident even: he wondered if she had already been in touch with the Bar Association Ethics Committee. Behind her, squatting in the slush, Prinz Rupert was oblivious of them. Instead he chewed Sutherland's sweat pants to ribbons, tearing off whole mouthfuls of cloth at a time and dropping them in a neat little pile. Other runners loped by, staring in mute perplexity at Sutherland's near-nakedness.

"That's a very serious charge, Mrs. Occhapenti. I don't like to put it this way, but people involved in divorce litigation are almost always under emotional duress. Their judgment is frequently unclear and distorted, to say nothing of being angry. Lawyers are used to this sort of insinuation. They become obvious targets for abuse as the process goes on—"

"Save it, Jimbo, okay? This is a lady publisher tycoon you're talking to, not some Newton hausfrau whose bottom just fell out of her life. The only kind of lawyers who matter for me are the corporate variety. You scavengers that feed on the trashy remnants of other people's lives are only a necessary evil in this archaic commonwealth as far as I'm concerned. When Manfredi and I decided on the divorce, we decided on the terms of settlement at the same time. It wasn't until you and your fellow shill, that loathsome tub of lard Morrison, started muddying up the waters and got poor Manfredi so confused that he couldn't remember what he'd agreed to in the first place, that our divorce became like everybody else's divorce."

"They're all the same, Mrs. Occhapenti. Some folks mount

big guns and other have a predilection for guerrilla raids, but when it comes down to the bottom line, there's been a war just the same." He was assuring her of this in his best chastening lawyerly voice—a voice he thought sounded tired and bored.

How many clients' arrows had he already deflected with that pitch? How many of them had he assured they were the hapless victims of an imbroglio larger than themselves that had to be played out to its own rhythms? You've been overwhelmed by nameless forces; otherwise you'd still have a marriage. See? He even had a special set of his jaw that went with the pitch. It was convincing, he knew, because he had often practiced it in front of a mirror. Now, impulsively, he reached up to check it. His jaw was in place, though sweaty. Only his client (well, almost his; his brother shill Morrison's actually) was not properly chastened. In fact, she seemed to be even laughing a little as she took out a cigarette and lit it. The same look of bemusement she had worn at the unnecessary depositions.

It had annoyed him at first, that look—the unflappableness, that complete lack of anxiety. Later it began to unnerve him and his mind kept searching around, looking for the one question, the nugget of a hot coal that would finally make her jump out of her seat in reaction. But he had not found it, she had not given way to emotion, and he had not forgotten her for it. Strange that he and this woman, who had been flitting in and out of his thoughts since then, should meet this way.

"Satisfied?" he asked, looking into her face again. He had been watching the toe of her boot tapping impatiently in the slush. He realized the tone of his voice was hopeful.

"Of course not. But what does it matter? The only reason you skinned me is because I let you, James."

"You paid for services rendered, Mrs. Occhapenti," he told her in a gruff voice.

She shrugged in response: "Have it your own way, James. I don't spend too much time looking backward. Not the way I suspect you do, that is. It only creates bitter spaces in the memory. The important thing right now is to get you home decently. Otherwise you're going to be the occasion of a lot of sniggering if you're seen trying to run up Beacon Hill in a jockstrap. Edith wouldn't like that, would she? Call me Jane, by the way, James."

"How do you know about Edith . . . uh, Jane?"

"I've asked around. Come on, James. I live in that building over there. You and Rupert and I can sneak down to the basement garage and I'll drive you home so you suffer no indignity."

They began walking toward one of the rampways that led over Storrow Drive to the tall, modern building where Sutherland would be living in less than a week. Rupert followed after them, dragging the unchewed remnant of Sutherland's sweat pants in his jaws. In some deference to modesty Sutherland pulled his sweat shirt down as far as it would go to cover his buttocks.

"What did they say?" he asked.

"Who?"

"The people you asked about Edith."

"Various things. But since most of them were said by other women who invariably thought no one had a right to be as beautiful as your wife, I took them with the grain of salt one must. One gentleman who's a mutual acquaintance of ours came closest, I think."

"What did he say?"

"Cool. But not sangfroid. 'Carrara marble' was his phrase for it. His name is Carmichael, by the way. It seems we both employ the same discreet accountant."

"Carmichael? Yes, he would put it that way," Sutherland thought out loud. Evidently you don't bite the hand that feeds you. But then he remembered something. "Carmichael wasn't your accountant during the deposition period, was he?"

"No. But he is now. His predecessor, in my opinion, was far too cooperative in supplying you with requested information."

"He had no choice," Sutherland told her. "I could have gotten a court order." He paused a long moment as they came to the end of the rampway that led down to the street behind her apartment building: "So you see, Jane, besides being the main event, divorce has a way of creating lots of peripheral severances, too."

"No more pontificating from you, Sutherland, or you run home. Just watch this lady's reaction to the sight of you, so you'll have an idea of how embarrassing that might prove. I know her. I guarantee you shock, outrage and titillation."

They had turned the corner of her building to the sidewalk that led to the garage doors. A matron in a fur coat strolled toward them, making for the crosswalk they had just left. She was evidently preparing to say hello to Jane when her eyes began traveling up and down Sutherland's form instead. Her mouth fell open, then began sputtering in its quest for words until the perfect words came out: "Mrs. Occhapenti . . . well, I never . . . and with a naked man of all things . . . this time—"

"Drop dead, Mrs. Brewster, will you? Put it in the building newsletter when you get your thoughts sorted out, why don't you? Only it better be accurate or I'll sue. His name is James Sutherland, a divorce-mill attorney, and as any fool can see he's half naked, not completely so. A mad dog unaccountably ripped off his sweat pants, but mercifully didn't leave any fang marks on his neat little ass, for which we have much to be thankful."

Taking a firm grip on his arm, Jane swung him about and patted his buttocks. Over his shoulder Sutherland caught sight of Mrs. Brewster's aghast face and started laughing. The woman reminded him of McGivern. Especially McGivern on the first real impropriety of his marriage to Edith, when she had opened the door late one night to find a very drunk Sutherland urinating on the doorstep.

"There are people in this building, Mrs. Occhapenti, who do not approve of the way you live. That business of you going off to work every day while Mr. Occhapenti stayed home did not sit well with a good number of people."

"I imagine, Mrs. Brewster. Especially not with that lynch mob of widows you pal around with. Given the fact that you all uniformly worked your husbands to death, you probably need every justification you can lay your hands on for sitting around idly battening on their willed portfolios. But of course, I didn't have the same options most of you did. Mr. Occhapenti was a very nice man, but never particularly ambitious. Oh, by the way, Mrs. Brewster, you'd better start calling me Ms. Winters, just to get yourself in the habit. My divorce will be final in about a month, no thanks to Mr. Sutherland here. He was Mr. Occhapenti's lawyer."

"You don't say!" She was no longer aghast or haughty. Like McGivern when she was after her prey, the eyes grew narrow and beady. "And . . . ?"

"And what, Mrs. Brewster?"

"Well, what are you going to do with him now that you've got him?"

"Take him home to his wife. He's already late for dinner."

"Oh, he's married." Her disappointment was keen.

"More's the pity," Jane sighed. "I'll be fully eligible in another month. This kind doesn't grow on trees, you know. They get scarcer as you get older."

"I know. My poor husband dropped in his tracks when he was fifty years old. I haven't had a proposal since then. One last question, Ms. Winters. Which car are you going to use? The Mercedes or the police car?"

"The police car I think. It's a sloppy night. Got it all now?"

"Oh yes, Ms. Winters. You've been so helpful. Good-bye for now. So nice to meet you, Mr. Sutherland. I do hope you get home safely."

She turned and hurried back toward the front of the building. Watching her, Jane released a long sigh: "Another rent in the fabric of Jane Winters Occhapenti is forthcoming when that woman starts in on the telephone tonight. God, what a pain in the ass she is! Oh, well, what does it matter? The only people who count for me are the maintenance guys and the doormen. They're all my friends."

But Sutherland was preoccupied: "What's this business about the police car? All I seem to remember from those depositions was a pretty posh Mercedes."

"It's a Boston Police reject I bought at an auction and use for zooming down bumpy country roads whenever I feel like letting down my hair."

"I have a pickup truck," he told her as she turned a key in

the electric lock and the building's garage doors began rising. "It's for pretty much the same reason."

"I know. It's blue and has four-wheel drive. I went for a ride in it last Sunday afternoon."

"Where?"

"Up in New Hampshire on your parents' farm. Your father took me out for a ride around the place after Sunday dinner. Your mother's a fine cook. It was a fantastic day. It was the first time in my life I was ever invited to Sunday dinner in a country kitchen."

They came to the Boston Police reject beside her Mercedes in a garage full of generally expensive cars. Sutherland looked across the roof line at her. He was puzzled but bemused at the same time.

"Why, may I ask, did you drive up to New Hampshire to visit my parents?"

"I didn't. I just happened to have a flat tire right in front of the place. I thought it was a remarkable coincidence, all things considered."

"You set this hound loose on me, too, didn't you?"

"I believe there are laws against that sort of thing, James." She climbed into the driver's seat and opened his door. Prinz Rupert bounded into the car before him and jumped to the rear seat. She started the junker and eased out of the parking place. In moments more they were on Beacon Street.

"I suppose you know where I live," he speculated.

"Yep. Nice house. Tell me something, James. How come your parents never get invited to your house for Christmas?"

"My wife and I prefer to spend Christmas alone."

"I guess. It would be rather embarrassing to have anyone else around when she starts tearing up the place the way she does every Christmas."

He whistled, his eyes beseeching upward: "Is it fair to ask how you know what you've just alleged?"

"There aren't too many secrets on Beacon Hill, James. Especially when you've got a battle-ax like that housekeeper of yours working for you. She talks."

Sutherland was laughing at the notion: "I'm astounded! I'm

absolutely astounded at that news. Dear Lord, Edith mustn't find out about it. It would be the ultimate betrayal. She'd absolutely pull the whole house down on us and Christmas is only two days away. Imagine that! Her devoted slave turns out to be the leak."

"The way I hear it, your devoted slave can't abide one-up-manship. She couldn't stand for anyone else in the house-keepers' corps to walk off with the cretinous mistress prize, so she blew the whistle on Edith."

They mounted the Hill in a roar of rusted mufflers and turned sharply into Sutherland's driveway. Jane stopped the car and shut off the ignition. McGivern was already at a window scrutinizing them. She wore her maid's uniform and Sutherland remembered with a wince that the Mortons would be arriving soon for drinks and dinner. He watched as she turned away from her spying and ran off to tell Edith that her husband was outside in a battered old car with a strange woman. At best though, she would be telling only part of the story: from her vantage point, the housekeeper could not have seen that he was not wearing his sweat pants.

"Thank you, Jane, for seeing me home."

"Aren't you going to invite me inside for a drink?"

"I would, but I don't think it's going to be particularly pleasant in there when Edith gets a look at us together in my condition. In fact, it's liable to be downright chilly."

"That's okay. I can take it. What I really want is a look at Edith."

"Suit yourself," Sutherland shrugged, climbing out of the car. Jane followed him to the front steps after ordering Prinz Rupert to stay. McGivern had the door open before he could press the doorbell. She almost collapsed as her eyes traveled up and down his bare legs.

"Good evening, McGivern. This is Ms. Winters. She was kind enough to drive me home after her German shepherd attacked me for no apparent reason and ripped my sweat pants right off me. I've invited her in for a drink."

McGivern put her finger to her lips and commanded silence. She came very close to Sutherland so that he could smell her cauliflower breath and her voice came out a harsh whisper: "God Almighty, Sutherland, don't let Edith see you like this! Hurry upstairs and dress for dinner! This woman'll have to come back some other time for her drink. The Mortons'll be here in a few minutes."

"Don't give me marching orders in my own house, McGivern!"

"Your own house? Find the deed! Find your name on it!"

The eternal refrain. How many times had she sung it to him or shouted it at him or whispered it?

"Out of my way, crone! Come on, Jane. What'll you have to drink?"

"A little bourbon and water would be fine, James." Her voice was not the least bit hesitant. There was a trilling sound to it that told she was going in to find what she had come looking for no matter what. As Sutherland went past McGivern she made a grab for his sweat shirt. She was desperate now. Her new warning was unmistakably fearful: "Sutherland . . . it's two days before Christmas. . . . I feel the holiday spirit comin' on quickly . . . if you know what I mean—"

"I know what you mean, McGivern. . . . So does Jane here. You've been gossiping a bit, old girl. The why and wherefore of the Sutherlands' secluded Christmas has spread all over the Hill and is making its inexorable way into every corner of the city by now. You've betrayed a sacred trust, McGivern. It's the Catholic hell fires for you, lady."

The beady eyes grew wide with an actual terror. But it had nothing to do with the hell fires: "Sutherland, please! If she finds out I'll be fired. Where will I go? What will I do? She needs me!"

"Catherine . . . ? Are the Mortons here?" It was Edith. She had come from somewhere in the rear of the house at the sound of voices, but Sutherland could tell she had not overheard his accusation of McGivern. For a long moment, giddy almost with the possibility of such cruelty, he thought of telling her, then decided against it. Pulling the rug out from under Edith like that might in the end produce a worse result than the Christmas homewrecking. And finally, being one up on McGivern was a tactical advantage no one who knew her should ever lose. It was that kind of three-member household he lived in, he thought sadly. Everyone needed some sort of leverage against the other two.

"Oh, she's beautiful . . . ," Jane Winters whispered beside him. Sutherland barely heard her. He was concentrating on the shock in Edith's face.

"James . . . Where are your sweat pants? Who is this person?"

"This is Ms. Winters, whose dog unexpectedly attacked me while I was running on the Esplanade and tore the pants right off me. She very kindly offered to drive me home to save us any embarrassment. That was a nice gesture, I think. I've very kindly invited her in for a drink."

"That wasn't wise. There's no time. The Mortons are coming," Edith snapped at him. He saw she was becoming quickly unnerved. She made plans for cocktails and dinners days in advance and ran them with stopwatch precision. The unexpected was her enemy and the unexpected had evidently just arrived in the form of her half-clothed husband and a strange woman who had no intention of leaving.

"James . . . Catherine shouldn't see you this way. It's very unsettling for her."

Since she stood right beside him, Sutherland turned to McGivern and asked her if she found his nakedness particularly unsettling. He saw her weighing her options carefully until she ground out the words: "Why, no, Mr. Sutherland. These sort of accidents can't be helped from time to time, can they? Thank the good Lord Ms. Winters was here to offer you a ride home."

"Good girl, McGivern," he congratulated her. "I really can't think of a reason not to offer Ms. Winters a drink, can you?"

He saw her scrutinizing Edith carefully. The planes and sharp angles of her boss's face were disassembling into the familiar sulk.

"Edith . . . ," McGivern begged. "It could have been

worse. . . . Think how many people might have seen him running through the streets like this. . . . We couldn't have that!"

In response, Edith spoke to Jane for the first time: "You really don't understand certain things, do you, Ms. Winters? I mean how it's best to withdraw when you sense that your presence is causing some sort of discomfort?"

"I guess I'm just plain lowbred, Mrs. Sutherland, and you'll have to forgive me for it. But I haven't found out everything I came to find out, so it's obviously not time to leave. See my point?"

"Who are you . . . ?" Edith whispered the words slowly, her voice laced with an edge like dread. She pressed the tips of her fingers tightly to her cheeks, draining pools of blood from around them, and the effect, accompanying the unnatural widening of her eyes, made her look crazed, Sutherland thought. He also thought the joke had suddenly gone too far and decided to put an end to it when, in the next instant, the doorbell rang.

"The Mortons!" McGivern hissed. "They're here!"

"I'll let them in," Jane offered, and before anyone else thought to stop her, she hurried to the door and opened it.

CHAPTER 9

Jane at First Christmas: The Mortons Are Good Friends

"Good evening, won't you come in? I'm Jane Winters," Jane beamed at Louie and Nancy Morton. "McGivern couldn't get the door because right now she's rigid with shock."

The Mortons, another of the desiccated sixtyish couples Edith favored, stepped through the doorway. Of all Edith's preferred circle, Sutherland supposed the Mortons were easiest to abide. They were nice drunks. There was no other way to say it. They were never quite inebriated, but they were never quite sober either. They came to parties and dinners and dances already primed, wearing identical pleasant half-smiles that never left their faces, made polite, unprovocative conversation, drank some more, then drove home, never once having recorded an accident. They were safe to know, Sutherland judged.

"Why is poor McGivern rigid with shock?" Louie Morton wanted to know.

"Because Mr. Sutherland insists on having dinner in his jockstrap and nobody can talk him out of it. McGivern's not sure it's correct."

There was no escape. Sutherland, standing between Edith and McGivern, watched fascinated as the pleasant half-smiles focused on him down the length of hallway. Then the Mortons broke into identical ringing laughter.

"Well, this is different!" Louie Morton said. "And here I thought we were in for another dull Edith evening with proscribed conversation and departure time. James, you look more comfortable than I've ever seen you! I think I'll take off my pants and join you for a drink. Nancy darling, is it okay if I take off my pants?"

"All right, dear, but only for drinks. I absolutely draw the line at wearing undershorts to table. It's unaesthetic, especially at your age and especially since darling Edith sets such a lovely table."

But Louie Morton was already wriggling out of his pants. Jane Winters stood beside him, holding one elbow to balance him. Tears of unrestrained laughter were coursing down her cheeks. Beside Sutherland, the anger broke out of Edith.

"This is my house! It belongs to me! If I want you to leave, you'll have to leave. What—what is it you've come to find out anyway, Ms. Winters?"

"Just how much effort it's going to require to make your husband my husband."

Sutherland whistled: "Jesus Christ, lady, you really get right to the point, don't you?"

"Unlike certain divorce-mill lawyers I know, yes."

"But why? . . . Why?" Edith was in full panic now.

"Because in about a month or so, Edith, with scant thanks to your husband, I'll be legally divorced and therefore eligible and looking for another husband. I've really gotten to like him, quite frankly, during all those unnecessary depositions he subjected me to. That's the only reason I let the foolish things carry on. To get to know him better. He's a very unhappy man, I think. Anybody that carries his kind of antagonism into his work would have to be. I think I'd be very good for him."

"So do I," Nancy Morton announced. "Are you Jane Winters, the lady who publishes *Antiquitaire Magazine?*"

"I am."

"I thought so! I once attended a lecture on period furniture you gave at the art museum. It was a fine lecture, but you've changed your hair since then."

"I used to wear it long to my shoulders, but it's so uncomfortable during the hot summer months."

"I know exactly what you mean, dear. I cut mine when I turned thirty and never looked back."

"He's not like cattle!" McGivern blurted out. "You just can't come walkin' in here and start biddin' on him!"

"Let's go in, pour our drinks and sit down and talk about it in a civilized fashion," Louie Morton proposed. He was out of his pants now, standing in long white silk undershorts that reached down nearly to the top of his garter hose. He still wore his camel's-hair overcoat and the sight of him resolutely enjoying himself caused Sutherland to break up into sobs of shuddering laughter as he led the way toward their drinks. Louie Morton, alive after all these years!

In the living room the fireplace was blazing. Sutherland set about making drinks as everyone took their places for the confrontation. It was McGivern who broke silence first, lurching to her feet out of the well of her chair to rail at Jane derisively: "What could you give him that his darlin' Edith couldn't? Do you own a house like this? Can you give him a Lhamborghini automobile every Christmas?"

"No, you old ninny, but I could at least give him a happy Christmas instead of what goes on here every year!"

"What—what do you mean?" Edith asked. Sutherland was handing out their drinks and he came to Edith as she asked the question. After she got the words out, she snatched the drink from the tray he proffered and took a great big gulp of it.

"I mean, Edith, we'll have a lovely dinner, lots of soft music and sanity as well. James won't have to watch you bludgeon your ancestors to shreds with a half-cooked turkey."

Edith's eyes were bolt wide: "How do you know— Who told you— Did you, James—did you betray me?"

Louie Morton interrupted then, getting up to make himself a second drink. "Oh, Edith, what does it matter? Everyone knows. Once the word got out you didn't want anyone around for Christmas, they were most happy to oblige you when it was understood what went on here."

"But no one really cares, dear," Nancy Morton hastened to assure her. "You deserve a little distraction from time to time. I mean, what's one day of unmitigated insanity compared to three hundred and sixty-four others of being just Edith? Affable, dependable, the perfect hostess, all that unstinting giving of yourself to charities and committee work and the rest of that bullshit. . . . And the consideration to perform your Christmas exorcism in the privacy of your own home without subjecting anyone but James and Miss McGivern to it. You know, Edith, people do appreciate those things."

But Edith was beyond listening. She stood abruptly and beseeched upward with clenched fists: "Who did it? Who betrayed me? Who betrayed Edith? James," she asked another time, "was it you?"

"No, Edith, it wasn't, I assure you. Do you think I wanted anyone to know I was the kind of husband who would put up with that madness?"

"Catherine!" McGivern had slunk out of the room and could be heard rattling dishes in the pantry. Edith rushed to the middle of the room and bellowed out: "McGivern, get your ass out here!"

"Edith, that's enough," Sutherland warned her as McGivern came fearfully toward them through the dining room. He had been too primed and spoiling for a revolt to realize that Jane's offensive against Edith, in which his ego had so luxuriantly basked, had spilled overboard into unwanted cruelty. He stood up, suddenly feeling absurd in his jockstrap, and pleaded with her to forget the whole business.

"Sit down, you, and shut up!" she commanded. McGivern came slowly into the room and stood before Edith, eyes downcast and whimpering like a child.

"So you did," Edith said simply.

"I didn't mean to, Edith. It's just that I couldn't think of anything to say—anything to make us seem special when I went out for tea with my friends on Wednesday afternoons. I just got so sick of listening to that witch who works for the Rutledges telling how awful they were with their fightin' and screamin' that I had to tell about us. It just came out, Edith. I couldn't stop myself one day."

"I guess we won the monster prize hands down, huh, McGivern?" Sutherland asked.

"Oh, Mr. Sutherland, I'm sorry. If you could only understand my plight. It's so hard to be a nobody. To have no identity."

"Granted, Miss McGivern," he told her, sighing heavily as he said it. "But now you're a somebody all right. In fact, we both are. Anyone that would aid and abet what goes on here on Christmas would have to be about as wacko as darlin' Edith herself."

When he said it, before Jane Winters and the Mortons, he realized he had just thrown in the towel. It was his first public disavowal of Edith. A collective sighing came forth as the remnant of Edith glided into the dining room and took her place at the table. Her miserably betrayed eyes began scanning the ancestor portraits. Sutherland knew Christmas was about to begin.

"I think I went too far," Jane said, rising suddenly. "I just came to test the waters, not blow up the whole dam."

"No, dear, I don't think you went too far," Nancy Morton assured her. "It was bound to happen, and perhaps it was best that it happened this way. There were a lot of people laying odds on a Beacon Hill ax murder one of these fine Christmases. Even a man that enjoys his creature comforts and status as much as James here does could only be expected to stand so much."

Sutherland did not wince at her judgment. He was already

looking to the future and he supposed that ever afterward he would count the Mortons as friends: "Now what do I do?"

"I think you should go home with this young lady, have a quiet dinner and stay the night," Louie Morton said.

"I'd like that fine," Jane said. "Though it really blows all those fantasies I had about clandestine meetings and all that."

"I'll help you pack a bag, James, while you get into a pair of pants," Nancy Morton spoke. "And don't forget your briefcase, so you can go directly to the office tomorrow."

"All this is happening too fast," Sutherland protested.

"Make your break deft, sharp and clean," Louie Morton urged. "Out of one house and into the other and don't look back."

"But I'm not sure—"

"You can't stay here any longer," Nancy Morton told him. "We've watched you for years, James. Your spirit, your capacity for love, even your good looks, are strangling in this house. You have the hardened face of a man whose life is under siege. Go with Jane Winters tonight and as Louie says don't look back. You won't find much here that you care to remember. Let's go get that bag now."

"I'll make some sandwiches for you," McGivern spoke. "A couple of turkey club sandwiches would be nice to take along on your trip."

"Why?" Jane asked. "We're only going to Back Bay."

"Bear with me, Ms. Winters. I need to do somethin' to steady my nerves. I'll be the one here with her when all the resta you are gone."

As she left the room there was a general nodding of heads for the truth of what she said. Then Sutherland went upstairs to dress and Nancy Morton went with him to pack a bag. When they came down McGivern was waiting with a bag of sandwiches. Louie Morton, still in his undershorts, had made himself another drink and Edith had somehow rallied and Sutherland was grateful that he did not have to go into the dining room to make his lone good-byes to her. She stood waiting for him beside McGivern, holding a bottle of champagne and a jar of caviar in her hands. She was smiling radiantly for his departure. He wondered how soon afterward she would descend into the Christmas madness.

Jane Winters took the champagne and caviar and McGivern's gift of sandwiches at the door. Then Sutherland and Jane descended the front steps to the battered old police cruiser while the Mortons, Edith and her companion housekeeper all stood framed in the doorway, waving and calling good-bye. The last words Sutherland heard before Jane turned on the ragged, noisy engine were Edith's: "Good-bye, James darling. Have a safe trip."

He did not look back.

CHAPTER 10

The Suicide on
the River Charles

It was almost four-fifteen. His body clock would be calling for
the return to sleep momentarily. In the window of the glass before him was the bright-orange reflection of the embers still
glowing in the bedroom fireplace. He opened his robe and the
image of his naked body was there also, and Sutherland turned
narcissistically about, admiring its hard, muscled thirty-seven-
year-old sleekness. Amazing, the elevation of the spirit: to look
better and feel better at thirty-seven than one had at thirty, at
twenty-five even. Plenty of exercise, no more hard drinking
(since the divorce from Edith he no longer hid out in bars
after working hours gloating in the company of crooked
brother lawyers because now it was much, much better at
home), and no more wenching either. For the past two years,
when he and his friend Frazier had taken their ritual fishing
trip to Gaspé, they had actually fished. Sutherland took a final
turn before the glass, betting he would look as lean as Pierre
Trudeau in his fifties, when he saw with a start that the apparition had returned again to the Esplanade below.

A poet? His mind leaped to the explanation. For some
reason that notion was now the only one that made any sense
to Sutherland: a man sleepless and driven to trudging through
the snows in an ecstasy of creative inspiration. The romance of

all this warmed Sutherland. He could only admire creativity. Writing a personal letter, one that did not politely threaten or cajole someone about a lawsuit or foreclosure, was a chore that caused him to break into sweat. His vision of the poet was interrupted momentarily by the grating passage of a snowplow on Storrow Drive, its blade audibly scraping on the roadbed. When it was past he saw that the man below had stopped and was facing their building again, staring up as he had imagined before to the level of their apartment. This time he waved and Sutherland's heart skipped a beat. He clutched at the edge of the curtain and held it tightly as he watched the figure turn suddenly toward the river and start out across the snow-covered ice. Some distant part of his mind judged that this made no sense at all.

On the other side, in Cambridge, if that was the man's destination, there was no way of scaling an approximately fifteen-foot wall to the walkway above. Sutherland peered closely after him as he disappeared beyond the range of the arc lights and into the white darkness of the storm. He awaited the poet's return. The man would have no choice.

In time he was back, retracing his own footsteps. About twenty yards from the riverbank, when he had just drawn into the range of the lights again, he halted and pulled the gun from his overcoat pocket. Even at that distance, Sutherland could see the unmistakable Luger profile with perfect clarity. Incredulous, he pressed his hands and face to the chill glass of the sliding door: the man who stood on the frozen river raised the gun to his lips and kissed the barrel in some parody of a reverential gesture, then hoisted it higher and pointed it straight at his right temple. Sutherland slipped open the sliding door and ran onto the snowy cold of the balcony.

Below, on Storrow Drive, another plow came lumbering past, working the middle lane this time. The man who wanted to kill himself still pointed the gun at his temple, but his face was turned skyward into the falling snow and Sutherland thought with a surge of hope that perhaps he considered heaven and was having second thoughts about his intent. Sutherland gripped the wrought iron of the balcony rail, heedless of its cold, and began screaming above the clank and scrape of the plow truck, the roar of its straining diesel engine.

"Stop! Stop! You don't know what you're doing! Nothing is ever as bad as it seems! Nothing is worth this! Please stop and I'll come right down! We'll talk! Do you need money for your children's Christmas presents? Is that it? I can help you! I can lend you the money!"

The plow went clanking and scraping out of hearing as the man squeezed the trigger. Horrified, Sutherland saw the bright spurt of blue flame that leaped from the barrel of the gun. The Luger sounded like a cannon in the clear, cold night. The man's head jerked sideways as if he had been walloped with the blow of a sledgehammer and he collapsed in a crumpled heap on the snow-covered river.

"For Christ's sake, this is Boston, after all," Sutherland uttered mutely to himself. He had absolutely no idea why he said it. He removed his hands from the balcony railing to return inside. He slid closed the sliding door and found Jane leaving the bed with a quilt wrapped around her.

"James, what's wrong? Why were you screaming out there?"

"You won't believe it, Janie, but some poor bugger just committed suicide out there on the river."

"What?"

"Look. No, don't look. It's liable to upset you too much and we don't need that right now. Why don't you get back into bed? I'll have to phone the police."

But she was already past him, pulling the quilt more tightly about her, squinting out through the window that had frosted over from the inrush of cold.

"Oh, James, that poor man. My God, today is Christmas Eve. What could have driven him to such despair?"

"I'll bet it had something to do with his children. I'll bet he was out of a job and couldn't swing Christmas. Come on, Janie," he took her arm gently, leading her toward the bed. "Lie down again. You need your rest. I'll go into the kitchen and call the police. Lie down now."

She lay down unprotesting and he arranged the covers over her again and kissed her forehead, telling her to sleep. He started out of the room toward the kitchen in the rear of the apartment when she clutched at his hand to stop him: "God Almighty, James, I'm too happy right now to even feel rightly sorry for the poor bastard. The guy's suicide feels like an intrusion. Why did he have to pick our little slice of the dirty old Charles to do himself in?"

Sutherland shrugged. "A dark angel's visit on Christmas Eve morning. A warning against optimism. I don't know. Maybe somebody's trying to spook us into religion. Let's don't forget to have little Ford Sutherland christened when the moment is propitious—or won't you Catholics indulge a name like that?"

"I don't know whether they will or not, James, but let's wing it on that business for a while, okay? I only joined the Church because Manfredi was a Catholic and his religion seemed to give him some sort of inner peace that frenetic, driven Janie Winters couldn't lay her hands on. It took me about two years to figure out that old Manfredi's daily inspiration came not from attending holy mass but from checking out all those little Government Center secretaries that popped in to light a candle every morning before they punched the time clock. Now why don't you go phone the cops, James? There's a guy lying dead out there, remember? And I guarantee your son won't be born tonight. It's a promise."

He laughed a little, embarrassed at himself, and tried to recall the name of the Indian tribe (in the Southwest? or South America?) whose husbands suffered identical labor pains to their wives giving birth. He bet on the Hopi, but then supposed he was wrong; the only safe bet really was that Janie was going to have an easier time delivering up little Ford Sutherland than Sutherland was. On his way out of the bedroom he paused to look out at the dead one once more. No one had found him yet, though a third plow moved past now in the lane closest to the river, its warning lights blinking eerily across the body that was already dusted with a covering of snow.

He closed the bedroom door behind him, walked the length of hallway to the kitchen and dialed the police emergency number on the wall phone.

"Yep? What can I do for you?" Someone, either a cop or a

male civilian dispatcher, yawned mightily into the phone. In the walk from the bedroom to the kitchen, Sutherland's disbelief had turned into a curious anger over the wasting of a life. He had forgotten his thirtieth year, the time of his own death wish.

"You won't believe this," Sutherland told the voice, "but some asshole just killed himself out on the Charles in front of my apartment."

The voice belonged to a black man. "For that he's an asshole? It sounds to me like he was pretty depressed."

"Look, I don't want to get into this. I could speculate with you until the cows come home. The point is he's dead and I'm sorry, but his body is being covered over by the snow and you really ought to send somebody out there to pick him up."

"Yes, suh! And who may I say is the provider of this unfortunate news?"

The lawyer in Sutherland coiled in reflex: "I'm just a public-spirited citizen. That's all I am."

"That won't do, Mr. Citizen. All sorts of nuts call up here. Especially around the holidays. People get lonely. I need your name and address."

"My name is James Sutherland. I'm a practicing attorney." He gave the man their apartment address and the telephone number and address of his office downtown: he did not want the police bothering Jane in her condition in the event they called back.

"I thanks you, James, and Merry Christmas. You'll be hearing from us if we need you."

Sutherland replaced the receiver in its cradle on the wall and thought of pouring himself a drink. But then he decided against it. What a pickle that would be: Sutherland trying to drive Jane to the hospital to deliver their firstborn through a foot of snow in a scotch-induced daze. He opened the refrigerator and settled on a leftover chicken leg instead to calm his stomach. Then he washed his hands at the kitchen sink and headed for the bedroom again. Before removing the robe and settling in beside Jane, he looked a final time through the window at the suicide on the river: The body was no longer there.

"What the hell . . . ?"

Somebody had already found him. That had to be the answer. Some police car cruising Storrow Drive had spotted the lump of body in the snow and rushed him off to Mass General or Boston City Hospital. The dispatcher he had just spoken with could not possibly have gotten an ambulance there so quickly. Then he saw the tracks coming off the river away from the depression in the snow where the man had fallen. The man still lived! He had only grazed himself perhaps and now was stumbling his way through the storm looking for help. Thank God and a Merry Christmas after all! Evidently the shock had done him some good and he had decided not to finish himself off.

Sutherland followed the stagger of new footprints through the lighted pools beneath the arc lamps. They led toward one of the rampways that crossed Storrow Drive to Beacon Street. The footprints ascended the ramp, then disappeared out of sight down the incline that led to the other side. He saw occasional bloodstains on the snow as well. Sutherland hoped the man had made it to the street and was able to flag down a passing car or a plow for help.

The snow fell steadily in the windless night and not a single thing moved out there now. Sutherland thought of phoning back to the yawning police dispatcher to tell him the dead one lived again, and was gone, but then he decided against it. He was too tired to put up with a black cop reading him the riot act about being a crank with a case of the lonely holiday blues. The police, when they arrived, would find the body imprint, the footsteps, and the bloodstains, and know at least that something had happened out there. They would probably follow the footprints and maybe even find the poor guy if he had not made it to the help he was seeking. If they were unable to find him in a snowbank somewhere they would start checking the hospitals. Sutherland had police friends. He would find out from them who had staged the memorable drama of this Christmas Eve morning.

He climbed into bed, not wanting to wake Jane. But she stirred anyhow and turned and kissed him lightly on his cheek.

The mound of her belly pressed into his and he patted at it softly with his hands.

"Call the gendarmes, James?"

"Yes, sweet, but the guy's gone."

Her eyes opened. She blinked away the grogginess, then squinted at him as if she had not heard correctly.

"Gone where?"

"To find a doctor, I hope. It looks like he changed his mind and decided he had better reasons to live when the bullet didn't kill him."

"God, James, the cops are going to think you're a loony. They'll think you've been drinking or something. First there's a suicide right outside your window, then there's no body. We'll have to invent a cover story to throw them off when they come ramming through the door with their unseasonal police irritation. We could tell them the body was carried off by a pack of sewer rats. Some of the ones I've seen out there on the Esplanade are probably big enough to do it alone. Or we could have Vogelmeister certify you insane. That always helps. You'll be declared unfit to stand trial—"

"Janie . . . ?"

"Yes, James?"

"Do you think you inherited your sense of humor from your mother or your father?"

"Oh, God, from Mother, of course. She died laughing. She had never died before and always got giddy about new experiences."

"Sleep, Janie, will you? Little Ford Sutherland needs his rest. So do you."

"James, I never thought to ask you before, but are we calling the impending little Sutherland Ford after the Henry or Gerald?"

"Neither. After my pickup truck."

She sighed heavily: "I thought that might be the reason. Oh, well, at least we don't have to name him in honor of your father. Archibald. Jesus, what an awful name! What time are your folks coming down from the farm, anyhow?"

"About late morning sometime. Speaking of Archibald, I'll

call him around seven-thirty or so and ask him to drive the truck down. For sure it's going to snow two feet at least. That four-wheel drive might turn out to be a wonderful help getting to the hospital if our fair city gets itself good and snowbound."

"Ugh. I swear I'll abort if I have to ride in that pickup of yours. I think the springs on the thing are cleverly disguised marble carvings."

"Sleep, wife."

"One last thought, James. That poor man. I hope he has friends or someone he can turn to for help if he pulls through all right."

"I hope so, too, Janie. It seems doubly awful to try to do yourself in at Christmastime. Night."

She fell back to sleep almost momentarily.

But Sutherland lay awake staring at the ceiling: the man on the Charles who put the gun to his head and squeezed the trigger was just about the most bizarre thing he had ever witnessed. It was like an omen, a disturbing premonition, and for Sutherland's purposes it had come at the wrong time of the year, to say nothing of the wrong time of his life.

And at whom was he waving?

PART II

A Snowbound Boston

CHAPTER 11

His Parents: Archibald and Marjorie

Sutherland woke from habit about seven-fifteen; Jane slept on, effortlessly as always, a vague smile about the corners of her mouth, as if she were enjoying a quite pleasurable dream.

Outside was the half-light of a very gray dawn and he saw with a yawn of resignation that it was still snowing. It seemed to be coming down even more heavily than last night. The wind had risen sometime since he had gone back to bed and was blowing the snow straight at the windows. He knew from the way the big glass panes rocked in their frames that it was coming hard and cold out of the northwest and that meant big drifts on the highways. There was no winning with the Boston weather.

He propped himself up, massaging his neck for a long moment on the headboard of the bed, then eased out from under the covers. He pulled on his robe and was going to his study to phone his father up in New Hampshire when he heard the clanking and scraping of a plow again and decided on a quick look outside.

The wind-driven snow was already a foot deep on the balcony. Down below, where the plow moved along the drive through mounting ridges of the white stuff, it was starting to look like one of the Colorado passes in January. A long line of cars, all with their headlights lit as in a funeral procession, moved slowly in single file behind the plow in the downtown direction.

Two of the uniformed cops swung what Sutherland supposed were metal detectors back and forth, probably looking for the man's gun. The thought had never occurred to him that the guy might have dropped or thrown down the weapon in his flight toward help, but Sutherland dearly hoped he had, because it would prove beyond a doubt that the good liberal barrister, James K. Sutherland, wasn't hallucinating.

Good luck, boys, he saluted the police. Find that nasty old Luger and I won't be the butt of any police jokes about poor overworked civil-liberties lawyers.

He went into the study to phone his father. He hoped he had not delayed too long watching the police at their work and that his mother and father had not already left for Boston in their battered old station wagon.

While he dialed the number on the phone at his desk he slid back the soundproofing curtains that helped keep out the traffic noises from the drive whenever he chose to work or read briefs in the study and glanced down at the police and their bloodhounds. They had found the place on the frozen river where the man had put the gun to his head and squeezed the trigger. Now the cops stood about nodding to each other for a few long seconds, then the dogs picked up the scent and took off toward the pedestrian ramp over which the man had crossed. The dogs leaped and bucked across the snow like the starving wild packs that Sutherland had often seen in February or March chasing the winter-weak deer into the flat stretches of field up on the farm where they were easier to trap and kill. The memory caused him to frown: often when he had gone out snowshoeing for exercise on the farm, he had slung a rifle over his shoulder in case he spotted one of the packs. He turned away from the window when he heard the sound of his mother's voice on the other end of the line. The storm was doing something to the connection. Marjorie sounded as if she were bellowing up from the bottom of a well. Her accent made it worse.

"Hello? I say hello . . . who is it?"

"C'est moi, maman. Ton fils de Boston."

She had been a Quebecker years before. A farmer's daughter from a dirt-poor place up in the northern part of the province that Sutherland always supposed must have been the limit of cultivation. The tundra, she had told him, began somewhere up at the end of the road. She had seen the jewel of the province, Montreal, but once—passing through the train station on her way south to work as a bobbin tender in the mills in Manchester and Nashua, New Hampshire.

Archibald had probably saved her from a worse life (depending on how you looked at it). He had proposed to her in Manchester, then married her in Laconia, then brought her to his farm on Winnipesaukee, where he had begun the reign of his omnipotent authority by forbidding her the use of her language and the practice of her religion. Marjorie became a Presbyterian who spoke badly accented English. She was an acknowledged local beauty who seemed to thrive on fourteen-hour days on the farm and bore up under her servitude uncomplainingly.

Sutherland and his sister, Elaine, had both learned French on the sly. At Harvard he had perfected it. When Archibald was not about, he honored his mother by addressing her in her own tongue. She used to respond to him greedily, though her son winced at the lightning speed, the clipped words, and ellipsed vowels of Québecois. Sometimes in the past when Archibald had been around and he and Sutherland were fighting like tigers over interpretation of that very same omnipotent authority, Sutherland had defiantly spoken French to his mother anyhow. Always at those times, often increasing her son's exasperation to tears, she responded in English, saying she really did not remember much of the old language. Giving a victory to Archibald was a habit of long, long practice.

"*Ah, mon petit cher! Je t'entend bien! Mais bon Noël, mon brave! Et petite Janie? Ça va bien chez elle?*"

"*Toujours bien, maman, mais rien encore. Où est le roi Archie?*"

"*Ah, dans la grange avec ses vaches . . . mais entend, il vien, je crois!*" Sutherland heard the little leap of panic in her voice. He knew she would finish the sentence in English: "Ah, here's your father, dear. Merry Christmas and we'll see you soon. 'Bye-bye for now."

Sutherland smiled to himself at the irony. He could not remember precisely when the consuming fire of his rage toward Archibald had finally gone out, been replaced by his sense of humor that now handled the old man like so much warm, soft putty. Probably the day he walked out on Edith for good, he supposed, for Edith saw the fueling of Sutherland's fire as a full-time job. She had despised Archibald, been mortified by his irreverent fartings, belchings and bellowings in her great and sacrosanct house, never once having the sense to realize that it was the very intensity of that mortification that turned Archibald's irreverence on full throttle. Well, Sutherland had lacked that same sense as well; in the beginning he had been far too impressed with what Edith came from to recognize what she actually was.

Sutherland waited for his father. He heard the plink of his morning chaw being jettisoned into his spittoon, then the wheeze of his breath over the wire.

"*Bonjour, mon père—*"

"Stop that shit, James!" the old man ordered his son on the morning of his thirty-seventh birthday. "Do you want me to have a goddamn heart attack? Is that what you want for your own father?"

Sutherland shook with laughter. He pounded the leather desk top with the flat of his hand.

"Well, am I a grandfather yet? Did Jane calf like she was supposed to? Is that what you're callin' to tell us?"

"Sorry, Archibald, not yet. Any day now, the doctor says. It might even be today."

"What if it was tomorrow? Wouldn't that be wonderful?"

The excitement rose in the old man's voice. Sutherland knew his parents had probably spent hours talking delightedly about that very prospect. "Little Ford Sutherland, born Christmas Day, nineteen seventy-nine. Jesus, you'd never forget that kid's birthday. Hey, where'd the name Ford come from anyhow? The President, right?"

Archibald was a Republican—to the core of his most recently metabolized cell. He had wept that midnight of Election Day when it was finally known that Jimmy Carter was the new President.

"Sorry, Archibald, but I'm naming him after my truck."

"That's what I thought," the voice came back at him sadly. "Hey, how do you know it's gonna be a boy anyhow?"

"The waiter in the Greek restaurant Janie and I always go to. He's got a foolproof system and everybody that works in the place swears he's about ninety-eight per cent accurate. He took down all the information about our ancestry and went back into the kitchen and figured it out. He was back in fifteen minutes with a two-page chart. It's going to be a boy. Definitely."

"Yeah, sure, Jimbo. And then you gave him a ninety-eight per cent tip for tellin' you what you wanted to hear all along. Right?" The voice that had been tinged with sadness was now dripping with the old Archibald scorn that he had always used so masterfully to goad his son into aggression. "Christ Jesus! For bein' such a smart boy you've got a lot of dumb parts to you, James. If that Greek's so bright what the hell's he doin' workin' as a waiter? He was probably sittin' back in the kitchen havin' a nip with the cook and laughin' his ass off at you and Janie while you was sweatin' it out waitin' at the table. All them Greeks know about is makin' money anyhow. They target a town and move in on it and before you know they've bought up half the place on the sly—"

"Archibald, I cannot stand a Yankee diatribe today," Sutherland growled at him. "Nor tomorrow or the next day either. And watch the raucous language when you get here, all right? Some people will be dropping in to visit. Now what time are you planning to leave up there?"

"Can't till Emmett gets here. That won't be till eleven fore-noon. He's goin' to watch the place and tend the cows while we're gone. But he went and got himself bagged for a little wiggly drivin' last night. The cops won't be finished with his arraignment till about ten-thirty or so. Then he gets sprung. Good old Emmett, huh? Heh. Heh. Heh—"

"Yeah, Archibald. Just great." Sutherland sighed at the old man's bemusement over Emmett drunk-driving in a blizzard. Life had its rhythms, evidently. After a certain time it seemed they became unalterable. Emmett was the hired hand from the Robert Frost poem. Once a handsome man, he had gone to hell in a bottle. Between benders he left his car with a married sister and slunk dejectedly back to the farm on foot and per-formed his chores like a penitent in exchange for his room and board and laundry. Archibald, who drank like a fish but never got drunk, lectured him sternly on the evils of drinking. Mar-jorie pitied him and supposed they would find him dead in his bed some morning. The thought of the three of them living to-gether and sitting before the fireplace on winter nights nod-ding gravely to the sageness of Paul Harvey and the news on the radio always prompted Sutherland to a head-shaking of an-other variety.

"You won't make Boston until three or four in the after-noon. Listen, before I forget why I called, Archibald, bring the truck down, will you?"

"Have to. It looks like goddamn Siberia up here. Besides, the car snapped a spring. I guess I put too much granite in the ass end to help out with the traction. Can't understand it, though. Some years I put in even heavier."

"Archibald, do you know what I'd really like to give you and Mother for Christmas?"

"What?"

"A nice shiny new nineteen-eighty station wagon."

"Nope. I can't accept no charity or welfare. I didn't send you to Harvard and you ain't givin' me some new doodled-up Buick or somethin' that everybody in Laconia knows I couldn't afford on my own."

"Your station wagon is of nineteen-forty vintage. That makes it thirty-nine years old."

"So what? It's a Packard, ain't it? They was built to last forever. One of the finest motorcars ever made."

"Really? I wonder why the company went out of business about twenty years back."

"Quality. Plain and simple. They built them so good nobody ever had to trade one in on a new model. So they got stuck with a backlog they couldn't unload. You don't need an economics degree to figure out what happened next."

"When Judgment Day comes, Archibald, I pity whoever's interrogating you. They're going to break down in an ungodly flood of tears."

"Don't get smart-assed with me, James. I ain't ready to pass the scepter yet. Now say good-bye to your mother and we'll be there soon as possible. Lord, it's gonna be somethin' to look forward to. Our first Christmas with you in ten whole years and a new grandchild on the way to boot. James . . . James . . ." The voice from New Hampshire faltered a little, then grew husky, and Sutherland felt an instant sadness at the certainty that Archibald was truly growing old and tired. He permitted himself the rare luxury of an emotion far more often these days. It was a sure sign.

"Yes, Arch?"

"James, we're happy, your mother and me, that you got rid of that damn Edith. Cripes, she was crazier than a loon. How the hell did you ever get mixed up with her anyhow? Anybody with ten cents upstairs could of seen her comin'—"

"Love is blind, Arch. Anyhow, it was long ago and far away and what's the use looking back? Put Mother on and I'll say good-bye. I've still got a bunch of things to do today."

Sutherland heard his mother chuckle into the phone. He knew the attraction that had kept her harnessed to his father all these years.

"A *bientôt, maman* . . ."

She nearly slipped, then rushed quickly to the safety of English. "Good-bye, dear. We'll see you this afternoon."

Then he put down the receiver in its cradle and pulled
back the curtain again to look out at the Esplanade. The
police were gone and there was only a solitary woman making
a giant's progress over the snow on cross-country skis.

Edith. How had he gotten mixed up with her, as Archibald
put it? It began humorously, he supposed, if anyone had
humor enough to see it. It began the late-August afternoon of
the summer before he left Laconia for his freshman year at
Harvard, when Edith's mother came upon him swimming
naked in the waters of Winnipesaukee. He had not heard her
approach on horseback, and once, when he came up for air
after diving several times to the bottom, he looked shoreward
and saw her. She was planted firmly in the saddle, astride one
of the big, nervous hunters that apparently traveled everywhere
with the Watkinses, and she was waiting for him to come
out. From where she watched, seated on the horse atop a ten-
foot rise of bank, he had no doubts she knew he was naked. He
was already flustered and embarrassed and the water was cold.

"Hello, Mrs. Watkins. Hot afternoon, isn't it?"

"Yes. Beastly. You're the Sutherland young man, aren't
you?"

"Yes, I am."

"I thought I remembered you. How's that awful tobacco-
chewing father of yours?"

He grew angry at her too easy judgment: "My father is quite
well, thank you. My mother is quite well also."

Florence Watkins enjoyed his anger. She smiled at the provocation she had managed while she slipped a cigarette into the
elegant silver holder that had become her trademark around
Laconia.

"We haven't seen hide nor hair of you Sutherlands in years,
it seems."

What do you expect? he wanted to tell her. After the way
you treated us when we first met. Three summers before, when
the Watkinses had purchased the neighboring estate of a deceased pulpwood millionaire and established it as their summer
digs, they had phoned the Sutherlands to invite them for cocktails one early June evening.

Only the colonel (who had made him a colonel anyhow? Archibald wanted to know; they were fuzzy on that score) and Mrs. Watkins were there, along with McGivern, who padded silently to and fro bearing plates of hors d'oeuvres. Sutherland had judged the new neighbors quickly. The colonel was a sot who frequently got his world wars mixed up. Miz Watkins (they were originally Southerners, evidently) he did not like. She was a lean, hard-muscled woman who had no softness around the eyes. She glared instead and took some sort of nameless delight in matching his stare, eyeball to eyeball, then smiled the pleasure of her triumph over a high-school freshman when he broke contact and looked away. Then she tried it on Elaine, but Elaine did not look away, and that seemed to enrage her and brought her around quickly to the point of the neighborly invitation.

The Watkinses needed a caretaker and cleaning lady and they offered the jobs to Archibald and Marjorie. In the hurt, stupefied silence that followed, it was Marjorie who somehow assumed control, assuring the Watkinses they had plenty enough work already and suggesting the names of some people from Laconia (pointedly not any of the local farm families, though the point was doubtless lost on the Watkinses) who might be interested.

In five minutes more they rose to say good-bye and the colonel compounded his missus' error by offering to buy the old Packard wagon since he was pretty certain it had some genuine antique value. Archibald, in a tight whisper of a voice that was strangled with anger, told them flatly that neither the Sutherlands nor anything they possessed were for sale. Then they had driven quietly home.

There, where everybody expected Archibald to explode with imprecations, he kept an ominous and uncharacteristic silence, broken only to warn them that they were to have nothing further to do with those foolish Watkins people. For Sutherland, it was one of those rare dicta of his father he was only too happy to abide by.

"I hear tell, young Mr. Sutherland, that you're off to Harvard this year. I didn't think your family had that kind of money."

"They don't," he assured her, angry enough to control the chattering of his teeth. "I'm a scholarship boy planning to make good."

"It doesn't matter," she dismissed his irritation with a wave of the long wand of her cigarette holder. "The point is you're going. This changes things."

"How do you mean?"

"I mean I have a daughter who's just come back from a Scandinavian tour and is starting to Radcliffe this year. I think you should meet her. Have you ever seen her?"

"No, I don't believe so."

"She's quite extraordinarily beautiful. She's been studying abroad every summer for years now. I never did see the point of her wasting her time around this place. There don't seem to be any of the right kind of young men. Dinner's at eight, by the way. We'll expect you about seven-thirty or so."

He remembered not wanting to go at the time, but deciding to acquiesce if for no other reason than that she might be satisfied and ride on about her business. But the horse did not move away. She even took binoculars from a case slung around her neck and trained them on him as he treaded water.

"You're wondering how long I'm planning to stay here, aren't you, Mr. Sutherland?"

"It has occurred to me."

"Well, I'm staying until you come out of the water and I get a good look at you."

"Can I ask you why, Mrs. Watkins?"

"I want to see for myself what we're getting."

With that rejoinder he decided his nakedness was now her problem. He swam quickly ashore and climbed out onto the little spit of beach below the bluff where she sat on the horse. He stood up, spread his arms wide and leered up at her: "Like it?"

"Very nice. Stop leering. This isn't a skin flick, this is serious. How tall are you?"

"Six feet even."

"That'll do. Turn around, please."

He did as he was bidden, putting his hands behind his head to show off the ripple of farm-work muscles in his back.

"That's fine. You can turn around now. Tell me about your parents. Your father is a New Hampshire Yankee on both sides, am I right?"

"Yes, that's right."

"And your mother? She is not, I believe."

"No, she's French-Canadian from Quebec Province, both sides of the family, by the way."

"That's not what I'd hoped to hear. Still, you don't look particularly Canadian."

He could only snort at that dumb remark. Perhaps, after all, she felt so much antipathy toward Archibald because they were so very much alike, so full of piddling prejudice. He too viewed the Canadians as a separate race and swore he could spot them a mile away. But this woman bore special watching. Archibald always managed to somehow live with the vilified object, once he was through vilifying it. Miz Watkins, he decided, could not and would not.

"I suppose she's Roman Catholic then."

"No, Miz Watkins, I'm afraid she's a forced convert to the Presbyterian church. I can vouch for it. We all go to services together every Sunday."

"Well, it isn't all bad, then. The colonel might buy the French-Canadian part as long as she isn't Roman Catholic. The two together would be impossible for him. He despises French-Canadian Catholics."

"The colonel sounds pretty dumb, then. You happen to have set up summer camp among a large nest of them."

"Yes, they do seem ubiquitous, don't they? We see their churches everywhere we drive. The colonel isn't dumb, by the way. He's obscure. There's a difference."

"I won't be able to make it tonight, Miz Watkins. Or any night, as a matter of fact."

"Did I say something wrong?"

He ignored her as he struggled back into his jockey shorts.

"Boxer shorts!"

"What?"

"I want you to wear boxer shorts from now on. Those things are obscene. I can't abide the idea of you taking off your clothes in front of my daughter and she having to see you in those things."

"Oh, God! Oh, wait until I tell that one at home! My poor French-Canadian Presbyterian mother will just die of mortification. She's been buying my underwear since I was a little kid. Have a nice ride, Miz Watkins."

"We dine at eight, Mr. Sutherland," she reminded him as she reined the horse about, preparing to return home.

"I told you I won't be there."

"I think you will. As I said, you haven't seen my daughter yet." Then she rode away without saying another word.

As it turned out, he dined with the Watkinses that evening. But only after he had gotten his first look at Florence's daughter. The seven-thirty invitation time had come and gone. He had already eaten dinner with his family and at five minutes to eight was seated on the front porch with Emmett, the hired hand, when she drove up to the house in the colonel's Cadillac with his self-inspired Hessian Horseman Farm motif—of a horse leaping over the sun—emblazoned on the front doors. Until then, Sutherland's resolve had been firm, and he reinforced it by telling Emmett a couple of times exactly how angry he was about the afternoon interrogation by Miz Watkins. Emmett in turn amplified Miz Watkins' heinousness by revealing a surprising wealth of anecdotes gleaned from people around Laconia who had had run-ins with her. Even living next to her Sutherland had no idea of what a local legend the colonel's missus had become. There were shops in town that refused to do business with her.

Edith got out of the car and started toward the house. She was a beauty. But there was something else about her, a sadness and evident shyness (the least imagined trait in any daughter of Florence Watkins), that he found instantly compelling somehow. He stood as Emmett stood at her approach when he had intended to remain rigidly seated.

"They sent me to get you. I'm sorry." She shrugged when

she said it and released a great sigh that was more like a groan as she riveted her eyes to the bottom step of the porch.

"I'm afraid I really don't want to go. I told your mother that today. Besides, I've already eaten."

"Look, you really don't know me, and there's no reason you should do anything for me, but if I don't come back with you in about five minutes, it's going to be very bad for me until I make my getaway to Radcliffe. Florence is on the warpath about everything that's wrong with me as per usual, but this time, instead of it being not playing tennis, not riding horses or not being first in my class, it's boys. She thinks I'm not aggressive enough and her newest theory is I'd smile more if I got myself laid more. Well, I don't care about smiling and I don't care about getting laid, but I do care about being yelled at and screeched at and being called a lesbian all the damn time!"

It came out of her in such an unexpected rush that he was wide-eyed and speechless in response. The fact that his parents had come out of the house onto the porch barely had time to register when she started in again.

"Look, I'll pay you! I have money left over from my European trip. I'll pay you a thousand dollars for the next two weeks if you'll just come around the house to see me and pretend you're enjoying it. Then it'll be time to go to school, and when we get to Cambridge we won't have to continue the charade any longer. But please come tonight! The colonel is over there now getting all bent out of shape and he needs his cannon fodder badly and you're scheduled to be it. It'll be terribly unpleasant, but chances are he'll pass out halfway through the meal and then you'll have a reason to leave. Only please come! I'll find a way to slip you the money tonight. I promise."

"Why would I be cannon fodder?" His mind had seized that phrase from out of the rush of her monologue. It had not even gotten to the part about the money yet.

She shook her head hopelessly in response, then shifted her eyes to his mother. The eyes were contrite. There was no mistaking it.

"Florence came home after she met your son, Mrs. Sutherland, and told the colonel that you were of French-Canadian extraction and that started him off. He even called the Presbyterian church office to verify that you were a church member because he couldn't believe you weren't a Catholic. I'm very sorry. Anyhow," she turned back to Sutherland, "that's why you're cannon fodder."

"*Allez-y! N'accepte pas d'argent!*" his mother commanded in the forbidden French. She had a ready pity in her for the Ediths of the world.

"But, Mother, I don't want to go. It doesn't make sense to go someplace where somebody is going to barf all over you the minute you walk in the door."

"Go with her, James. Do as your mother says," Emmett said tonelessly. In those days, before he hit the bottle so badly, Emmett still had something of a shareholder's say in family matters.

"Yes, go with her, son," Archibald encouraged, "and if anybody over there tries to barf on you, just nail their mouth shut with a punch. And if you need help, call and we'll come runnin'."

Now, nearly twenty years later on a Christmas Eve, Sutherland smiled at the memory of going off to the wars against the Watkinses. In the car, rumbling back to Hessian Horseman Farm, Edith broke into a sudden flood of tears and wailed at him piteously: "I don't want to marry you!"

"Who said you had to?"

"Florence. She's got you all picked out. Oh, God! Run and save yourself! She came home all out of breath this afternoon and announced you have a body like Michelangelo's *David*. I'm supposed to start sketching you early next week." She turned to him, the tear-stained face already miserably bloated. "I don't want to sketch you stark naked!"

"Why not? I don't mind."

"Because it's sick, that's why! The sketches are for Florence. She wants to take them South with her when they leave next month to show to all her friends, a bunch of sex-starved Amazons who drink too much in the afternoons after tennis! I can just hear her now, 'And this is the young man my daughter is shacked up with. Doesn't he have a gorgeous body?' Oh, it's so sick! Doesn't it just make you want to vomit?"

If it had made him want to vomit, he supposed it would have spelled the end of Edith then and there. But it had not, and the inexorable march toward the altar, albeit seven years thence, was thus set in motion. Florence had chosen her man well. She had realized that a vast narcissism lay dormant like a hibernating snake in the good-looking neighboring farm boy who was overloaded with chores and schoolwork and athletic competition, a lonely out-of-towner who had no real society but his own family. She brought the serpent to life and baited it skillfully for years. In the same skillful way she managed to keep him everlastingly off balance until he learned to live with the axiom that nothing the Watkinses ever did was as expected. That first night with Edith was a perfect example.

He had gone to their dinner with a sense of foreboding, and walked away from it thinking he had turned it into a literal triumph. They had planned it that way. Before they sat down, the colonel read him the riot act about observing the punctuality of the 8 P.M. dinner hour. In response, Sutherland stood up, told them he had eaten, bade them a cordial good night and started for the door. Florence had hauled him back and exchanged a grave, approving look with the colonel.

Over gazpacho, the colonel began a merciless needling about New Hampshirites and the French-Canadian segment in general, and Sutherland energetically denounced him as a bigot who ought not to ramble on in that vein outside the safety of his own house. This time Florence and the colonel passed judgment in a grave, approving grunt language that apparently only they understood.

"Give me a young man with balls any day," the colonel opined.

"I told you, Colonel," Florence spoke. "I told you when he answered back this afternoon that he was a young man with spine. He's not the type to take anything lying down."

"Oh, God, please stop it, Daddy!" Edith begged.

"Let Daddy handle this, Edith dear," the colonel told her.

Over the ham and candied yams, the colonel began taunting him again about the French-Canadian segment in general and his mother in particular. Sutherland told him to go fuck himself three times and once threatened to knock all his teeth down his throat. The colonel and Florence loved it. They laughed like hyenas and slammed the table with their fists like hillbillies. Their heartfelt endorsement of him was a monster that filled the room, driving Edith from the table to a nearby powder room, where she vomited audibly. Sutherland hardly noticed. Now he was playing the colonel's and Florence's game —their curious stratagem of inducing backhanded compliments—and liking it. Over the chocolate pie when they excoriated Archibald for poisoning the roots of his own family tree by marrying Marjorie, Sutherland spent nearly a half hour calling them every name in the book. They reveled in the abuse. They never seemed to get enough.

It was time for Sutherland to leave. Edith was called from hiding to drive him home. At the door, as he prepared to say good night, the colonel offered him money so he might take Edith to "nice places." Sutherland wound up and punched the colonel right in the stomach. But the colonel's stomach was unexpectedly hard, and though he gasped a little, the punch did not knock the wind out of him. In response he clamped a heavy hand on Sutherland's shoulders and told him gravely: "A proud man and a good man! It takes one hell of a man to knock the wind out of me, but you almost did it! You'll always be welcome in this house, sir!"

At seventeen, Sutherland remembered, it was a heady, heady night. He said good-bye, and Florence gave him a gift-wrapped present for his mother.

In the car, returning him home, it was Edith's turn to be angry: "Goddamn you, you're so stupid! They love you! They'll never leave you alone now!"

"They weren't so bad," Sutherland judged lamely.

"Oh, you poor fool. You poor, poor shitkicker. You peasant."

But that was all. He left the car without trying to kiss her and went into the house as she roared out of the farmyard and back along the road to her parents.

Inside the house, he narrated the Sutherland triumph with

gusto. When his mother opened the gift box that contained three pairs of new boxer shorts, they had howled at the patheticness of that Watkins woman, and not seen the gift for what it was. The next day when he walked over to see Edith, he carried the same gift box in return. Only now it contained three clean pairs of his oldest jockey shorts. Florence had smiled in pretended embarrassment, but actually she was smiling in victory. But he had not understood that: in his own mind he had won the skirmish of the night before.

. In the years to come he would be allowed to win many more skirmishes, but ultimately lose the war. He and Edith were married seven years later in the summer, a month after he finished law school. His defeat had cost him dearly, he considered: later, when it became apparent that Edith had many more problems than anyone suspected, his friends the colonel and Florence were nowhere to be found. As parents they had gone into retirement, and the problems of Edith were now Sutherland's problems. It was time for them to start living; they had had enough of Edith. For years he was bitter about that neat trade-off. The knowledge that he had been so neatly set up for a fall and blindly acquiesced to it burned within him like a volcanic fire never far from eruption. It was his chief source of self-loathing.

But what of it now? he considered after two years of knowing Jane Winters. That loathing had been the recrimination and self-derision of an immature man whose only recourse to the problem of Edith was a pathetic self-pity that asked an eternal stupid question: What if I had only done it this way? Jane had turned his mind around and propelled it toward the future. He had bought her primal philosophy of never looking back. She had made him more of a man if only because she had caused him to cease his self-flagellation over the unchangeable past. Quite simply, the time came, early on in their relationship, when she would not suffer hearing any more.

She was a consummate optimist, Jane was, he thought affectionately as he watched the woman who passed by on her cross-country skis making her giant's progress now in the opposite direction. No wonder everyone liked Jane.

CHAPTER 12

Their Friends: Maggie and Otis

Jane was up and in the kitchen making coffee by eight-fifteen. Sutherland joined her about five minutes later when the first cup was ready to be poured. He had already showered and shaved and survived the worrisome morning ritual of carefully scrutinizing the advancing thinness of his hair. It was his special fear: baldness, in part hereditary and transferred through the mother, apparently skipped a generation. Sutherland had seen photos of Marjorie's father, old Armand Gervais, who had been bald as an eagle. Unless he had had the good fortune to pick up an errant recessive gene someplace, he decided he was going to end up a distinguished elder bow-tied Boston lawyer whose head reflected the courtroom lights. But this morning he beamed at himself in the mirror. His hair was still thick and covering well. It was no worse than it had been last Christmas.

He dressed in corduroy pants, his green chamois shirt and his favorite alpaca ski sweater, then pulled on his hobnail boots that were best for snowshoeing. When he walked into the kitchen Jane was already sipping at her coffee. Seated on a stool at the counter, she looked very big with child indeed.

"James, you look like a hick from New Hampshire."

"I'm just conditioning you, my sweet. The real McCoy is on his way. You should hear his roar in the hallway about three-thirty or four this afternoon."

"There was no trouble getting to him? The lines weren't down anywhere?"

"Nope. Still up and singing away."

"How about the police? Did you call them back?"

"No. There's no point to it yet. The cops were out there with bloodhounds only about an hour ago. The dogs picked up the scent and headed off at a gallop across the footbridge toward Beacon Street. I'll phone one of the detectives I know down at headquarters later in the afternoon. They should have had time to put something together by then. I'll phone from the office. Unless, that is . . ."

"Not to worry, James. Today is not the day. That's a further promise. Besides, Maggie and Otis are coming over in an hour or so to start the fixin's for all that delicious Christmas garbage you lucky folks are going to get to eat tomorrow. They'll be here in case little Ford Sutherland starts trying to score a field goal later on. So hop onto your snowshoes and have a nice trudge downtown."

She lifted her coffee cup to her lips with her right hand; impulsively the left hand that would have held her cigarette if the doctor had not forbidden smoking during her pregnancy followed after it, perched above the rim of the cup for a moment until she realized what she was doing and dropped the hand irritably to the counter with a slam. Her husband laughed at her, then pretending fearfulness moved his own stool a few inches away.

"Shut up," she said. "I'm dying for a damn cigarette."

"Soon, Janie," he tried soothing her, feeling guilty about all the onus of childbearing that fell on the woman while the man usually got off with only a case of the jitters. But she was already preoccupied elsewhere. She stared out the kitchen window that looked down the Charles toward the Harvard Bridge. Sutherland could just see the bridge's vaguest outline through the universe of squalling snow. He saw the lights of an MBTA bus inching across and was surprised they were running.

"God Almighty, James, that poor guy last night. I can't stop thinking about it. I hope he made it to help. Maybe you should have gone down and tried to find him."

"Look, good wife, I'm a three A.M. insomniac, not a doctor.

By the time I could have gotten myself together and dressed
and downstairs he was probably long gone anyhow. I did my
civic duty, after all. I did phone the police, didn't I?"

She shrugged. "Have it your way, husband. This is no time
to irritate the baby's father. He might desert me. Now, I've got
a bunch of phone calls to make before Maggie and Otis swing
by. There's no point in that caterer showing up at the office
today for that Christmas party if there's nobody there to party.
I'll just leave word that anybody who does show be my guest
for lunch at a bash down at Rudolfo's on the waterfront and
let Rudolfo put it on my account. Cripes, I hope none of the
out-of-towners try driving in this slop. I'd rather bring out the
next issue late than not at all because the Art Department got
itself wiped out in a series of simultaneous skids somewhere.
Now eat your grapefruit, dear, and don't forget your whole-
wheat toast. You'll need your strength for that trek downtown."

The telephone rang as she stood up. She started across the
kitchen for the wall phone: "I'll get it. It's probably somebody
from the office."

He began eating the grapefruit as she lifted the receiver
from its cradle.

"Hello? Hello . . . ? Hey, who is this? Stop that crazy laughing and talk if there's something you have to say!"

Sutherland spun round on his counter stool and read the
baffled look of Jane's face. He left the stool in annoyance and
took the phone from her when the look changed to her special
impish mask of comic disparagement that she always reserved
for drunks. That was all the holiday needed, Sutherland
decided—a Christmas loony on a bender who had the wrong
number that he would dial incessantly until he finally passed
out sometime that evening.

Sutherland took the receiver from her and put it to his ear.
A shrill, maniacal laughter cascaded into his ear. Its perpetrator
did not sound drunk to Sutherland; he sounded quite, quite
mad.

"Hey, knock it off, will you? You've got the wrong number,
mister," Sutherland protested. But then the line went dead
and the laughter was gone and Sutherland was left gazing in

impotent consternation into the receiver as if he somehow expected to see the nuisance caller.

"What was that all about?" Jane asked.

Sutherland threw up his hands: "Some kids, I think. Probably getting their holiday jollies. I hope the hell they've got a few other numbers to work today so they don't keep phoning back."

"I wonder if it could be . . . No, it's been such a long time."

"Who, Jane?"

"Oh, about a year before we were divorced, some nut kept calling up almost every night and laughing like that. We finally resorted to taking the phone off the hook before we went to bed, and then after about a month when we put it back on, I guess the guy was shopping new territory. He never phoned again, and it was just as well. I think Manfredi would have strangled him if he could have found him. He used to get positively apoplectic on that phone trying to get the guy to stop laughing and say a few words. That's probably the only reason the nut kept calling back. He knew he had Fredi's goat and was milking it for all it was worth. If this one keeps coming back for more, promise me you won't lose your temper, okay, James? They love that. It absolutely turns them on."

"I promise, wife. It won't be hard. What do you imagine our obscene laughter is worth on the scale of one to ten compared to some of the courtroom heavies I've been up against that I've really wanted to bludgeon to death?"

"I take it you've never had the pleasure of living with your own personal nuisance caller for a couple of months, eh, barrister? Well, they can get to you, let me assure you. It gets so bad before you finally give up and take the phone off the hook that you lie wide awake at night after the hardest working day just waiting for them to phone. You actually feel incomplete until they do and you say good night."

"Whoever they are, they'll encounter nothing but reserve and indifference from this house if they choose to phone again. We'll turn this classic American game around. We'll make them beg us to pretend outrage with them. We'll turn the lush, fetid garden of their insidious art into a veritable desert. We'll—"

" 'Bye, James." She waved to him. "Mother has to touch base with several realities this morning."

He slapped her ass as she went past: he was crazy about Jane. An hour after she had the baby she would be on the phone barking orders into the office. Jane Winters Occhapenti Sutherland was *Antiquitaire Magazine,* a high-gloss quarterly on the antiques trade. She was the magazine's founder, editor in chief, chairman of the board and president all at once (a corporate boondoggle if Sutherland had ever heard of one, but he had sent his curiosity into permanent exile: it was the single thing she required of him), and he was frankly in awe of her intelligence, but even more so of her efficiency. She seemed to get more accomplished in any given day than anyone he had ever encountered.

He poured himself another cup of coffee and started in on his grapefruit again. Jane did her telephoning in the living room. Sutherland vaguely heard the measured tone of her business voice at first and supposed she had gotten someone at the office. But when the voice sputtered in excitement and rose a whole octave and he smiled at the certainty that old Rudolfo had answered the phone down at the restaurant and she was practicing her Italian on him.

Italian was the legacy of her ex-husband Manfredi. She had found him in Rome when she had gone on a shopping vacation for some baroque pieces to add to her private collection. At about the same time she allowed herself to be gigoloed by Manfredi, she stumbled on a crumbling minipalazzo near Orvieto owned by an old widow despairing over the government and its tax agents. The contents of the palazzo had nearly caused her to faint, and she ended up buying every last stick of furniture in the place. Then she got out of Italy as fast as she could, lest the bureaucracy somehow speed up and the tax men pulled the old widow's file for another go-round.

She sailed home on the *Leonardo.* In the hold were the baroque treasures that decorated every room of the two floors of their apartment. Up top, abed with his new wife, Jane, was the flesh-and-blood treasure (again, depending on how you looked

at it) she had brought home from Rome. All in all, a successful vacation, many people thought.

Manfredi was a handsome man. He admired his own face. In Italy, where a more cautious sport evidently existed, he had been an aspiring prizefighter, or a "pugilist," as he referred to himself. In America, where he had checked out the circuit and seen some of the black heavies in the ring and the battered, punch-drunk remnants of veterans hanging around the gyms, he had resigned his art. His new career was as a private tutor of Italian. One of his star pupils was his own wife, Jane Occhapenti, and a good thing, too, for even after six years of marriage, Manfredi had never quite gotten the hang of English. After two glasses of wine, he was invariably trapped in the present tense.

Despite himself, Sutherland had always had a fond place in him for Manfredi Occhapenti. He wondered if it was right to be fond of your wife's ex-husband, if it did not represent some refined form of incest. But then his thoughts were interrupted by the chimes of the doorbell. Maggie and Otis were there earlier than expected, the snow already shaken from their clothes, but their faces were still wet and running from the melted flakes. Sutherland drew them inside and urged them out of their coats. Then he bussed Maggie warmly, as he always did. When he released her, Otis impulsively reached up and straightened the wisps of Maggie's perfectly coiffed hair that Sutherland had accidently displaced.

Maggie Hanson was *Antiquitaire*'s managing editor. She was also Jane's oldest and closest friend; they had grown up together in the western Massachusetts town of Stockbridge and gone on to graduate from the same U. Mass. Amherst class. Otis, her live-in lover of five years, was a hairdresser and an enigma because he had no other name but Otis. He was in love with either Maggie or her opulent, stunning blond hair and Sutherland chose not to speculate on which possibility. The first time Sutherland was introduced to Otis was the first time Janie had given a small dinner party in the apartment for Archibald and Marjorie. They learned that Otis always referred to himself in the third person, as if he were an abstraction that had stepped out of himself but always hovered close by in full view. Sutherland, just back from his office and tired and still squirming in a vested suit, had asked Maggie's lover somewhat perfunctorily, "Well, have you got a last name, Otis?"

In response, Otis had shaken his also blond, angelic head in a sad and wistful way, as if trying to find out his last name were the consummate searching of his entire life. For no good reason he could remember except that he had had about three or four scotches by that time, Sutherland imagined Otis peppering the personals columns of newspapers in the Midwest where he was born, begging for anyone to come forward and tell him his surname. A small desperation was growing on Sutherland then: he was still new to Jane Winters and not yet divested of Edith, and the edginess he felt in transition made him want to blurt out, "But then if Otis isn't your last name, it must be your first name, right?" The lawyer in him had to get to the bottom of this.

But it was Archibald who had usurped the question, except that he said Christian name instead of calling it a first name.

Again the sad and wistful shake of the blond, angelic head, "Otis is just Otis. That's all he is."

"He's just Otis," Maggie had assured them quietly.

"Just Otis," Jane had concurred.

"Ah, I see," Sutherland had answered, using the polite, understanding smile he reserved for near-demented departing partners leaving the courtroom in divorce cases. Only it was not good enough for Archibald. Later, on the pretext of remembering that he needed to make an important phone call that involved a legal affair, he had maneuvered Sutherland into the privacy of Jane's bedroom. Together, they paged madly through the Boston telephone directory, and there, at a Commonwealth Avenue address, it was listed for all the world to see: Otis.

"Well, I'll be goddamned," Archibald had judged, shaking his head at the wonder of it. Thereafter, Archibald viewed Otis with a curious kind of awe, and Otis, if he cared about it at all, had gained a lifelong friend and supporter in New Hampshire. It was hard to tell what Otis cared about, actually. He was about the most inscrutable person Sutherland had ever met.

Maggie seemed to do all of his thinking and most of his talking for him.

"Is young Ford Sutherland going to happen today?" Maggie asked.

"Your boss says no. We're apparently safe for the time being," Sutherland told her.

"Lucky lady. I wouldn't want to have to go speeding off to the hospital in this slop. This is going to top the blizzard of eighty-eight or whatever that legendary one was. The only things moving out there now are the snowplows. We had to walk down the middle of the street to get here. Are Archie and Marjorie going to cancel out?"

"No, they're coming down in the truck. They shouldn't have any trouble in four-wheel drive."

"Oh, good," Otis enthused. "Otis has got a wonderful Christmas present for Archibald. He'll just love it."

"That's good of you, Otis. Nice of you to remember old Arch. What is it?" Sutherland asked him.

"An earring just like Otis's. Only it's gold instead of silver."

"He'll faint," Sutherland judged lamely. Otis was bisexual and managed to throw the fact of his two-handed preference into every conversation, whether there was room for it or not. Maggie let him out one night a week to tour the gay bars, but demanded he go to a free gay-activist-sponsored V.D. clinic twice a month for a checkup. Archibald, who had as little tolerance for homosexuality as he had for most other things, made a single exception in the case of his friend Otis. In his left ear, Otis wore a silver earring and one of Archibald's occupational delights was tugging on the earring and turning Otis in slow circles about him in a bizarre pas de deux they never seemed to tire of. Sutherland tried to picture his father wearing a gold earring on the streets of Laconia, New Hampshire, but the image refused to be conjured.

"It won't fly, Otis baby," Sutherland warned him.

"Otis reminds you that that's what you said about the mezuzah he gave him last year. But Otis knows he never takes it off. Sometimes he even wears it outside his shirt. And he doesn't like Jews either."

"That's true," Sutherland agreed: the part about the Jews, but the part about the mezuzah also. He stared off into space for a long moment and all of a sudden the image of Archibald wearing his gold earring on the streets of Laconia did emerge and he knew it was going to happen. He knew what the reaction would be also. If it was good enough for Archibald Sutherland, then every woodchuck in town would be wearing an earring by New Year's Day. Maggie had the same thoughtful faraway look on her face.

"They say the country's getting more conservative every year, but sometimes I just don't know," she said at length. "There are no more constants. Nothing you can depend on. I mean, even Archibald is changing."

"Otis is certain we'll have a woman president by the end of the century," Otis said. "He intends to tell Archibald what he thinks, too."

Sutherland smiled weakly at the hairdresser lover. It was no use telling him that Archibald would start slavering over that one. He already knew. He loved goading the old man almost as much as the old man liked being goaded. But Sutherland counted on his father not to demur from any politeness. The son had his prejudices, too. He thought Massachusetts might have a woman governor in the not-too-distant future. Neighboring Connecticut already had one. But he did not think America would have a woman president before the year 2000, was not sure he wanted one either. Still, the talk of women reminded him of going to the office. He had taken on a class-action suit against a downtown bank for refusing credit cards to women who were adequately salaried and mostly debtless and he still had the brief to write.

"Listen, I'm going to snowshoe my way down to the office and try to catch up on some work for a couple of hours. Janie's in on the horn fixing up an alternative to *Antiquitaire's* Christmas party, which isn't going to be very well attended, if at all. The folks should be in from the boonies about three-thirty or four or thereabouts. If anything develops give me a call at the shop, okay?"

"Will do, squadron leader," Maggie saluted as he left them

and went to put on his parka and ski hat. He picked up his briefcase and snowshoes and headed for the door, stopping for just a moment to blow a kiss to Jane, who had finished talking to Rudolfo and sat in the living room leafing through a pile of papers on her lap. Maggie and Otis were in the kitchen pouring themselves some coffee. As he opened the door to leave, the telephone rang.

"I'll get it," Otis called out.

It was the laughter again. Sutherland left the door and walked into the kitchen when he heard Otis trying to elicit some words from the caller.

"Hey, who is this? Is there somebody you want to talk to? Speak up!"

"Otis, is it a guy laughing?"

"It was," Otis said with a shrug. "He just hung up. He didn't say one word. He just kept laughing. Do you have some client who's particularly angry with you, James?"

A variant of the hate call? He had not thought of that possibility. But who could it be in this prime time of his life's happiness when he did not consider that anyone had a proper enough reason to hate him? If the calls were truly intended for him, then it had to be somebody from the old days before Jane. Edith perhaps? Preparing for the Christmas housewrecking during a year in which his may have joined the ancestor portraits in her dining room? The depression she felt in the aftermath of their divorce might have focused by now into a real hatred of him. He may unwittingly have helped propel it along by phoning her to tell her the good news in the midst of his ebullient, forgiving mood on learning he was to be a father. For Edith, it had not been welcome news. She had stuttered her way through a cursory congratulation and when she had hung up he knew she was crying.

"Are you sure it was a man, Otis?"

"Positive. Otis is especially attuned to men's voices. This one was shrill, but male. Why? What were you thinking?"

"Edith, maybe. Tomorrow is her day to go bananas. She might be getting an early jump on it."

"That wasn't Edith. That was a guy for sure." It was Jane.

She had evidently picked up the phone in the living room at the same time as Otis. "If that guy calls one more time today, I'm getting in touch with the phone company to see what they can do about it. Crank phone calls are not Edith's style, by the way."

"Then who?"

"A crank. Who else?" Jane answered. But the moment she spoke, the real possibility came to him. It might be John Worth, the husband of a client he had represented in a divorce some four or five years back. Worth, a borderline psychotic pushed over the edge by his divorce, especially after Sutherland and his brother shill Morrison played tin gods and decided Worth was going to take the fall because he had lots of money and could pay for it. Worth had made no secret of his hatred for divorce lawyers before his family finally took the step of committing him. He had rammed Morrison's car from behind on State Street and put his own counsel in a neck brace with a bad whiplash. He had come after Sutherland with a chair in a downtown restaurant and missed only when a waitress spoiled his aim with a pitcher of water to his face. But Sutherland had gradually put him out of mind and possibility when it became apparent he was going to be hospitalized for a long time to come. What luck. What if he was running loose and vengeful now with that psychotic strength of his? It had taken Sutherland and three cops who rushed in from the street to wrestle the madman Worth to the floor so they could put the cuffs on him and take him away. If he had just been released, then to Sutherland's mind his timing was impossibly wrong.

"I think somebody just happened on our number in the phone book," Sutherland told them. "I haven't antagonized a client I know of since I quit the legal racketeering game."

"I can't think of anyone either," Jane said. "It's been ages since I had to fire anybody."

"Crank, then," Maggie decided. "Just stay cool and they'll move on to somebody who can indulge them with a temper tantrum."

"Yeah, you're right," Sutherland agreed. But the sense of

unease was uncurling inside of him. He had to find out if Worth was still in the state hospital.

"Listen, Otis, do me a favor, okay? Please don't get stoned until your friend Archibald gets here, okay? I don't want you off in Tibet or Nepal or someplace like that if there's an emergency and I'm not back yet."

"Otis can cope, straight up or stoned," Otis said, stung, righteous. "And listen, James, Otis has one very interesting bit of news for you."

"What's the news?"

"The baby. It's not going to be a boy. It's going to be a girl. So you better start thinking about your favorite little-girl name."

"Don't be nasty, Otis, just because I told you to stay away from the dope," Sutherland begged. "It's going to be a boy and its name will be Ford."

"Otis isn't being nasty. Otis is prescient. That Greek in the restaurant was funnin' you, James. If that little baby comes out wearing a penis, Otis will give you a free hairstyling, facial and manicure."

"I don't want to hear this, Otis. I want a son. I've been planning on it all along."

"Otis is never wrong," Otis said with a convincing finality that made Sutherland's stomach sour a little.

"I've got to go now, you two. I can't stand to listen to any more of this stuff. There's fresh coffee in the kitchen if you want it."

He left them, Maggie nodding after him sympathetically and Otis's face the mask of irrefutable Truth. As he opened the door to leave, Otis called out to him, "Annabella."

"What did you say, Otis?"

"Otis thinks Annabella is a nice name for a girl."

"Shut up, Otis," Sutherland told him and closed the door behind him. Still, by the time the elevator arrived, he conceded to himself that no matter how you viewed it, for genuine, nonremitting attractiveness, Jane's friends, who were now his friends, beat the hell out of Edith's old gang.

But who was doing the telephoning?

CHAPTER 13

Some Bostonians: Moskowitz and Mallory

Sutherland snowshoed his way happily up Beacon Street toward the State House. The big-bladed plows were working everywhere in town, but the new blower plows the City had just purchased were, too. Their job was the parking lane nearest the curb where the stack-up from the blade plows was heaviest, and with apparent effortlessness they whirled up the accumulation and spewed it onto the sidewalks. There was no place else for it to go. The storm had put down about twenty inches so far. The plows had added an easy additional two feet.

The wind had fallen off again and that would at least help by easing the drifting problem. The snow fell straight down now, as it had most of the night before. Some teenage kids came walking down the middle of Beacon, and Sutherland knew from the giddy, impish grins of their faces that they were about to unleash a salvo of snowballs at him. They did, then started to run, and he assured them they were a bunch of little bastards, but he was laughing when he said it. Life was very fine, Sutherland loved winter, and he knew the hairdresser Otis was absolutely wrong about the sex of his yet-unborn child.

Up ahead, across from the Public Gardens, was a fire engine, its red dome light whirling in the whiteness. But there was no fire; instead the firemen were shoveling clear the hydrants in case one occurred. The engine moved slowly down the street from hydrant to hydrant, a gaggle of three weary figures in full fireman's uniform and carrying long-handled shovels trudging after it. Even from a block away, Sutherland could hear audibly the repetitive clack of a broken cross-link on one of the engine's tire chains against the fender well. When he came upon the three, they had stopped for a moment to pass a warming flask among themselves. When he wished them a Merry Christmas, they offered him a nip and he took it, deciding it was a silly time to play patrician taxpayer.

The firemen moved on and Sutherland stood for a long moment staring across the street into the Public Gardens. A young father perhaps, or in any case a man in his mid-twenties, lurched through the knee-deep snow, dragging a bucking toboggan behind him that had two small children and a very large dog all squeezed onto it. Sutherland smiled easily on the scene: the man was whooping and howling, the children were screaming their shrill delight, the dog was barking nonstop and Sutherland had no idea how the dog kept its balance on all fours.

He stopped smiling abruptly when he saw the would-be suicide of the night before, and his heart gave a little leap of fear. The man, barely discerned, stood at the far edge of the Public Gardens near the Boylston Street entry and appeared to be staring directly at Sutherland. Squinting through the snow, he could just make out that the other's head was bandaged and saw, or thought he saw, a bloodstain on the bandaging above the right temple. It had been only a flesh wound then, a crease in the skull numbing enough to have knocked him out for almost as much time as it had taken Sutherland to phone the police. Impulsively Sutherland stepped down from the curb and started across the street to the Gardens. But the man began a quick retreat onto Boylston Street, turned a corner and vanished from sight as Sutherland charged into the Gardens through the wrought-iron gates screaming after the fled one.

"Stop! Hey, stop! Do you need help? Is there something I can do for you? Have you seen a doctor yet?"

In the middle of the Public Gardens Sutherland hooked one snowshoe on the other and went sprawling facedown in the snow. When he stood up, cursing and brushing the snow from himself, he knew he had no chance of overtaking the man. He walked the rest of the way to the Boylston Street entrance and searched the direction in which the man had fled. There was not a trace of the would-be suicide anywhere and Sutherland could not imagine why he had run away.

One thing disturbed him now. It was too much coincidence even if Boston was a relatively small city. As with the suicide attempt, he had the nagging sense that the man was somehow trying to communicate with him and the name John Worth came to him again. If he was no longer in the state hospital and out roaming Boston now, then Sutherland had an enemy at large and this might be exactly his kind of caper. The telephoning and the pretended suicide, calculated attempts of some rational part of that deranged mind to bait a trap that would entice Sutherland? But in the last analysis he doubted it. The John Worth that he remembered was not given to calculation. He was a prisoner of blunt rages that overwhelmed his hugely muscled frame and sent him hurtling at the hated object like a battering ram. Witness the attacks on Sutherland and his crony Morrison. Witness Worth's punching bag of a wife, who had desperately wanted out of her marriage and appeared in court with a wired jaw the day the judge quickly terminated it.

He fought to control his growing sense of unease and snowshoed his way at a fast walk out of the absolute stillness of the Public Gardens. He had a need for reality and when he reached Beacon Street he searched for the three firemen and their truck with its whirling dome light. He spied them about a block away where some students from Emerson, who had evidently not gone home for the holidays, had volunteered to help dig out the hydrants. The firemen handed over their shovels with a kind of elegant bowing and the students attacked the snow as if they were in competition with any previ-

ous shoveling record the firemen had ever established. Sutherland chased the apparition from his mind and smiled easily
again because he understood what the firemen had certainly
known from the beginning: the students could not last very
long. They were good for a reprieve, a couple of free hydrants,
but that would be it.

Still, Sutherland thought, it was the gesture that counted.
He closeted his anxiety by permitting himself one of those
warm, expansive emotions, the kind he always got in the beginning when he had too much to drink. This time he thought
that Boston was a fine, civilized town in almost every respect.
It would be finer still when the races wearied of beating each
other over the head with lead pipes because of the busing
issue. He loved walking its throbbing downtown streets to the
office each morning. He could not think of another place he
wanted to live in America. He felt safe here.

The memory of the man who had wounded himself on the
Esplanade the night before crept back into his mind while he
stood there. He shook the memory away in annoyance and hurried on toward the intersection at Charles Street.

He started up Beacon Hill. Someone who looked like an expert was skiing straight down trafficless Beacon Street. He was
in a racing crouch trying to get up some speed on an incline
that would not even rival a decent beginner's slope, but he
screeched and yodeled as if he were skiing the Bugaboos and
Sutherland laughed with delight when the skier shot past. He
wondered if they had a law on the books that covered skiing
out of control on city streets. The guy reached the bottom,
made a neat, sharp turn onto Charles and was gone.

The Boston Common appeared to be completely empty of
people except for two stark-naked young men who played
lacrosse in the white dimness while a bareheaded girl in a
sheepskin coat took flash-camera pictures of the insane event.
In front of the State House Sutherland came upon one of the
capitol security guards who watched the lacrosse players with
an unblinking squint.

"Looks like somebody's trying to put together a very memorable Christmas album," Sutherland said to him.

"If they're for real, then it's their fuckin' pneumonia, not mine. Cripes, every year I live in this town it seems to get crazier. I'd move someplace else if I didn't think I'd die of boredom."

"State House in session today?"

"Naw, they're all home. It's too bad they're not in session though. If somebody could convince them to move outside they could melt the storm away with all the hot air they generate and save the poor taxpayers some money for a change. Well, Merry Christmas to you, sir."

Sutherland, laughing, shook hands with the man, "Merry Christmas to you also, and a fine New Year." He was about to trudge on when he took a last look deep into the Common downhill beyond the naked lacrosse players. The would-be suicide was there again, but this time the sight of him did not cause Sutherland to start. He was somehow resigned to the other's presence now and his real reaction was the sensation of an inner strength beginning to ebb away: The guy—John Worth or some other grudge-carrying former client—was definitely tracking him.

"Do you see anyone standing down there, a couple of hundred yards beyond the players?" Sutherland asked the guard. He wanted to be still more certain when he was already convinced.

"No, but it don't mean there isn't somebody standing down there. I don't see so good. I can hardly make out the two guys and the girl over there."

"Oh, I'm sorry," Sutherland told him, staring at the bulge of the guard's revolver strapped to his hip beneath the jacket and wondering if the man was a political appointee. It seemed ludicrously unprofessional to issue firearms to a cop who didn't see so good.

Sutherland started down the harbor side of Beacon Hill toward Tremont Street. At Tremont he paused a moment to scan the street in both directions for his shadow with the bandaged head, but the other was nowhere to be seen. There was no traffic moving here either, but across the way, in front of the Parker House Hotel, three taxis waited in the cab line with their engines idling, the smoke of their exhausts in the cold curling up around the rear windows so Sutherland could not even tell if their drivers were inside or had gone into the hotel coffee shop to wait for a fare.

Boston would have a sweet, festive Christmas Eve no matter what the weather. But it was Sutherland's own sweet, festive Christmas he found himself worrying about now: with Jane about ready to deliver, guests for the holiday and the would-be suicide stalking him around town, with no real way of knowing what the man was about, Sutherland decided the Christmas stew pot was already too full of ingredients. He checked once again for his tracker and, seeing nothing, hurriedly crossed the street.

When he passed the entrance to the Parker House, one of the regular doormen in his colonial-period livery was just coming out and they nodded and smiled as they always did and wished each other a Merry Christmas. As he walked farther along, he found himself thinking about Washington and his colonial armies wintering at Valley Forge until he vexedly chased the thought away by remembering what it was he had come downtown to do today. He still was occasionally perplexed about some of the unaffiliated thoughts that flitted through his mind. Before he had gotten to Vogelmeister for help he used to be certain it was a symptom of madness.

He turned down State Street toward the building where he had his offices and was again surprised to find that Moskowitz's Deli was open. The lights were on but he could not see inside because the steam tables had the big plate-glass windows all fogged up. He could still read the cheerless season's greetings banners that hung in identical drooping arcs against the inside of the panes though. One read "Merry Christmas" and the other proclaimed "Happy Chanukah," and they had reappeared faithfully every December first for the six years since Sutherland had taken the offices on State, and probably for forty or more years before that. The listlessness of the banners always reminded him of the shabby tinsel and twisted green-and-red crepe-paper-and-plastic trees they invariably put up in seedy bars where only drunks would gather on Christmas Day

because they had no families to go to. It also reminded him of
the owner, Mordechi Moskowitz, who was only fifty-eight, but
looked seventy-five because he was sick and dying. Sutherland
knew he would be working well into the afternoon, so he decided to pick up a sandwich while it was still convenient and
he would not have to leave the office to look for someplace to
have a quick lunch later on. Down in the financial district in a
snowstorm on Christmas Eve, there might be nothing open.

Moskowitz's was usually open only for the five-day business
week. It did a brisk breakfast and lunch trade with the secretaries and brokers and ambulance-chaser lawyers and bank
clerks and claims adjusters that flooded into the area in the
mornings, and it was always closed up tight by five o'clock,
being scrubbed down in preparation for the next day. Sutherland, who had given up on liquored lawyer lunches when he
had given up on Edith, enjoyed lunching there when his work
schedule was not overly tight. He had learned to like delicatessen food during his years at Cambridge and at Moskowitz's
it was very fine. The coffee was the best in America.

Old Mordechi was his friend and always gave Sutherland the
corner table he reserved for himself and his sons or their wives
when they dropped by occasionally. While he ate it was
Sutherland's chief pleasure to study the clientele and smell the
rich smells of Jewish cooking and listen to the pandemonium
of the cooks and long-aproned waiters and cashiers and some
of the customers screaming at each other across the steam
tables and sandwich counters and pastry cases. For Sutherland,
it was a kind of voyeurism. For himself he coveted order, but
he loved to study pandemonium, and Moskowitz's at lunchtime he always likened to an initiation rite for a cult of whirling dervishes, so incredible was the frenzy of activity. Today he
stomped the snow from his boots and went inside through the
revolving door. Except for the occasional clank of a fork on a
plate, there was almost a breathless silence in the place.

Only the old people were there today. He had not thought
about them in a long time. Old Jews, men and women on
inflation-ravaged pensions, who filtered into the deli in the afternoons about three or three-thirty, after the pandemonium

had gone back to the offices, for their single decent meal of the day, which was sometimes only a bowl of soup. He had happened upon them the first time one day when he had to skip lunch and the craving for his favorite corned beef sandwich struck at about three-thirty. The sight of the old ones with shaking hands carefully picking at measured portions of food had depressed him. It was hardly the tingle of voyeurism he felt. When it happened the second time, he understood that they came there every day, so he resolved that it was Moskowitz's at lunchtime or not at all, and he stuck faithfully to that resolve ever after.

He saw Moskowitz sitting at the corner table and went over and shook hands, then sat down.

"Happy Chanukah, Mordechi."

"Merry Christmas, James. Still coming down out there?"

"Like the dickens. Not a sensible car and driver anywhere on the streets."

"Pa used to say the winters in Odessa were hell. He should have lived to see this one."

"I didn't think you'd be open today, Mordechi."

Moskowitz took the cigar from his mouth, the ones Sutherland was sure were helping to kill him, and gestured toward the old ones: "They have to eat. But it's over at one o'clock. Tomorrow we're closed all day. Want some breakfast?"

"No, just a corned beef on dark rye to go. I have a few things to do at the office, so I thought I'd take one along for lunch."

Moskowitz gestured to one of the old aproned waiters to come over. "A corned beef on dark rye with hot mustard to go for Mr. Sutherland and a nice pickle, too." He spread the thumb and index finger of his left hand to about a four-inch span to indicate the corned beef should be generous. The man nodded and headed off to the sandwich counter.

Sutherland surveyed the delicatessen. Moskowitz's was in the dining room of an old hotel long defunct. It always reminded Sutherland of a hotel dining room he and Edith had once eaten in on a tour of Russia, though he could never remember in which city the hotel had been.

Today the sea of old people in dark, heavy winter clothing at the white-covered tables recalled Russians in Russia to him also. He had found the country cheerless and dreary and he could barely wait to leave the place and get back to Paris and raise a little hell. Moskowitz's was so quiet because the old ones concentrated on their food. A few sat together and occasionally spoke to one another, but most sat alone and there was a kind of vital energy to their eating. Mordechi Moskowitz was practically a charitable organization. The old people got larger portions and paid less for it. By the time they began shuffling in in midafternoon, gaunt specters who seemed to wear heavy clothing in even the most stifling weather, the soups had already been thickened, the fatty cuts of brisket that they appeared to crave were ready for carving and the larger wedges of bread had been sliced. Moskowitz's in the afternoon was a soup kitchen with dignity.

Loneliness pervaded the air. A lot of the men wore their hats as they ate and that somehow added to it, though Sutherland could not exactly say why. Cripes, some of these people had to have families, but look how they lived! Where were the sons and daughters? Where was their sense of responsibility? The notion of this kind of abandonment was anathema to Sutherland. If anything happened to Archibald or Marjorie both he and his sister Elaine would be up to New Hampshire in a flash. It was hard to think about it, but he suspected Archibald was going to go first, and when that happened Marjorie would move right in with either him or Elaine. There had never been any question of that. He frowned at the sight in Moskowitz's dining room, then turned to face the proprietor. Moskowitz seemed to be reading his thoughts. "Let's hope nobody ever dies in here, James. They say it's bad luck for a place. The chandeliers might start dropping on customers or something like that. Let's talk about life for a change. The wife about ready to give you your son?"

"Any time now. It might even be tomorrow."

"Christmas Day, huh? Hallowed event in the making. Your folks make it down from New Hampshire for the holiday?"

"They're on their way by four-wheel drive. How about you,

Mordechi? What are you going to do tomorrow? Sleep all day?"

"No, me and the wife are going to celebrate Christmas. At the youngest son Aaron's house. You know, the one who married the Japanese girl? I swear, I can barely wait. It's the only chance I get all year to sit on the floor at the table, drink Manischewitz from saki cups and eat turkey chow mein or whatever the fuck she's going to surprise us with this year. Then, instead of watching a football game on TV like I want to, I am further submitted to the indescribable torture of roughhousing with my slit-eyed little grandchildren, who do not look very Jewish to their grandparents. It usually takes about a month to recover from the children and sitting on the floor."

Sutherland shook with quiet laughter in Moskowitz's sad, sad deli. Mordechi was one of the funniest men he had ever met. The knowledge of his own impending death, if anything, had sharpened his sense of humor. What was there left to be desperate about? Sutherland had first met him about the same time he had cashiered Edith and the man had proven to be a kind of tonic for him. Even then Moskowitz had known his would be an early dying. By degrees, like Jane, he had broken down the rigidity of Sutherland's awesome reserve at the same time that Vogelmeister worked at putting his head back together. God! To think that there had even been a time in his past when he thought there was something improper about knowing a person like Moskowitz!

The waiter returned with the sandwich in a warmer bag. He started to write out a check, but Moskowitz waved him away: "It's Christmas, James, your wife's about to have a baby, et cetera, et cetera. Have one on me."

"Thanks, Mordechi." Sutherland looked in the bag. He doubted he could open his mouth wide enough to take a bite of the monster.

"Anything else new in your life, James?"

He told Moskowitz about the man who had tried to kill himself on the Esplanade that morning.

"Crazy business," Moskowitz judged. "Suicide is the saddest

thing there is. A man's really at the end of his tether when that happens. Years ago, when the word got out that Moskowitz had a glad hand with the victuals and these old codgers started coming in, I used to think some of them were prime candidates. But they never do. They're tough as nails, these bastards. They're born survivors."

"There he is," Sutherland said quietly. As Moskowitz spoke, Sutherland's eyes had been slowly traveling the clusters of wrinkled faces bent intently over the plates of food when he suddenly saw his tail at the window, peering inside and rubbing the glass with the palm of his hand as if he failed to realize that the condensation of the steam tables that obscured his view was on the interior of the pane.

"Who, James?"

"Last night's attempted suicide. This is the third time I've seen him today. We've been getting some crank phone calls at home—really off-the-wall crazy laughter—and now I think it's him. Look over there, Mordechi. In the big window to the left of the Chanukah sign. See him?"

Sutherland pointed toward the window and Moskowitz had time to catch a quick glimpse of the apparition before he apparently realized he had been seen and moved quickly away.

"Yeah, James, I saw him. A heavy-set guy with a scarf wrapped around his head, right?"

"The scarf is bandaging, I think. He must've just grazed himself when he squeezed off that shot last night, otherwise it stands to reason he wouldn't be around to dog my tracks today."

"You seem remarkably calm, James, for a person who might have a real problem on his hands."

"What else can I do? I can't ask the cops to arrest a man who hasn't done me any real harm I know of. They might decide I was some sort of paranoid loony and haul me off for a bit of observation instead. No, it's curiosity that's got me now."

"Why don't I send three or four of the waiters outside and see if they can corner the guy and haul him in here so we can ask him a few questions about himself? I'm curious, too."

Moskowitz raised his arm to get the attention of one of the waiters, but Sutherland reached over and hauled the arm down.

"No, Mordechi, no way. I appreciate your wanting to help, but I'd be carrying around a bad conscience for a while if anything happened to one of your waiters. Our man was packing something for his own dispatch last night that looked convincingly like a German Luger and he might still have it with him. Besides, my chief suspect is a former client's ex-husband who I'm hoping is still in the state hospital up in Danvers. Because if he isn't, he wouldn't need a gun to do somebody some harm. The guy was a real psychotic bulldozer. He's the crazy who rammed my buddy Morrison from behind with the car and put him in a neck brace that time."

"Jesus, I remember. The same one who came after you in the restaurant, right?"

"Same guy, Mordechi. Very fucked up."

"Take care, James. Take very good care of yourself, huh? Especially now that you've got the good wife you always wanted and the kid on its way. Get yourself a gun permit if it turns out that guy isn't in Danvers any longer. You may need it, pal."

Sutherland shrugged, stood up and shook hands with his friend, and marched out the door with his briefcase, his snowshoes and his corned beef sandwich. It still snowed like the dickens.

He signed in at the guard station in the office building's lobby, wished the guard a Merry Christmas, asked him to telephone Sutherland first and then the police quickly thereafter if a disheveled, overweight man with a bandaged head showed up looking for him, and went upstairs.

He took the papers he needed from the briefcase, then sat down at his desk to wait until the coffee was ready. Sutherland looked about his office and thought for perhaps the thousandth time how much he approved of it. It was rich-looking with paneling and leather-bound volumes on the bookshelves. Jane had furnished it as a birthday surprise the second year they had known each other. He walked in one Monday morn-

ing and there was a genuine Bokhara on the floor and a
leather-topped teakwood desk. There were campaign-style
cabinets and plush leather chairs for the clients. He remembered being nearly delirious because he thought she had forgotten altogether about the birthday. He stared fondly now at the
gilt-framed photo of Jane that graced his desk. When he was
married to Edith, her photo had lasted about two months on
his desk. Then he had shoved it in a drawer and never looked
at it again for about three years until he resigned from the firm
and was cleaning out his desk. Then she went out in a trash
can the office building maintenance people provided for his
cleanout and ended up, Sutherland supposed, dying in the
flames of the building's incinerator.

He turned to look through the window. He could still discern the docks and warehouses on the near side of the harbor,
but the lights of Logan Airport on the other side were only a
vague blur. A ship moved in the harbor, just arriving, evidently. It was a tanker, long and low in the water, and fes-
tooned with lights, and he watched its slow progress as it was
nudged by two tugs toward the tanker port. Just as it edged
out of view the buzzer went off on the percolator. He went
into the conference room, poured himself a mug of coffee,
then returned to his office to sit down and work on the brief.

Three cups of coffee and approximately three hours later,
Sutherland called a halt and began his attack on the corned
beef sandwich from Moskowitz's Deli. It was the friend-of-the-
management special, all right, and rather than dislocate his jaw
by trying to eat it in single bites he separated the two halves
into four open-faced sandwiches and put them on a plate the
secretaries also kept in the conference-room cabinet. He carried
the plate to the window and stood eating as he looked out into
the storm.

It seemed to him to be diminishing a bit, though he could
have been mistaken: a clock gong sounded twice and he decided that for two in the afternoon it was uncommonly dark,
like the darkness of an eclipse. Squinting out into the harbor
he could see little. Logan Airport had vanished without a trace,
and the warehouses on the Boston side were blurred hulks

without the detail of windows or doors, their roofs covered uniformly with a blanket of snowlike white icing on a long row of wedge-shaped cakes.

Almost directly below, on the Fitzgerald Expressway, a tractor-trailer had jackknifed and two police cars were there diverting the few vehicles that moved around the wreck in the single lane that remained open. The trailer was tipped precariously as if it were about to go over on its side. Under the glow of the overhead lights Sutherland could read its bright-orange nomenclature clearly: Sewanee Belle Citrus Groves, Titusville, Florida. He hoped the driver had not been badly hurt or killed and he even felt strangely apologetic: the rig had been moving South and he imagined the driver was a black man hastening home in time for a warm Christmas with a family in Titusville; sweet New England had just struck down another somebody who did not know enough about driving in snow.

He watched the scene as a huge wrecker drew near, then maneuvered in reverse, intending evidently to try winching the trailer upright so it could be moved away. Two men left the wrecker and began conferring with the police for a few moments, when all of a sudden the trailer gave up and fell over on its side with a loud crash that was even audible to Sutherland eleven stories up in an hermetically-sealed office building. The cops and the two men who had brought the wrecker scattered everywhere across the highway to safety.

"Merry Christmas!" Sutherland judged and got off a long, low whistle.

"And a Merry Christmas to you, sir," a voice said from behind him. Sutherland whirled about so startled that he dropped the sandwich plate and it shattered on the floor. His fear was real: someone stood in the door of the pitch-dark conference room with hands thrust into the pockets of his overcoat. Sutherland could not see his face, but it came to him with a bowel-churning terror that he was now in the same room with the would-be suicide of last night on the Esplanade who had somehow gotten past the guard downstairs. The man's portly build was exactly the same.

"Who are you? What do you want? Worth, is it you?"

The figure salaamed with his hands extended in front of him now.

"I have come, O Brahmin Prince, to wish you a Merry Christmas as I have already done and then to ask you a few questions about that little incident you witnessed on the river last night. . . ."

The voice walked forward into the light of the desk lamp and Sutherland sighed relief like air issuing slowly from a bellows. It was Mallory, the detective from the M.D.C. Police. He was also a friend since Edith was gone.

"You Irish miscreant bastard, you! I almost went through the window from fright. Merry Christmas yourself. Don't you believe in knocking on doors?"

"I did. About ten times. Then I opened it because you forgot to lock it, saw the glow of a light in your office and crept forward to find you since your wife said you'd be here most of the day. Does working in total darkness except for a small desk lamp somehow improve your concentration?"

"Not really. I just got going on some work and didn't notice how dark it was getting out there. Take a look out the window here at this cute little Christmas Eve spectacle on the expressway."

"A chorus line of naked college girls is dancing in the snow to commemorate the birth of Christ? Am I right, Sutherland? Tell me I'm right."

"No, detective sir. It's a little less entertaining than that, I'm afraid."

"Oh, well, it's going to happen one of these years," he shrugged as he moved toward the window. "In this eccentric village of ours, it's just a matter of time."

Mallory peered through the glass. He had put on a lot of weight since Sutherland had first cross-examined him in court years before. He was an honest cop and funny like Mordechi Moskowitz, but it was a different kind of humor—the kind some cops surrounded themselves with like a protective glaze to inure themselves against a career of looking up society's anus. Mallory scanned the highway, and then spotted the tractor-trailer.

"Ah, that's the Florida truck, I'll bet. They were dispatching the wrecker when I was on my way down here. I caught it on the radio."

"I hope the driver's okay."

"He's dead. D.O.A. When they got him to Mass General. Some throttle jockey spade barrel-assin' his way back to the land of sunshine in a blizzard. It's damn lucky he didn't take a bunch of innocents with him. . . . Which reminds me, James, speaking of death, let's you and I turn on some lights, sit down for a couple of minutes and talk about that suicide caper last night."

Sutherland flicked on the ceiling lights, then went to one of the campaign cabinets, pulled out a bottle of scotch and two glasses. "A little nip for Christmas, Michael?"

"Why not? I can use the fortification. Everybody's on over-time tonight. There is much concern down at headquarters about banditry by snowmobile this sweet holy night."

"Did you find that guy?" Sutherland asked with pretended nonchalance. It was the only way to plumb Mallory, to find out first what he knew or was willing to tell, before Sutherland might have to lay bare his suspicions about John Worth and invite the police in to help deal with his growing anxiety. He poured two rock glasses of scotch neat and passed one to the detective.

"Nope. He got over that footbridge onto Beacon Street, turned off his blood-making machine, and vanished into the obscure night."

"Then maybe he got to help. Maybe he was able to fashion some sort of tourniquet. God! It made me so sad to think of somebody trying to kill themselves in the middle of the Christmas season. What depression he must have felt."

"This may be the Christmas season, but that guy was still celebrating Halloween. Somebody was funnin' you, James. It was a prank."

"But, Mike, I heard the shot. I saw the flash of gunfire. When he ran toward the footbridge he was bleeding like a stuck pig."

"Correction, James. He was bleeding like a just-slaughtered

chicken. More like three of them, as a matter of fact, according to the lab boys. There wasn't a drop of human blood anywhere around."

"That bastard!" Sutherland forced a laugh. "That's got to be one of the oldest practical jokes in the world." He raised his glass in a toast to himself, shaking his head at the incredible irony of timing: a determined, evidently now calculating enemy had resurfaced at the worst possible moment of his life: "Sutherland is a good man. A toast to Sutherland, gentlemen. His humanity was tested and was not found wanting."

Smirking, Mallory raised his glass also. "A toast to the Police Department, gentlemen. Their duty was called upon and not found derelict." Then the detective lowered his glass. "Boy, would I like to get my hands on that son of a bitch! Ten cops, four lab technicians, and two fucking bloodhounds we had to borrow from the staties. I hate wasting the taxpayers' money, particularly since I'm also one of them. Tell me, what did the guy look like?"

Sutherland told him, but Mallory shook his head in the negative.

"No. Too heavyset. Too tall. The loony I'm thinking of who might get his jollies from something like that is about five feet, one inch and thin as a rake." Mallory downed the rest of his drink in one gulp and stood to leave: "Well, let's hope he got his rocks off last night and settles for midnight mass tonight instead. It was probably one of those damn M.I.T. kids who didn't go home for the holiday break. I'll bet somebody put him up to this on a dare. A bunch of them probably spent the whole morning laughing their asses off in a dorm room at the spectacle of a platoon of cops about to find out they were tracking down a bleeding chicken. See how stimulating higher education can be? Since the honorable peace was achieved in Vietnam and they no longer have any reason to throw rocks at the pigs, the new methods they come up with for harassing the thin blue line of civilization are inventive beyond belief. Well, Merry Christmas again, James, and say hello to the wife for me. I've got to move on."

"Wait up, Michael, and I'll ride down with you," Sutherland told him with more studied carelessness. After the fright Mallory had given him he no longer wanted to be alone, and he wanted to tell the detective about Worth, but was not sure he had sufficient reason. He was trained as an attorney and panic was anathema to his profession. There was no real evidence that the crank phone calls and the would-be suicide who shadowed him were connected, and the man had not attempted to harm him in any way. In the complex of Sutherland's private ethic, there was a generous space for caution: you only went to the mattress with the police as a last alternative. It served no purpose to bare a layer of the self just because a man felt queasy. They were a tribe of curious people, the police.

The phone rang then and Sutherland thought first of Jane.

"Hello?"

It was the crank laughter again.

"Hello, who is this? What the hell do you want?"

There was no response save the laughter. Sutherland made his decision and handed the phone to Mallory. The cop listened, raised his eyes and puckered his lips a little in response, but did not speak. In moments more he handed the phone back to Sutherland.

"Hung up. How long's this been going on, James?"

"Started today. But this is the third time in two different places. It can't be some guy trying potluck with a number he lifted randomly from the phone book. Whoever's doing this knows something about me. Too much."

They sat down again. Both stared out the window through the early darkness toward the blurred glow of lights at Logan. Sutherland suddenly felt a dull ache from tension in the muscles of his shoulders. The kind he always got before his final summation in a jury trial.

"What's up, James? Who's Worth?"

"How did you know about Worth?"

"Boy, you are rattled, barrister. If you remember back just a little, you thought I was Worth when I came in and almost scared the socks right off you."

Sutherland sighed heavily and decided he was going to stop

playacting for Mallory's benefit. No use in jeopardizing this friendship: Mallory had the scent now and it would be only a matter of time before he found out what he wanted to know. The cop would be annoyed if Sutherland made his work that much harder.

"Mike, I knew that guy who pulled the suicide-for-fun caper last night wasn't dead. I've already seen him three times today with a bloodstained bandage wrapped around his head. And I'm not hallucinating, either. The last time was up in Mordechi's deli, and Mordechi saw him, too. Up until now I didn't really put too much stock in the possibility of a connection between the crazy phone calls and the crazy on the Esplanade, but now I'm beginning to. Mike, I think that guy put on a performance for my benefit last night. Mike, he actually waved at me before he put the gun to his head! Can you believe that's just a coincidence?"

Mallory was looking across the desk at him now. An indulgent smile played at the corners of his mouth. "I became a father when I was only twenty. The stress of birthing a baby for the first time, plus witnessing that prank this early A.M. would be enough to spook any jittery new daddy."

Sutherland scowled at him: "I'm thirty-seven, not twenty, and I've lost plenty of hide to experience in between, Michael. I don't spook that easily."

"All right, then, who's Worth? You might as well tell me because you know I'll find out. I don't give up that easily either."

"Worth is . . . Well, when the phone rang the second time this morning at our apartment I started checking back over the enemy list, and even considering the minimal gratitude divorce lawyers can expect from clients' spouses, the only one who rang a bell as being demented enough for this kind of fun and games was a very battered client's husband named John Worth. He's the one who went after my crony Morrison with his car that time and almost murdered me with a serving tray in a restaurant—"

"Hmm. I remember that. You were nearly beheaded. Any idea where this guy is now?"

"They sent him up to the state hospital at Danvers about four years back. If he's not in there, Mike, he might be out here getting set to wreak vengeance on me. Any way you can find out?"

Mallory reached for the phone on the desk, pushed a button for an outside line, then dialed a number.

"James, any aliases you remember on this guy? Recall where he lived before Danvers?"

"No aliases I remember. They lived out in Westwood, but the wife got the house and sold it and later left the state. She ended remarrying in the Southwest. Either Arizona or New Mexico, but I don't recall exactly which."

Someone answered Mallory's call: "Who's this? Jean? Hello, Jean darling, and Merry Christmas to you. . . . Yes, it's Mallory, Charlestown's most distinguished export and unrivaled delight of—You want me to can the bullshit because tomorrow's Christmas and you already have a headache? . . . Okay, but I'm complying only because you sound like you mean it. . . . Listen sweetheart, run me a quick tracer on a subject, John Worth, no known a.k.a.'s, last known address the state funny farm at Danvers, committal date about four years gone. Call me back as soon as you know something, okay? I should be able to hang out here for about fifteen more minutes."

Mallory gave Sutherland's office number to the M.D.C. clerk, said good-bye and returned the phone to its cradle. He poured himself a little more scotch from the bottle on the desk, then returned to looking speculatively out the window into the midafternoon darkness.

"James, what about your wife's ex-husband? What was his name anyhow?"

"Occhapenti. Manfredi Occhapenti. No, no way. We had a bad go-round with him last spring that you may remember me mentioning to you, until the Immigration people deported him to Italy and got him out of our hair. But once he went back he was quick to bury the hatchet. He's not the brooding type. He married an American girl before he left and she went over with him. They're happy and living in Rome and we exchange letters with them a couple of times a month. All's forgiven. No,

Michael, I'm putting my money on John Worth. Besides, even if Manfredi were still carrying a grudge, there isn't much he could do about it. He's barred from ever entering the States again because of that arson charge the feds nailed him with."

"Hmm. Grisly business that was, if memory serves me. Okay, so Occhapenti's defused and we concentrate on Worth. If he's sprung and it turns out he's the guy who seems to be harassing you, then it stands to reason we ought to be able to ensure he goes back in again. If my tracer confirms he's loose, a tail goes on you right away."

Then the phone rang again and Sutherland impulsively reached for it, but was waved away by Mallory. The detective picked up the receiver and listened. It was the woman named Jean from M.D.C. headquarters, when Sutherland was certain it would be the laughing crank. He listened as Mallory responded now in monosyllables.

"Yep, Mallory. Hmm. When? Hmm. Where? When? Sure? Okay. Thanks. Merry Christmas, pal."

"What's up, Michael?" Sutherland asked as Mallory put back the receiver.

"Scratch suspect John Worth, unless it's his ghost. He died at Danvers of a heart attack about seven months back and was buried in a family plot out in Westwood. There's a coroner's report on file. He's very dead."

"Cripes, who then?"

"How about your wife? Any torpedoed ex-suitors around who might have gotten burned?"

"If there were, I don't remember any. She came and plucked me out of my first marriage one night and I've never seen another eligible man anywhere around since then."

"How about anyone who ever worked for her that was handed his walking papers? Any possibilities there?"

"We talked about that this morning. She can't think of anybody." Sutherland threw up his hands in consternation. "My wife doesn't have enemies, Mike. She doesn't believe in them. To my knowledge anybody who ever got canned at the magazine left with a good letter of recommendation and a hot tip on a new job, and there've been very few firings over the years. I don't think that's the right direction to look."

"Then I don't know in what direction to look, James. And now that we're certain Worth isn't after you, I really don't have enough reason to have you shadowed on a nuisance complaint. Keep in touch and let me know if the phone calls continue or if you see that guy with the bandage again. I'm betting you're the victim of a one-day plague, and tomorrow it'll all be gone. Even pranksters get tired of their own pranks. Well, I've got to move on now, James."

Mallory stood to leave another time and Sutherland prepared to go with him. He packed his briefcase, put away the scotch, picked up his parka and snowshoes and closed down the rest of the office, remembering to lock the door this time. They rode down in the elevator and exchanged a little banter about the Celtics, said good night to the building guard and were outside in another moment, instinctively scanning the sky. It was almost completely dark now, but the snow was definitely tapering off, as the Weather Bureau had promised.

Mallory's unmarked department car was parked almost in the middle of the street. It was an unobstrusive blue Chevy that wore shiny new chains. They shook hands good-bye and Mallory sighed, looking toward the flashing lights of the wrecker up on the expressway.

"Too bad about the Florida nigger, huh, James?"

"Black person, Michael. Black person."

"Aw, shit. Sorry about that. I always forget."

"I'll bet," Sutherland winked at him. But that was all. He began walking up the middle of State Street toward Washington, where the inevitable plow rumbled past while Mallory started the car and headed off in the opposite direction.

Sutherland understood Mallory's game. Affecting near-indifference by relegating the bandaged prankster and the crank phone calls to nuisance complaint only meant that Mallory's curiosity had been seized. Sutherland guessed he was now the bait that would bring out the quarry Mallory had just set his sights on.

CHAPTER 14

Other Bostonians

Late in the afternoon of Christmas Eve the downtown shopping area of Boston was an eerie place. The stores were all closed by now, but their display-window lights still burned and cast multicolored reflections on the heaped-up snowbanks. Not a vehicle moved anywhere; not a single pedestrian any longer had a reason to trudge the streets as Sutherland did. He felt a little like the lone survivor of a city that had died of an epidemic.

He decided it was a perfect time and place for the would-be suicide to reappear and he was not at all surprised when the man materialized out of the shadows of the covered walkway before Woolworth's and stood in the middle of the street. Sutherland surmised that their face-to-face confrontation was going to happen here and now and started walking toward his shadow that was almost two blocks away. When he had cut that distance down to little more than a block and Sutherland was able to see what a large overweight man his stalker really was, the other bolted for the sidewalk with surprising speed, turned a corner of Woolworth's and was gone. Sutherland ran after him, yelling out in the silence that was broken only by the sizzle of neon lighting: "Stop! Stop and tell me what it is you want!"

But when he reached the end of the Woolworth's building and looked down the street where the stalker had fled, there was absolutely no one to be seen. Then the anxiety quickened in Sutherland again: he felt vulnerable in playing this game completely by someone else's rules. He suddenly wanted out of this deserted shopping area. There was not another person to call to for help. He turned about and started to run.

He stopped running at Tremont Street, where he found some people. The engines of taxicabs still idled in front of the hotels and their drivers sat inside reading newspapers. The lights were on in King's Chapel and Sutherland could see figures moving behind the stained-glass windows.

He started up Beacon Hill. The Christmas lights had been turned on at the State House and reflected against the gold leaf of the dome. The sidewalks around the capitol had been cleared sometime that afternoon evidently, and the new snow from the additional fall was only an inch or two deep. Sutherland left the street and clambered over a snowbank to the sidewalk. In front of him, right before the State House main steps, was an anomalous sight.

Ahead, about a hundred yeards away, were two women standing motionless in the middle of the path, staring far off and upward at what he supposed must be the blinking temperature-clock atop the Edison Building that said the time was 5:05 P.M. and the temperature had dropped to nineteen degrees. Both women wore furs and remained as rooted to the spot as statues and when he was about twenty yards nearer them, the moment of recognition arrived and an involuntary wrench of dismay passed through Sutherland and he thought of turning around.

It was Edith, his ex-wife, to whom he had not spoken in more than two years except for the phone call to tell her about the baby's impending birth. He had seen her during that time —once at a charity benefit, and once at Quincy Market on a Saturday afternoon when he and Jane had been shopping for cheeses and prosciutto. They were about to leave when Edith's dark-blue chauffeured Mercedes had swept up to the curb. George, the black driver who had worked for Edith and her parents before her as long as McGivern, had opened the door and a woman who should have been some emperor's empress emerged. An awed cluster of people looked on as always and

Jane, who stood beside him, said simply, "I wonder if there's such a thing as being too beautiful? It must get to the point where it starts being a liability."

Edith moved toward them. Sutherland prepared to say hello, shifting the package he carried to his left arm so he might shake her hand. But she moved past, unseeing, and he turned, like just another innocuous member of the gaping crowd to follow her progress. A stab of hurt went through him like a knife, but he could not say why. Perhaps she had really not seen him, but he suspected she had. Edith missed very little, despite giving the impression of being three quarters ethereal. Janie sensed the hurt instantly. She nudged him. "James, say hello to the driver. He's smiling your way."

George stood beside the Mercedes and smiled a cautious smile. He kept a wary eye on Edith's distance until she disappeared inside the market, then his face broke into a wide grin.

"Mr. Sutherland! How are you, sir? It's been such a long time since I've seen you."

Sutherland shook his hand warmly and asked after his family. He had always gotten on well with George. During the sustained warfare of Sutherland's marriage to Edith, he had somehow managed a delicate tightrope act between the two camps, and unlike McGivern never openly declared an allegiance. Sutherland was grateful to him for that. That Saturday afternoon at Quincy Market he was also grateful, restored even, to learn that George still thought kindly of him.

The two women had not yet moved. Edith wore the Russian sable cape. The hood was down and occasional flakes of snow fell lightly on her beautiful hair. In either hand she held the leash of her two sleek black Dobermans and the dogs lay quietly on the path, staring—much to Sutherland's fascination —in the identical same direction as Edith and the woman who accompanied her. Perhaps they were looking for the appearance of the Star of Bethlehem and not at the Edison temperature-clock at all. Inane thought, Sutherland chuckled to himself. But it was followed by another.

Sable-clad Edith and her splendid Dobermans were a living, breathing advertisement. For what? For anything, he supposed.

Russian sable capes, fine Dobermans, winter vacations in Boston, New England snow gift packages for your friends in Florida, cosmetics, health spas . . . The list of possibilities seemed endless to him. Stick Edith and her furs and her matching Dobermans next to a winter-white Rolls-Royce and that financially groaning British old lady would be off and charging with a new lease on life. Yes, that was it. Edith was not real. She was fictive, an advertisement. She belonged in the high-fashion, high-priced come-ons in the pages of *The New Yorker* or *Vogue* that a certain breed of women traipsed through faithfully, skirting the meat of any worthwhile literature therein. But Edith did not belong in life. She was too anomalous. What a curious flash of insight after so many years of knowing her. Christ, it was turning into a crazy Christmas.

He drew closer. Neither of the women had seen him yet. Nor had the Dobermans, who were members of a supposedly alert breed. When Sutherland had moved out, the Dobermans had moved in. For protection against her estranged husband, who was given to violent abuse, was the word Edith put out. Sutherland thought she had gone mad: in all those awful years of marriage he had never laid a hand on her. Banging women around was not his ethic, and at that time, carrying around so much anger inside him that not even Vogelmeister could diffuse it, there seemed to be no dearth of full-grown, angry men in Boston bars and traffic jams to oblige him by taking the first swing.

Still he slinked around town by day, afraid of meeting any of Edith's preferred society who knew him as James Sutherland the wife-beater. Only there had been no reason to slink anywhere. Edith's tale had backfired on her, and not a few other people thought she had gone mad, too. He found this out one early evening from Louie Morton. He and Louie belonged to the same club and chanced upon each other in the bar, though Sutherland, who spied Louie first, had tried for a getaway.

"I'll tell you, James, it's all bullshit. Everyone thinks she's really gone daft and no one will go to the house any longer. They're all afraid. That Nazi witch McGivern's got those two creatures roaming the place to guard against some sort of imminent attack she thinks is coming from you at any moment. Somebody's gone mad in that house. I tell you they're attack dogs, the same sort riot police would use for crowd control or God knows what. . . ."

Edith's Dobermans became famous. Sutherland began hearing about them everywhere. But gradually the stories changed. McGivern apparently relaxed her vigilance after a time, feeling foolish perhaps, because Sutherland communicated with Edith only through his lawyers. McGivern's dogs then became Edith's dogs in the true sense of ownership. If dogs really assumed the quirks and personality traits of their owners, then Edith's Dobermans were worth a study grant. They mellowed. The aggressiveness that had been bred into them receded by degrees until, full-grown monsters in appearance, they were about as mean as puppies and, by all reports, about as vacuous as their mistress. They pined to be petted at cocktail parties and slept at the foot of Edith's bed. People made jokes about their safety if they were ever attacked by another dog.

Ten feet away from them, they were still unaware of his presence. He finally spoke: "Hello, Edith. How are you?"

Four heads turned toward him with the same slow simultaneous motion: Edith, the woman companion Sutherland did not know, and the two Dobermans. The women smiled identical smiles that verged on enigma, and the Dobermans looked as if they had somehow just lapped up a whole bowl of Christmas eggnog. Edith seemed not to have aged a day since the first time Sutherland laid eyes upon her.

"Oh, hello, James. Merry Christmas. You look quite well. These are Desmond and Bill," she explained, introducing the Dobermans. "And this is my friend Catherine. You do remember Catherine, of course?"

Sutherland smiled a greeting to the woman, then removed a glove to shake her hand. He looked at her closely. She was sixty-five perhaps, but well preserved and groomed and not the least overweight. She had the thin, finely boned face of an older woman who must have been a great beauty in her youth. Her snow-white hair was cut short and perfectly coiffed in a way that would have brought forth gushes of admiration from

Otis the hairdresser. Kindly green eyes smiled back at him. She wore a full-length mink coat and there was a tasteful, simple string of pearls at her throat where the coat lay open. She must be a new friend, Sutherland surmised. None of Edith's old gang had a hope of surviving this well.

"No. No, I'm sorry. I'm afraid I don't remember you, madam."

"But, James, you must," Edith insisted. "It's Catherine McGivern. Our Catherine. Remember?"

"Jesus Christ!" Sutherland spurted involuntarily.

"Hello, James. It's so very nice to see you again," the woman companion told him in a soft, cultivated voice.

Sooo: McGivern had moved out of the kitchen and into the parlor. Despite himself he shook his head in wonderment at the transformation. Henceforth he would believe in miracles. The potato-faced puffiness and the harsh grate of the brogue were gone. He suspected she might have abandoned her vociferous Catholicism as well. He could not think of a single thing to say for the moment, but his mind worked feverishly nonetheless. The new McGivern, after a fashion, was a final judgment on Edith. Her promotion from companion-slave to companion-friend meant that Edith had called it quits on hunting for Sutherland's replacement. The feverish age of American materialism was on the wane, he had read somewhere, and his friend and shrink, Vogelmeister, delightedly concurred with that idea. That implied that the number of fortune-hunters in circulation who might pursue Edith's fortune as dedicatedly as Sutherland had in his day must be diminishing; and no man with any more than a peapod of a brain would pursue Edith for anything but her fortune. Her mind was a desert of shifting sands and her fantastic beauty, as far as Sutherland was concerned, was about as ill-starred as Helen of Troy's. Any guy who thought it worthwhile to own a tuxedo would understand this. And anybody who did not own one would not make it into Edith's house.

So McGivern was the replacement; and after McGivern died there would be another McGivern, and the chronicle of Edith Watkins' life (she had taken back her maiden name after the divorce) would also be a chronicle of McGiverns coming and going. On Christmas Eve, Sutherland felt a very great sadness for his ex-wife indeed.

To fill the void of silence he told them the bizarre story of the phony suicide on the Charles early that morning.

"Oh, James, how interesting," Edith said.

"So very interesting. Yes," McGivern concurred.

He grew a little panicky, but could not explain why.

"Have you and Catherine been here for a time, Edith?" he asked desperately. "The Common is very lovely tonight, isn't it?"

"We've been here almost two hours, James. We're watching the thermometer temperature on the Edison Building drop. It's quite fascinating. It falls precisely two degrees each half hour. Isn't that right, Catherine?"

"Exactly so, Edith. Precisely two degrees."

On Christmas Eve! Sutherland might have wept for them. Where were their men? The drinking of spirits toasting the season before a fireplace? The trimming of a tree? He wanted to go home. To race home: he wanted to be near the vibrant reality of Jane, of Maggie and Otis, of his parents, Archibald and Marjorie . . .

They seemed to him of a sudden to be the loneliest people he had ever encountered. The idea of suspecting Edith of making the crank phone calls now seemed to him an absurdly paranoid notion.

He bent down, knowing it would be all right now, and kissed Edith on the cheek. He kissed McGivern also and she hugged him warmly. The Dobermans rose from the ground for theirs, and he patted at the sleek smoothness of their coats.

Then he fled from them all, trying to make it seem as if he were not actually running.

PART III

The Suicide
Returns to the
River Charles

CHAPTER 15

The Christmas Eve War

Sutherland made it home from his chance meeting with Edith and the reconstructed McGivern without catching another glimpse of the bandaged stalker who had frightened him into a run from the deserted stillness of Washington Street. Archibald and Marjorie had already arrived and were upstairs in the apartment. He knew because he went down to the garage first and his Ford truck was parked and dripping snow in the slot he had reserved for it next to the Jaguar.

The welcome sounds of laughter came from inside the apartment as Sutherland opened the door. The five who awaited him were in the living room and he entered to the by now familiar spectacle of a howling Archibald turning a very stoned and moronically grinning Otis about the room by his earring. Otis moved in a slow circle like an ox driving a wheel, his rhythm a variegated high-stepping gimp that reminded Sutherland of buck dancing. Sutherland smiled a tolerant smile and wondered how long this obtuse ritual had been going on. A long time, he hoped. None of the others ever seemed to tire of it the way Sutherland did. Perhaps Jane did: but then she would condescend to any silliness that gave her new father-in-law pleasure.

He smelled a forest smell and turned to see that a fresh-cut and very full blue spruce hauled down from the farm had been set up in one corner of the room and Sutherland guessed that it had probably been about three feet taller when it came through the door because its top ended near the ceiling in a sawed-off nub about six inches wide. He wondered if they had enough lights or ornaments to decorate even half of it.

He kissed his mother and wished her a Merry Christmas in English. Then he shook hands with his father, who extended his left hand somewhat perfunctorily to his son since the right was absorbed in twirling his friend Otis about. For a long moment the three of them revolved in a slow circle like folk dancers in a reel until Sutherland left off in response to the meaningful glance Jane made at her watch. He pulled off his parka to hang it up, then went to put his snowshoes and brief-case away. When he returned he sat down on a sofa with Jane and Maggie and watched what he hoped was the dancers' last gasp.

Archibald looked very tired and drawn despite the childlike smile that illuminated his face. He seemed somehow shorter and paler and had definitely lost weight since the last time Sutherland had seen him, a month before, at Thanksgiving. He was short of breath, too, from the mild exertion. The sight of him now only served to reinforce Sutherland's judgment of that morning on the phone when his father's voice had quivered with emotion: He was truly growing old, acceding to the inner crumblings that meant the wind-down had begun. His shoulders were stooped, he walked with a limp that grew more pronounced every year and his eyes teared for no reason. Even at seventy-two, though, the end might be a good while coming, Sutherland speculated. A life of hard farmwork and a proper diet had to count for something. There was still a strong grip in that hand the old man had proffered only minutes before.

He stared at his mother for a long moment while she was absorbed in watching her husband and his friend. Unlike Archibald, there was no appreciable change in her since Thanksgiving. She was locked into one of her phases—long-term periods of predictability in dress and taste and style during which she always seemed to maintain a uniform weight and hair color. When she entered another phase the change was always abrupt and startling, a clear marker on her pathway to growing old. Two years before she had become sixty. Her hair that was flecked with gray seemed to turn unaccountably white overnight. She gave up on her monthly trip to a neighboring woman who cut and set the hair, and when Sutherland next saw her that year, at a Fourth of July picnic in Laconia, it was tied back into a neat bun. Except for a simple pants suit she looked exactly like the last photo Sutherland had seen of her mother, long since dead and buried in Quebec.

Jane turned to him and spoke in a quiet voice: "The laughing crazy didn't call here after you left for the office, James. Anything happen down there?"

"No, nothing," Sutherland lied. There was no need to dampen anyone else's holiday spirits with the specter of a menace that seemed directed at Sutherland alone.

"Good. Maybe he lit out for fresh territory and is bugging somebody else right now."

Maggie reached over and tapped him on the shoulder: "Mike Mallory called this afternoon, James. Did he get to you down at the office?"

"Did he ever! Suddenly appeared in full darkness and almost scared me right out the window."

Otis had apparently overheard. He reached out to haul down Archibald's hand that gripped the circle of his earring.

"Enough, Archibald. Otis is tired now and wants to hear James's news. We can dance some more tomorrow. What did the police find out, James? Were they able to locate the guy?"

"Nope. But that was the good news. The guy was some kind of a prankster. All that blood he left on the snow out there belonged to three recently butchered chickens."

"Well, I'll be goddamned!" Archibald, seated now, slapped both knees at the notion. Practical jokes delighted him. During one hunting season when Archibald returned dejectedly empty-handed, a neighbor had bagged an eight-point buck and pridefully slung it up on a timber tripod before his house. In the dead of night Archie had cut down the deer and stolen the tripod and put it all back up again on the front lawn of a minister in Laconia who railed ceaselessly against hunters and guns and man's inhumanity to the defenseless creatures of the forest. For whatever disappointment the act assuaged in Archibald, it did far more for the minister. He switched his pulpit rantings from man's inhumanity to animals to man's inhumanity to man and his congregation overflowed the church each Sunday to be spellbound by the passionate oratory of his sermons. Archibald, who attended the minister's church every Sunday for months thereafter when his own Presbyterian service was done, was the only smiling face among the awed listeners.

"Thank God!" Jane and Maggie said in unison.

"Better pray to Him instead. If Mallory catches that bird he's liable to wring his neck. It was probably some college kid who did it on a dare."

"College does seem like a fun place to be," Archibald spoke somewhat wistfully. "I wish I'd a had a chance to go. But there was no money in them days and somebody had to work the farm so there was just no chance—"

"It is probably just as well," Marjorie suddenly blurted out. "You might have found out you didn't have enough brains either."

Jane traded a quick wink with Sutherland. Marjorie, who rarely touched alcohol, was sipping at a glass of sherry this Christmas Eve and the effect, as ever, was an almost instantaneous sea change. Her accent was thickening and Sutherland guessed they would yet hear some of the old language of Quebec sometime this night. Archibald glared reproachfully at his wife; he was used to complete loyalty. He surged determinedly on.

"Mother and me went to the U.N.H.-Dartmouth game last fall. Some young fellas who was bare-ass naked went runnin' right across the field at half time. Streakin' they call it. The crowd just loved it. I never laughed so hard in years."

"I thought it was indecent," Marjorie said. "*Absoluement dégoutant.*"

Archibald pretended not to hear the French. "Well, it

looked like fun to me. Anybody ever do that when you was at
Harvard, James?"

The question that would have sparked a bitter reply from
him in the past now encouraged Sutherland's own variety of
wistfulness. The memory of slugging his way through undergraduate years on scholarships and part-time jobs and the recall
of the drudgery of law school returned to him pridefully now.
Now it was an achievement; then it had been a barely concealed fury at the constant struggle to somehow stay above the
default line in the ledger. So he smiled at his father. "No,
nobody did things like that in those days. Times were different.
Eisenhower was still president when I started school, and Ken-
nedy had short hair and wore dark suits and Lyndon Johnson
wouldn't be caught dead wearing a gold earring like you are
about to, Archie. You remember how it was. Things weren't
like they are today. . . ."

Archibald recalled the past with a perplexed look on his
face. Maggie got up and put some soft Christmas music on the
stereo. Sutherland guessed that one reason she did it was to
fend off another long, rambling Archibald reminiscence about
Eisenhower, the kind in which he invariably got all of the
dates and most of the names wrong. A framed, personally
signed photograph of the dead Republican President rested on
the fireplace mantelpiece at the farm in New Hampshire. In a
Protestant household, bereft of idols to worship, Eisenhower
was the bold smiling god who had ruled the country during the
favorite time of Archibald's memory.

On the stereo, Bing Crosby crooned about a white Christmas. Maggie, still standing, caught Sutherland's eye and nodded toward the liquor closet and he nodded his head in assent.
When she emerged carrying his scotch and soda, Marjorie held
up her empty glass. Maggie raised her eyebrows, returned to
the closet and emerged, this time carrying a bottle of sherry in
her other hand.

"Anything interesting happen here today?" Sutherland asked
after he had taken his first swallow of the drink.

"Maggie and Otis got the fixin's ready for tomorrow's feast,
Arch and Marjorie showed up at three forty-five exactly with

that fantastic tree, nobody showed up at Rudolfo's for the office Christmas party and Otis is serving us veal scallopini for supper. Otherwise, all was peace and contentment, nothing stirred inside me, and it snowed all damn day," Jane told him in a singsong lilt. "How about you? Anything interesting happen downtown besides Mallory?"

He could not tell them about the crank with his unknowable motive and the bloodstained bandaging on his head, so he told them about stopping to see Moskowitz and the free sandwich.

"Well, I tell you it's a once-in-a-century event when you can get something for nothing out of a Jew," Archibald spoke. "What's the matter, James, did he run out of change?"

Sutherland winced. Archibald was a bona fide bigot with an infinity of racial, religious, ethnic and political prejudices who had no use for anyone not of his own caste. And he had no restraint about mouthing them either.

"Mordechi's a good friend and a generous man, Arch. And we don't stand for any talk like that in this house," Sutherland told him levelly. "Try a new subject."

"Okay. What do you think of this here business of trying to put in a state income tax back home?"

"I think it's a good idea. If memory serves me correctly, New Hampshire is either dead last in the country in aid to education and state services or fighting Mississippi for the honor."

"Well, I think it's a foolish idea. I tell you, what we need is to put Meldrin back in the State House. Meldrin'll put his foot down on that business. You can bet your burial plot on that!"

"I guess so," Sutherland sighed, sipping again at his drink. Meldrin was Meldrin Thompson, ex-governor of New Hampshire. Archibald worshiped the man and his politics, and so, it seemed, did a lot of other Granite Staters. The man and his politics quite plainly baffled Sutherland.

Marjorie drained her second glass of sherry in one gulp and poured herself another while they all looked on in collective disbelief. Her eyes grew fibrous and distended. She puckered her mouth as if she meant to spit in disgust, then took a squinting look at Jane's expensive Bakhtiari on the floor and evidently decided against it.

"Bah! That one! I never voted for him! Not one time!"

Archibald slowly put down his glass on a table. The betrayed look on his face said he had just been delivered history's most insidious kiss since Judas. "You told me you did, Marjorie! You lied to me!"

"*Tu es fou, toi!* Eh? I have the right as a citizen to a secret vote! That is one right you cannot take away from me!"

Sutherland grew dazed. Where was all this coming from? Why the revolt of Mother after all these years of quiet servitude? And why now, at this time of all times when the crank was perhaps getting set to blow a hole in the sweet promise of his and Jane's future? He looked at his parents and suddenly felt he had become father to the child. He thought of spanking them and sending them to bed without supper.

"Otis thinks we should have some of Otis's very delicious veal scallopini pretty soon," Otis proposed in the silence while the others watched the stung, then wrathful faces of Archibald and Marjorie. The outcome might depend on who first broke down into a flood of tears. Sutherland supposed it had to happen that way. They had not been bickerers, his parents, unlike some of the parents of friends he remembered from high school who seemed to go at it nonstop. The sheer infrequency of the times they fought was an indication of how intense their confrontations had to be when they finally came. Someone always cried, but usually it was Marjorie.

"I don't like Eye-talian food! You know that damn well, Otis!" Archibald barked at the hairdresser.

"You don't like anything!" Marjorie hurled at him. "Except your cows!"

"Otis will panfry you a wonderful steak, Archibald," Otis tried again. "Very well done and all dried out. Just the way you like it."

"Come on, break it up, you two," Jane kidded the contestants. "Maggie, do me a favor, will you? Put *The Messiah* on the stereo. I could stand a little inspirational music right now and old Bing just isn't making it this Christmas Eve."

Maggie got up to comply with her boss's request. At the same moment Archibald and Marjorie skulked off in opposite directions—Archibald to Sutherland's study and Marjorie upstairs to her room, taking the sherry with her. It was a predictable pattern Sutherland recalled, the retreat to a neutral corner to await the next round when their children became couriers between adversaries hopelessly bound together despite themselves by the immutable interdependence of farm families. During one cold, awful February Archibald stalked off to the barn for three days. Sutherland had carried his meals out to him in a picnic basket. He quit the hay loft only when Marjorie relented first because some pipes had frozen in the house that needed attending to.

The remaining four sat wordless in the aftermath of the departure as the first strains of *The Messiah* came from the stereo. It was Otis who broke the silence.

"Otis doesn't like it when people fight. Otis needs to begin preparing supper. It will help to calm Otis's nerves."

"Good idea. We'll help you," Jane said. They all stood and the other three followed Otis single file into the kitchen.

There, where *The Messiah* still trumpeted through extension wall speakers, Otis turned to face them gravely.

"Once two women started fighting in Otis's salon and one stabbed the other with a pair of clipping scissors. Police came and broke them up. They took one lady to the hospital and the other to the police station. One of the cops was an absolute knockout. He agreed to meet Otis in a certain bar the next night but was shot to death during the afternoon by a criminal. That's why Otis doesn't like fighting. Because of the gorgeous cop who died. Did Otis ever tell you that story?"

"No, no, I don't believe so," Sutherland told the hairdresser. He saw his own reflection in the stainless steel of the double-door refrigerator. The image was slightly blurred, yet clear enough to show the studied confusion of a man supposedly picking over his memory—the look Sutherland always resorted to to mask his embarrassment when Otis began conjuring his self-justifying, mostly erotic tales out of thin air. Their advent was totally unpredictable, they could happen anywhere, and the chief beneficiary of any harm done by lying was usually Otis himself. Most people who had not known him for years actually believed him. Later, when they made reference to the story, he assured them he did not know what they were talking about. Otis had a knack for getting dropped like a hot potato.

Otis warmed the already prepared veal, Sutherland opened the wine to let it breathe, and Maggie and Jane set the dining-room table. Sutherland made an avocado salad for six. Otis began panfrying the flavor out of Archibald's steak in a cast-iron skillet.

When dinner was ready, Jane called the warring twosome to the table and diplomatically sat them apart. Except for the solo voices of the oratorio there was no noise but the clanking of forks and knives until Sutherland made his second mistake of that Christmas Eve.

"You'll never guess who I saw on the Common tonight. Our old friend Edith and her buddy McGivern. Except you should have seen McGivern. Believe me, miracles are absolutely possible. I didn't even recognize her at first. Edith must have shipped her off to charm school for a year or something like that. She's now very much the companion-friend. Tasteful clothes, soft cultured voice, and about a hundred pounds scaled off somewhere along the way. I don't know how it was done, but Tugboat Annie has now become a lady."

"And Edith?" Jane asked. "Ravishing as ever, I suppose?"

"A Russian empress in sable cape with matching no-aggression Dobermans. But really out on cloud nine. More vacuous than ever."

"Were they friendly in any way? Did they at least say hello?" Maggie asked through a mouthful of salad.

"Oh, they were friendly enough," Sutherland told them. "The past has evidently been buried. But somehow I felt very sorry for them. They'd been standing there on Christmas Eve alone together for more than two hours comparing the temperature drop to passing time on the thermometer-clock on the top of the Edison Building. I think my dear ex-wife has given up on the search for a new husband and McGivern's become the surrogate."

"What was the rate of fall, James?" Otis wanted to know. He had that kind of mind. It seized on wisps of things, on the fragments. Sutherland's painting was of Edith and McGivern standing in a magical place on a magical night, mesmerized by a goddamned clock-thermometer of all things. Yet Otis wanted to know about that bunch of grapes almost off canvas, way down in the left-hand corner.

"It was dropping two degrees each half hour, Otis. The information was precise."

"How interesting," Otis judged.

"Yes." There was a mumbled near-general agreement on that. Behind them, from the stereo speakers the hundred voices of the Mormon Tabernacle Choir boomed out in full chorus. Archibald was next to speak.

"I always kinda liked Edith a little, even though I used to torment the hell outta her. There was something down there and you kinda felt if you could just get to it and unlock it, she'd be okay, that she'd be a good wife to James."

Marjorie had brought her liquor to the table. The now half-empty bottle of sherry stood before her. She took her slug and, not unexpectedly, exploded. Then the nagging intuition came to Sutherland that his known world had somehow begun the irreversible process of dismembering itself.

"Bah! I hated her! She was awful! I would not go to her house and I would not have her in mine!" She addressed herself now solely to Jane. "She could not even cook, Janie. *Même pas la cuisine!* Not even a sandwich could she make! And the cuffs of James's shirts! Always dirty! I saw them myself."

The eternal complaint of a farm housewife about someone who had not been raised to be a housewife at all.

"Mother, control yourself, will you?" Sutherland implored. "This is Christmas Eve, after all. Edith never cooked because she didn't have to, and she never did my shirts because a laundress came in and did them. If my cuffs were soiled, it was because you always saw me after I came home from the office, where I was slopping around in ink and carbon paper. Believe me, when I left home each morning the cuffs were impeccable. And believe me further that you didn't have to worry about

barring Edith from your house. She wouldn't go there anyhow."

Sutherland had always considered that his mother had only
one venomous place in her (though tonight it seemed a few
more were coming to light). Marjorie despised Edith in the
way only a married son's mother could and had never made
any bones about it from the beginning.

"Marjorie, please try to calm down a bit, all right," Jane
tried soothing her. It worked evidently, and the scowl of her
face relaxed. But then Marjorie adored her son's second wife.
She had never made any bones about that one either.

Archibald went for full contrition. "It was all my fault. Everything from the beginning. It makes me ashamed that I
didn't work harder after money so James didn't have to struggle so hard all those years in school and come out bound and
determined to marry a rich wife so he could make up for what
he never had. He never even looked at what he was gettin'. All
that interested him was the financial statement."

Sutherland might have wept for the certainty of what he
said. But what was the point of it now? The past was indeed
past, Edith was gone and the Irrefutable Truth that should
have been confronted then was now a historical mistake in the
pages of Sutherland's life chronicle. He rarely looked back at it
these days.

But it was not enough for Marjorie.

"Idiot! *Vache!* Stupid Yankee! Tight like a clam he is! He
can't owe nobody money, he says." Her voice was dripping
with scorn. Her accent was now thick as syrup; her words
began hyphenating. There was no shutting her up. "He won't
go to the banks for loans so he can't buy a modern equip-ment
or fix up the old stuff so we barely squeeze a liv-ing out of the
place! We must be the last farm in New Eng-land to plow
with horses! That's how we could make the money! We could
charge the tourists to come see how a New Eng-land farm was
one hund-red years ago! He's so stupid he don't realize he
could buy two cars more with all the money he put into that
old Pac-kard to keep it going!"

Marjorie hiccuped then. Archibald looked as if he were

going to cry. Jane, who sat across the table from Sutherland, moved her empty wineglass forward with a determined plunk. "James, I want another glass of that nice calming Soave. Then I want you to do something about this before I finish my supper in the kitchen."

He hesitated about the wine and traded a questioning look with Maggie. He would get to his parents in a moment.

"Jane, do you really think it's all right to have some more wine?" Maggie asked her boss. "I mean tonight could be the big night—"

"Tonight is the big night as far as I'm concerned. But I'm not talking about the baby. It's not going to happen tonight. Now pour, husband," she demanded. He poured her the wine.

Otis hastened to reassure everyone: "Otis is also certain tonight is not the night. Tomorrow a child will be born. Otis is certain little Annabella Sutherland will be born tomorrow in the afternoon."

Both of Sutherland's parents were suddenly transformed. Good old Otis: Marjorie's gusher had apparently been capped. Both warring factions actually beamed at each other.

"Are you sure, Otis? Are you absolutely sure about the day it's gonna happen?" Archibald begged.

"Otis is prescient. Otis is never wrong. If Otis cared about football, Otis would be a very rich hairdresser indeed. Otis could call the odds dead right on every pro game of every Sunday of the season."

But then the realization caught up with Archibald. "But you said Annabella . . . That's a girl's name . . ."

Otis shook his head emphatically.

"Why call a boy Annabella?" Otis queried. "Unless you're bent on raising him to be heavyweight boxing champion of the world and want to start him in training right from the beginning."

"But, James, you said it was gonna be a boy," Archibald sputtered. "You told me the Greek in the restaurant told you just so and that he was right most ninety-eight per cent of the time—"

"Annabella Marie-Joseph Suther-land," Marjorie pronounced

slowly. She had a trancelike faraway look in her eyes when she said it.

"That's what the baby should be called. Marie-Joseph was the name of my mother in Québec."

"That's a French name!" Archibald thundered. "She should have an American name! And I don't want a girl! I want a grandson with an American name! I was countin' on it!"

"*Merde!*" Marjorie was off again. "Always the law of Arch-i-bald! *Le fermier qui parle à ses vaches!* You should run for king of New Hamp-shire! All the cows will vote for you and there are more cows up there than people!"

From the voice of the stereo the Mormon Tabernacle Choir boomed out the mighty strains of the Hallelujah Chorus. From instinct—or impulse perhaps because he had witnessed it performed so many times—Sutherland stood at the table to ramrod attention; Maggie and Otis did the same. Sutherland saw a further possibility in the reverential act. It might help to calm the storm. The way he had once seen the playing of the national anthem break up a donnybrook among some delegates at one of the state Democratic conventions. But it did nothing. At the instant of the most militant repetition of the word "Hallelujah!" Marjorie flung the contents of a full glass of sherry straight into Archibald's face and Sutherland felt the entire universe tremble in response.

"Maggie, Otis wants to go home!" Otis pleaded. "Otis is frightened!"

But Maggie was otherwise engaged; she sprinted around the end of the table to disarm the fury-faced Marjorie, who was brandishing her knife with its serrated blade menacingly toward her husband. Archibald, for his part, wiped the stinging sherry from his eyes with his napkin, put his head down on the table on his crossed arms and broke down in wracking sobs. Jane sat calmly, sipping at her Soave, the unfathomable look of her face suggesting that her mind had not really absorbed what her eyes had seen.

Sutherland thought of a messenger arriving from a distant place on a sweated horse to announce that the Empire of Rome had just been overthrown.

"Better separate the contestants, James," Maggie spoke to him with an urgent voice.

He walked around his end of the table, pulling his father to his feet. "Let's go, Arch. Let's go for a walk. A little cold air will clear the head."

He urged the old man toward the hallway closet, bundled him unprotestingly in his fleece-lined hunting jacket, and tied his hat with the earflaps under his chin, while the King sobbed bottomlessly all the while. Then he slipped into his own ski parka and they went out the door of the apartment to the elevator.

CHAPTER 16

The Passing of the Scepter

The snow had stopped completely now. When Sutherland looked up, the heavy clouds were moving quickly eastward out over the Atlantic, and occasionally, through a rift that appeared here and there, he saw a cluster of a few stars, the first he remembered seeing in nights.

He had gotten Archibald out of the building unseen, even past the doorman, who was busied with trying to hail a cab for an elderly woman. Rather than head down Beacon Street and encounter any carolers on their way to the City Hall Plaza Pageant, he steered Archibald around the next corner toward Storrow Drive and the Esplanade, where he doubted they would meet anyone.

His father still cried as they went up the ramp and over the footbridge that traversed the drive. Below, only an occasional car crept past. The wind had risen again and the piled snow beside the drive blew across the glow of the cars' headlights.

When they touched down on the Esplanade, where the wide paths had already been cleared, Archibald stopped his crying. He wiped his eyes with the sleeves of his hunting jacket and blew out his nose in the way that had always made Sutherland apoplectic when he was a kid: flailing out the snot by holding closed first one nostril then the other with the press of his finger. He finished that work on the sleeve of his jacket also.

"Sorry about that one, James. Your mother kinda caught me off guard tonight. She doesn't raise her voice too often, you know."

Sutherland smiled at him. "I didn't think she ever did it."

"Oh, every once in a while. The time I burned the barn down a while back for the insurance and she found out about it. Had to get down on my knees to her for that one. She swore she was gonna go to the sheriff and tell him. She meant it, too."

"Well, you're not spending Christmas in the state reformatory, so you must still be a highly persuasive man."

His father sighed deeply as they trudged along, heading toward the lights of the Harvard Bridge. His voice was phlegmcoated. For a seventy-two-year-old man, it had a tone of hurt like that of a child.

"There was concessions had to be given. She can be a hard bargainer when she's holdin' an ace."

"What kind of concessions?"

"I had to let her take her test and renew her driver's license again. She passed first time."

"That sounds intelligent. What if something happened to you on the farm? She could drive you to a doctor or to the hospital in an emergency."

"I also had to concede that she could talk French to her sister and her brother when she phones them up in Quebec Province." His father turned to face him, his eyes glazed and rheumy from the crying. He shook his head gravely. "She didn't forget none of it. She always said she did, that a language goes after five, ten years, and then you don't remember it. But she didn't forget a Jesus Lord word! She can still jabber along a mile a minute like a chipmunk. She prays in French, too. I hear her every night. . . . I think all those years she was just pretendin' to be a good Presbyterian. . . ."

Sutherland shrugged as they continued walking. "She went underground. That's all."

"What?"

"She went underground," he repeated. And now, perhaps, she was coming out again.

The moon appeared for the first time in a wide starry blank

between the clouds. It reflected brilliantly on the everywhere-white covering of snow, outshining even the glare of the arc lamps that swayed in the wind above them. Sutherland looked across the frozen river toward the lights of M.I.T. and Cambridge. The physical world seemed extraordinarily beautiful to him tonight.

"Don't it just seem to you like the world is comin' apart around you sometimes, James?" his father asked.

"No," he said despite the earlier intuition he had had. "For the most part the center seems to me to be holding especially well these days." He was aware as he said it that he was scanning the Esplanade for his bandaged prankster.

"Well, it does to me. I think I'm not long for it. It's probably just as well. I can't stand all of these goddamn new movements, the way they come at you so fast and furious. Take this women's liberation horseshit, for instance. I think it's that business that's unhingin' part of your mother. She reads a lot of magazines and gets pamphlets and stuff in the mail about it—"

Sutherland laughed at him. "You're slippin', Arch, old boy. I'm surprised you haven't tried censoring her reading materials."

The old man seemed not to hear. A flicker of rebellion leaped up in him.

"Now you take this woman Phyllis Schlafly, out there in the Midwest. Now there's a woman with her head screwed on straight!"

"I think she's a bit misdirected," Sutherland said reflexively.

"And all these other movements," Archibald surged on. "The niggers and the Chicanos and the unions . . . You know somethin', James? I think there'll be a nigger in the White House before the end of the century."

"Better check with Otis on that one, Arch. He's putting his money on a woman."

"I'd vote for the nigger first," Archibald said flatly.

Sutherland did not laugh. He found himself trying to think of the name of a short story by Flannery O'Connor about blacks and whites on a bus in the South, but the title would not come to him. He gave up trying when they reached the

Harvard Bridge and decided it was time to turn around. They did and his father was silent for a time until he gave out with a long, deep sigh like defeat.

"I think maybe it'd be a good thing to die soon. To get away from all this change."

Sutherland was laughing again. He extended his hand and when his father took it, Sutherland pumped vigorously. "Well, good-bye, Arch, old boy. It hasn't always been fun knowing you, but it sure as hell hasn't been dull."

"No, I mean it, James. I'm gettin' tired," the other said seriously.

Sutherland shrugged. "Well, anyhow, don't worry about Marjorie. Elaine and I talked that one over years ago. She can move in with either one of us she prefers, though I think it'll be me, seeing how she's so crazy about Janie."

"There's neither of you has to worry. As soon as I'm in the hole and covered over, she'll grab the next bus back to Quebec."

"Back there? Why? She's an American citizen."

"She's got her ear to the ground on this Quebec liberation bullshit like you wouldn't believe. Listens like a hound for every scrap of news she can hear about it, gets all sorts of pamphlets and magazines in French from Canada just like the women's lib business. You'll never guess what the last little bit of needlepoint she did was."

"What?" He thought he knew already.

"The Laurentian flag. Her brother and sister send her pictures along with their letters sometimes. They both got it run up on flagpoles in their front yards. God! Them French Canucks play a good game of hockey, but they sure are a crazy bunch of bastards. Can you imagine them gettin' loose and governin' themselves right next door? It'd be like America got a bad boil on its flank. That Trudeau better get crackin' the whip up there."

Sutherland smiled. So what if Quebec got loose? He preferred it to the rest of Canada anyhow. The cosmopolitan bustle of Montreal, the quiet, twisting streets of old Quebec City. He remembered the way the wind swept the early-autumn leaves along the promenade on the cliffs above the St. Lawrence . . .

"What was the name of Mother's village up there? She told me once, but I've forgotten."

"St. Etienne de la Neige," Archibald pronounced carefully in surprisingly well accented French, probably because he had practiced it so many times.

St. Etienne of the Snow. What a beautiful name for a place that was supposed to have been so hardscrabble. So: a generation was culminating then. Archibald had pronounced his death sentence (and Sutherland believed him, too; he suddenly looked very old and tired) and Marjorie would end hers by going full cycle. He bet when the bus of her return made its final stop it would be in the village of St. Etienne de la Neige. Her brother still lived there. She would shuck off the veneer of her forty-five years as a Presbyterian and resume the Catholicism of her youth with a vengeance. He pictured her henceforth—a little old Catholic lady in black winter coat trudging her way to daily mass through the snows of a French-Canadian village—and shook his head at the wonder of it. What immense power of a dream must survive in those of us in life who are only refugees!

They walked on in silence disturbed only by the howl of the steadily rising wind and the squeak of their boots on the snow. When they were nearly to the place where they would have to turn off to recross the drive on the footbridge, his father suddenly halted. The wind had blown down the rotted limb of a dead tree on the pathway. It had shattered into many pieces and Archibald reached down and picked up one of the pieces about a foot long and thick as the grip of a baseball bat. He handed it to Sutherland.

"Here, James, take it. It's time now."

"What's this?"

"The scepter. I'm passin' on the power to you now."

It was Sutherland who felt like crying now. "Bit premature, isn't it, Arch?"

"Nope. Deathbed scenes are a damn nuisance. It's your time, that's all. Tomorrow, or soon anyhow, you'll be a father . . ."

A sudden delirious smile came onto Archibald's face, making him look now like he cried from happiness. He wound up and punched his son hard in the arm. "Just think of it! Three generations of Sutherland males alive and kickin' at the same time!"

They started walking again and his father said earnestly, "Good Lord! When you came home one of them times and said you decided to contribute your share to zero population growth, I got sick for a week. You say that Greek in the restaurant has about a ninety-eight per cent batting average, huh?"

"I hope so. But I also remind you that Otis, the oracle, said baby Ford's going to be an Annabella. He's pretty keen on his predictions, too."

"Oh, him! Pshaw!" The old man waved it away. "I mean he's a ladies' hairdresser, not a goddamn computer." His father turned to look at him knowingly. "To which you can add the fact that he's not quite all there. He likes the boys, too, you know. I didn't know if you knew that."

Sutherland chuckled. "Of course I knew it. Everybody does. The world doesn't exactly want for clues. It always surprised me that it never seemed to ruffle you or Marjorie particularly." They descended the footbridge ramp to the street.

"Well, you know your mother. Easy come, easy go. If a Martian walked into the house, she'd set a place for him at the table." He did not volunteer any information, however, about how he had shunted aside this one of his fanatical intolerances in the case of Otis. Sutherland wondered what the old man's reaction would have been if he had turned up gay. In another moment, as if he could read his son's thoughts, Archibald answered the question for him. "If you'd turned out that way, you wouldn't be alive right now."

Then there was no more. They turned onto Beacon Street and into the apartment building and Sutherland wondered how best to preserve the rotting wood scepter of the dynasty of Sutherland that he would pass onto his son when the time came.

* * *

They had put Marjorie to bed when she finished her bottle of sherry, and she had apparently gone instantly to sleep. Mother was drunk for the first time in her life.

"I sure do hope this ain't the beginning of a drinkin' problem for Marjorie," Archibald said gravely as he poured himself a glass of rye and filled it right up to the rim. "I got enough problems now with Emmett hittin' the sauce every coupla weeks without Mother climbin' aboard on the other shoulder. If old Emmett thought he got himself a new drinkin' buddy he'd start bringin' the stuff right into the house and there'd be a bender every night."

"I think you can relax on that score, Archibald, my boy," Jane smirked at him. "This was a one-shot deal. Marjorie had some things stored up inside her that just had to get out. And if you want some advice, you'd better stop writing those letters of support to your friend Meldrin against passage of the ERA legislation or you're liable to wake up some morning with a pipe sticking out of your head."

"That bad, huh?" Archibald quizzed, his face screwed up in consternation. "Why didn't she just come out and tell me? Why does she always keep so many things to herself?"

Jane shrugged. "A lifetime of habit, I guess. Listen, do you want me to remassacre that steak of yours?"

"No, thanks, Janie. I lost my appetite. I'll just finish this here hooch and pack it off to bed."

They watched, a trifle incredulous perhaps, as he raised the glass to his lips and drained it to the dregs in one continuous swallow, his Adam's apple bobbing in staccato motion as the stuff went down. Finished, he wiped his lips on the sleeve of his shirt and pronounced himself ready to sleep.

"It would be most diplomatic, Archibald, if you spent the night in the back bedroom," Jane told him. "Maggie set it up for you. The only way we could get old Marge into her nightgown was to agree to let her take her knife along with her. She's keeping it as a souvenir or something."

"Ow," Archibald winced, then kissed her forehead, said good night to Maggie and Otis, who were busy trimming the Christmas tree, and headed off toward the stairs. He climbed them slowly, taking a heavy grip on the rail. He looked truly old and tired, Sutherland thought for the second time that night.

"I've kept your plate warming for you, James. Want some food?"

"Yes, I'm starving."

"Set yourself up one of those TV tables and you can eat in here with us. I'll bring in your plate and some wine. What's that piece of wood you're carrying? Somebody try mugging you out there this sacred night?"

"I'll tell you when you get back."

He set up the table where he could watch Otis and Maggie at their work. They had solved the problem of too few lights and ornaments for too large a tree by backing the tree right into a corner and decorating just the front of it. Otis was in his element: Maggie was up on a stepladder stringing lights and Otis stood back from the tree, one hand on hip, and told her where to place them. From the stereo came the sweet voices of the Vienna Boys' Choir singing German Christmas carols. Sutherland sat down behind his portable table and fingered the scepter of his new kingship. He thought how nearly everything in life seemed so wonderful to him right now.

Jane brought in the food and a half bottle of the Soave and sat down beside him. She asked again about the piece of rotting tree limb and he told her. In response, she removed the fork from his left hand, raised the hand to her lips and kissed it.

"Oh, wow! Isn't life exciting? I was once married to an Italian, but never to a king. Does this mean I have to walk three paces behind you now?"

"If there's anything I can't stand, it's an irreverent subject. Seriously, though, what can we do to preserve this chunk of wood? You know about those things."

"I know a guy who'll do a good job on it. Remind me about it after whatever it's gonna be gets born. Hey, you two," she called to Maggie and Otis. "How about an eggnog break? We'll get the fraternal toasts over with, then I'm hitting the rack. Expectant mother needs her bed rest."

When Sutherland had finished his supper, Maggie brought

out the bowl of eggnog. They did the Christmas toasts, then Jane bade them all good night and went off to bed. Sutherland put the flip side of the Vienna Boys' Choir on the stereo and sat down to watch Maggie and Otis finish their work. He sipped a little at the last of the wine until Otis pronounced himself satisfied. The tree was beautiful. It reflected the feeling in the house of Sutherland perfectly this season, a distant part of Sutherland thought. Maggie announced it was time to leave.

"Why so early, you two?" Sutherland asked.

"Otis has the urge," Otis proclaimed. "And unless James is a secret voyeur and would enjoy watching a tryst of two magnificent bodies on his living-room floor, Otis and Maggie had better get themselves home."

"James has been celibate too long to watch any two bodies trysting. The result might be the turning of pleasure into unwanted pain. Better you should run along."

He helped them into their coats and saw them to the door, putting on the night lock when he closed the door behind them. Then he took his scepter to his study, cached it in a desk drawer for the time being and ferreted out Jane's Christmas gift that he had hidden behind some books on a shelf.

It was a music box of carved mahogany inlaid with ivory that had been crafted in Portugal more than a century before. He had a friend who owned an antiques shop in Cambridge and when he had begun thinking about a Christmas gift for Jane some two months before, he phoned her and asked her to keep an eye out for the perfect "something." Neither of them had any idea what the "something" was, but she promised to send out the scouts. When she found it, she had him dragged out of an important conference in another attorney's office. Her voice was breathless.

"Found it, James! But don't have it. I think we can get it, but it'll cost a bunch to shake it loose. Only we have to move quickly."

"What is it?"

"A Portuguese music box about a hundred years old. It's incredible. The workmanship must have taken half the carver's lifetime. Only problem is, it's in the collection of a rich couple of idiots whose cocktail party I finally had to go to last night because I'd run out of excuses. They allowed as how it might be for sale after a couple of rounds of negotiations. That's apparently how they get their jollies and ward off the boredom of having too much money and too little to do."

"When do I get to see it?"

"Tonight. Negotiations begin over drinks at six-thirty. Don't bother to bring your checkbook. I know this kind. They'll play it out until you're about ready to keel over from exhaustion."

Love at first sight. Two more rounds of drinks and two dinners later they brought down the wonderful prize. Later, when he picked it up, he took it over to the Conservatory of Music to identify the few bars of a Vivaldi concerto it played when the top was opened. One of the professors recognized the correct work in moments, pulling a recording of it from the conservatory that they listened to in its entirety. Then the man begged him to sell the music box. Sutherland told him politely no, then made a donation to the conservatory and left.

He had the Christmas gift specially packaged and wrapped. Now he thought of opening the package to admire the thing and listen to the few bars of Vivaldi one more time, but decided against it. Like most men, he was lousy with wrappings and would inevitably do a sloppy job putting it back together. He took it into the living room and put it beneath the tree, nestling it inconspicuously among the other presents that Maggie and Otis had already placed there. Then he turned off the winking tree lights and the stereo and headed for the stairs, turning off lights as he went along. He paused a moment to look outside and saw that the night was cloudless and clear and the moon shone brilliantly now.

He slid into bed without waking Jane and quickly drifted off to sleep, surprised a little to find that the image of Manfredi Occhapenti standing bareheaded in the snow before St. Peter's in Rome had returned to his thoughts once more.

CHAPTER 17

Encore

At 3:30 A.M. he was bang-awake.

He got out of bed while Jane still slept, put on a robe and quietly left the room, closing the door behind him. He went downstairs to the living room and, on an impulse, switched on the winking lights of the Christmas tree. He smiled for a long moment in the warm, multicolored glow that covered the spruce in the otherwise darkened room before going to stand before the windows that looked out on the river. The moon still outshone the arc lights on the Esplanade. From all the stars in the very clear sky, it looked as if Christmas Day would be perfect and full of sunshine. He decided he would try some cross-country skiing on the river to work off Christmas dinner in the afternoon. He was on his way to a storage closet off the hallway where the skis were kept when he heard the sound of someone descending the stairs. The figure crossed the room toward him, stumbling just a little on the hem of her nightgown, until she came within the perimeter of light from the street. It was Marjorie. Her hair, always so neatly done up in a bun, hung lifeless and gray to the level of her shoulders. Her face was splotchy and she looked quite ill. Sutherland's mother was suffering from her first hangover in sixty-two years of life.

"*Bon Noël, maman.* Feeling better?"

"*Bon Noël, mon fils.* Better in the mind, I think, but the rest of me wishes it was dead."

"Want a little nip more? Biting the hair of the dog is supposed to be a help."

"*Plus d'alcoöl?*"

"*Oui.* A little sherry?"

She shuddered. Her hands twitched visibly before her face.
"*O mon Dieu, non!* Don't even speak of it or I will be sick."

He laughed, but then he felt sorry for her when she stepped
close to the window to look out and was caught up in the
white light of the moon's illumination. Marjorie looked just
plain ghastly. She wore a bathrobe over her nightgown and a
knitted blanket covered her shoulders over the robe. She
seemed to him suddenly very tiny and old.

"Well, *maman*, you really evened up the score with old Arch
tonight."

"Oh, I had so much anger against him inside me, but now it
is gone." She turned to face him, frowning a little. "I've been
reading these books . . . these magazines about the liberation
of the woman. . . . Before there was never time with all the
work we had to do. But these books, they give me ideas I never
thought about before. . . . I never even heard of them. . . .
Perhaps I should stop this reading? Perhaps these ideas are too
dangerous to think about."

"How can an idea be dangerous unless it condones bigotry
or nonsensical violence? Besides, it's not right to tell someone
not to think."

"For me, it could be dangerous. Look what happened tonight. I almost stabbed your father at the supper." But then
her face broke into an impish grin that worked despite the
awful hangover. "*Très française, eh?*" She nudged at his elbow.

He grunted at the joke and put his arm about his mother's
shoulders; it was not often that Marjorie acknowledged something to be amusing. "I thought you were being marvelously
calculating, Marg, old girl. Anyhow, it did the trick. It brought
down your man. Peace negotiations should start before breakfast and your deck is stacked right now. Keep on reading,
maman . . . now that you have some time."

She seemed satisfied with the advice and turned to look out
the window again. He remembered how she had had no time

to read: it was nonstop from work to sleep. He could not even recall her eating one continuously seated meal. On his occasional weekends home from Harvard, she listened hungrily to his talk of teachers and courses. Even then, when he recounted for her the plots of novels he had read and their characters (the talk she really enjoyed hearing most) her rough farm woman's hands flew at darning or knitting or repairing some item. She had the compulsion of a genuine workaholic, but for all of it, she never really got too far ahead in life, he thought sadly. Merely kept up with life, that was all.

"Archibald thinks you're going back to Quebec when he kicks off."

She snorted a little. "He does? At last he has an intuition. Too bad so late. Yes, I am going back. To St. Etienne de la Neige to live with my brother and *ma belle-soeur*. You must keep the farm, though. It should never leave Sutherland hands until there are no more Sutherlands. You must promise me that and find a way to tell him that also. Put tenants on it or keep it for yourself for vacations and weekends. Hire a caretaker to watch it when you're not there. You can afford it. When the time comes, give it to your sons. Promise me," she ordered, raising her hand for the taking of an oath.

He raised his hand also. "I promise, *maman*." He felt like crying again, for the second time that night, the moment was so profound. Then: "You don't want any of it? No compensation at all?"

She turned back to the window, sighing heavily as she looked again.

"None of it belongs to me. I just worked there for thirty-nine years. Your father was a cow most of the time, but always an honest cow. That counts for much. Besides, there is some money for me, too. You know how the old Yankees are. Always a sock in the mattress you find out about later. He kept one, too. It will be enough."

Sutherland frowned at the news: he doubted there was very much money in the sock.

"You promise me one thing, too, *ma mère*."

"*Quoi?*"

"That you won't let your Quebec separatist ardor get the best of you and end up donating all your new little fortune to some radical bomb-chuckers up there."

She had the foxy sort of look that came easily to someone who had lived most of an adult life in a prison of reserve. She turned that gaze on him now and studied his face askance.

"How do you know about that business?"

"Your friend the cow understands more French than you think he does. He knows what that literature that comes from Quebec is. He knows what the Laurentian flag means, too."

"Hmm. Perhaps I underestimated him. Perhaps he grows more liberal, like you and me, as he grows older. He said nothing about it to me. And he used to tell me what I could and couldn't read."

"I heard tonight on our little walk that you had a certain very sharp ax hanging over his head. That you'd found out he burned the barn for the insurance and were going to the sheriff."

She smiled just a little and there was a small glint of triumph in it.

"Are you crazy? Do you think I would be responsible for putting my own husband in jail?"

"Better not tell him that, then. Or your subscriptions might be canceled."

"Don't worry. And I promise not to give all the money to the separatists. Just some. There are other ways I can help. I know how to shoot a gun and I am a good shot, too. Your father taught me and he taught me good. He always said I must know how in case someone bad came to the farm when he was not there—"

"Jesus Christ, Mother!" Sutherland shook his head in wonderment. "Do you actually imagine it'll come to guerrilla warfare?"

But the power of the dream inside her was too great and it burst out of her all over him; God only knew what her fantasies consisted of: perhaps she saw herself picking off Mounties with a 30-30 from the window of her brother's farmhouse.

"Just think of it! It's possible! *La libération! Une nouvelle nation française-parlante!*"

A new French-speaking nation. A parliamentary democracy with an old royalist flag fluttering over it. With enough passion, Quebeckers like Marjorie ready to take to the barricades, they might just pull it off.

He tried to calm her down a little. "Trudeau might send in the army, *ma mère.*"

"Let him!" She almost spat. "It's the best favor he could do for us. How long can they stay? Forever? And it will unite Québec once and for all. The minority who would not want the separation because they fear the economy will collapse will join us after that provocation. And it will not be easy for the army either. They will suffer more than a few flat tires!"

Radicalized at sixty-two: Jesus Lord! as Archibald always profaned. In her own mind, she had it all figured out though he hoped she was not on her way to becoming a disillusioned romantic. All the counterarguments in preparation for the antagonists. And they grew in intensity until the time would be reached in her scheduling for the rifles to come down from the gun racks. How wrong he had been all these years to think of her as the methodical, plodding mother he loved!

"You'll take back your old religion, won't you, *maman?*"

"I never left it," she said simply, staring out the window toward Cambridge. "Every night for these thirty-nine years, I have said the Catholic prayers in French. I sang the hymns in the Presbyterian church because they were beautiful and they were to the same God as the Catholic God. But during the preaching, I always prayed the rosary. Archibald, even if he had been intelligent, still could not read minds." She paused a moment, pressing her fingers to the glass, then the impish grin came back to her face and she jostled him again with her elbow. "Good act, *eh, mon fils?*"

He said nothing. He found himself thinking instead of the Moriscos, the Jews of Spain who had been forcibly converted by the Inquisition. They preserved the ancient, preferred part of themselves by tagging the Catholic prayers with a Hebrew ending. The thought of the subterfuge made him angry. "Why the hell did you let him do it to you? Why didn't you tell him to drop dead?"

"It was one of Archibald's two demands. The other was the language. I had no choice." She sighed wearily. "Those were hard times. It was the Depression then and when the Depression came to Québec what was already bad became worse. I was lucky to get a job in the mill in Nashua through a cousin of mine, and there was no question of going home then. My father cried when he wrote me letters telling me I must stay in the United States when I was so homesick, but he already had too many mouths to feed."

She stopped to wipe two tears from the corners of her eyes, but Sutherland was too entranced for pity or sorrow. She had never opened up this way before. He doubted his sister, Elaine, had heard any of it. He doubted any other person had, not even her brothers or sisters, and she had no close friends that he knew of.

"When it came time to marry, there were two choices. One was a Canadien-Français, also from Québec, who worked in the mill with me, and the other was your father. I think I loved the Quebecker . . . but he meant a life in the mills when already I was having trouble breathing from the cotton dust, and he would have turned into a wife-beater, I am sure. So I chose your father even though I did not love him then. He had the farm, and if the life would be hard, at least it would be healthy."

She turned and smiled at him; the tears were gone now.

"So you see, *mon fils*, in the beginning your father was a convenience, and when one marries a convenience, one must be prepared to make concessions. And he did not hit women, I was sure of that, and I was right. He has not laid a hand on me in thirty-nine years. And later I learned to love him and the life was not so bad. Sometimes it was even very happy after you and Elaine came along."

She chewed at the end of a finger and her eyes had the myopic look of someone remembering the past.

"The one thing I still regret was the day of my marriage.

Not one person from my family had the money to come to New Hampshire. Not even my father to give me away. The man who gave me away was a Quebecker, a foreman at the mill, and we said to Archibald that he was my uncle. To this day, he does not know the man was a friend instead."

Sutherland marveled: it was truly a bright, clear night of revelations besides supposedly being silent and holy.

"Does anyone else know this?" he asked her. "Does Elaine?"

"No. Only Janie knows because I trust her. She is the kind of woman that if you tell her something and say it must go no further, it will not."

"Yes," Sutherland agreed. She was that kind of woman. It came to him suddenly that he was proud his parents had both lived long enough to see that he was finally capable of making an uncompromised choice in a wife.

"I think it would be a fine thing if we had the baby baptized in the Catholic Church," he told her after a time. "Janie's a Catholic and I've started thinking I might take instructions and join."

"No. I don't want this," she said emphatically, shaking her head at him. "The religion of the Sutherlands is Presbyterian. Your children should belong to that church also, at least until they're old enough to decide whether they want to stay with it or leave. And Janie is not a Catholic. She became one at a time of confusion in her life because she thought it was her first husband, Manfredi's, religion that made him so calm and gentle. It was not. He was just that kind of man. Besides"— she appraised him with an enigmatic smile—"you do not have the right mentality to be a good Catholic. You think like a Protestant. It is how you were raised. Your mind could not accept the Catholic mysteries."

Side by side, they stood together now and stared out the window. The refugee from Quebec who meant to return and her son who was banished forever from the incense-sweetened liturgy of the Catholics. Then his heart skipped an actual beat when he saw the figure walking on the cleared path of the Esplanade below. The suicide prankster of the night before had returned. There were no bandages on the head now.

"Mother—my God, look!"

"*Quoi? Lui?*"

"Yes. The one from last night—he's back!"

"But he does not look hurt at all—"

"I told you what the detective told me. It was all a prank. A practical joke."

They watched as he left the path and bucked his way through the deep snow toward the frozen river. But tonight he did not disappear into the dark void beyond the range of the arc lights. The moonlight gave no concealment. He fought the deep snow to the middle of the Charles, turned suddenly about and started back toward the riverbank.

And then he did it again. He stopped in approximately the same place as the night before, the eyes beseeched heaven for the long moment, he waved at Sutherland another time, the Luger came out of his pocket and went up to his temple, the blue flash of flame spurted out of the barrel and the figure crumpled into the snow. Sutherland's mother grabbed urgently at his arm. "James! Perhaps he really did it this time!"

"We'll know in a couple of minutes whether he did or not. Otherwise this was just another practice run."

He was amazed at his own coolness. But then he remembered he had said "practice run." What if the guy got up and walked away, only to return nightly pretending to commit suicide until the night he actually did it? Did that mean that Sutherland's duty to his fellow man had shifted from informing the police to attempting prevention? It was clear that the other wanted something from Sutherland. They watched in silence as the stain of blood from his head gradually enlarged on the snow and then, sure enough, he got up, made for the path on the Esplanade and ran up to the crosswalk ramp, went over and disappeared out of sight, copiously dripping blood all the way.

"Let's make a bet on what kind of blood he used tonight. Human obviously doesn't qualify," Sutherland proposed.

"Tonight was a pig," his mother giggled as the relief surged through her. Then: "But seriously, you must phone the police and tell them."

"If I phone the cops with that same story as last night, they'll haul me off to the funny farm." He thought for a moment. "I know what to do. I'll give Mike Mallory a call. He's my detective friend. Then I'm going back to bed and get some sleep."

He went into his study while Marjorie stood waiting at the door and found Mallory's Charlestown number in the directory. He dialed the number and the phone rang for perhaps forty seconds until the receiver was lifted and a woman's voice groggy with sleep came over the line.

"Hello. Who is it?"

"Is this Mrs. Mallory?"

"Yes. Who's calling?"

"I'm sorry to wake you, Mrs. Mallory. This is James Sutherland. I'm afraid I need to speak with Mike. Is he there?"

"You're his friend the lawyer, aren't you? Yes, he's here. Is this call absolutely necessary, Mr. Sutherland? He's dead to the world. He had to work overtime; we just made midnight mass, then he came home, had half a drink, and went out like a light on the sofa downstairs. I couldn't wake him so I covered him over with a blanket and left him there."

"Well, maybe a message is okay. Just so he knows. Did he say anything to you about the guy who pulled the suicide stunt on the Charles last night?"

"You bet he did. He was mad as hell about all that time and energy wasted. I hope he doesn't get his hands on that kid."

"Well, you can tell him the nut strikes again. Same time, same station."

She was wide awake now. "Cripes! He must be crackers or something. Hang on, he'll wake up for this one. I'll put him on the extension in the kitchen."

She put the phone down on something with a clunk and he heard her open the bedroom door and disappear through it. In about a minute the extension was lifted and Mike Mallory yawned into the receiver.

"James, dear James. How good of you to call so early, at exactly four-fourteen A.M., to wish me a Merry Christmas and congratulate me on my valiant and untiring efforts on the force."

"Sorry, Mike. I told her a message was enough."

"So our friend showed up again, huh? Exact same game as last night?"

"Yep. The walk to the middle of the river, then hello and farewell. He went down for the count, then took off over the drive, leaking something's blood all the way. And no hallucination either. My mother saw the same thing I did."

"Did he wave at you like yesterday morning, James?"

"Yep again, Michael."

"Hmm. Any more phone calls since this afternoon, James?"

"No, nothing more."

"Hmm. That might be a dead letter then."

But that was all. Sutherland heard the wife's voice whispering to Mallory. "Ask him . . ." He could not make out the rest.

"James, my good wife would like to know if the guy was wearing a hat or not. She actually does all the detective work and I just go in to pick up her salary. Anyhow, she's got a theory he keeps the blood that comes from his head in some kind of plastic bag under his hat."

"Sorry to blow her theory, but he was bareheaded. No hat."

"Shit, you've just ruined Christmas dinner in the Mallory house. That calls for a new theory, and when she gets preoccupied with formulating one, food burns. I'll have to tell one of my daughters to keep an eye on the bird in the oven while her mother's at work. Listen, James, for your penance for getting me up in the middle of the night, I want you to go out now on the Esplanade with a container, a Mason jar or something, and get me a sample of some bloody snow. Then leave it someplace so it will melt and I'll send somebody over at a decent hour to pick it up for the boys in the lab."

"Mike," he begged. "It's almost four-thirty in the morning." He did not mention he was afraid to go out before daylight, afraid that that was exactly what the prankster wanted him to do. To draw him into the other's hostile environment where he could menace Sutherland according to his own rules. But perhaps Mallory understood then. Perhaps he was sending out the bait.

"Exactly, James. Exactly. Merry Christmas to you and your wife. Today the big day maybe?"

"We've got a hairdresser friend who says yes."

"He's probably right. You'd be amazed at what those guys know. Part of their job is to listen while they snip. You wouldn't believe what some women tell their hairdressers that they wouldn't tell anyone else. Well, 'bye for now. Hope it's the son you want. I got four darling little majorettes in a row before I finally got my linebacker. 'Bye again."

" 'Bye, Mike."

He replaced the receiver and told his mother he was going out for a blood sample. He accompanied her back upstairs, stepped into his bedroom to dress and out again without waking Jane. He took a plastic container from a kitchen cupboard and went out into the chill moonlit darkness for the sample. On the Esplanade he looked in every direction for the prankster, then stooped to his task and hurried back inside the building without looking behind him.

He put the sample on the desk in his study and closed the door. Then he went upstairs, undressed and got into bed without waking Jane this time either.

Then he lay awake for perhaps half an hour searching through the gallery of his mind for another John Worth.

But nobody came to his thoughts as a proper replacement for the dead John Worth.

PART IV

Christmas Day: A Child Is Born

CHAPTER 18

Sutherland's Child

The warmth of sun woke Sutherland on Christmas Day. It filtered through the skylight above their bed and before he opened his eyes he knew it was already midmorning from the way the warmth traveled across his face. He heard vague sounds of movement on the floor below, then reached over to touch Jane, who had left the bed. He decided the rest of the house was up and about.

He sat up against the headboard, rubbing the sleep from his eyes, then staring a long moment across the river to Cambridge, where the windows of the M.I.T. buildings shone with a reflected sun. A dazzling day for Christmas, he thought, and he smiled on the promise until he permitted himself to remember the telephone calls and the prankster's encore and his growing intuition that they were somehow connected. One thing was certain, he knew, as he experienced the first uneasy churnings of his stomach: intrusions had to be suffered in life. But these were especially badly timed, particularly with Jane about to give birth and his parents announcing their future travel plans within hours of each other, plans that spelled the end of the one constant he recognized in his life: a farm near Laconia, New Hampshire, tended by two hardworking, very stubborn people.

Archibald had declared himself, and opted for his mortality. Marjorie seeking her own liberation had decided to liberate Quebec. He remembered reacting to their pronouncements with a certain levity at the time, but in truth he was deeply touched. While he slept he dreamed of Archibald's burial in the old family graveyard on the knoll above the lake. There was deep snow everywhere in the fields and he wondered if the snow meant this winter or next.

He left the bed and went over to the window to look down at the Esplanade. There were no police this morning and no bloodhounds. Only a few people strolled along the plowed pathways. No one paid any particular attention to the blood the prankster had pumped onto the snow. It dulled the reflective snow, a deep red stain through which someone had already sliced with a pair of cross-country skis.

He showered and dressed and went downstairs.

Archibald and Marjorie sat quietly side by side, holding hands on a sofa in the living room, their peace evidently made. They watched a televised replay of the cardinal's midnight mass on a portable TV they had wheeled in. Archibald wore the clip-on gold earring Otis had given him and Marjorie was somehow completely restored, her hair done up in the familiar neat bun once more. The draperies were drawn to darken the light around the television and the Christmas tree and it made the room unexpectedly somber when the others adjoining it were bright with sunlight. He greeted his parents quietly, then went to the kitchen for coffee.

Jane was on her perch at the kitchen counter, sipping coffee and watching Maggie and Otis load the turkey and mincemeat pie into the oven.

"Our friend paid us a visit again last night, I hear tell," Jane said after he had kissed her.

"Yep. Right on time, too. Marjorie saw the whole thing with me, so I know now I'm neither loony nor hallucinating. Who is it, Otis? Are you getting any vibes on this one?"

"Otis is remarkably prescient, as Otis had always insisted. But trying to divine which of perhaps one million students in the greater Boston diploma mills is the prankster is beyond even Otis's capabilities."

"Marjorie said that you phoned Mike Mallory at four-thirty this morning," Jane winced at him. "I bet he just loved that."

"Oh, well, you know Mike. He could turn Armageddon into wry Irish humor. And I did the cops a favor, too. I went out and got a blood sample for their lab men. Somebody should be over this morning for it."

"Somebody should be here momentarily," Maggie said, tasting a sauce she was concocting. "They called from headquarters about ten minutes ago. Any bets on what kind it is?"

"Marjorie says it's hog's blood, but she's wrong," Otis told them. "About that Otis is feeling prescient again. It's bunny-rabbit blood. Definitely."

"Bunny-rabbit, huh? That's kind of a rare item. Where would somebody be likely to come by a couple of quarts of that stuff?" Sutherland asked.

"Otis can think of about five different ways right this instant. But if the prankster who is getting boring was a student as the cop thinks, the most obvious place was a school laboratory where they use bunny rabbits to try to find out about cancer and stuff like that. Or in the North End, where they slaughter rabbits for the Italian people." Otis narrowed his eyes and hunched over into what was a familiar dramatic pose; the tips of his fingers came lightly together as he began to draw a scene, conjured from the psychic wavelengths. "Otis can see it clearly now. There are evidences of Satanic cultism in all of this. Two little bunnies were ritualistically slaughtered —decapitated—then hung up by their little heels as the blood drained into an iron vessel adorned with the symbols of witchcraft—"

Jane brought Otis to a halt with her laughter. "Leave it to good old Otis to spice up Christendom's holiest day with a message from a Satanic cult."

Otis looked hurt. "Well, if you don't want to hear the story the way it happened, Jane, Otis won't waste his time. Otis is quite sure the police would be interested and they're the ones who really count. Otis will take himself to the living room and join Archibald and Marjorie in watching the archfoe of Satan perform his witchcraft down at the cathedral."

Then the phone rang and they all stiffened reflexively.

"We ought to be used to this by now," Maggie said as it rang a second time. "When the police phoned this morning we thought it was he, too."

"Let me take it before Arch or Marjorie answers in there and it does turn out to be he," Sutherland said. He lifted the receiver warily to hear a familiar voice and released a little sigh of relief.

"Mr. Sutherland, sir? Merry Christmas to you and your wife. This is George, the doorman. There's a police officer here to see you," the voice said somewhat uncertainly.

"It's okay, George. He's expected. Send him up, will you? And a good holiday to you also.

"Just the cops sending over somebody to pick up that blood sample. I'll go let him in."

He went to the door to look for the policeman and the man emerged from the elevator in less than a minute. He was young and an oriental and took off his hat as he shook hands with Sutherland. "Mike Mallory thanks you, Mr. Sutherland, and says he'll phone you as soon as he knows anything from the lab."

"Fine. Want some coffee?"

"No, sir. I'll just wait here while you get the sample. I have to get right downtown with it."

Sutherland nodded and walked into the living room on his way to the study. The snow in the container had melted down to about a third of its original volume and the bright red of the blood was faded now to a pinkish tint and he wondered seriously if it would be of any use to the lab men. When he returned to the foyer, Otis had already cornered the cop and was telling his witchcraft hypothesis to a stony, politely nodding oriental face.

"Yes, sir, you can be sure we'll check into everything. Thank you very much for your help." The man took the container from Sutherland and shook hands again as he prepared to leave. He answered Sutherland's wink with a shrug. "It'd just knock you right over how some of the free advice we get turns out to be absolutely straight. Well, Merry Christmas, gentlemen."

When he was gone, Sutherland and Otis returned to the kitchen. On the television, the cardinal was distributing communion to a very long line of worshipers.

"Well, we should know before too long if there's anything they can do to that watered-down sample I gave them,"

Sutherland said as he settled down to his grapefruit and more coffee. "Otis, baby, your whole career is on the line this morning."

"Otis will be vindicated," Otis said flatly.

He was. Mike Mallory called back in less than two hours.

"James, greetings. Say, do you think that hairdresser friend of yours would consider a contract offer for official psychic in residence with the Boston Police Department?"

"You're kidding. He was right?"

"Bunny rabbit, he said, and bunny rabbit it was."

"Oh, shit. That means my linebacker is going to be a majorette named Annabella. Otis even preempted that paternal privilege. He chose the name and I don't have a strong alternative."

"Oh, well, let's hope your line doesn't run high to women like mine did. I got the traditional Catholic overpopulated family from sheer desperation, not belief in unbridled fertility. Listen, James, what are the chances that this guy Otis is having a little Yuletide fun at your expense? I mean, you just don't look at a reddened patch of snow and call it dead right without a lab test."

"Maggie," Sutherland called to her, holding the phone near so Mallory could hear. "Mike Mallory would like to know what the chances are that Otis might be our prankster?"

"My Otis?" She guffawed at the notion, came over, and took the phone from Sutherland. "Detective Mallory, I'm Maggie Hanson; Otis is my lover, we live together on Commonwealth Avenue, and I will swear on a stack of Bibles that for the last two nights of the endearing prankster from about midnight to seven A.M., said suspect was wrapped around me in a very warm bed. Otis doesn't like the cold, and he's afraid to go out alone at night. And he really is psychic, believe me. His tips on the stock market and the ponies out at Suffolk Downs are unerring."

She listened for a moment, then her face assumed a look a feigned righteousness. "My God, Mallory! Of course I don't use a bookie. What sort of person do you think I am? I'm a businessperson of the highest moral character. Like all businesspersons, I even pay my taxes."

Then, smiling broadly, she handed the phone back to Sutherland after a moment during which Mallory had evidently turned on the charm.

"I want you to know that I never even considered propositioning your friend Maggie, James," the detective volunteered. "This is no time to be unfaithful to my wife, even if it is Christmas. There are at least two murders in Boston this year that she hasn't solved yet and the department can't afford her alienation. Anyhow, continued good wishes and do give me a ring if our friend returns tonight. But not until a reasonable hour of daylight, please."

"Why don't you just send two cops out there around three-thirty A.M. and pick the guy up and find out who the hell he is?"

"Of course. On Christmas night in the middle of a snow emergency when there will be automobile accidents, fires, all sorts of drunks falling into snowbanks unaware they are dying of hypothermia, robberies and suicides who will be calling in droves like they always do when their holiday depressive spiral hits top gear. All men, you know, James, are not wearing the identical happy boots you find yourself in this season. In addition, there will be family quarrels in profusion and an astounding number of runaway kids who didn't get what they wanted from Santa Claus. Of course, none of this low-rent roughhousing will be going on in your privileged enclave over there in Back Bay. No, there you get just cranks who specialize in ear-splitting phone calls and then hang up and pranksters who leave a calling card of chicken and rabbit blood, then run away. Meanwhile, back in Charlestown, where I live, is the nitty-gritty. Not only will I be on duty when I'm on duty, but I'll be on duty when I'm off duty. Because everybody in C-town knows I'm a cop who keeps his nose clean and tonight when the fights and wife-beatings and butcher-knife skewerings happen, they'll call me before they call the precinct. Can you believe that, James? People actually find a reason to stab each other on Christmas Day. No," the detective sighed wearily, "I won't send two cops out there at three-thirty tomorrow morning to ask some weirdo why he's playing games with you. Why don't you get up some guts and do it yourself?"

"Mike, I get the idea. Enough." Sutherland begged.

"Lastly, James, I really don't much care any longer except to know what kind of blood he uses tonight if he hasn't gotten bored with himself by now and actually does show. 'Bye, and let me know what happens."

" 'Bye, Mike."

Sutherland replaced the receiver and answered the questioning arc of Jane's eyebrows with a shrug. "Mike thinks my idea of sending out the cops tonight is a waste of time better spent. He's probably right, too. I'll bet the guy doesn't show."

"Oh, he'll show, James," Otis said from the doorway. "Otis is quite certain about that. You'll have your regular appointment at three-thirty A.M. sharp."

"When will the baby be born, Otis?" Jane asked the seer.

"Otis sees darkness and a full moon. Tonight's the night. Otis knows. Otis feels labor pains."

"Jane doesn't feel anything," Jane mimicked in response.

"Jane must give nature a chance," Otis advised.

*　*　*

Annabella Marie-Joseph Sutherland entered the world at six-oh-five that evening, weighing eight pounds and two ounces.

The telephoning crank who admitted he was the Esplanade prankster telephoned in the middle of Christmas dinner not ten minutes before Sutherland took Jane out to the hospital. Sutherland pretended ebullience at his daughter's birth, but he was too worried about the prankster's unknowable motive to enjoy the event.

The presents under the tree had all been exchanged by late morning, the Portuguese music box an unqualified success as he had anticipated, and they had drunk a single cocktail before the meal and then taken their places at the table. Sutherland, who was carving the turkey, was the first to notice the change in Jane. Light beads of perspiration had broken out on her upper lip and forehead and she had the sudden look of someone nauseated by the rich odor of food.

"Janie, are you all right?"

"*C'est l'heure, Janie?*" Marjorie asked.

"No, not yet." She smiled down at the plate of bland dietetic food her doctor had ordered. "It's just that the smell of all this wonderful chow you people are about to wolf down is making me a little queasy. I could pick up the scent of that oyster stuffing Otis ought to be marketing about a block away from here. I think I'll just go upstairs and lie down for five minutes or so."

She rose from her chair firmly enough, Sutherland thought, but he went with her anyhow, helping her ponderous, measured ascent up the stairs, then through the door into their bedroom where the phone rang. Jane said it in the same instant Sutherland thought it: "Oh, no, not that ugly fuck!"

Sutherland lifted the receiver and heard the manic laughter. The laughter infuriated him: "What do you want? Goddamn you, my wife's about to have a baby! The last thing we need right now is the certain expectancy that it's going to be you every time we lift the phone . . ."

His voice trailed off as he heard himself speak the words. He realized he had succumbed, had the universal desperate reaction to this kind of harassment. He was convinced that a terror was intruding on his life. Jane reached up from the bed and took a hard grip on his arm, shaking her head no. He calmed himself after a deep breath.

"Listen, friend, are you the same guy that's pulling the suicide prank out on the Esplanade the last couple of nights? Just say one word. Yes or no?"

"Yes," the hollow faraway voice told him, then the line went dead.

"Yes," Sutherland told his wife as he hung up.

She studied his face for a long moment: "Let's saddle up, James. The hour has nearly arrived anyhow. It'll be safe in the hospital with all the staff and guards there. He can't know what hospital I'm going to, for God's sake. And take the car, okay? You know, the one with the nice comfortable suspension. The roads are clear and there's no wind so there won't be any drifting to worry about. Just pull up in front and I'll be waiting in the lobby. I'll get Maggie to ride down in the elevator with me."

He went for his parka and keys while she readied her bag. None of the four at the table asked about the phone call, but he guessed from the look of their faces reading his that Maggie and Otis knew.

"Sorry to break up the party, folks, but Jane wants to go to the hospital now. Maggie, will you go up and help her along?"

She got up quickly from her dinner as Sutherland went through the door heading for the elevator.

Downstairs in the garage that was always overheated, especially on the coldest days of winter, Sutherland grew calmer as the Jaguar's engine sprang instantly to life and settled into its comforting purr. In another minute he parked the car on Beacon Street with the engine idling and went to the lobby, where Jane and Maggie were talking with George, the doorman.

"I hope it's the son you wanted, Mr. Sutherland," George greeted him.

"It's going to be a girl. We're quite certain of it now," Sutherland told him. "A friend of ours who knows all about these things and a lot of others says so, and he's never wrong."

George prepared to mourn, but Sutherland suddenly found humor in himself and laughed. "Her name will be Annabella Marie-Joseph Sutherland. I didn't have anything to do with the baby's name. The friend and my mother copped that privilege. I wonder if I had anything to do with this baby at all."

"Oh, you did, Mr. Sutherland. I promise you, you did," George chortled, familiar with Sutherland for the first time ever as the doorman clapped him warmly on the back while James was being ushered to the car.

Jane was laughing as she eased her way into the passenger seat. "Don't forget to give George a cigar, James. It's not to keep tradition, either. It's his reward for our finding out that that old sourpuss doorman actually has a sense of humor down there."

They waved to Maggie, who stood on the sidewalk with only a sweater thrown about her shoulders, and headed off down Beacon Street with the single admonition from Jane that he relax and drive slowly since there was time. She turned on the stereo radio and the soft voices of English carolers came forth from the FM classical station from which the dial never moved. Jane hummed along and sometimes sang when she knew the words and they made the hospital in about twenty minutes along lightly traveled streets. Sutherland was astounded at his wife's composure. He had expected to see the bandaged prankster at any number of places along the way. But the man had not appeared, and when they entered the front door of the hospital he was ready to concede that Jane had been right: there was no way the guy could know what hospital they had gone to, or even that they had left for a hospital. Jane was safe here.

Sutherland waited four hours in a lounge with two other expectant fathers until his daughter arrived. He gnawed nearly nonstop on candy bars to assuage his hunger and the leapings of his stomach and reflected that he could not remember ever having been so nervous in a courtroom. Not even at his first jury trial, and that had happened only three months after he first began practice. This child meant a stupendous amount to him, he decided, and much rode on a successful delivery. It might be their one and only. In terms of a mother's ideal childbearing age, Jane, after all, was no spring chicken. And Sutherland had grave doubts about his own thirty-seven years being prime time for beginning parenting. He studied the other two men he waited with closely. One was white, the other black, and he experienced a curious emotion that he recognized as jealousy when he realized he must have at least fifteen years on the black man and even more on the white, who sipped nervously from a silver pocket flask: what wonderful years they might know with wife and children until they became as old as Sutherland was now; the same years that he often joked he had spent riding across life on a lame horse.

The three nervous men became fellow travelers. The first's new son was born at 2:50 P.M., to effusive congratulations from the other two. The second's son was born at 5:13 P.M. After the first had gone his way, promising to write and forgetting his silver pocket flask in his excitement, the second confessed to Sutherland that the birth of whatever was coming would be second to the relief he felt at not having to be in the delivery room when the baby was arriving.

Sutherland, for his part, confessed to the opposite: he had wanted to be there, assisting at the birth, but Jane had vetoed the idea and was absolutely adamant about it in the face of almost a month of persistence. Bugliosi, her doctor, convinced him that the veto had to stand, arguing that he was putting undue pressure on an already pressured situation. He had met with Sutherland in Cambridge for lunch, told him gravely across his dieter's salad about the high risk in over-thirty pregnancies. Bugliosi sweated in an early-June heat wave. He drew a statistics curve on a paper napkin and swept flies from the tablecloth of the open-air restaurant in annoyance. When he argued he raised his voice and tapped his pen sharply on the table for emphasis. Heads turned and a woman at a nearby table leaned over to assure Sutherland the doctor was exactly right. She had lost one after a surprise pregnancy at age thirty-five. Her IUD had been incorrectly implanted. It came out with the baby. Sutherland expressed his sorrow. Now he waited away from the delivery room with another man whose chief emotion was blessed relief.

At about five-twenty a nursing nun came to tell him that he was wanted on the phone. He was alone in the lounge now and growing more nervous still as the wait became longer, so he left with her gratefully, glad for the distraction and confidently expecting that the call was from either Archibald and Marjorie or Maggie and Otis. He thanked the nun and lifted the receiver to his ear. He heard the terrible laughter and staggered a little and grabbed at the nurse's desk to steady himself.

"How did you know . . . ?" he whispered hoarsely, checking his tendency to scream because he did not want the nun to raise her head from her work at the far end of the desk. The laughter continued to peal mocking and shrill in its awful cadence.

"Happen yet?" the voice suddenly spoke.

"No . . . no . . . not yet. Listen . . . you can't come into this hospital. I won't leave it while she's here. I'll notify the police. Do you hear me? I mean it, you bum!" He had hurled the last louder than a whisper and the nun raised her head and looked at him questioningly. He smiled weakly and shook his head no and she bent again to her charts.

"Come to the river tonight and we talk. No police."

"And if I don't?"

"You will. If you do not, Jane is no longer safe. Until then she is." Then, as before, the line simply went dead. Sutherland was too stupefied by everything to be even startled that the prankster had called Jane by name. He stood there a long moment, his eyes squinted closed, as he replayed the voice of the terrible shrill laughter through his memory. Deep, husky and carefully enunciating, not at all the voice of the laugher. Not a voice that recalled anyone to him. He thanked the nun and returned to the lounge. There he bought a pack of cigarettes from a machine and sat down to smoke one thoughtfully. It had been more than ten years since he had smoked his last cigarette.

At five forty-five, Archibald, Marjorie, Maggie and Otis showed up. Sutherland smiled gamely through the anticipated round of jokes about expectant fathers, then managed to maneuver Maggie outside the lounge for a quick question.

"Did our loony laugher phone anytime after we left this afternoon?"

"Nope. Your sister Elaine and her husband Hank were the only ones to call. Let's hope he's trying every two minutes right now and going out of his mind with frustration trying to figure out where his targets have gotten themselves to. Hey, James, he didn't phone here, did he, by any chance?"

"No, I don't think we have to worry about that."

"I mean, that's what I figured, James. How could he possibly know you were here? Even if he knew enough about you to have your building staked out and saw you leaving today with a very pregnant lady, he'd have to have a keener science than old Otis to know you were out here in Waltham."

"Yeah, I think we've heard the last of that bird, Maggie. Let's go back in, okay?"

At six-ten, Annabella's birth was announced and they all got their first look at Sutherland's daughter about half an hour later through a plate-glass window in a room full of cribs and sleeping babies. She was held up to view by a masked and heavy-hipped black nurse whose eyes were laughing above the top of the mask. The reaction was a universal silence.

"That kid looks like a little spic," Archibald finally pronounced in judgment.

She was unaccountably dark-complected with hazel-almond eyes, whereas Sutherland's eyes were blue and Jane's were a pale gray. Sutherland actually raised his hand to check its coloring. Though darker than Jane, whose skin was very fair, his own was shades lighter than the baby's.

"Maybe she's got the wrong baby," Sutherland said after a long moment. "Is that possible?"

The nurse apparently was hearing them over an intercom system and shook her head emphatically in the negative. She raised the baby's arm to show a wristband identification tag and the tag read: Baby Sutherland.

Marjorie laughed with delight and clapped her hands, then reached up to peck Sutherland a kiss of congratulations on his cheek.

"You lose this one, Archibald. You got yourself a little French-Canadienne, *mon fils*. She has the exact coloring of the Gervais family. I was the lightest, but all my brothers and sisters have the same as the baby. My mother and father, too. We have Iroquois blood in us. Oh, I cannot wait to send her photo to Québec! I am so proud of you, *mon fils*. She is so beautiful."

Sutherland grinned, asinine with pleasure at the perfect sense of what had to be the explanation. He had seen photos sent down from Quebec of his aunts and uncles, and they did indeed seem darker than his mother. Then they were all smiling and calling the baby beautiful and Sutherland's father was pummeling his back with a clenched fist after his fashion of congratulations.

"Well, I'll be goddamned!" Archibald intoned. "A recessive gene! That's very rare, I hear tell," he assured everyone with head-shaking earnestness.

"How a recessive gene?" Marjorie demanded. "Your son whose name is Sutherland is carrying half of me in him, too, after all. Are you saying that if I was as dark as one of my sisters, you would not have married me?"

"Well, no, Marjorie, that's not what I meant at all," Archibald whined. "I'm not like that, you know."

"Not since yesterday. No, you have definitely changed, Archibald."

But then they were all smiling and waving again at the baby, who yawned in response.

"Otis could have told you what the little baby's complexion was going to be like if only you had thought to ask Otis," Otis said. "Then there wouldn't be any shocks like today. Otis knew that Annabella would be dark."

"Maggie would never have guessed in a million years," Maggie said simply.

"*Alors,* stop mooning over your daughter and go and kiss your wife," Marjorie prodded Sutherland's arm. "It's all right?" she asked the nurse. The woman nodded her head.

"Yes, go and see her and don't be a chickenshit like your old man was," Archibald said. "Cripes, I had to get about five snorts of hooch in me before I could see Marjorie after you and Elaine was born! Go and we'll wait here for our turn."

Sutherland, burying his apprehension over the visit he had to make early that next morning to the Esplanade, went off to see his wife while the other four ogled his newborn daughter.

Jane was in a private room. Sutherland knocked on the door and then went in in response to her tired voice. The blinds were drawn and the room was dark except for a single gooseneck lamp on a bedside table. Even though she lay in shadow, Sutherland could tell how exhausted she was. She looked very small and frail.

He approached the bed beaming at her and saw that she watched him with an unsmiling, never-before-seen uncertain look as if she needed to hear his reassurance that she had given him the right thing.

"She's beautiful! I love her! Thank you! Thank you! Thank you!"

She smiled openly now. When he bent to shower her face with kisses, she threw her arms about his neck. After a long moment, she began laughing and playfully pushed him away. "Enough! Enough, James! If you keep it up, I'll invite you to spend the night in this narrow little bed with me."

"I will! I will! Just ask me!"

"You won't! You won't! One, mother is absolutely shot

tired, and two, if one of those nuns walks in here and catches us, I'll have to spend the night on my knees in the hospital chapel for a punishment." She studied his face closely again. "Are you a little sad, father dear, that you got an Annabella instead of a Ford?"

"No! She's just fine. The only thing is I'll never doubt the outcome of Otis's predictions again. God, I wish that guy was my broker. He claims he even knew she was going to be dark-complected."

"She is kind of darker than one might have expected," Jane admitted.

"Old Marjorie wins another. She says our Annabella is a Gervais. We got ourselves a little French Canuck."

She clicked her fingers and smiled at the suggestion: "Now I know who she reminds me of. All those photos of Marjorie's family up in Quebec. Oh, boy! Archibald must be sputtering out there."

"Are you kidding? He's ga-ga. They're all waiting to come in with their congratulations."

"Oh, no, I'm so tired," she groaned. "Okay, kiss me good night and go play with your daughter and tell them to come in. But emphasize brief visit to them, will you? I need to bag it for a couple of hours at least."

"I'll wait around. Maybe I can con the nurses into letting me in when you wake up."

"No. You owe me a favor now. I want you to go home, finish that slice of turkey you were working on, then celebrate by getting drunk. Only promise you won't go joyriding in that truck of yours when the elation hits high gear. Promise?"

"Promise. I'll be back first visiting hour tomorrow."

"Lovely. And I want you to look good and hung over for me. And please bring a little something for Mrs. Crawford, the nurse. She's a real sweetie."

"Will do, General."

Then her face clouded over for a moment and she took a sudden grip on his arm. "James, that nut didn't call here at the hospital did he . . . ?"

"Of course not, darling. How the hell could he know we're here?"

She smiled at the reassurance, a little chagrined even, he thought. He kissed her, rose from the side of the bed where he sat, clicked his heels together and saluted. Then he backed out of the room, waving and smiling all the way and his wife waved her good-byes in return.

He went out again to the waiting room where Marjorie, Maggie and Otis were laughing at Archibald, who invoked his gift of tongues and baby-talked to his granddaughter.

"You're on call, folks," Sutherland interrupted. "But make it a quickie, okay? She's exhausted."

They departed in a collective rush and Sutherland took over talking to his daughter, who now lay yawning in a crib. In about three minutes, Archibald, Maggie and Otis were back smiling and giggling at something Maggie was saying, but Marjorie was not with them.

"Where's Mother?" Sutherland asked.

"Your mother is privileged to have a private audience with her daughter-in-law and Maggie, Otis and Archibald are very jealous. Marjorie is required, by the way, to make you hand over your truck keys for safekeeping and Archibald is charged with helping you to get drunk."

"You two coming back to help us party a little?"

"No, James. Otis has the urge now and wants to go home," Otis said flatly. "We came here in Maggie's car, so we can drive back ourselves. Otis offers you his sincere congratulations for the twentieth time, but really must be going now. 'Bye-bye, little baby."

Maggie groaned. "Oh, God, Otis. Promise me if you ever get me pregnant you'll at least be good enough to marry me."

"Otis promises. Let's go."

Maggie kissed Sutherland a last time, waved to the baby and allowed herself to be dragged off down the hallway.

Marjorie's audience lasted five minutes. When she returned, her unsmiling face had a thoughtful, somehow annoyed look on it, Sutherland thought.

"Hey, *ma mère*, you look like your daughter-in-law just told you never to darken her doorstep again."

"Eh? Oh, I'm sorry, *mon petit*. I was trying to remember the name of someone." She brightened into a smile when she saw the baby once more. "He was a friend of my father's from Québec City, but I can't think of it and I get angry with myself when I forget things like that. It makes me think I'm getting to be a senile old lady. Well, had enough of your daughter? Why don't we go back to Boston now? Your father is to encourage you to get drunk, and I am to sleep with your truck keys under my pillow."

They left after thanking the nurse, Mrs. Crawford, and on their way to the parking lot Sutherland asked his parents to remind him in the morning that he was to bring her a gift. At the car, Marjorie asked his permission to drive and he acquiesced. She drove back only a little more slowly than Sutherland had driven out, handling the gear changes expertly, silent while Sutherland and his father joked and talked nonstop. In thirty minutes, they were at the entrance to the apartment-house parking garage on Beacon Street.

Upstairs, Sutherland was too excited to eat and after ceremoniously handing over his driver's license to his mother, he sat down with a glass of his favorite scotch and sipped at it slowly while Archibald worked at building a fire.

When the fire was blazing Archibald leaped to his feet and tried launching a celebration party with a comically grotesque and gimping dance about the room for which Sutherland gave him little encouragement.

"Arch, please, it's been a really strenuous day."

"Aw, c'mon, James. Get up and stretch your bones a little bit. I never been a grandfather before."

"Arch . . ."

"Archibald, come now for your dinner and leave James alone for a while. Can't you see he's tired and doesn't want to play?"

His mother dragged Archibald into the kitchen and a sad smile flickered across Sutherland's face as he watched the retreat. His parents were at that most poignant age for their children, he thought—the age when one partner's senility in the face of the other's continuing mental acumen made that senility all the more painfully obvious. See them now: the thundering voice was a whimper. The whisper became certain authority. In the kitchen Archibald begged to know what he had done wrong. Marjorie's voice searched for a quiet, diplomatic way to tell him. Sutherland knew she would put him to bed soon.

He heard them loading the dishwasher as he put a record of Mozart serenades on the stereo. Halfway through the strains of *Eine Kleine Nachtmusik* they congratulated him a final time and bade him good night. Archibald looked tired as though he had been drugged.

In an hour more he kicked off his shoes and went to sleep on the couch. He came bang-awake again with an awesome headache and rose, mystified as to why his head should ache until he remembered the phone call the afternoon before at the hospital. He stood and headed for the window to look for the prankster, certain he would be there because Otis had told him so.

At three-forty or thereabouts, he showed and turned toward the river as always. Sutherland threw on his parka and headed out of the apartment for the elevator. In the lobby the doorman slept at his desk. Sutherland made it over the footbridge and touched down on the Esplanade just as the prankster returned from his trek across the ice to the outer perimeter of light from the arc lamps.

"Hey, you!" Sutherland called out to him. "Who the hell are you? You're driving me around the bend with this little caper of yours!"

The figure stopped and spoke to him. "Hello, James, how you are?"

Then he pulled off the wig and the mask that gave him the look of a puffy-faced, heavy-set man and Sutherland staggered a few feet backward from the shock: it was Manfredi. Sutherland was more afraid than ever.

CHAPTER 19

Manfredi's Child

"I see you still have the wakefulness, James."

"What the hell are you doing here, Manfredi? How did you get into the country? The Immigration Service will deport you right back to Italy again if they find out you're here."

"They will not find I am here, James, because I am not in U.S. as Manfredi Occhapenti. False passport in Italia is easy to get. I have other name now and I keep that to myself. The only way they could find out is if you are to tell them, and I do not think you will tell them."

"Bullshit, pal! I'll go right in there now and phone them. You'll have another ticket on the next Alitalia flight out of here. We don't need any more trouble from you, friend."

"Do you want your father to go to prison, James?"

"What are you talking about?"

"Do you recognize the name Emmett Tyson?"

"He works for my father up on the farm . . ." Sutherland knew then that Manfredi had found out about the barn.

"This Emmett also drink too much. One night he shoot off his mouth in a bar up in Chicopee where Marlena's two brothers go for a drink. He tells everybody about how funny is that his friend Archibald Sutherland burn down his barn for insurance money, then build brand-new barn for nothing. The same barn you accuse me of burning and get me deported for. So call Immigration Office if you want. They may send me back to Roma, but not until I get new trial, and there are fifteen witnesses in bar that night and the Avgerinos brothers know all. Your father go to prison for sure. I have talked to lawyers in Roma about this."

So: Emmett, that stupid bastard! The very evidence they had used to hang Manfredi (and Sutherland had been convinced of its truth at the time) was going to hang Archibald instead. Sutherland's mind was boggled for a long moment of silence; he could not think of a way to defend his father. He thought instead of killing Manfredi, proving to the police that all these nights of the caper on the River Charles had indeed been practice runs. But Manfredi seemed to sense his thoughts. He pulled the Luger from his pocket and pointed it straight at him.

"I would not to do that, James. Tonight I thought you might come. Tonight the gun is loaded. But I would not need it. I am fighting again in Italia. I am in very good condition, you will see."

"I could offer you a lot of money to go away, Manfredi. I know you can't be making a lot of money, and Marlena doesn't come from a rich family."

"I do not want money, James."

"You want to come back to the States, then? I can help you. I can arrange for your visa to be reinstated. You'll be allowed reentry."

Manfredi shook his head in the negative. "No, in Italia is better for me. I stay there."

Sutherland raised his hands in a plea to the other.

"Manfredi, why wreck our happiness? You had six good years with Jane. You both wanted out when you came to me for a divorce. It'll kill my father if he has to go to prison. Even if we pay the insurance company back in full, he'll still have to serve a term. You're not that kind of man. You're not a vengeful person. There must be something you want."

"There is. Today my baby girl was born here in Boston. I want to take her back to Roma with me. You want to call her Annabella, but I want to call her Angelina."

"Are you crazy? Are you losing your mind? That's not your child! You weren't even married to Jane when that baby was conceived! You—you can't talk about my wife that way!" The echo of his fumbling words had not yet died in the clear, frigid silence of the Boston night when he realized how perfectly ineffectual they had been. He studied Manfredi closely. That very handsome Latin face had always been a motile mask of expression in the past. Joy and anger, sadness, depression, elation and curiosity—sometimes it seemed the face flew through the whole range of them in seconds. Only now the mask was calm and purposeful, tinged perhaps by a shade of the pity he felt for Sutherland for what he was telling. Sutherland felt something strain, then begin slipping inside him: the unequivocal trust he had come to feel for his wife, Jane. Manfredi would offer proof now. No one would come so far and at such a risk without much certainty. Sutherland would not listen.

"We had the lovemaking two times before you had me deported, James, before you were even married. Otis write me and tell me this is true."

"Otis! That nutty faggot! He's got a sixth sense about a lot of things, but knowing something like that is just plain impossible!"

"This not the magic art of Otis. This is truth. Ask Janie. She tells Maggie when she is sure because she needs to talk with someone and Maggie tells Otis. Otis write to me because he does not think is right for me. Call the hospital and ask the blood type of the baby. Between you and Janie it is not possible, James." For the first time a smile, childish even with its delight, Sutherland thought, leaped across Manfredi's face: "James, Otis say the little bambino even look like me . . ."

Sutherland stared blankly at the Roman, only arriving now at the real threshold of reaction to the notion of such a betrayal on Jane's part and not yet at the moment of convulsion that he knew had to come sometime later on. The forepart of his mind, the part he reserved for confronting reality, hoped Manfredi might even be a little mad right now, standing before Sutherland with a loaded Luger in hand. The power of his dream, pressed fruitlessly on his Janie for six long years, had to be greater even than the strength of Marjorie's dream that she had carried so long in silence. What else could have impelled him back to America, where he was an automatic fugitive, determined at any cost to carry off the prize the dream had promised as if there were no one else involved, no one else who mattered? And that long-barreled Luger was not the only weapon in his arsenal that had to be disarmed. He had come with enough ammunition—witness Archibald—to destroy a few other people into the bargain if he did not get his way and quit the country with Sutherland's daughter in his arms. Mad, yes, but not in conventional parlance, and that made him even more dangerous in Sutherland's estimation.

"Manfredi, we have to resolve this somehow, I mean, having or not having this child doesn't mean your world is complete or totally incomplete, you know. I mean, Marlena's a young woman. She could give you lots of children, lots of little bambinos. Ha. Ha. Ha."

The pitying smile returned to Manfredi's face and Sutherland knew what he was going to say. It was pity for both of them now, not for the silly, panicked, patronizing words he had just uttered.

"Ha. Ha. Ha, yourself, James. I am sorry you are so desperate. But now you will be more desperate. Marlena cannot to have children. It is not possible. Three doctors have told us this."

"Ah . . . I'm sorry," Sutherland told him simply. He looked across to Cambridge at the luminous outline of the darkened M.I.T. buildings. A weather-scouting searchlight probed the sky above them. He heard the resounding clang of fortress gates being closed against him in the night.

"Yes, I do not doubt you are sorry. But I am not the Shah of Iran. I cannot to change wives when I wish because they give no childrens and I love Marlena as much as I love Janie so she do not leave."

"Then what can we do?"

"We wait. When the baby is enough strong to travel, Marlena will come from Roma. Then we will take her home."

Sutherland found he had shoved the middle of his index finger between his teeth and was chomping on it hard to keep under control. He was dizzy with frustration because he had never felt so completely trapped before. He just knew that Manfredi was not taking the realization of James Sutherland's also long-anticipated dream back to Rome. He would find a way to stop Manfredi.

"I have to go, Manfredi. I have to think about all this now. I have to make certain that what you say is true."

"Make a telephone call to any doctor, James. Find out what is the type of the baby's blood and tell him what is the type of you and Janie's. Then you are certain. *Ciao, paisan.* I am sorry because I like you so much. I think now you will not to sleep all the night, not just the one hour like before."

"I'll manage. I always make a point of getting my rest no matter what the problem. Tell me one thing. Where does the blood come from? A detective friend of mine is eating burned food because his wife is preoccupied with trying to figure that out."

"Burned food?" He shrugged his puzzlement. "Anyhow, the blood comes from here."

He opened the voluminous overcoat and, predictably enough, there was a clear-plastic bag that was Manfredi's padded stomach slung by a strap around his neck, holding about two gallons or so of the police lab technician's low-stakes betting material for that day. There was a hose that climbed up to the level of the coat collar and another hose with a fist-sized ball pump attached. Sutherland smiled, guessing it would not take Mallory's wife too long to figure this one out.

"Why did you think you had to stage all this routine, Fredi? I'll bet it just grabs your Italian flair for drama."

"What am I to do? Ring the doorbell at the Christmas dinner and to tell six people I want my baby who is not born yet? No, I needed just the one. You."

"What's in it tonight, Manfredi?" Sutherland asked, gesturing at the bag.

"It is not important, James. I will not to use it this night. When your friend this Irish detective—his name is Mallory, yes?—calls you, you will tell him nobody comes tonight so he will not to interfere."

"Let me decide what to tell him. I gather you're in contact with our friend Otis, huh?"

"Yes. I stay in a little apartment he keep for his boys above his coiffure shop. Even Maggie do not know it is there. He tell me about this Mallory."

"I'm going to take care of Otis when all this is over," Sutherland gnashed his teeth. "That rotten little pederast! Sitting down at a man's table for Christmas dinner while he's orchestrating this little theater of the absurd at the very same time! Funny how internecine treachery always makes so much more interesting drama than just plain old indifferent treachery—"

"What is inter-necine?"

"You know. Deadly to both sides. Heavy casualty. Especially because it's at close quarters like in the family or among friends."

"Oh, like the old *Romani*"—he frowned for a moment—"like the new *Romani* also, I guess. Like everybody."

Sutherland sighed, "Yes, I guess. I have got to go now, Manfredi."

"I will walk a way with you, James. I go home to sleep now."

They set off side by side walking toward the crosswalk rampway. When they were halfway across and a car passed below them on the drive, Manfredi spoke a last time.

"Maggie knows nothing of what Otis does. She does not betray you. You must not to harm Otis either, James."

"Again, let me do my own thinking."

"What you can do? Kill him? Then everything is finished for you. You can to have more *bambini*. You will. I must to have this one. It is so simple. I leave now. Let us make congratulations on all our good *fortuna*. Is all same family!"

He extended his hand, the Luger pocketed when they had begun walking. Sutherland thought of trying to make a grab for the gun. But Manfredi, reading his thoughts, stared at him levelly and shook his head no.

"I don't want to shake your hand, Manfredi," Sutherland said. "We're not all the same family. You're an intruder and you're breaking up my family." And then he said it, though he did not know why he said it, "We're not all Italians."

Manfredi showed his hurt, then he shrugged the hurt away. "You do not hate Manfredi Occhapenti. This you do not to understand about yourself." Then quickly he was disappearing around the corner of a building. Sutherland trudged wearily into the apartment house and took the elevator upstairs. The truth of it was he did not hate Manfredi Occhapenti.

He knew he could not sleep. He paced and tried to think. He considered pouring himself another scotch, but decided against it and settled for a cup of instant coffee. He paced between the lighted tree and the opposite wall along the expanse of window and looked out on the scene of the most bizarre confrontation he had ever experienced.

Lord God, the unexpected way in which this had all come to pass!

Manfredi the Roman was back in America illegally, garbed in the most invincible armor Sutherland had ever encountered, demanding that the girl child born to the father Sutherland the day before be handed over to her rightful father. It had all happened so suddenly. He could only pray there might be at least some room for maneuvering. As long as he believed the room was there, then he might cherish hope. Manfredi had to be wrong about the baby's blood type; if not, then he had to be unhorsed. Sutherland would find a way.

But first things first. In the morning he would phone Mike Mallory to put him off the scent lest Mike turn up again asking questions.

Next the hospital for the baby's blood type.

Lastly, he would put in a casual call to his doctor, Lon McBane, with a question about blood types, and hope that Manfredi really had only one iron in the fire: his knowledge that it was Archibald who had torched the barn, the very crime, wrongly judged, that had ended Manfredi's American career and sent him into exile to Rome.

That done, McBane consulted, Sutherland might try a little delicate probing with the insurance company to see if they would forgo prosecution in the event of full repayment of the claim. It might not be inconceivable. Insurance companies were not in the business of revenge, after all. It was his guess that Archibald's advanced age would save the day. The insurance company would take its money and interest and call it quits.

Then there was the Immigration and Naturalization Service. Manfredi would get his hearing all right. And once the evidence and witnesses were presented he would get his acquittal on the charge of burning a barn to the ground in New Hampshire also. But that would not necessarily mean an automatic reversal on the Immigration Service's decision to deport him. There were other smudges on his ledger. The barn-burning charge had been simply the third strike that put Manfredi out of the game and brought on the deportation order. Sutherland recalled them now, and the remembrance of Manfredi's violent and fearful harassment of Sutherland and Jane made him certain that there was still reason enough to return Manfredi to Italy.

How wrong Sutherland had been to judge Manfredi Occhapenti a comic buffoon. He had mistaken the man's real passion for a manic personality, and the mistake had almost cost him dearly.

CHAPTER 20

Marlena Avgerinos, Childbearer

With Manfredi Occhapenti, children were an obsession. On the street he plucked them from their mothers' arms to kiss them and sometimes bought them presents on impulse. He spoke their language so readily, Sutherland thought, because they liberated him from speaking English. He imprinted himself indelibly in Sutherland's memory when at their first client-lawyer interview he managed to bring home the emptiness of Sutherland's own life by asking to see photos of Sutherland's children. But perhaps all Manfredi's excursions into the world of children were merely symptomatic of a starved man. In the six years of his marriage, Manfredi's pleadings that Jane bear his child fell on deaf ears. When that marriage was over, he went shopping right off in a very businesslike fashion for a new wife to be the mother of his children. To Manfredi's mind, he had wasted years enough already.

He first worked his way through the very limited list of eligibles he and Jane had known, then through another list, some of them staffers at *Antiquitaire*, provided by Maggie Hanson. Then there were the singles bars, all of them depressing and pointless because Manfredi asked all the wrong questions to the throb of stomping music. The singles-bar detour had cost a valuable two weeks.

He then turned to the newspapers. To Sutherland's mind it was at once a funny, pathetic, desperate and ultimately narcissistic act, since each advertisement was headed by Manfredi's own favorite, four-year-old photo of himself. He solicited for a wife in the Personals columns of the Boston *Globe,* the *Herald-American,* and the *Real Paper.* He had composed a different profile of himself for each newspaper, predicated on Manfredi's canny analysis of each paper's readership. The reaction was, quite simply, overwhelming.

Sincere women candidates, a few eligible, but most sadly ineligible; the inevitable fraternity and sorority house and neighborhood barroom jokers; bored housewives anticipating their own divorces, mothers proffering their daughters, a woman anticipating her husband's suicide, a Combat Zone hooker named Millie Smith who wanted to go straight. Sutherland, the new friend privy to it all, had no idea that there were so many kinds of desperation out there. There were hundreds of letters in response to the first week's inquiries, more than a thousand at the end of three weeks. Each and every one was accompanied by the photo Manfredi requested. Each week the responses, by virtue of Manfredi's bizarre logic, were narrowed to ten finalists he deigned to answer by personal letters, including his own photograph in glossy reproduction and telephone number.

The selection process was an interminable time of decision that Manfredi played like a game of solitaire, laying out all the letters with identifying photos in lettered rows on the oriental rug that Jane had given him as a farewell present. (She also paid the rent for three years according to the divorce settlement, a fact about which Sutherland could scarcely quibble since he had been Manfredi's lawyer for the proceedings and had demanded that it be included in the terms of the agreement.)

Among these rows of numbered photos, Manfredi Occhapenti, free agent, padded like a panther in stocking feet, magnifying glass in hand. Occasionally he stopped to scoop up a photo and examine it carefully under the lens, checking for close-up evidences of concealed aging and blemishes. For the first couple of days, the rejection process went along at a measured pace. Then the pace quickened until the afternoon of the sixth day of each week.

By the afternoon of the sixth day, there remained only ten photos in a single unlettered line on the carpet. On the evening of the sixth day, he came to Jane's apartment where the lover Sutherland was already ensconced, it being three months since the divorce, and more than eleven months since the legal separation the laws of the Commonwealth required. He came for Jane's approval and her help in deciding how to rate the candidates. Nothing had really changed. There was not one iota of slippage in the intensity of love Manfredi felt for his ex-wife. They were simply not married and he no longer had any claim on her.

From uncertainty and interest, Sutherland always made a point to be there at the same time. Christ Jesus! he remembered as he paced now like a panther himself, it had all been so incestuous! What reason had he to be uncertain about Manfredi? They were friends, lovers, everything—an incongruous threesome who spent hours traipsing around the city everywhere together, Sutherland invariably trailing in the wake of Jane's and Manfredi's vast energies. They were a working team, those two, and at that time they seemed to be working their darnedest to teach him how to laugh again. Manfredi especially, Sutherland thought. He thought the greatest compliment he had ever received had come from Manfredi. The day outside the lodge at Aspen when Sutherland had laughed long and hard and effortlessly at someone's joke and Manfredi had turned to him and told him simply that now he was ready for his marriage to Jane. A terrible pity that their friend Manfredi was showing up once again in Boston like this.

The name and face of Marlena Avgerinos appeared in the third week's finalists. Sutherland by then was tiring of the game, but Jane never seemed to lose her enthusiasm for it. While she and Manfredi took their places on the stools at the kitchen counter to begin that final week's countdown, Sutherland was in the dining room eating a late dinner. He heard

Jane exclaim sharply when the judging could not have been more than a minute old.

"Oh my God, Fredi! She's beautiful! She's the one! Forget the others! Forget the twenty you wrote to! This is the woman you're going to marry!"

Jane was up and pacing excitedly up and down the kitchen; Manfredi was in skipping step beside her.

"You think, Janie? You think so, huh? I think so, too! I look at her picture and I fall in love! Like that!" He snapped his fingers repeatedly in his excitement. "She's Greek. From New Hampshire. Good family. Very religious. Greek Orthodox, but it doesn't to matter. I already called the priest. Janie, what if she doesn't to like me?"

"She'll like you, Fredi. Don't worry. If she doesn't, call me and I'll give her a pep talk. Lady to lady. James, take a gander at this."

Marlena Avgerinos passed above Sutherland's shrimp scampi. He bolted his glass of wine to clear his throat. "Gorgeous! She's fantastic! She's one of the most beautiful women I ever laid eyes on! Where was this up in New Hampshire when I needed it?" He almost added, why would anyone like this answer a newspaper advertisement for a wife, but then thought better of it. He hoped it was not somebody's idea of a joke.

"In Chicopee," Manfredi informed them, but he mispronounced it. "Janie, what do you think I should do?"

"Write her a polite letter and tell her who you are and how attractive you think she is. Invite her to dinner at Rudolfo's sometime next week. And, Manfredi, one thing," she cautioned. "With this girl, you've got to be extra honest. None of this woppy figura. No exaggerations. Don't tell her anything you aren't or haven't got. Remember."

"Promise. Absolute promise." He lectured himself sternly in the dining room's massive wall mirror. "You must not to exaggerate. You must not to exaggerate. It is forbidden to exaggerate."

They sat down at the dining-room table while Sutherland finished his meal. Her photo lay on the tablecloth between them. Sutherland studied her carefully. She was a sloe-eyed

Greek beauty, her olive face framed between twin curtains of very dark hair. But somehow she reminded him of his wife, Edith, whom he was still trying to divorce. She had the same look about the eyes—the innocence, the passivity, the shyness that called out for protection. But this girl was different. She didn't have the very fine, delicately chiseled features of Edith. This girl's were broader, stronger somehow to Sutherland's eye. There was a suggestion in them that if Manfredi got her and occasioned to step out of line, she had the will to let loose a flight of harpies in his direction.

Manfredi talked himself out as Sutherland ended his dinner.

"Janie, can I borrow the Mercedes the night I take her to dinner?"

"No way. You own a Fiat, you're a Fiat man. A car won't make you any different than you are. No pretenses, remember?"

"What if she doesn't think I make enough money?"

"Come and see me about that. Maybe I can help."

Sutherland gazed resignedly into the future. He saw Manfredi with four kids and never enough money to support them, running to Aunt Jane for a periodic handout. And she would give it to him, too, if she had it. But about that Sutherland had no real doubts. She speculated to him once in an uncharacteristically open moment about her very private business affairs that she could probably unload *Antiquitaire* the next day for about fifty times what she had started it with.

In time, Manfredi left. Sutherland and Jane sat having a last glass of wine before the fireplace.

"You'd do anything for that guy, wouldn't you? As it is, you mother him too much," Sutherland told her.

"I won't sleep with him and I won't remarry him. Just about anything else is up for grabs. And I don't mother him. I merely read directional signs for him. There's a difference."

"You'll never be rid of him."

"I don't want to be rid of him. Manfredi's the most honest man I've ever met. He's far more honest than you are, by the way."

"Give me a chance. You can't undo half a lifetime of professional deceit overnight."

"Anyhow, Manfredi gave me six very good years and, as you can guess, there was never a dull moment. The only thing is I didn't give him the one thing he wanted most, and that means I'm still on the debit side of the ledger. And no more of this veiled criticism of my ex-husband. He's your friend, too, remember? You said so yourself."

Marlena Avgerinos accepted Manfredi Occhapenti's invitation to dinner at Rudolfo's. Before he drove there to meet her, Manfredi dropped by for inspection and a courage drink. It had just turned spring. The snow was gone and the ice on the river had long since broken up. Manfredi wore a cravat and incessantly patted his hair into place as he shifted his drink from one hand to another. Behind him, through the plate glass of the windows, was the wide bank of an incredible sunset.

"Janie, how I look?"

"How do I look. You look fine. Gorgeous as the day I married you in Rome. Now calm down, Fredi. You're thirty-four and you've been through all this once before. God! To think the thing that impressed me then was your sangfroid!"

Manfredi walked before a mirror, adjusted the cravat and squinted menacingly at himself: "Sangfroid. Yes. Very good. I have that."

He threw his belted raincoat over his shoulders, checked out his sangfroid one more time in the mirror and left to meet his new wife.

"God, I feel like his father. Like we're seeing him off to a high school prom or something," Sutherland told her. "Let's go out to a movie tonight, okay?"

"Can't, James. I've got to get a look at her. She might be one-legged, after all. There's got to be something wrong with a girl who looks like that and answers an ad for a husband that's running in the newspapers. I'll give Manfredi a half hour or so, then get out the car and run down to Rudolfo's for a squirt."

"Cripes Almighty, Jane! Give the guy some room to breathe, will you? What if he sees you peering in the window? You might ruin his evening if he thinks you're spying on him."

"I won't be peering in the window. I'll be sitting on a well-placed stool at the bar having a quiet drink and watching the action. Manfredi might see me, but he won't acknowledge me because he expects me to be there snooping. It's part of our working relationship. Later, we compare notes. Fredi did it for me. He shadowed us the first two or three times we went out together."

"Why? That doesn't make any sense to me. You both already knew who I was. Manfredi was a client and I'd already tried putting you through the wringer at those depositions and in court."

She had remained standing after Manfredi left and was staring out the window at the sunset that was fast disappearing behind thick dark clouds from the northwest. She shrugged her shoulders and fixed him with an apologetic smile: "Forgive me for that one, James darling, but Manfredi insisted on it. He wanted to see how you acted other than professionally, because he suspected you might be violent with women. Because of some of the things you said about them to him those times you met alone in the office."

It was Sutherland's turn to shrug: "Sounds to me like Manfredi really took the bait, then. That was all part of my standard spiel from the days of my much-compromised ethics when I did divorces. If you'd been the client instead, I would have turned it around and put the jinx on the detestable husband. Most of the people who showed up in my office were genuinely distraught and seemed to find it comforting. I expect my crony Morrison tried to use something of the kind on you."

Jane had come across the room and stood beside his chair rumpling his hair with her fingers.

"He did, but I turned him off in no time flat. It hurt the dear crook terribly, I think. His ego, I mean. He couldn't comprehend anyone who had no use for that aspect of his expertise. Yes, I think I had the man genuinely rattled. Why else would he have showed up for our first day in court with the wrong case file? God! I thought that lady judge was going to fall off the bench from laughing so hard. Remember how enraged Morrison got when Manfredi couldn't answer those questions about last year's profit statement for his sporting goods chain or the value of his house in Wellesley? And you!

James, I wish you could have seen the look on your face. It was priceless, believe me. Equal parts confusion and terror. What did that judge say to you anyhow when she recessed court and hauled you and Morrison back to her chambers? I couldn't make it out sitting in the courtroom, but there was a hell of a din coming through the wall."

"She humiliated us," Sutherland said, rising abruptly to straighten the hair Jane had been fingering. "She threatened us with the Ethics Committee and I went out of that place absolutely certain she was going to do it. I was shaking in my boots for about a month before I realized she'd completely forgotten about the incident. . . . Jane, do me a favor, all right? You can talk about my current practice until you're blue in the face. But I don't want to hear anymore about my former practice, especially the part where you figure into it. I've told you before I don't do divorces now."

"Sorry, friend. I forgot about that precarious male ego. Yours especially. Okay. I promise not to speak about any of the dishonest, prurient, miserly and loveless parts of your past anymore. Even if that doesn't leave us with much to talk about."

"I notice I never seem to drag up any unpleasant aspects of your past. I mean just by way of comparison."

"That's because there aren't any unpleasant aspects to drag up. There's not much I've done in my life that I have to turn my back on. Anyhow, cheer up, lover. The present will be the past soon enough, and a present so notable for its dedication, lovingness and charitable good works is going to make for a marvelous recent past to reminisce about. Pretty soon we'll actually be able to talk to people about some of the things you've done for others, instead of to them."

"Jane?"

"Yes, darling?"

"Is there anyone alive you've ever touched who hasn't been forced to develop a sense of humor?"

"Offhand, I can't remember anybody. But so far, you're looking like the first holdout. You know, I've just realized something, James. It's not you I love. It's your morbidness."

"I can't answer that, Jane. There's no humorous way to answer that remark."

"There is. There are several of them. But we haven't got time for it now. Come with me down to Rudolfo's. We'll spy on Manfredi. We'll see how genuine pure intention and lightness of spirit captivate the lovely princess. We'll see how a real mover moves."

The clouds had brought rain and it was pouring as they left the garage and drove down to Rudolfo's on Atlantic Avenue. Rudolfo welcomed them excitedly at the door and helped them out of their coats.

"Jane, wait until you see her! Lovely hair, eyes like a Madonna, a shy, soft voice, a queen's nose! She's Italian, I think."

"Sorry, Rudy dear, she's Greek. I know. What lovely, quietly romantic corner as far as possible from the scrape of violins did you stick them in?"

"Right where you told me, Jane. Right where you could get a look at her from the bar. How are you this evening, by the way, Mr. Sutherland?"

"Fine, Rudolfo. Thanks for noticing I was along."

"Mr. Sutherland . . . I'm sorry, Mr. Sutherland. You'll have to indulge an old man's excitement. It's just that I've known Jane and Manfredi for a long time now, and since they're very dear friends, I'm afraid I get carried away in my enthusiasm for the things they do. I hope I come to know you for as long a time, Mr. Sutherland. It would give me great pleasure."

"I'm sorry, Rudolfo, also. I didn't mean for it to come out the way it sounded."

"You're in luck, Rudy. You will get to know him for a long time because I intend to marry the bastard as soon as I manage to drive a few of the spooks out of his head and calm him down a bit."

"Hmm. The ex-wife is still roaming around in there, huh, Jane?"

"Like you wouldn't believe, Rudy. On horseback. The dummy has a sad habit of keeping a lot to himself, and he's paying for about ten years' worth of silence right now. We all are, as a matter of fact."

"Make him laugh, Jane. Teach him how to laugh the way we do."

The two friends, Jane and near-eightyish Rudolfo Montavi, stood about ten feet away from him eyeing him rather analytically, Sutherland thought, perhaps speculating as to whether it was possible ever to drive the anger out of him. His every instinct was to inform Jane that his psychological condition was none of Rudolfo's fucking business, but he knew that was impossible. Their communion was too deep. Jane, who had never known her own father, had long ago chosen the warm and wise Rudolfo as a surrogate. Sutherland, who very much wanted her, knew he would never get her if Rudolfo did not approve of him. Behind the friends, Rudolfo's very own string quartet began playing the Spring movement of Vivaldi's *Four Seasons*. Muted voices hummed with talk and occasionally laughed at the candlelit tables beyond the forest of palms that separated the dining room from the entryway. Sutherland was suddenly very glad he had come along.

"Soon I'll be the funniest man in Boston, Rudolfo. You'll laugh to see me coming. Wait and see."

"You'd better become the funniest man in Boston, James, if you want to marry my daughter. Come on, I'll show you to the bar."

He followed after Rudolfo and Jane, who held hands as they walked around the periphery of the dining area. Halfway along toward the bar, Rudolfo nodded across the room to where Manfredi and Marlena Avgerinos now sat. The very beautiful girl was evidently speaking, smiling shyly at Manfredi and rotating her hands slowly just above the white linen of the tablecloth as if she were somehow trying to encourage the words out of herself. Across the table Manfredi looked shell-shocked. He sat staring myopically at the beautiful face across from him, occasionally nodding his head in response to what she was saying. His hands were joined before him on the tablecloth. Then he removed his right hand from the clasp and promptly knocked over his wineglass. He did not even look away when a waiter showed up almost immediately to help the girl mop up the spilled wine.

"*Dio mio*, I've never seen our Manfredi like this," Rudolfo said. "I've never seen him when he didn't have something to say."

"I have," Jane said. "In Rome, when we first met. He sat down at my table in an outdoor trattoria to gigolo me and promptly forgot his lines and went blank. Gentlemen, I'm going to confess to you a very closely guarded secret. When Manfredi and I first met, I was the aggressor. He was so damn beautiful I almost raped him."

"He'll never get this girl that way," Sutherland said. "She's painfully shy to begin with. Even from here you can see what a difficult time she's having trying to make conversation."

"Let's go to the bar, Rudy. With any luck, she'll get up and go to the john and I'll have time to rush out and kick him in the foot or something to snap him out of it. Oh, God, doesn't the drip realize this girl is no Jane Winters? She'll give up in sheer exasperation if he doesn't open his damn mouth sometime tonight. And nobody would much blame her either. Damn it!"

Rudolfo led the way into the bar: "Jane, are you going to want dinner tonight? I'm sure I could find you a table with a good vantage a little later on."

"No thank you, Rudolfo," Sutherland told him. "We'll watch the action for a couple of drinks, then head on home for a quiet supper."

"I guess not, Rudolfo. The man I want to marry has just spoken."

"Very good, James," Rudolfo said. "I wouldn't let my daughter marry a man who couldn't take proper control of a situation."

Rudolfo left them and Jane started for the bar. Two stools nearest the waiters' service area were best for watching Manfredi, but the stools were occupied by two men who were turned staring into the dining room. Jane marched right up to the man nearest the service area and introduced herself.

"Hello, my name is Jane Winters. I wonder if you'd be

kind enough to let me have your seat? I'm here to keep an eye on my ex-husband who's meeting his prospective new wife for the first time and you're sitting in the best place for watching the action. I'd stand, but Rudolfo the owner doesn't allow ladies to stand at the bar. He's a dear man, but he's pretty old-fashioned about some things."

Sutherland whistled his exasperation as the two men traded a look for a long moment, then began laughing in their amusement. The one she had spoken to left his stool and invited Jane to take it with a courtly bow. He wore a rumpled striped suit, white socks and badly scuffed tassle loafers. There was a large grease stain in the middle of his striped tie.

"Have a seat, dear lady. I couldn't refuse to give my place to anyone with such an important mission. Which guy is he, by the way?"

"He's the very handsome man at that table over there on the right next to the room divider. He's sitting with the gorgeous girl with the long black hair and he looks like he just had a lobotomy. Can I buy you gentlemen a drink for being so kind?"

"Thank you, that would be very nice," the one who had kept his seat told her. "Can I ask you why you're keeping an eye on your ex-husband? Don't you approve of him meeting another woman? You did say you were divorced, didn't you?"

"On the contrary, I approve very much, and yes, we are divorced. The only reason I'm here snooping is because he asked me to do it. I'm supposed to check out the prospect, but my main concern right now is my old ex. He's thunderstuck and that means he's in love, but the lady'll never know it unless she can read minds. I mean, I hope Manfredi at least remembered to introduce himself."

"That's his name? Manfredi? It sounds like an Italian name," the seated one said.

"He is Italian. For six years I was Mrs. Jane Winters Occhapenti. Now I'm just Jane Winters."

Sutherland got the bartender's attention and ordered another round for the two men and drinks for Jane and himself.

He leaned against the bar, nibbling on peanuts and watching Manfredi as the seated one spoke again.

"Why did you and this Manfredi divorce? Wasn't he a good man?"

Jane looked at him quizzically for a moment, then told him: "Hey, isn't this getting a little heavy for casual bar patter?"

"Of course. Please forgive me, Jane."

Sutherland looked at the seated man closely. He sported a vested double-knit suit and a loud polyester tie. He was balding, in contrast to the other man who was bushy-haired. He reminded Sutherland of a used-car salesman. These two were definitely not Rudolfo regulars.

"Well, actually, there's no reason not to talk about it," Jane unexpectedly started in again as their drinks were served. "Manfredi wanted children badly and I didn't want them at all, so we agreed to divorce. And yes, he is a good man. A priceless man. Honest and kind and loving and not a man to hold a grudge against anyone. Ours started out to be history's most amicable divorce until James here started muddying up the waters. James was Manfredi's lawyer. I'm going to marry James."

"This is getting complicated," the one who had given up his seat opined. "Maybe you shouldn't have asked," he told the other. The other threw up his hands and shrugged in response. Then he asked another question.

"This Manfredi, Jane. What about his income? What does he do? Could he support a family? It's a practical matter, after all."

"Fredi could wing it all right if the family didn't get too large. He picks up a nice bit of change giving private Italian lessons and I take care of his apartment rent and I'm scheduled to make monthly alimony payments for about five and a half more years. So he will have a steady source of income for that much time at least."

"You pay the alimony?" the bushy-haired one who stood wanted to know. "I never heard of such a thing. I thought the man always paid the alimony."

"There are some exceptions," Sutherland said in his best dry, lawyerly voice. "In the case of Manfredi, he was simply too busy being honest, kind and loving to bother with making anything like a decent income. I hope this girl's not out to marry money. If so, she's going to be sorely disappointed. Fredi's pushing love and babies."

"If they married, where would they live?" the seated one wanted to know.

"In Back Bay. Manfredi's apartment is certainly large enough. It's a great place, too. Bright and sunny. I picked it myself and decorated and furnished it. Oh, God, James, Fredi just smiled. He just said something, too. And look!" she said, gripping his arm. "The girl is smiling, too! They're both laughing and talking now. Oh, I'm so proud of him. I knew he could do it. You know, James, there's just one thing still bothering me about all this. From here that beautiful girl looks like she's got all her parts and faculties nailed on the right way and in good working order. Why would a girl like that answer a newspaper advertisment for a husband? There must be something wrong."

"Nothing physically or mentally wrong. Our mother just prefers that she do it this way," the seated one answered. "It's the way it was done in the old country. My name is Stavros Avgerinos, Jane. This is my brother, George."

"I'm Jane Winters, as I've already told you. James here is James Sutherland."

"I'm flabbergasted," Sutherland said as he shook hands with the brothers. "How did you know, Jane?"

"I was pretty certain. It was the first time at Rudolfo's I've ever seen two guys turned around in their chairs and staring raptly out into the dining room. Somebody had to have a reason for doing exactly the same thing I intended doing."

"Would you like to meet our mother?" George Avgerinos invited. "I know she'd like to meet you."

"She's here?" Jane asked.

Stavros, the balding brother, swung around on his stool and pointed to a table in a dimly lit corner where an old woman, a veritable transplant from one of the craggy Aegean islands, sat spooning ice cream into her mouth. She was dressed all in black, her head covered by a scarf, and through the dimness Sutherland could just see the gaping holes in her mouth left by many missing teeth, and the set of her face which was a perpetual scowl. He could not believe that a beauty like Marlena Avgerinos had come from this woman.

"Is she Marlena's natural mother?" Sutherland asked.

"Of course," George answered. "She's the real mother of all six of us. Of our other brother, Michael, and our two other sisters, Martha and Helena. Come meet her. She'll have questions for you."

Sutherland and Jane followed the brothers Avgerinos to their mother's table. They arrived just as the old lady finished the last of her chocolate ice cream, dumped the spoon into the bowl with a loud clank and emitted a great burp that had a hint of satisfaction to it. She was very fat and up close they could see thick folds of her skin erupting from the too-tight clothing she wore. There was a thick mustache covered with a residue of chocolate ice cream above her upper lip, and Sutherland could barely resist the temptation to wipe it clean. She had elephantiasis too, he decided. Her legs were two heavy logs that ended abruptly in dainty feet shod in black patent leather little-girl pumps. Stavros introduced them, apparently in Greek, and she nodded and scowled her greetings. After a long moment of embarrassment Sutherland retracted his hand from the air when she had declined to accept it.

They sat down around the table just as the bar waitress went past with an order of drinks. The old lady stopped her and held out the empty bowl.

"You, bring more ice cream now," she commanded.

"Mama, I've asked you to say please," George told her in English. In response she gave him a black look that promptly withered her son, then turned the look on Jane. She asked a question about Jane, evidently in Greek, and once shifted her beady eyes to Sutherland, then returned to Jane. Stavros answered the question in Greek, gesturing once toward Sutherland and a number of times at Jane.

"He's a divorce?" Mama asked Jane as she pointed out into the dining room at Manfredi.

"Yes, Mrs. Avgerinos. I was his wife."

"Why no childrens, missus? He's a something wrong down there?" She pointed emphatically toward her own pubis.

"No, not that. I didn't want any. That's why we didn't have any."

"He's a rich?"

"No, I'm afraid not, ma'am."

"He's a no rich, he's a no Greek, he's a divorce. We go now. I don't want him."

"But, Mama," Stavros begged, "these people say he's a wonderful man. Look how nice he and Marlena are talking now."

"I don't want him. Come now, we go home," Mama ordered as she lurched to her feet.

"Mama forgot her ice cream. Mama doesn't eat enough to fill a fly," Jane said in a voice dripping sarcasm as Mama began waddling her way toward the dining room. Son George sprinted after her and grabbed his mother's arm: "Mama, please don't. You're going to make Marlena so unhappy. If you keep finding fault with every guy she meets, she'll never get married. You can tell he's a good man. So what if he doesn't make a lot of money? We can help them out."

"Don't want," Mama rumbled, then to emphasize her point she hauled off and struck him with the flat of her hand. Instant tears flashed to George's eyes as Jane leaped to her feet, knocking over everyone's drink at the table: "You fucking ogre, you! You big pile of shit! I won't let you ruin my Manfredi's happiness either!"

Jane ran after Mama, who had already reached the first row of diners and started barreling through toward Marlena and Manfredi. Jane caught up with Mama when she had only ten feet to cover before she reached the now startled twosome. Jane reached out to grab Mama's scarf and when she yanked it off, Mama's wig came with it. Mama, seemingly heedless of her own baldness, stood in a roomful of laughing restaurant patrons bellowing at her daughter Marlena: "You come now, we go home. You no marry him. He's a no rich, he's a no Greek, he's a divorce. I no want him."

Marlena looked as if she were about to faint from mortification. Her two hands were pressed very tightly to her face and as Sutherland reached the first row of tables with her two brothers, he could hear her pleading with the old lady.

"Mama, please! Please don't do this to me! He's a very nice man, Mama! You don't have to be afraid for me, Mama! He won't beat me like Daddy beat you! He's not that kind of person!"

"I no want him! You come now!" Mama ordered as she grabbed Marlena by the arm and pulled her to her feet. Manfredi stood also, perplexed and speechless, and in a blind reaction to Mama's attempt to drag Marlena out the door with her he took a firm grip on her other arm and refused to allow her to budge. Sutherland and the Avgerinos brothers converged on the scene and pleaded with Mama to be reasonable. Mama responded by spitting repeatedly at Sutherland and her own two sons, her very bald, shiny head whipping back and forth on the short, squat fulcrum of her neck like a turtle snapping at flies. She hit Sutherland exactly in the center of his forehead, and as he wiped with a napkin at the trickle of saliva that had started down the bridge of his nose, Rudolfo came rushing up to them to find out what was happening.

"What's happening, Jane? What's wrong?"

"This is Mama, Rudolfo. Mama just canceled the wedding. Here's Mama's hair," she said as she clapped the wig back on the old lady's head, making a dull hollow sound like a thud. Mama seemed to stagger a little under the renewed weight of the wig. She pulled out an extra chair from the nearest table and collapsed into it with a mighty sigh, planting her elbow firmly in a serving dish of Lobster Fra Diavolo. The couple seated at the table Mama had chosen laughed so hard that they both held their napkins to their eyes. Their laughter and that of the other patrons seemed to enrage Rudolfo out of all proportion. His face turned white and his hand shook as he pointed his finger at Mama: "I want that person taken out of my restaurant immediately!"

"You wait, mister," Mama said. "I'm sick. Look how you make me sick, Marlena. I'm so tired."

Marlena did not respond. Mama had released her when she sat down and now her face was pressed tightly against Manfredi's chest and she was crying. In her chair the old lady's face had gone chalky white and sweat oozed out of it. She breathed very heavily and the sound of her breathing was a dry rasp. Sutherland thought for a moment to advise Rudolfo to phone for a doctor, but then decided against it when Mama, apparently realizing for the first time that her elbow was mired in someone's Fra Diavolo, removed it, and popped a large piece of lobster into her mouth as well. In response the couple who sat across from her increased the pitch of their laughter to the near hysterical. The look of Rudolfo's face increased to the near apoplectic.

"Out! Out you troll! How dare you eat the food from my customers' plates!"

Mama helped herself to another morsel, then rose ponderously to her feet.

"We go now. Good-bye, mister," she said to Rudolfo through the lobster. "Good-bye, people," she said to the laughing couple at the table. She started for the exit and Sutherland saw that she was weaving a little as she walked, so he hurried to catch up and took her arm to steady her: "Why don't we talk about this in Jane's car, Mrs. Avgerinos? I'm sure you're making a terrible mistake. Manfredi would make a first-rate son-in-law for you."

"No mistake, mister. I no want. He's a no rich, he's a no Greek, he's a divorce."

"Yes, yes, we know all that business. But it's not really the most important consideration if you just think about it for a minute."

"No think now. Too tired. Just go home."

They were outside now, and it still poured rain. Mama jerked her arm from Sutherland's grip and headed in the opposite direction from Jane's car where he had been trying to steer her. She waddled up to the rear door of a battered old Cadillac and ordered Stavros to open it. He did and Mama sat down heavily on the edge of the seat, her feet propped up on the curbstone and one arm braced against the open door. Mama's head was bent far down as if she were going to retch between her legs and the rain was fast turning her wig into a sodden mop. She was breathing rapidly again in a hoarse rattle. It came to Sutherland for the first time that she might be suffering a coronary.

"Marlena," she gasped. "You a nurse. I'm very sick. I think I'm gonna die now."

"Are you sure this time, Mama?"

Sutherland was startled by the coolly analytical tone of her question when he had expected apprehension or outright panic instead. He turned to see Mama's three children standing side by side in the pelting rain staring down at the old lady with nearly identical pursed lips and speculative gazes. Jane stood off to one side between Manfredi and Rudolfo. The collective look of their faces was positively hopeful.

"I think we should call a doctor and ambulance," Sutherland said.

"Doctors are so expensive," Stavros said.

"She pulls this trick all the time," Marlena said. "Nearly every time there is some possibility she won't get her way."

"Perhaps there's a doctor in the restaurant," Sutherland tried again. "Rudolfo, do you remember if any of the reserved tables were taken by doctors?"

"All the tables were reserved tonight, James, and none of them by doctors," Rudolfo told him stonily. "There are no doctors in the house tonight."

Sutherland looked along the length of Atlantic Avenue and saw a police car turn out of one of the North End streets and start slowly toward them. He thought of flagging the police for help, but then decided against it. What was the point of it really? They were all willing Mama to die, and as a practical consideration it looked like the only way the union of Manfredi and Marlena was ever going to be sanctified. So he watched the police car in silence as it slid by, apparently unaware that the old Cadillac was parked next to a fire hydrant. The police moved off, their taillights blurring in the rain and fog, as

Mama lay back in the seat and began her earnest dying. In less than a minute her glassy eyes were wide open in an unflinching stare at the car's roof and the hoarse rattle of her breathing was over. Stavros bent over her and listened for the beat of her heart.

"Mama's dead," Stavros said.

"Oh, poor poor Mama," George said.

"Now we can be married, Manfredi," Marlena said. "God, are we lucky! If you turned out to be acceptable, she was going to live with us."

"James, do you believe in God?" Manfredi asked.

"Yes."

"I do too. Now more than ever I did before." With that he took Marlena into his arms and they locked in a passionate embrace right there on the sidewalk in the rain not five feet from where Mama lay dead. Jane and Rudolfo began clapping in a spontaneous reaction, and Sutherland, not knowing what else to do, began clapping also. After another moment Stavros and George joined in as well.

"Will you come to dinner in Chicopee on Sunday, Manfredi?" Marlena asked when Manfredi finally released her from the embrace.

"Oh, yes, I would like that very much."

"But, Marlena," George spoke, "Mama's dead."

"That's what I mean, Georgie. Now we can enjoy Sunday dinner for a change. Call me tomorrow night, will you, Manfredi? Then I'll tell you the directions and time for Sunday. We'd better go home now and take Mama to the funeral director."

"Well, better late than never," Jane spoke. "My name is Jane Winters, Marlena. I had the wondrous good fortune to precede you as Mrs. Occhapenti. This is my boyfriend, James Sutherland. Pretty soon I'll be Mrs. Sutherland. And this is our friend Rudolfo Montavi, who owns Rudolfo's."

"Oh, hello to all of you. Manfredi has told me everything about you. About how wonderful and kind you are. And, Rudolfo, we're very sorry about what happened in there. Mama was . . . Oh well, what does it matter? She's dead now and won't be causing public disturbances anymore." She turned to the younger of her brothers: "I want to sit up front, Georgie. You can sit in the back with Mama because you were her favorite. Well, good-bye for now, everyone. And again I'm sorry about the ruckus in your restaurant, Rudolfo."

"Don't think about it, Marlena. My customers would probably all agree with me that a little laughter is good for the digestion. When do you two plan to marry, by the way?"

"As soon as we can to do it," Manfredi said.

"Sooner, if possible," Marlena said as they locked in another embrace. While they kissed, Stavros, George and Sutherland sat Mama upright and tucked her heavy legs inside the car. Then they closed the door and locked it and Mama obligingly settled against it with an aspect of peaceful sleep. In another minute all the Avgerinoses were inside the Cadillac, Marlena and George waving and calling good-bye as Stavros maneuvered it out of the parking slot, made a U-turn in the middle of Atlantic Avenue, then headed north toward New Hampshire. When they were gone, their receding taillights only two dim specks in the distance, the four friends finally quit the sidewalk in front of Rudolfo's and went inside to towel off their dripping heads.

CHAPTER 21

The Commonwealth of Massachusetts' Annual Greek Festival Day

How perfect and old fashioned and first-love-like it had been! Sutherland thought, smiling despite himself as he paced back and forth before the living-room windows. He checked his watch, then stopped to stare outside at the early-morning darkness, wondering if it was late enough now to find the morning star or the first trembling edge of dawn on the north slope of Beacon Hill. But it was not the hour yet, apparently. The same stars that hung in the sky at the time he had spoken to Manfredi on the riverbank were there now, and they seemed disinclined to go away.

What a friendship theirs had been, Sutherland thought, before it changed so suddenly, before it was transformed by

Manfredi's implacable enmity toward them—an enmity that seemed all the more heinous because of the deep bond of feeling it had so savagely erased. Before it there had been nothing like it in Sutherland's life. There was nothing he trusted so much. But then, the lid blew off before thousands of people at the Annual Greek Festival in City Hall Plaza a week after Bugliosi had phoned to confirm Jane's pregnancy.

They had arranged to meet Manfredi and Marlena at the festival about two o'clock on the afternoon of a cloudless, sunny Saturday in late June. Sutherland worked in the office until just before two, then left to meet Jane, who was shopping in Quincy Market. She was already waiting when he arrived, leaning against the old brick of Faneuil Hall, looking up toward the parapet of City Hall Plaza where Greek and American flags fluttered in the breeze and the sinuous wail of bouzouki music could be heard. Even from the back side they could see that the plaza itself was wall-to-wall people and Jane surveyed the scene with a grimace.

"Oh, Lord," Sutherland moaned, "I didn't think there were that many Greeks in the state."

"They're not Greeks, lover. They're everybody. There's a busload of tourists from Texas who're supposed to be over here checking out the history, but instead they're over there checking out the ethnics. That disgruntled-looking guy sitting on the steps of that bus over there is trying to be their guide."

"Well, what say we shoulder our way up there, grab a souvlaki or something and a glass of wine and try to find the lovers."

They crossed the street and started working their way up the rear steps to the plaza. Once there they had no difficulty finding two souvlaki and two plastic cups of retsina among the myriad stands vending Greek foods and pastries. Then they inched around the edge of the vast crowd toward the higher Cambridge Street side of the plaza, where the vantage was better. Sutherland and Jane leaned against a concrete trash disposal and ate their souvlaki and sipped at the wine. Before them a sea of people, uninterrupted except for the space required for three rings of swiftly moving dancers, clapped to the amplified music of a band on an elevated stage erected against the City Hall façade. In the midst of much pandemonium, Manfredi and his Marlena were not hard to find.

They were dancing in a ring with perhaps a hundred other people. The sight of them, of him really, in the circle caused tears of laughter to flow down Sutherland's cheeks. A handful of Greek sailors leaped and clowned in the center of the ring, laughing and pointing toward Manfredi repeatedly.

Marlena was a very unconvincing peasant girl in a long skirt and vest and kerchief. Manfredi was dressed like an evione, one of the Greek palace guards, in pointed shoes and pompon hat and the short skirt that was little more than a tutu and revealed a flaming red pair of bikini underpants every time he jumped or bounced. He wore no leotards as the Greeks did and instead Manfredi's great hairy soccer-player legs emerged from the bottom of the tutu to complete the comic disaster. He did not actually know the dance, but it did not seem to matter since he improvised energetically, and the look of his face told he was off on cloud nine on Mykonos someplace anyhow.

Finished with his souvlaki, Sutherland joined in the clapping. Only he stopped after a minute when he looked aside and noticed that Jane was not smiling as he might have expected, but rather was staring in Manfredi's direction with a very pensive, somehow sad look on her face.

"What's the matter, Janie my love? Having second thoughts about having given up on that very vital, funny ex-husband of yours?"

"No, it's not that, James." She turned to face him. "How are we going to tell Fredi about the baby? We have to, you know. Or sooner or later he's going to find out anyhow without anyone having to tell him. Are you still planning to marry me next month?"

"Yes. Are you getting cold feet?"

"No. I guess I don't have much choice after I let you and Bugliosi talk me out of that abortion. But the point is he has to know by then. It's the only right thing to do. Otherwise he'll be very hurt and possibly very angry."

"Well, let's just think about it for a little while. One thing though, I'm pretty sure we can downplay the being angry bit. He's got Marlena now and sure as hell they both want children. It's not like you're absolutely depriving him of something he can never have again. . . . Hey Jane, do you know something?"

"What?"

"See that happy, crazy guy dancing down there? He's in a new relationship now. The past is behind him. I bet he'll even be happy for us when he hears the news. Let me take care of it if you're feeling a little squeamish. I'll ring him up and propose a boys' night out. I'll even find an oblique, lawyerly way of telling him. I'll make a moral dilemma: Jane is pregnant and wants to have an abortion. What would you do in my shoes, Fredi old buddy?"

She clapped her hands now and began smiling instantly at the notion: "Hey, yeah! That's perfect! I can tell you right now exactly how that churchgoing Catholic ex-husband of mine is going to react to that news. He'll leave you standing at a bar someplace and come charging over to the apartment and threaten to pulverize me if I ever dare abort your baby. Yeah, James, that's it! Come on, lover, let's go down and meet those two nice people."

They made their way through the crowd toward Marlena and Manfredi. The dancing had ended and now through the loudspeakers came a discordant cacophony of plinking and scraping noises as a new band tuned up in preparation for a singer. When they came upon the couple Manfredi stood signing autographs for a group of Texans who had deserted their guide. Marlena was speaking Greek to the cluster of sailors who had played clown in the middle of the dancers. She laughed effortlessly with them and turned occasionally to point toward Manfredi, and it occurred to Sutherland that now, at twenty-nine, barely a month after Mama's felicitous death, she must be enjoying a kind of freedom she had never thought possible before. She caught sight of them and hurried over. It was only the third time they had met, but

Sutherland felt he cared for her as if he had known her for years.

"Jane! James! Come with me, please, and help me drag Manfredi away from all those adoring Texans! I think they're trying to take him home with them or something like that!"

They were able to rescue Manfredi only after he and Marlena agreed to two minutes of posing for the camera-wielding Texans. Then they made their way to a makeshift taverna at the edge of the plaza, found a table and ordered a bottle of retsina and a plate of calamari. From outside they heard the voice of a female singer who was on the stage with the band. Inside there was soft, lilting bazooki music coming from a tape deck behind the bar. Sutherland remembered that had he felt very much at peace and among friends that day, five minutes later Manfredi Occhapenti became the most terrifying enemy he had ever known.

It had begun innocently enough, Sutherland supposed, with Marlena talking about the wedding date they had settled on and the number of children they wanted before she suddenly turned to Jane, who was wolfing down the calamari and called for a second platter.

"I swear, Jane, you're eating enough for two people. Are you pregnant or something?"

"Yes," Jane answered. It was an involuntary reaction. Sutherland could see the shock at what she had done register on her face.

"Why did you say that?" he demanded angrily. "We talked about how we were going to handle this."

"I don't know. But it doesn't matter. It's out in the open now."

The news had about the same effect on Manfredi as a mugging with a sledgehammer. For a long moment he was shocked and speechless. Then he began to stir, a slow trickle from the headwaters of his anger that swiftly grew until Sutherland could feel its actual transference through the table between them. When he finally erupted it was with such an obsessive fury that the words came out sputtering and nearly incoherent. Sutherland thought he had never seen a man so angry.

"Six . . . ! Six years . . . Janie! Six years I am your husband . . . ! A good husband . . . ! Never once I am unfaithful to you . . . ! Six years . . . ! And you refuse always to give Manfredi a baby . . . !"

"Manfredi, please!" Jane begged. "Please stop screaming! Let me explain! This is embarrassing! Everyone is looking!"

"I do not care! Whore! You give this lawyer—this crook a baby . . . ! You are not even married to him . . . !"

He spat first and hit Sutherland right in the face. Jane began her run to the safety of the car and Manfredi started after her. Sutherland, knowing there was no other way he could stop the giant, tackled him from behind and brought him down about halfway toward the door. Around them, the taverna was in an uproar. People leaped from their places, knocking over chairs as they backed away against the walls. From the corner of his eye, Sutherland caught sight of the proprietor coming around the end of the bar with a nightstick in hand. There was no rage in the man's face. He was chalky white and fearful-looking instead as he ran up sputtering obscenities and started kicking Manfredi hard in the thigh.

"Get out, bastards! Get out of my establishment, cocksuckers! Out or I call the police!"

Sutherland took advantage of the distraction provided by the proprietor to untangle himself from Manfredi and a collapsed table across which he had fallen. Marlena helped pull him to his feet.

"It's all right, James! She got away! He'll never find her in that crowd! You go too, James! Hurry! I'll try to keep him here!"

Just then Manfredi made his feet after groping his way upward with the help of a table. Sutherland began backing quickly off into a corner, expecting Manfredi to come after him in full charge. But instead he turned his incredible anger on the proprietor, who had been kicking him, wresting the nightstick from the other's grasp and whacking him repeatedly on the back as the man ran away, pleading and screaming in Greek. When he reached the wall he turned about and extended his arms in a pleading gesture toward his attacker. But

Manfredi gave him no quarter as he slashed viciously at the extended arms and Sutherland gasped as he heard the actual snap of a bone breaking. The man stared at his broken arm for a moment, his face a mask of absolute disbelief, then fainted dead away from the pain, falling into the plywood wall behind him with its tacky array of Olympic Airlines Grecian Scene posters and knocking it over into the surprised patrons and vendors in the next stall. Sutherland and four other men were on top of Manfredi an instant later. It took more than a minute to wrestle him to the ground and take the nightstick away from him. When they turned him face up for the first time, he was staring into the muzzles of the guns of two policemen. To Sutherland, Manfredi's face seemed unexpectedly peaceful now, as if he had just gone through a great catharsis.

"I'm sorry, Manfredi, that you had to learn it this way," Sutherland told him quietly. "Let's let a little time pass and then Jane and I will try to explain things to you."

"There is nothing to explain, James," Manfredi said, his voice very calm now but somehow even more menacing. "It will be very bad for you when I find you."

"I'm sorry," Sutherland said. Then he said it again to Marlena when he shook hands good-bye.

"You'd better go, James. He'll calm down," she told him. "My brothers are here. We'll take him home."

"Is anyone pressing charges? Are you?" one of the police asked Sutherland.

"No. I'm not. It was a very unfortunate misunderstanding. Please keep him until I can get out of here."

"Are you?" he asked the proprietor.

"No, no. Just make him go away."

The cop nodded and Sutherland ran away.

When he came to the car behind Quincy Market, Jane was seated inside with the doors locked, the tips of her fingers pressed to her eyes as if she were trying to drive away a very bad headache. She started with fright when he tapped the window glass for her to open the door.

"What happened?"

"Well, the place is pretty well wrecked, I'm fairly certain

Manfredi broke the proprietor's arm, and when I made my escape there were two cops with guns drawn sitting on top of him. Lastly, I've got a bad case of the shakes."

"I've never seen him so angry, James. I've never seen anyone so angry. What are we going to do?"

"Hope he calms down and comes to his senses so we can have a chance to talk with him." He sighed a long sigh, then switched on the ignition. "Let's take a ride. Let's get out of town for a few hours and find a long beach and take a walk on it. The last thing I feel like doing right now is going back to the apartment."

They drove up onto the Fitzgerald Expressway and headed north on I-95 that led to the New Hampshire seacoast and Maine. After crossing the Tobin Bridge neither spoke all the way through the miracle ten-mile strip of Saugus and Lynn, crowded with its fast-food drive-ins and shopping centers, gas stations and bowling alleys. Jane was first to speak.

"Newburyport's not far. Why don't we go to Plum Island? There's plenty of beach for walking there."

"Okay, sounds good to me. I'd like to stick my head in that icy surf and leave it there for about an hour so it would forget what happened back there."

They turned off at Newburyport and crawled through the Saturday-afternoon traffic that moved between the elegant clapboard houses built during the heyday of New England whaling. At Plum Island they left the car in a Nature Reserve parking lot, took off their shoes and walked over the dunes to the beach. There was little surf and a low fog hung over the water about a hundred yards off shore. They could hear the rumble of a lobsterman's engine moving slowly through the fog. Sutherland picked up a flat stone and sent it skipping across the water.

"What a way for things to botch up," Jane said at length. "I wonder when I stopped thinking."

"I'm going to try to see him tonight. I'm going to talk to him before this business somehow reaches the point of no return and we lose our best friend."

"We may have lost him already," Jane said wiping tears

from her eyes with the back of her hand. "I thought I knew everything about that man, but until today I never imagined him capable of such anger."

"He'll calm down. Nobody can stay angry forever," Sutherland assured her. "There's always Marlena, too. If we can't talk to him, at least we can talk to her for starters."

They walked about three miles along the beach before they turned around to go back to the car. When they left the Nature Reserve they drove to the opposite end of the long sandbar that was Plum Island to look for lobsters. Among the spindly, still houses perched on the final edge of land they found a pound where an old woman sold them three chick lobsters then invited them to have coffee with her. The coffee and cake and the woman's defiant pride about not having been across the causeway to the mainland in more than five years was somehow mollifying, Sutherland thought, a tonic that helped shove the memory of the afternoon of Manfredi's rage to the back of his mind. They returned to Boston with a timorous optimism that peace with Manfredi was in the works for that very night.

Sutherland drove into the parking garage and slid the Jaguar into the space beside Jane's car. Then they carried the lobsters and Sutherland's briefcase upstairs. When the elevator doors opened they stopped short at the sight of a large pool of water that had coursed out from under the apartment door and soaked the hallway rug.

"Oh, shit!" Jane exclaimed. "I'll bet the cleaning lady left the water on in the kitchen. Oh, what a mess it's going to be!"

They were unprepared for the mess they found: water flowing from everywhere upstairs and down. Slashed paintings, broken furniture, one of the oriental rugs badly burned by a fire that had thankfully burned itself out. The drapes were all torn down and the walls splashed and stained with some of nearly everything that was in the refrigerator.

"Manfredi did this," Jane said simply. "He's the only one who could've gotten past the guard downstairs and he still has the keys."

"Why does he still have the keys? He doesn't live here anymore."

Jane sighed for a long moment: "He has the keys because it simply never crossed my mind to ask for them back. He's been here dozens of times for one reason or another while we were away at work."

"Well, it's quite obvious we'd better change the locks rather than ask him for the keys. Why don't you phone downstairs and put the guards on alert for now, since we probably won't get a locksmith until Monday. I'll check upstairs and see how bad the carnage is there."

As he started for the stairs the thought came to him for the first time that Manfredi might still be in the apartment. He looked around for a weapon and spied a leg cleanly broken from one of the lovely baroque chairs. He picked it up, thinking to use it as a club, then put it down with a derisive snort. What good was a club against Manfredi's awesome strength? A feeble defense at best, and, it might only serve to antagonize him.

He went upstairs and first turned off the taps in both bathrooms. In the bedrooms the destruction was as expected: overturned dressers, broken mirrors and slashed mattresses. Except for Sutherland's and Jane's own bedroom. Absolutely nothing had been smashed and yet it was easily the most frighteningly sinister manifestation of Manfredi's handiwork. Only their bed had been touched. In its center, like an occult sign of warning, the huge Samurai sword that had hung on the wall stood upright, the tip of its blade plunged through the mattress and into the bedboard below. Sutherland yanked it out and went quickly downstairs to find Jane.

"Jane . . ."

"What's wrong? What did he do up there?"

"We've got to hire a bodyguard for you. Manfredi intends to abort the baby."

CHAPTER 22

Il Minaccia

Jane refused to press charges and she refused to consider hiring a bodyguard despite all Sutherland's desperate pleadings. The apartment was cleaned up, the furniture sent out for restoration and the irreparable paintings went down on the books as a tax loss. Manfredi waited a few days to make his next move. Then, evidently certain that there was no warrant out for his arrest, he locked up his apartment and moved to a furnished room in the North End. They found this out one afternoon when Jane, acting on an impulse, left her office and went to the apartment to find him. It was the building manager who had given her Manfredi's forwarding address.

"That makes no sense, James. Why would he do that? Why would he leave a perfectly fine apartment and move up there? I mean, he used to shop in the North End and all that, but he's never shown any particular passion for the company of brother Italians."

"I don't know," Sutherland told her. "I'm as confused as you are." His mind envisioned gangs of very tough Italians waiting for Manfredi's command to strike at them. He could find no movie romance in their purpose. Sutherland copied down the Hanover Street address and decided to go to the North End himself the next morning to try talking sense into Manfredi.

In the morning about ten-thirty he drove along Hanover looking for the number of the building that housed Manfredi's room. But he saw Manfredi first from the car, standing on the sidewalk talking gravely to a group of grave-looking men. Sutherland double-parked the car and started toward him, calling out his name. When he caught sight of him, Manfredi stopped speaking in midword. His face assumed a heretofore-never-seen deadpan look. The ring of men parted to let them face each other.

"Manfredi, could we talk for a few minutes? We could go into that café over there and have a cup of espresso if you like. It won't take very long for—"

Manfredi spat right in his face for a second time. Some of the men started laughing as Sutherland fished for a handkerchief to wipe away the dripping saliva, but one of them, middle-aged and nearly as burly as Manfredi himself, shoved him rudely against a parked car.

"Go now! Go back to where you come from! He doesn't wanna talk to you!"

"Fredi, you've got to come to your senses! Look, I understand how hurt you must feel, but this isn't you. You're not an animal. Don't you realize how you're hurting us too?"

In response the silence was broken only by the sound of horns from the traffic moving behind him on Hanover Street. The one who had shoved him caught his eye and nodded sharply toward the car. Sutherland shrugged, returned to the car and drove miserably out of the North End back to his office. He did not tell Jane about either his mission or the incident.

They hired the bodyguard a few days later when Jane and Maggie, who were on an afternoon shopping expedition in Back Bay caught sight several times of Manfredi ominously stalking them. He remained silent when they tried to speak to him, and stood absolutely motionless when Jane, breaking down into exasperated tears, buried her head in his chest and begged him to say something. It was Maggie who had described that scene so graphically, shaking her head in continued disbelief when she told of the utter lack of expression in Manfredi's eyes. Then Sutherland was adamant about the guard and Jane concurred in a small, tear-stained voice.

The guard's name was Dunphy. Dunphy was a pro and Dunphy was perfect because he looked bigger, tougher and much, much nastier than Manfredi, and he had a permit to carry a gun. Sutherland remembered cross-examining him one time in a particularly bitter divorce case when Dunphy was testifying as the wife's bodyguard. He was a courtroom prima donna who gave expert testimony and, to Sutherland's dismay since he represented the husband, the judge awarded the judgment to the woman. When she realized she had won, the woman kissed Dunphy, not her lawyer.

Dunphy picked Jane up in the mornings, drove her to *Antiquitaire,* stayed with her all day in an outer office, accompanied her to business lunches, where he kept watch on her from the bar, and brought her home safely in the evenings, waiting with her until Sutherland returned from the office. Then he went home to his family. Dunphy was a family man. He had Sutherland's complete confidence.

The arrangement lasted for about a week until the morning that Manfredi resurfaced from wherever he had been keeping his own counsel. Dunphy arrived according to schedule to drive Jane to work in her Mercedes. When they reached the magazine's offices Manfredi stood waiting near the front entrance. Later, when she was able to compose herself, Jane gave Sutherland the awesome details of the massacre that ensued.

"Mr. Dunphy, that's my ex-husband standing there by the doorway."

"So, he finally shows, huh? Wait here, Ms. Winters, while I go have a little talk with the gentleman."

Dunphy left the car and sprinted onto the sidewalk, not breaking stride until his two ham hands clutched at the lapels of Manfredi's jacket. When the bodyguard opened his mouth to deliver his warning, Manfredi brought his hands up so quickly into a clasp that caught the bottom of Dunphy's chin that the tip of his tongue was ground off between his teeth. Then, Manfredi literally lifted the much heavier Dunphy off the ground and dumped him on the hood of a parked car, where he began to work over the bodyguard's face brutally.

Jane, in her retelling, professed to be much less appalled at the actual beating than at the incredible smile of Manfredi's face—sinister and cold-blooded, a smile more frightening still because it was slight and determined as if its wearer were not just enjoying his handiwork of the moment but looking far beyond. Dunphy lost eight teeth and suffered a broken nose and a severely traumatized left eye before Manfredi was done with him. As a final contemptuous act before he sauntered off he removed the gun from the bodyguard's shoulder holster and dumped it down a storm drain. Jane had aided a weeping Dunphy to the car and rushed him to the emergency ward at Mass General. When Sutherland caught up with them Dunphy promptly tendered his resignation. His speech was sadly changed; the moxie harshness of the Southie accent sounded now like a halting fight for words because of the lost end of his tongue. It would take Dunphy a long time to forget the name Manfredi Occhapenti.

* * *

After Dunphy left they were defenseless except for an ineffectual court restraining order. Sutherland went everywhere with Jane, driving her to work and picking her up as Dunphy had done, taking time off from his client meetings and court appearances to shadow her business lunches, even accompanying her to the monotonous trade cocktail parties. But for perhaps two weeks they saw nothing of Manfredi, only felt his dreadful presence everywhere, until one night about three weeks before Sutherland and Jane were to be married, when he chalked up the second strike that was to serve as evidence against him at his deportation hearing.

They were having a quiet dinner at about nine-thirty at their favorite table at Rudolfo's when Manfredi looked through the window and saw them. Apparently he had stood there for a long time with his face pressed against the glass before Sutherland or Jane knew he was there. Sutherland saw him first, but only after he realized there was some commotion going on at the tables directly in front of the window. He heard a woman's voice say distinctly, "Do something about him, will you? I can't enjoy my meal with him stuck against the window like that." He turned when he heard the scrape of her partner's chair being moved and the man's assurances—"Don't worry. Don't worry. I'll tell the maitre d'. He can send out a waiter or call the police or something."

Sutherland would never forget the look on Manfredi's face. Somewhere since the day of Dunphy's beating the expressionless mask had fallen aside, as if the roilings of his inner furies had won the upper hand and forced their way outward. Now Manfredi wore his soul on his sleeve. More than anything he looked lost and confused. Staring at him thus it occurred to Sutherland for the first time that Jane was no longer the object of his fixation. Now it was Sutherland himself, the man who had somehow gained all that Manfredi had ever wanted.

In the next instant Manfredi leaped through the window. Shattered glass rained down on the two tables before the window and staid, old-worldly Rudolfo's broke into pandemonium as Manfredi picked himself up and headed for Sutherland.

He attempted to say something before he attacked, but the words came out more of an anguished howl instead, and then he was on top of Sutherland, who had had barely enough time to get out of his chair. Sutherland threw a blind punch that landed feebly before Manfredi took a viselike grip on Sutherland's throat and fell on top of him on the floor. Sutherland thought he might be killed before anyone could come to his aid.

A part of him went passive: from the corner of his eye he saw old Rudolfo grab Jane and hustle her away someplace. He wondered vaguely if she was being taken to the kitchen for safety. He saw the desperate faces of two men behind Manfredi who were straining to pull him off. He saw too, with minuscule clarity, the slivers of glass in Manfredi's hair from the broken window, and the red-faced chef charging toward them with a butcher knife. He thought hopefully that Manfredi would have to stop choking him when that very lethal-looking blade arrived. Because he apparently passed out, he did not see the head barman sneak up on Manfredi from behind with a nightstick he kept behind the bar and put him out cold with a deft, hard whack at the right spot on the skull. Manfredi, when he went out, went out right on top of Sutherland, and they did not remove him until his hands and feet were tied.

With the help of a doctor Sutherland gained consciousness before Manfredi, and Jane and Rudolfo helped him sit at a table, where they had a glass of sherry waiting for him. The waiters had turned Manfredi over, and as they watched he gradually came to, blinking repeatedly and swiveling his head as he tried to orient himself. When he caught sight of Sutherland, he apparently remembered, and the same resolute look he had worn in the aftermath of being overpowered at the Greek Festival came over his face. Resignedly, Sutherland decided they were in for more as he watched Rudolfo pleading with Manfredi.

In time the police came and took him away, but again no charges were pressed. Rudolfo assured the police that Manfredi had been drinking and it was all a mistake. Jane paid for the window and placated the glass-showered diners at the nearest tables by buying them a few drinks to calm them down and paying for their dinners. Sutherland could only smolder on the outside of their conspiracy to protect the most dangerous man he had ever met.

Then, before they were married, in the middle of July, the barn burned to the ground up in New Hampshire one fine, clear night and there was no way Jane could restrain her prospective husband from pressing charges. She did not try. Manfredi's vendetta had spilled over into the lives of innocents and he had to be stopped.

About six o'clock the morning after the fire, Marjorie phoned to give Sutherland the news and asked him to drive up since the fire chief was outside checking the ruins and making ominous rumbles about the possibility of arson. Sutherland left Boston immediately and made it to the farm in about an hour and a half. When he drove into the farmyard, the firemen were wetting down the last smoldering embers of the barn that had burned right to the ground. When he had spoken with his mother on the phone Sutherland had not thought to ask if any of the stock had been saved, and as he climbed out of the car he saw with a rush of relief that all, or nearly all, of the cows and the two horses were standing at the top of the big pasture behind the barn, staring down at the remnants of their home. His mother came out of the house to greet him, pointing, as she walked toward him, at the blistered paint on the front of the house. Archibald hovered over the fire chief's shoulder, apparently dispensing advice as the chief poked through the ruin.

"*Bonjour, maman.* Was it arson?"

"It must have been. It went up so very quickly. I was over helping Anna Marshall with some sewing when we saw the first flames. We drove back as fast as we could and when we got here it was completely gone. Every part of it was burning. Thanks to God the cattle were outside for the night after the milking."

The fire chief and Archibald were walking toward them now, the chief carrying the unmistakable remnant of a five-gallon jerry can that had caved in from the heat. Archibald was arguing with the man, but his argument seemed to be scoring no points: "I tell you, Malcolm, it has to be that old wirin'. What else could it be? There wasn't no lightnin' last night, 'n' sure as hell there ain't any kids around here fool enough to go playin' with matches in a hayloft."

"Oh, Archibald, shut up 'n' let me do my job, okay? When we got here last night this place smelled like a gas refinery. The goddamned ground was even burnin' where they went 'n' spilled some of it. It's arson. I'm openin' an investigation. Hello, James, how are you?"

"Fine, Malcolm. When are you opening your investigation?"

"Today. Right away. Why?"

"Because I have a name you might be interested in knowing. A gentlemen named Manfredi Occhapenti who lives in Boston. He's the sore loser ex-husband of the woman I'm about to marry and he knows this place exists because he's been here."

"Manfredi?" Archibald and Marjorie spoke the word in identical disbelief.

"But, James, Fredi's a good old boy. He wouldn't do nothin' like this," Archibald said.

"James, it's not possible," Marjorie said. "Manfredi is simply not like this. It would never cross his mind to do a thing like this. He is not capable of it. Not to us, certainly."

"Manfredi has changed, Mother. He's deranged these days. We've been having a lot of trouble with him. We even had to hire a bodyguard to protect Jane, and Manfredi beat him up so badly the guy quit. I'm certain he did it. He's the only one with motive enough."

He watched their fear become real: two old people who drew perceptibly together and began searching the hills around the house with frightened eyes, suspicious now that Manfredi might be lurking anywhere near, waiting to do them harm when they were alone again. The fire chief and Sutherland turned about in slow circles, searching also. Manfredi must be out of his mind with laughter at the sight of them.

"Write that fella's name out on paper, will you, James?" the chief asked. "I ain't too good on Italian names."

Manfredi, when they caught him, stood trial in Laconia District Court. A state fire inspector gave testimony that the fire had been deliberately set, and Manfredi proved to be his own worst enemy by panicking and running off to hide in Providence when he heard there was a warrant out for his arrest. He was adjudged guilty and the deportation order came next.

That part had been effortless: Manfredi was not an American citizen. He was not even in the country legally. He had married after the citizenship-by-marriage privilege had been quashed by Congress, and had failed to register once yearly with the Immigration Service as the law required and had somehow never been apprehended. He was not even in the process of naturalization. He was forever going to begin, but had not quite gotten around to it. Two U.S. marshals handed him over to Italian authorities in the Alitalia office at the airport, and on the last day of July he departed in custody on the morning Alitalia flight to Rome. Sutherland and Jane had both tearfully watched the departure from the airport observation platform. Marlena, his wife, would follow in two days on the same morning flight with her aunt.

The two women stayed the night before they left in the

apartment with Sutherland and Jane, and the Sutherlands saw
them off the next morning from the Alitalia waiting lounge.
Manfredi and Marlena had been hastily married the Saturday
before in a Greek Orthodox church in Manchester, New
Hampshire. His best man was a fellow Italian with whom he
played soccer nearly every Sunday afternoon and a U.S. mar-
shal, with a revolver under his tuxedo jacket, had been one of
his ushers. Manfredi, Sutherland thought as he sat beside Jane
with head-shaking wonderment in the last pew of the church,
did nothing halfway. Neither Sutherland nor Jane had been invited to the wedding.

* * *

Sutherland stopped his pacing and went to look out the window one final time before he returned his coffee cup to the
kitchen. It would be dawn soon and this time he was able to
find the morning star. He smiled at its emergence and felt a
kind of comfort grow within him. He was certain he held the
ace. Manfredi was going back to Rome. For even though the
original strike three against him was trumped up, he had replaced it with another. He was in the country not only illegally
this time, but with a false passport to boot. This time Sutherland would be behind the prosecutor again, flagging him on as
hard as he had before.

He went upstairs to go to bed. As he dozed off he saw the
great snow-covered square before St. Peter's in Rome once
more. Only Marlena was there this night, not Manfredi. She
was crying softly, with a shawl drawn closely around her head.
The nuns he had seen the night before were there, too, five or
six of them, weeping and wailing all about her. They were
lamenting the sad, sad fact of Marlena Occhapenti's bar-
renness.

CHAPTER 23

Final Solution

His father shook him awake about 9 A.M. with the news that Mike Mallory was waiting on the phone to speak with him. He rose groggily from bed, threw on a robe, frowned at himself in the mirror with the memory of the night-before encounter with Manfredi and picked up the bedroom extension.

"Ha, ha, James," came Mallory's judgment. "I see I'm getting even for your four A.M.er to me. Congratulations, by the way. Your father told me the good news."

"Thank you, Michael. I've got even better news for you. Our man didn't show last night."

"Good. Even crackpots get tired of being loony, I guess. Sounds like he won't be back. Well, my food's about to take a turn for the better. Give my best to the wife. 'Bye, now. Take care of that hangover."

"'Bye, Mike."

He showered and dressed and went downstairs for breakfast with his parents. Archibald continued to feel unwell and settled for a cup of tea laced with honey. Sutherland drank about half his coffee, then excused himself to make a phone call in his study. He sat at his desk after staring out at the river a moment, then dialed the hospital and asked for Mrs. Crawford at the nurses' desk. She was paged and came on after perhaps a minute.

"Good morning, Mr. Sutherland. Enjoying your hangover?"

He went along with her. "Am I ever! It's the best yet, Mrs.

Crawford. Listen, my parents got me a little spooked this morning. Do you happen to know the baby's blood type? There's some kind of a rare blood disease in my mother's family that rears its ugly head every so often and I was a little worried."

"Oh, the baby's perfectly healthy, Mr. Sutherland. But wait, the medical record is here someplace. Yes, here it is. The baby's an O-negative."

"It looks like we're okay, then. Thank you so much. How's Mrs. Sutherland doing?"

"She's much stronger today. She's already been on the phone to some people at her magazine. I picked up a copy on my way home last night. It really is a good magazine. She should be proud. Will you be by this afternoon, Mr. Sutherland?"

"Yes, I've got a bit of work to do, but I should be there at four o'clock. Tell her I send my love."

"All right, Mr. Sutherland. 'Bye."

"Good-bye, Mrs. Crawford."

He phoned Lon McBane at his office. His receptionist offered her congratulations. Then she told him, "Hang on a sec, Mr. Sutherland. He said to interrupt if you called. I think he's hot for a game of squash today sometime."

"He's about to be denied."

"You'd better tell him gently. He's going to be disappointed."

Lon McBane's voice was preceded by the heavy slam of his fist on his desk top.

"James! Congratulations, my man! Not quite what you wanted, but not bad either. How about a quick game of squash during my lunch break?"

"Can't, Lon. I celebrated in typical delirious father fashion last night and I'm paying for it this morning."

"Oh, come on, we'll sweat it out together. I've been sticking rectal thermometers up you long enough to tell by your squeal of pain how badly it hurts. You're pretending."

"No go, Lon. I've got a bunch of work to do today before I

go out to the hospital. Listen, answer a quick question for me, will you? It has to do with a case I'm preparing."

"Shoot."

"It's a divorce case and there's some question about a child's real parentage in the custody agreement. The kid's blood type is O-negative, and—"

"And yours is B-positive and Jane's is A-negative," McBane sighed deeply. "Better sit down, James, if you aren't already. You didn't father that child. I've known it for a couple of months."

"Life seemed very fine to me yesterday, Lon," Sutherland said after a long pause when he stared across the river at M.I.T. "Today it seems like I'm nothing but a cuckold. Does all of Boston know?"

"Janie's doctor, Bugliosi, and your shrink, Herr Doktor Vogelmeister, plus two friends of Jane who are also friends of yours. That's all. Listen, James, I could come right over and give you a sedative—"

"I don't want a sedative, Lon."

"Suit yourself, James. The baby's father is Manfredi Occhapenti, by the way. Just so you don't end up going off half cocked out at the hospital when you see Jane."

"Is he? Old Manfredi, huh? My, my."

"What can he do, James? He doesn't know it, he won't know it, he can't come back to the country and he's got a new young wife of his own. You've got a problem on your hands and the solution lies in your ability to find the tolerance in you to accept it. So do me one favor, friend."

"What, Lon?" There were tears rolling down his cheeks. He could taste their salt when they hit the corners of his mouth.

"Call Vogelmeister before you talk with Jane about this. He's waiting for you. I recommended him to you and I still think he's the best in the business."

"I'll think about it. Thanks for your help, Lon."

"Don't withdraw, James. There are people out here who care about you and nobody's laughing at you."

"I'll have to think about that one, too. See you when I stop crying. 'Bye for now."

He hung up the receiver and tried to think what to do next. His impulse was to pick it up again and phone Vogelmeister, but he thought he might sound desperate and incoherent so that Vogelmeister would come running and he did not want Archibald and Marjorie to know anything was amiss. He stared out the window at the Esplanade again, where a pack of perhaps twenty cross-country skiers glided over the snow, and decided to wait out the day until he confronted Jane. For now he wanted to take a long walk.

He wiped his eyes and went back to the kitchen for another cup of coffee. His parents both looked up when he entered and his mother eyed him closely.

"*Mon fils*, you've been crying."

"Just a little sentimentality. I was talking with Janie in there."

"Oh, how is she this morning?"

"More rested and back barking orders at the folks down at her office."

"And the baby?"

"Just fine. Listen, I think I'm going to go for a walk. It should clear up the buzz in my head."

"Let me go with you a ways," Archibald said. "It might help me get a little appetite back. If I get too tired, I can always take a cab back."

Sutherland shrugged, "Suit yourself—about five minutes, okay?"

"Okay. I'll be ready."

Sutherland finished his coffee and pulled on his parka and ski hat. Archibald wore his hunting jacket and cap. They left the building and started walking up Beacon Street, keeping to the street because the sidewalks were still impassable. As yet, there were very few cars moving anywhere.

"You seem kinda quiet today, James," his father said. "Tired out from thinkin' about all that belly dancin' and booze you was supposed to be enjoyin'?"

Sutherland took a deep breath then blurted it out. "You know, pal, I wish you hadn't burned down that fucking barn last summer."

"Oh, James, not you, too. Your mother's been beatin' me over the head with that one since July. Cripes, it helped you out, didn't it? I mean, it got rid of Manfredi for good. And if that old barn was still up for this storm the stock'd all be dead. The barn woulda collapsed on them. Besides, the insurance company's got lots of money and nobody's gonna find out I did it."

"Somebody already has, Arch. About fifteen guys in a bar up in Chicopee. Your good buddy Emmett was off on a bender shooting off his mouth about how cool you were to burn down your barn for the insurance. Two of the fifteen guys were Manfredi's brothers-in-law and they wrote and told him. You'd better start praying he doesn't write the court up in Laconia or you're going to be in the slammer. Not the nice comfortable one where they send all your brother Republicans, either. The real one where the Democrats go is where you'll end up."

Archibald scowled at the thought. Then his face brightened, "Hell, James, Manfredi's a good old boy himself. He's got to be calmed down by now. I mean, we was pretty friendly before he got so mad that time. You know how those Eye-talians are. They blow up sometimes, but they usually calm down a little later. You know, forgive and forget."

"Yeah, like the Mafia, most of whom are Eye-talians, by the way."

They trudged on to Charles Street in silence. Three cabs stood idling at the cab rank on the corner and Archibald made his good-byes, preparing to take one of them back.

"I'm not feeling so well again, James. I'll take a taxi back and try to get a little sleep. I think I'll pass on goin' out to the hospital, too. If I'm still asleep when you leave, give Janie a kiss for me. Your mother'll want to go."

"Okay. See you later, I guess."

He started up Beacon Hill and before he reached the State House decided he was heading for the North End. He would walk through the Italian district to the waterfront, circle around the yacht marinas, and return to the apartment through the theater district. That distance ought to tire anyone out and he thought then he might grab a nap for a half hour or so before he went out to the hospital. It came to him distantly that it was no use thinking about Jane, for he had absolutely no idea what he was going to say to her.

He took the familiar route past Moskowitz's Deli, where the windows were as fogged with steam as ever in the winter. He went in, not sure why he was doing it, because he felt depressed enough without needing to increase his depression at the sight of the old ones hunched over their cut-rate breakfasts. They were there, more than a hundred of them perhaps, the place curiously soundless except for the dirge music of their knives and forks clanking on plates. Mordechi Moskowitz sat at his familiar table puffing on his cigar and he waved Sutherland over.

"How's your hangover, James?"

"How'd you know, or do I just look that bad?"

"Mike Mallory was in for his morning kipper before he went on duty. Many congratulations. What are you going to call her?"

"There are two schools of opinion. One wants Annabella and the other wants Angelina."

"Annabella's prettier. Call her Annabella."

Sutherland stared at the deli owner for a moment and the paranoid notion flashed through his mind that Mordechi was also in the coven of those who knew about Manfredi. But Mordechi merely grinned at him and turned away to beckon a waiter to the table.

"What'll you have, James? A little coffee and breakfast?"

"Just a coffee, thanks."

The waiter left and Moskowitz spoke again, "Your Christmas must have been a bit hectic, James, what with running out to the hospital and pacing the expectant father's waiting room."

"It was. In more ways than one. My mother launched the first revolt against anything in her whole life and almost sliced up my father with a carving knife. The old order of a lot of things seems to be coming apart, Mordechi, all of a sudden."

Sutherland was silent for perhaps a minute and did not

remember to thank the aproned waiter when he brought the coffee.

"What's up, James? You seem depressed like a man shouldn't be whose long-awaited first child was born yesterday."

Sutherland's memory flashed back over the six years he and Mordechi Moskowitz had been friends, then he found himself telling the deli proprietor about Manfredi, who had returned claiming his daughter.

"Crazy business," Mordechi judged. "James, you got to call the boys over at Immigration and get that guy run out of here. He's trouble 'cause he sounds like he's around the bend someplace."

"There's a Catch-22, Mordechi." Then he told the other about his father torching the barn.

"Phew. I know you won't mind if I say he's maybe a little stupid, that father of yours, for telling people what he did because my bet is you've already told him that. I know very devout, heavy contributors to my temple who I am almost certain torched a few of their own businesses, but you can bet your sweet tushie the only one who's going to know about it is the Big Man upstairs. You've got to do something, James. That baby doesn't belong to him. He was already long since divorced from Janie, and if the trip down the chute still takes nine months like it used to, then he wasn't anywhere around. And I know a good woman when I see one. She wouldn't play games on you. I could tell she had it bad for you the first time you introduced us. Do something."

"What? You tell me. I'm flat up against a wall." He was vaguely aware he was halfway across the table actually pleading with the other. Moskowitz leaned close also and his cigar-smoke breath flooded into Sutherland's face.

"A contract, James. You need a contract on that Manfredi. Otherwise he's going to completely destroy that old order you think is just crumbling right now. I know guys could set it up for you. If he's been playing at suicide, they could make it look like the real thing. Then your troubles are over."

"A contract . . . Mordechi, what the fuck are you saying?"

"James, I am saying this: Mordechi Moskowitz is a dying man, but considered by many to be a good man, a charitable man, a religious man and a family man. But if anybody got that threateningly close to my life and family as your Manfredi then I'd step outside the law pronto to play tennis on his court. You, my friend, are just going to have to meet him half-way."

"But, Mordechi, he's a friend. He and Janie and I—it was like a ménage à trois. We were crazy about each other."

"He's a friend? I'm your friend and now I know your old man torched a barn up there in the sticks. But do you think I'm going to call the cops and tell them? You were smarter when you were a crooked lawyer, James. Your new ideals have gotten the best of you."

Sutherland sighed. "It just doesn't make good sense, Mordechi. If I'm running the risk of one guy blackmailing me now, what good does it do to increase the odds against myself by replacing the one with two or three others who could blackmail me with something even worse?"

"Don't be silly, James. These guys are pros. They try something like that and they lose their professional standing and maybe a few other things, too. Does a bookie stay a bookie if he welches on his payoffs or, worse, can't collect? Remember what happened to that guy Morrison who was running that divorce-mill shakedown with you and ended up in the shark tank at the aquarium when he tried to muscle the mob around? Call Mike Mallory and ask him if they solved that one yet. It took the cops more than a year to even find out what happened to him. If they hadn't cleaned out the tank that time and found his belt buckle that the sharks thought was indigestible, they still wouldn't know whether he was dead or alive. And I bet they never find out who did it, either."

Blank-eyed, Sutherland stared into the past. Once, some weeks after they finally knew what had happened to Morrison, Sutherland snorted coke for the first time with Jane, Maggie and Otis. He had lain on the floor, howling with irreverent laughter at the thought of fat, double-knitted, stupid and unscrupulous Morrison with whom he had actually sunk to collaborate, railing about in final payment for his sins in the jaws of kindred-spirited sharks. My, the efficacy of the mob! Talk about finding the punishment to fit the crime. Even Morrison's widow had thought it was perfect.

Then he began to laugh, remembering that the mob had sent a prior warning to Morrison's Westwood home before they finally had recourse to doing him in. Sutherland and Edith had even eaten some of it at a barbecue in the pavilion beside Morrison's swimming pool—a steer whose throat had been slashed and dumped into the water in the dead of one June night before the August in which Morrison had been committed to the shark tank. Morrison had ignored the warning. Instead the carcass was raised from the bottom, certified almost freshly dead and butchered. In the quickly dying evening light, his face florid and sweating and reflecting the glowing charcoal over which he presided, Morrison boasted of his resourcefulness to his twenty or so guests. Edith—she had sensibilities that one had to admire after all—rushed deep into a thicket of Morrison's overgrown shrubbery and vomited audibly. Sutherland had had to drive her home shortly thereafter.

"You're smiling, James. You're maybe liking my idea?"

He grew serious again, "I'll think about it, Mordechi. I'll let you know. If I run out of options, then it may be the only option I have."

"You know where to find me."

"Yes, thank you."

Then, as he was about to leave, the first person ever to die in Moskowitz's up and did it. An old man wearing a felt hat stood up abruptly, tottered a few feet away from his table and fell out on the floor. A few others of the old ones stood, but there was no real alarm. Many continued to eat as if nothing had happened. Two waiters hurried over and one tried the man's pulse and listened for a heartbeat, then looked to Moskowitz and shook his head in the negative. Mordechi signaled with a wave of his hand toward his office and the two waiters lifted the shrunken old body and began carrying it off. Sutherland had not even risen to help.

"So, the curse that nobody's eatery needs has finally come to the house of Moskowitz. An augury perhaps. You see, James, death isn't such a big thing. From here it looks easy. I'll bet it's even easier if somebody helps you along. Well, I must go in and phone the police. Congratulations again on little Annabella."

" 'Bye, Mordechi."

Sutherland walked out of the cursed house of Moskowitz with a curiously buoyant step. Because now he was certain he had the hope he needed . . .

CHAPTER 24

Jane

He went with his mother to the hospital at about three-thirty that afternoon. Archibald had complained of feeling too ill to go with them. They drove in silence for perhaps ten minutes until his mother switched on the FM stereo.

"*Alors*, if you don't want to talk, at least we can listen to some music. I can't stand this peculiar silence."

"Sorry, I'm just doing some thinking."

She switched off the radio. "Well, what are you going to do about him?"

"About whom?"

"About Manfredi who you met out on the river last night. I had a feeling it was him and when I heard you go out I got up and watched."

"He wants the baby. He wants to take her back to Rome. His wife can't have any children."

Marjorie stared out the window for a long moment. They were crossing the Charles into Watertown and she seemed to be watching a bunch of kids playing hockey on the frozen river.

"You have to stop him, James. If he is here, it is not legal. Call the government and make them deport him again."

"He didn't come emptyhanded, *ma mère*. He knows Archibald burned down the barn. He'll go to the police first and Archie might have to go to jail."

"*Merde!* How does he know this? No one knows this who cannot be trusted."

"Your trusted friend Emmett knows this. And when Emmett gets drunk, as he did one night in the wrong bar, he talks. Manfredi's brothers-in-law were there and they wrote him in Rome."

"*Salaud! Con!* When I get back home I will strangle him!"

"Save it. I've got too many problems today that I didn't have yesterday without having to go up to Laconia to arrange for your defense in a murder trial."

She sighed deeply as he halted the car for the traffic signal at Watertown Square.

"*Qu'est-ce qu'on va faire, mon fils?* What about Janie? What are you going to say to her at the hospital?"

"Are you one of the coven, too?"

"What is a coven?"

"A band of witches. And as far as I'm concerned, everybody who knows what I didn't until last night is exactly that."

They started through the square heading toward Waltham.

"You must be good with her, *mon fils.* She is full of remorse, but everybody makes one mistake they should be forgiven for. You must find the way. You will never get another woman like her."

"How long have you known, *ma mère?*"

"For months. Janie told me when I stayed with her alone for that long time you had to go to Washington."

"I must admit that was a very clever little story you came up with about Manfredi's olive-skinned daughter being a French Canuck."

She shrugged, "How do they say it? Necessity is the mother of invention. But you should not worry. There are very few who know about this and they will say nothing. There is only myself, Maggie, Otis, your doctor Monsieur McBane, another doctor called Vogelmeister and Jane's doctor, an Italian whose name I don't remember. No one will say a thing."

"Someone already has broken the code. Our dear friend Otis wrote Manfredi with the interesting news that the baby wasn't mine."

"Otis! *Sale pédéraste!* I'll kill him, too!"

Sutherland ground his teeth to control himself.

"Not if I get to him first. Let me take care of Otis, *ma mère.*" Then: "There's one other person who knows about this. His name is Moskowitz, a friend, a restaurateur. He knows some guys that could put out a contract on Manfredi and end that little problem forever! A contract, by the way, is a professional killing by some person who's a friend of the mob."

"Do it!" she hissed, startling him with her intensity. "Tell this Moskowitz person to go ahead and arrange it! Manfredi has the power to wreck everything for you! Especially now when you are finally happy with your life and rid of that foolish Edith!"

"Who's crazy now, Marjorie, old girl? I'm supposed to be trying to lock those guys up, not get into bed with them. No. It's out of the question. That's murder."

She grabbed his arm so fiercely that she almost caused him to sideswipe a car in the adjacent lane. "Look, James! Nobody ever has accused you of being stupid! Misdirected, *peut-être*, when you were chasing all that money and married that idiotic Edith. But not stupid! If you save your father, you lose your daughter. If you save your daughter, you might even kill your father. *Au diable avec ses ordeurs d'idéalisme!* This is the family, where everything begins and ends! Remember that or never speak to me again!"

He pulled into the hospital parking lot, found a slot, and turned off the ignition.

"I need to talk to Jane alone Mother."

"But of course. Say what you have to say to her so there is less pain after you say it. But remember one thing. Manfredi is your enemy and this Moskowitz is your friend. Talk to your friend about how to deal with your enemy."

They left the car and walked into the hospital. The nurse, Mrs. Crawford, greeted them at the nurses' station.

"Hello, Mr. Sutherland. Hello, Mrs. Sutherland. Jane's just finished nursing the baby and is waiting for you."

"I'd like to see her for a few minutes alone, Mrs. Crawford."

"Of course, Mr. Sutherland. I understand."

She came from behind the nurses' station and walked with them to a small waiting room about fifty feet from the entrance to Jane's room. Marjorie took a seat on a leather couch and Crawford sat down beside her. The two women began talking immediately as Sutherland walked toward Jane. He knocked once on the door, then opened it and walked in.

There was only a single gooseneck desk lamp, beside the bed, burning in the room. Jane sat propped up in pillows reading a book. Or pretending to, really: Sutherland could see by the cover that it was upside down. He closed the door behind him and she put aside the book. The look of her eyes was fearing and then she dropped them with a long sigh of defeat and Sutherland knew that she also knew.

"Lon McBane called this morning, James. I guess you didn't buy Marjorie's story about Annabella looking like a Gervais, huh?"

"I bought it completely. I had no reason to suspect anything. I was in the habit of completely trusting you, but a little bird started whispering about how I ought to check some blood types. So I did, and now I know."

"Who told you?"

He still stood near the door staring straight at her. Then he turned and began slowly pacing along the wall.

"You'd better brace yourself, Janie baby, for some bad news. Manfredi Occhapenti is back in Boston."

"How? Why? Why did he come now?"

"How? By virtue of a false passport. Why? Because he wants to take his daughter, whom he wants to name Angelina, back to Rome with him. You see, my sweet treacherous wife, Marlena is barren. She can't have any children. And since we're all such good friends, and since you've always maintained you're on the debit side of the ledger, Manfredi has come to collect what he feels is owed him. And what's a friend for, after all, but to help out another friend in need? As usual, Manfredi's reasoning is near-moronic. He takes this one and since you're evidently nice and fertile, we get whatever else we can come up with."

She started whimpering a little, "But I won't let him. We can't let him. If he's here, he's here illegally. Call the Immigration people and have him thrown out again. We can be rid of him tomorrow."

"You're the third person to suggest that same simple remedy, Janie dear, but unfortunately it isn't quite that simple." He turned again and started pacing back in the opposite direction. "You see, Manfredi has our—correction, my—ass over a barrel. He found out that it was Archibald who burned down the barn, the very same barn-burning we successfully accused Manfredi of. So if you don't hand over that kid that I no longer want, my father stands a very good chance of going to the slammer. And I would divorce you, effortlessly, before I'd allow that to happen. *Comprends, ma chérie?*"

She was sobbing now, two clenched fists pressed to the sockets of her eyes.

"How did he find out? About the barn and the baby?"

"Treachery is everywhere around us these days, it seems. Correction again; I mean around me. Marlena's brothers up in New Hampshire found out about the barn and you'll never begin to guess how he found out about the baby that isn't mine. Otis told him. Not Maggie. Just our dear favorite faggot, Otis, who seems to have quite a soft spot in his rotten little heart for Manfredi. There you have it, *ma chérie.*"

"Oh, my God, no! There must be a way out of this. You've got to help me, James!"

"The way you helped me? Whore. Boy, did I get suckered in. Who else did you take a roll in the hay with besides old Manfredi while you were pledging eternal love and fidelity to me?"

She sobbed bottomlessly now. "Oh, James, I'm so sorry. It only happened twice with Manfredi. We got drunk and sentimental and I was off the pill trying to have your baby. It happened those times you were in New York or Chicago or wherever it was. It just happened, that's all I can tell you—"

"Just happened, huh? That's bullshit, Jane. Things do not just happen with you. You're one of the most determined and programmed persons I've ever met. Neither I nor anyone else who knows you has ever seen you out of control. If you balled Manfredi, it was because you wanted to ball Manfredi."

"James, please! Haven't you ever gotten tipsy with a woman and gone to bed with her when you thought you had no intention of ever doing so? Not with one of your secretaries or one of your clients or a woman you met in a bar someplace?"

"Yes. When I was married to Edith, whom I absolutely despised. I fucked everything I could lay a hand on and had a full-time girlfriend to boot. But not when I was living with, then married to, you, whom I adored until approximately nine-thirty this morning."

"James, don't say that! I beg you! That hurts more than anything anybody has ever said to me in my life! Don't wreck everything for us! There has to be a way out of this!"

"Everything is wrecked, traitor! Irrevocably so. And the only way out of this that I can see was proposed by our friend Mordechi Moskowitz. Except it's highly illegal."

She stopped crying and narrowed her eyes the way she did when she got down to brass tacks at the end of a business lunch.

"What is it?"

"A contract. Mordechi knows guys who could waste Manfredi and make it look quite innocent-seeming. You see, Manfredi is the crazy who's been pulling that fake suicide caper on the Charles these last three nights running. What these professional gentlemen would do is help things along so the capers would seem like a dress rehearsal. Why, it just plain smacks of the perfect crime. The reality of Manfredi's suicide would come to the suddenly sobered attention of Mike Mallory, and there, for all police intents and purposes, it would end. The only extra distance it might go would be to the confessional of poor Mike's parish church, because even cops get remorseful from time to time."

"Do it!" she hissed, just as Marjorie had done not fifteen minutes before in the car.

"Do it. . . ." He stood facing her with hands on his hips, shaking his head in mute disbelief. "Jesus Christ, no wonder you and Marjorie are such good buddies. You're both instinctual killers. . . . You're garbage, Jane. Absolute garbage. You cheat on the man you're married to and you're agreeably ready to kill the one you used to be married to. Both of whom you ardently professed to love—"

"Hit me, James! For God's sake, do something to punish me, will you!"

He was staring out the window when she said it. In the middle distance, towering above a neighborhood of old clapboard houses, were the four onion-domed spires of some Eastern Rite church. The church's walls were grimy with age and the copper sheathing of the domes was dark green and badly streaked with water stains. Against the low clouds of a glowering sky that threatened more snow, Sutherland thought the image depressing and foreign, as in a place of interminable winters somewhere east of the Vistula. He pointed out the window as he spoke: "I wonder what sort of church that is over there, Jane?"

He heard the sheets on her bed rustle as she slid off one side to stand on the floor. He heard the astonishment in her voice when she spoke: "What church? What fucking church are you talking about at a time like this?"

"That one. With the onion domes up there on the hill. It must be Russian or Armenian or something like that."

She took a quick, disbelieving look out the window in the direction he was pointing in, then reached up and slapped him fiercely across the face. "Why don't you say something? Why don't you try to murder me? I'm your wife and I just had another man's baby!"

He shrugged in response: "What is there to say, you treacherous whore? You've said it all. The only punishment that really fits this crime is to let you live out the rest of your life with that knowledge. What's whacking you around a bit going to do?"

She hit him again, but this time pummeling his face and neck and chest with her fists while he laughed so hard that his body shook and tears of merriment began rolling down his cheeks. He was vaguely aware of the door whipping open behind him and the sound of feet running toward him. "Mrs. Sutherland, stop it! Are you losing your mind? Stop it!"

It was Crawford. She came up behind Jane and in another moment deftly pinned her arms to her side. Jane tried a few feeble kicks backward at Crawford's legs until the nurse told her in a low, menacing voice: "Careful, Jane. I used to be a matron at Suffolk County before I went back for my nursing degree. I'll put you right out cold if I have to. Come on, back to bed with you."

"No, wait, Crawford! I have more to say to him. I haven't said everything I have to say."

"You've said enough for now. Say the rest later when you're calmer. Come on, James, we should go now."

He turned to see his mother. A perplexed-looking security guard with a nightstick stood behind her.

"Everything okay in here, Crawford?" the guard asked.

"It's okay, Charlie. The lady just got a little excited. You can go now. Thank you."

The guard turned and left and Jane suddenly spoke in a very timorous voice: "Are—are you going to divorce me, James?"

"I'll tell you in the morning, lady. If I do, I'll employ some very upstanding barrister. Not the kind I used to be and will probably become again."

Then he simply followed his mother out of the room.

He spoke to her in the hallway: "Sure you don't want to speak with your coconspirator, *ma mère?*"

"No," she said at first, then suddenly changed her mind. "*Oui.* I'll be only a few minutes."

"I'll be in the car. You can drive."

She nodded and walked past him toward the room, where he could hear Jane crying now. He walked by the guard, whose face still wore the same perplexed look, then past the nurses' station, where two nurses eyed him somewhat uncertainly for a few seconds, and he supposed the guard had already told them what happened.

Outside he climbed into the Jaguar and sat in the passenger's seat. Marjorie joined him in about three minutes and they did not speak. She evidently had no intention of telling him what had transpired in her meeting with Jane. He was already crying by the time she pulled into the street from the hospital parking lot.

Going up in the elevator from the apartment house parking garage, she finally broke silence: "Most men would have hit her and I am proud you didn't. You're as good a man as your father."

PART V

The Second Night
of Christmas

CHAPTER 25

Alternative Jane

He had no appetite for dinner. Marjorie made soup for Archibald and a sandwich for herself and took them upstairs to the guest room, where Archibald was still abed, too sick to come down to the table. Sutherland poured himself a glass of wine and went into his study to phone Vogelmeister. He was prepared for the shrink's answering service, but Vogelmeister lifted the receiver.

"I thought I was going to get that nice lady who takes your messages, Herr Doktor."

"I haven't left this phone all day, James," came the heavily accented voice. "You've been anticipated."

"I suppose you've heard by now about the tête-à-tête at the hospital this afternoon?"

"*Oh, ja,* I heard. Feeling a little better now?"

"Not really. I'd still like to kill someone."

"Vell, if you're lookin' for a hard time, it's an easy thing to find. There's always somebody will oblige you. I would suggest an Irish bar in South Boston or a black bar in Roxbury where they don't serve whites. There'll be somebody big and mean in either one of those places with his own ax to grind. Otherwise I would suggest we get together and talk."

"Tomorrow. I've got some business to take care of tonight."

"Don't kill him. If the cops find out, everything is ruined for you. What you got for a problem is bad enough without making it worse. Where do we meet?"

"At the aquarium. How about eleven o'clock?"

Vogelmeister moaned, "Oh, James, those sharks are so boring. All they do is swim around in circles and always in the same direction. You're not thinkin' what I think you're thinkin', are you? The world was maybe better off when the sharks gobbled up that crook Morrison, but Manfredi's a friend."

"He's supposed to be Archibald's friend, too, but he'll see him in prison in very unfriendly fashion if he doesn't get what he wants."

The shrink gave off a lengthy sigh, "So? *Nu?* Vell, James, don't forget to take his belt off because the sharks don't like the buckles. Remember?"

"I remember."

"And one parting favor for your old friend and shrink, Mendel Vogelmeister. Don't call up Janie and start that business about a divorce, okay? Otherwise I got two nuts named Sutherland on my hands instead of the one I got already."

"How about one James Sutherland and one Jane Winters?"

"Stop that shit, will you? Never was there two people who should be together like you two. You walk into a cocktail party together and suddenly it becomes a real party. They could turn off the lights and you two would provide the illumination. You got a problem, but I told you already a million times nothing is as bad as it seems. We just have to talk and figure a way to solve it. That Manfredi has to go back to Rome carryin' nothin' more than the suitcase he showed up with. Now watch the television or read a book or get plastered or somethin', but stay off that telephone. See you at eleven in the mornin' at the aquarium. Good night."

"Good night, Mendel."

He went out for a walk instead.

He had no real idea where he was going. He started up Beacon Street and instead of thinking of Jane and betrayal as he supposed he would, he found himself thinking of Manfredi and wondering what he would say to him when 3:30 A.M. rolled around. His mind obliged with a list of alternatives, but none of them were satisfying and only one promised a final solution. That one was the shark tank at the aquarium, and the notion smacked so much of Keystone Cops high jinks or Mafia melodrama that he even started to laugh a little.

By the time he reached Charles Street he was convulsed with merriment and even had to hold on to a blinking yellow traffic light to keep from falling down as a result. People who passed joined in the laughter though they could have no idea why, and Sutherland declined to tell the one man who actually stopped and asked. He had done that once before in a crowded bar and the general reaction to his story about Morrison taking his last swim had been the suggestion that there were elements of his private humor that were downright heinous.

Halfway up Charles Street toward the Longfellow Bridge the soft lights of a onetime favorite bar illumined the snow-banks. It had only a beer and wine license, and in the days of being married to Edith he had frequently taken a nightcap there, leaving the house with briefcase in hand on the pretext of needing to return to the office for some work. It was there he had found his girlfriend, Maureen. Tonight he decided to go in for a glass of wine, so he crossed the street and opened the door to the place and the first person he saw was none other than Maureen herself. She looked a little drunk and very depressed.

"Hi, Reenie," he told her fondly and kissed her cheek.

It seemed to take her a few seconds to put him into focus. "James . . . Oh, I look so awful."

"Well, I've seen you looking better. Why so blasted?"

"It's a seasonal thing. It starts about Thanksgiving and ends on Valentine's Day. Then I head up again. St. Patty's Day is pretty good and the Fourth of July is the top of the curve. After that it's gradually downhill and the real terror of the season is around Christmas and New Year's. Keeping a buzz on seems to help."

He ordered a glass of chablis. "I knew you when you were very funny and a consummate optimist."

"That was before I discovered something curious about myself."

"What's that? That you were getting older like the rest of us?"

"No, that I'm a one-night stand. I can't seem to hold on to

a man, and the only men I can attract are disgruntled husbands like you when you were married to Edith." She paused and took a long gulp of her beer. "Why are you here, by the way, James? Are you disgruntled again?"

"Yes."

"I knew it. It had to be. When your old drinking gang from this place kissed you good-bye at your wedding to Janie, we all figured that was the last we'd see of you. Well, welcome back. Your sense of humor is very much appreciated when you're disgruntled and getting bombed at the same time. What happened?"

He ordered another chablis and told her, only mildly concerned that someone might overhear him.

"Yow! You must be disgruntled. You know what I'd do if I were you?"

"What, Reenie dear?"

"I'd waltz on over to Cambridge and see our old buddy George Konstantinos the sandwich man. He knows a lot of different kinds of people, and those Greeks are pretty good when it comes to putting the muscle on somebody."

"I'd be the last one to tell you before I get bombed and therefore funny, but I seem to be in the situation I'm in because a bunch of Greeks helped put me there."

"Hmm. You sound like the original dead-end kid. Is your self-esteem low enough to sleep with me tonight? I showered earlier."

"Sure. I'll always help a friend in need. Got anything to drink at your place?"

"No. The cockroaches are all alcoholics. They keep stealing it."

He shrugged, "My place then."

"Your parents are not going to like this, James."

"That's their problem. They're all grown up, after all."

So they left the bar and Sutherland led a wobbling Maureen back down Beacon Street to the apartment and into the bed of his marriage that he shared with Jane, where he made love to Maureen for revenge.

At 3:30 A.M. he was already out on the Esplanade waiting

for Manfredi. The Roman sauntered toward him about ten minutes later. He was his usual trim self tonight and had not bothered with the wig or the makeup. His only prop was the Luger and Sutherland could see its warning bulge in Manfredi's overcoat pocket.

"How are you tonight, James?"

"Just delirious, Fredi, old buddy."

"You should not to make Janie cry today, James. It was not necessary."

"I'm the one who's married to her. She abused her wedding vows so I took it upon myself to abuse her a bit. That's one privilege I retain that's no longer any of your business anyhow."

Manfredi said nothing. They walked together onto the frozen river and into the darkness beyond the range of the arc lights. There was no moon or stars to be seen and the clouds overhead were pregnant with impending snow.

"I take it you phoned Jane today, huh, Manfredi?"

"Yes. Early tonight."

"And she said?"

"She said no. Absolutely no. So I tell her what I know about Archibald and she said no again, but tells me to come to the hospital in the morning and we will talk more. I am agreed to this."

"And if she continues to say no?"

"Then you and me meet one more time tomorrow night. And if you say no, too, then I go back to Otis's secret apartment and telephone *la polizia* and next morning Archibald goes to the prison. It is just like that."

"Archibald is very sick, I think, Manfredi." He said it matter-of-factly. He was not pleading any longer and that was the only thing about all of this that pleased him.

"I am very sorry for Archibald, James. You know I care for him very much. But prisons have doctors."

"You're a generous person, Manfredi, to be so warm and thoughtful. What will you do then? Go home and sleep the sleep of the just?"

"No, I go to the airport. Marlena comes from Roma the day

after tomorrow. Then I call the Immigration Police and wait for them to arrest me. Then I get my trial and perhaps they do not deport me anymore. I have thought about everything."

They started walking back to the riverbank. "It's a neat package, I must admit, Fredi, my man, and I'm supposed to be a good lawyer."

"Yes. I think I have, as they say, missed my calling. But the fighting is good, too. I think soon I will be a famous pugilist in Italia and will make my daughter proud."

"I wish I could find something complimentary to say, but I'd rather you'd make your godchild proud instead."

They began mounting the crosswalk over Storrow Drive. "I am always sorry for you, James, but you know I will love her just as you would."

Sutherland had to admit it. "Yes, I know that at least."

"You must to sleep, James. You look very tired."

They were descending the rampway now.

"Don't worry, Fredi. I've got a little somebody in there warming the bed right now."

He frowned his disapproval. "Tsk! Tsk! Who is?"

"Maureen, my old girlfriend."

"Oh, James, is awful, Maureen. I see her on Charles Street yesterday and she is so drunk she does not even know me. You must not to tell Janie this."

"Night, Fredi. Again, let me do my own thinking."

The other shook his head and walked away out of sight and Sutherland went back upstairs to the apartment.

In the morning when they came downstairs, his parents were already eating breakfast. Archibald drank a cup of tea with trembling hands and Marjorie ate a cheese omelette and drank coffee. Sutherland introduced Maureen, who told them all she wanted for breakfast was a Bloody Mary. Marjorie responded to Maureen with a very chill but polite tight-lipped smile; Archibald apologized for not standing, but told her he did not feel too well. It was evident he did not understand what Marjorie understood and thought simply that Maureen was an overnight guest. But when Sutherland made Maureen a Bloody Mary and sat down beside her to his first cup of coffee and tipsy Maureen began running her fingers through his hair, Archibald did understand and had no way of concealing his confusion and shock.

"Marjorie, I think I want to go home today, okay? You're gonna have to drive."

"*Oui. Je comprends bien.*"

"We have good doctors here in Boston, too, Arch."

"They're just as good in Laconia, James, even if we are a pack of country hicks. I been doctorin' with Shepfield for thirty years now. He'll know what's wrong with me. Can we leave soon, Mother?"

"After I call James's wife to say good-bye."

Archibald nodded. "I'd like to say good-bye, too." Then he got up from the table, leaving his cup of tea unfinished, and walked out. Marjorie finished her omelette and coffee and took the plate and cup to the kitchen.

"Oh wow," Maureen judged. "The polar icecap comes to Beantown. I told you they weren't going to like this, James."

"And I told you I don't give a rat's ass."

She shrugged. "How about another Bloody, then."

"Sure. I'll even put in a double shot of vodka for you."

"Thank you, James. That would be very nice. You're always such a kind and thoughtful person."

He made her the drink and started in on his grapefruit. Marjorie and Archibald were ready to leave in ten minutes more and he saw them to the door.

"I ain't gonna mince words with you, James," Archibald told him as they waited for the elevator. "I don't like this business one bit. It ain't right. You wasn't raised this way. You get rid of that lush 'n' get out to that hospital to visit your wife and baby today or you ain't welcome at the farm anymore. Hear?"

"I hear, Archie. I'll decide what to do. Have a good trip. Hear?"

The elevator arrived and they stepped inside. Marjorie stared thoughtfully at the floor and Archibald looked as if he was about to start crying. Then the door closed on them and they were gone.

CHAPTER 26

Vogelmeister

He finished his grapefruit as Maureen started in on her third Bloody.

"I've got to meet Vogelmeister at eleven o'clock at the aquarium, Reenie, and have to make a few phone calls first, so I must leave you."

"Can I stay, James? Your apartment is so much nicer than mine and I don't have to go to work today."

"Well, okay, I guess it's all right. But no cigarettes if you feel yourself getting tired, okay? I've got enough problems now without having to host a fireman's convention."

"No smokes. Promise."

"Okay. Don't forget."

He left for his study and telephoned the hospital first. It was Mrs. Crawford who answered the phone in Jane's room. She was not happy to hear his voice.

"Keep it clean, Mr. Sutherland," she warned him.

"I shall be the model of perfect decorum, Mrs. Crawford."

"All right then. Here she is."

"Hello, James," came the tired voice. "Too bad Arch and Marjorie had to leave so soon, huh?"

"My old friend Maureen stayed the night and the Granite State Republican got a bit irate."

"Well, what can I say? Tell her hello for me, will you?"

"Of course. I hear our Roman friend phoned you yesterday."

"He did and I told him no way. He's coming here today and I'm telling him no again."

"Have it your own way. But Archie is going to the slammer tomorrow morning."

"If I had a gun I'd kill Manfredi this afternoon."

"If you do that, then you go to the slammer instead."

"Right now, it would probably be the best thing that could happen to me. You just can't hate me forever, James. I'll die. I'll do a Madame Bovary trip to myself if you don't find a way to forgive me."

"I've got to go, Jane. I meet Vogelmeister this morning at the aquarium."

"The sharks, huh?"

"Yep."

"Well, give him my love. 'Bye, husband."

"Good-bye, Jane."

He phoned Moskowitz next. Mordechi took the call in his office.

"What's up, Mordechi?"

"All set up. They'll nab him tonight if you want."

"What are they going to do to him?"

"I don't know. They're quite imaginative gentlemen. They'll think of something interesting. But the aquarium is out. You'll have to give up on that fantasy. Since Morrison became fish food the place is impenetrable. It's so bugged that if a fruit fly got in at night every cop in Boston would be there with a fly-swatter in about two minutes."

"How's the fee look?"

"Tank of gas and a nice Italian dinner for three guys. The mob at heart is nothing but a pack of romantic idealists. Also, you successfully defended the daughter of one of the gentlemen involved in Suffolk Court and he is eternally in your debt. The only thing is, you should not try to remember who she is."

"Understood. Thanks, Mordechi."

"Anytime, James. Drop by tomorrow when a lot of your problems are over and have a nice corned beef and beer."

"Will do."

"If I'm not here, call me at the house when you make up your mind."

"Okay. 'Bye for now."

He put on his parka and left to meet Vogelmeister. He walked to the waterfront, threaded his way through the files of schoolbuses out front, paid his money and went inside the aquarium to pick his way through the hordes of school children on field trips.

Vogelmeister was already there. Sutherland found him on the second level, smiling at a school of silver fish that darted all about and glowed luminescent in the dark waters of their tank. The shrink spoke when he saw Sutherland's reflection in the glass of the tank. As ever, his white hair with the curious nicotine-yellow streaks was windblown and standing on end as if he had been electrified.

"Zo! The problem kiddo is here. How are you feelin' today?"

"A little better. A partial solution is looming on the horizon. I talked with our friend Manfredi again last night." They were being elbowed by a crowd of excited schoolchildren, but there seemed no real reason to move their conversation to a quiet corner of the building. There was very little chance of their being overheard.

"And he changed his mind? Yes?"

"No. Not that."

They started mounting the stairway to the open top of the circular shark tank.

"Then what? If he didn't change his mind, how is anything better?"

"A couple of gentlemen are going to change it for him."

"You crazy? They muscle him around and he's really got you over a barrel. You're just giving him more ammunition."

"That's not quite the game plan. They were thinking of cement boots. Tonight is Manfredi's last night in the free air above the earth."

They were at the lip of the shark tank. Sutherland stared down at the great parade of hammerheads, tigers, nurse and marlin sharks that swam in an eternal counterclockwise motion. Vogelmeister stared down at the concentration-camp tattoo on his hand, then his eyes beseeched heaven. "*Oh mein Gott*, no! James, I swear I'm gonna have you committed! Not only are you a party to murder, but you're settin' yourself up for a blackmail what's gonna haunt you till the day you die. Every time those thugs need money, guess who they're gonna telephone?"

Sutherland shook his head in the negative, "No way, Mendel. One of the heavies is, I am pretty sure, a guy from East Boston named De Santis whose daughter I got sprung on a pot rap a couple years back when Nixon was trying to clean up everybody's act but his own. It was a plant job and her old man knew it. He is very grateful."

"You're gonna be back in intensive therapy, you know that? Not only are you gonna need to get your head straightened out on your problem with Janie, but once your killer instinct subsides and you realize what you've done to Manfredi and his wife, your remorse is gonna be just like St. Peter's was when he betrayed that Jewish friend of his."

They started down the rampway that wound around the thick glass walls of the shark tank. The sharks swam past them in profile now. Sutherland stared down to the bottom of the tank, wondering vaguely about the segregation of species: the sharks ruled the upper levels; the giant sea turtles kept their distance near the bottom. Vogelmeister slapped the glass wall in anger and a startled hammerhead darted away from the perimeter. "*Mein Gott!* How did you ever contact these kind of people anyhow? These killers!"

"Through a very dear mutual friend of ours who owns and operates the best Jewish deli in Beantown. He suggested it, condoned it and set it up."

"Mordechi? Mordechi did that?" Vogelmeister seemed dumbfounded.

"Yes."

"I think perhaps I'm a very gullible man, James. I think maybe I've deluded myself for many years. We shrinks have a high suicide rate. I wonder if I should do myself in? It's a noble tradition in the profession after all."

"Oh, Mendel, don't be an idiot. One sacrificial victim in this bullshit affair is enough."

They were outside now, staring at the seals that played and cavorted in their pool, whose water steamed in the frigid air. Vogelmeister suddenly had a faraway look in his eyes.

"You know, James, when I was in the camps during the war I despaired of mankind. From there it looked like the men of the future, of the time we live in now, would be spiritual and emotional robots. But after all everything survives intact. Only the clothes styles and the music changes. Man's instinct to protect the family remains just as intense, even if the family has mutated a bit. Gott dammit! He's the wrong victim, James. It's Archibald should take the dive. He committed the crime."

"No way, Mendel. Don't go one microspace further with that argument. Manfredi isn't completely guiltless either. He screwed my wife and started this whole problem and I'm still convinced that before we got him deported he wanted to abort that kid."

"Let's go watch the dolphins, James. They always help when I get depressed. The show starts in a couple of minutes."

Sutherland moaned, "Yeah, and when it starts they lock the doors and if you get bored you can't get out. Make my apologies to the dolphins, will you? I've seen that show about thirty times already. Archibald at least five times, my sister Elaine's kids and kids of every married friend who ever shows up in Boston. Sometime else."

"Come on. Do your poor old suicidal shrink a favor, okay? I've done lots for you."

He shrugged, "Oh, all right. Let's get it over with."

They went into the dolphin show, which was full of excited school kids, and minutes later the guards announced that they were a captive audience for forty-five minutes and that anyone who wanted to leave should do it now. But nobody left, so the doors were closed, the lights were dimmed, a screen descended from the ceiling, and the preliminaries began. They watched a narrated film on migrating whales making their hegira from the Bering Sea to the bays off Baja California. Then came the comic antics of bull sea lions and their harems and the more-comic-still waddling about of penguins in Antarctica. The kids loved that one and Vogelmeister positively roared with laughter; turning, Sutherland saw tears streaming down his cheeks. Sutherland all the while wondered if Manfredi would phone that evening after he left the hospital: he meant to tell the Roman he would not be meeting him at 3:30 A.M. this time. He had nothing more to say.

The lights came on as Vogelmeister wiped the tears of his laughter from his eyes and the kids clapped and stamped their feet for more. The screen went back up into the ceiling, the pretty girl in her tank suit came to the edge of the pool with her buckets of herring reward for the dolphins and a young man brought out the props of her act. A trapdoor opened underwater and the two dolphins shot onstage and the kids and Vogelmeister went mad with delight.

The dolphins jumped through hoops, balanced beach balls on their snouts, lunged out of the water to do graceful one-and-a-half or double flips in the air like Olympic divers on their way down from high-tower springboards. They stood nearly erect on the surface in human posture, using their tail fins as feet, and mimicked the notes of popular music and the cadence of a human voice that suggested they were but a membrane's thickness away from outright communication. For all this they were paid off in raw herring. Then they leaped, flipped, raced all about the pool again in tandem like the incarnation of perfect joy and beauty, and Sutherland realized all of a sudden that they had gotten to him, touched a part of him that he never knew existed, possibly because in the past he had always taken too much pleasure in the joy of his charges, be they Archibalds or children, to enter the spirits of the dolphins.

He was crying, and in a moment more sobbing bottomlessly with the rage and hurt and tension that the events of the last few days had put into him. Vogelmeister turned to stare at him, and then some children who looked astonished to see an adult breaking down and all at once Vogelmeister hissed at him, "James! Stop it! Come on, we've got to get out of here!"

They were sitting near the end of the bleachers and Vogelmeister shoved him toward the stairs that led up to the exit doors, took his arm when they made the stairs and started him upward. The guards caught them at the door.

"Gentlemen, you can't leave. You heard the announcement."

"Guard, I'm this man's doctor. He's got to leave. He's lost control of himself. There's just been a death in his family."

The guards looked at each other a moment; then they pushed open the doors and the shrink propelled him into the lobby. In another few seconds, they stood outside in the frigid air once more.

"Put on these sunglasses, James," Vogelmeister ordered. "And try to stop crying. Look at all these little kids lookin' at you."

More schoolchildren were unloading from buses and Vogelmeister took the outside route around the buses and started for the end of adjacent Long Wharf. They moved quickly past the restaurants and apartments that now occupied the old China trade warehouses and gained the fenced-in parking lot at the end of the wharf. After the last parked car, they were staring down into the filthy water of the harbor. The tide was moving swiftly out, carrying the harbor garbage and a high-riding empty tanker with it. Sutherland regained control when he looked across to the airport and saw a gleaming Delta jet swooping gracefully down to the runway. He thought he would like to be flying somewhere far away from Boston this very day.

"Sorry, Mendel. The dolphins just got to me today."

"*Ja*. The dolphins and everything else is what got to you. I can't stay too much longer, James. What you gonna do?"

"What I have to do. Archibald is not going to take the dive, and that baby is ours. Manfredi gets wasted. There's no alternative. But I want to know one thing from you. Are you going to put the law on me?"

Vogelmeister sighed, then shook his head. "No. I promise you that. We can talk about this standin' up or lyin' down or whatever until the cows come home, but I gave you the only alternative I can think of and if you can't buy it, then you get yourself a new shrink is all. Have a good time indulging that primal instinct for retribution. It lives in your mind's nonreasoning region that I'll never penetrate. I won't call the cops. Good luck."

Then Vogelmeister turned and walked quickly away, his shoulders bent as if he were very tired. It occurred to Sutherland for the first time that Mendel Voglemeister might die soon. The Nazis could not kill him and he would never kill himself. Time would kill him, that was all. The beloved shrink had to be nearing his mid-eighties. They would bury him in twenty-four hours the way the Jews buried their dead and the only thing that was wrong with that was that the hundreds of others who claimed him as their spiritual father the way Sutherland did would never have enough time to gather themselves in Boston for the final farewell. Sutherland turned to look across the harbor one more time to the pier where the *Constitution* was docked and was amazed that the eternal long line of tourists was there waiting to go aboard in near-zero cold so soon after Christmas. He smiled on the scene a moment longer, then started walking back to the apartment to wait for darkness.

Maureen was passed out on a couch in the living room. She had dispensed with a glass somewhere near the end of her bender and had been swigging straight vodka from a bottle when the lights went out. The bottle lay tipped over beside the couch and some of the vodka had run out onto the Bakhtiari. The rich carpeting was wet, but he doubted it would stain. The colorless components of the liquor whose taste he could not stand were something to be grateful for, he supposed. He picked up the bottle and put it away, then covered Maureen with a blanket. He would have to phone Lon McBane about her soon. But he would cross that bridge tomorrow.

He went to the study and phoned the hospital. Jane answered immediately.

"Well?" he asked her.

"The ball's in your court, James. I told him no deal."

"I hope you made your proper good-byes."

"Yes. I kissed him for us both. It wasn't a Judas kiss. It was just good-bye."

"Good-bye, then."

He replaced the receiver and looked out the window to the Esplanade and the river where the darkness was gathering and the arc lights had just blinked on in anticipation. There was nothing to do but wait. He stood up and walked to the kitchen and decided to prepare a light supper for himself and for Maureen if she woke up and he could convince her to eat something.

He removed some of the leftover Christmas turkey from the refrigerator and started experimenting the way he always did when Jane was not around and he was lonely or had a particularly vexing legal problem he was trying to unravel. He sautéed the turkey in some white wine and began chopping vegetables —tomatoes and celery and onions and peppers—and then threw in some canned mussels and frozen peas with water and bouillon cubes and a little salt and decided it was starting to smell nice and pungent and might go well over a bed of rice. He was peeling a few cloves of garlic he meant to mince and dump in and was even humming a little and dreaming his elite little restaurant dream he always kept stored in the back of his mind when Manfredi phoned. He cocked the wall receiver between his shoulder and ear and kept at skinning the garlic.

"Hello, James, how are you tonight?"

"Cooking, Fredi, old boy. Want to come over for a little supper?"

"Tsk! Tsk! Tsk! Frivolous man. You must not to forget the Italian mind is trained always to remember the Borgias. Especially Lucrezia. You might put poison in my food."

"Tsk! Tsk! Tsk! yourself, my man. And you must not to forget the American mind is trained always to be sporting, gracious and generous."

"If so generous, why you do not to give me what I want?"

"Because it doesn't belong to you. That's the simplest and most truthful answer I can give you."

"We will talk later tonight, James."

"No, we won't, Fredi. I have nothing more to say to you and it's damn cold out there. You've already got our answer."

"I will wait for you, James. I will wait until the dawn if I have to."

"Then prepare to freeze your ass off, because I'm not coming out."

"If you do not to come by the dawn, James, you know what I must do."

"Do whatever you think you have to."

"I wait for you."

His voice cracked now, choked a little. "Ciao, Fredi. Ciao, my dear, dear friend."

He hung up the phone and took the garlic cloves to the chopping block and began mincing them. He was crying again by the time he threw them into the bubbling experiment and began stirring it with a ladle. That was the moment Maureen chose to stagger into the kitchen.

"James . . . you're crying. What's wrong?"

"These fucking onions. I love to eat them, but peeling, chopping and cooking with them breaks me down into an unmanly flood of tears every time."

"I know what you mean. Same with me."

"Like to try a little chow, Reenie?"

"Ugh! Don't even talk about it. Okay if I make another drink?"

"Sure. Why not?"

PART VI

The Most
Important Night
To Be Recorded

Reprieve

This time when Maureen went out, he put her to bed in the guest room. After he watched some television and caught the late news that promised slightly higher temperature and more snow, he went to bed himself, setting the alarm for 3:15 A.M. The phone rang before he fell asleep.

"James, did I wake you?" It was his mother.

"*Non, ma mère.* What's the matter?"

"I'm thinking more clearly now than I was the day we drove to the hospital, *tu sais.* I want you to stop those men from killing Manfredi."

"Why this now?" he snapped, suddenly prickly with irritation at the capriciousness of other people's motives for him. "It's all set up for about four hours from now."

"Because it may not matter any longer. Your father is very sick and what can they do to a man who is so ill? The doctor came this evening and told me we must expect the worst. Another reason is that I am afraid for you. About these people and what they could do to you with what they know. I would live in fear of the telephone ringing for the rest of my life if I was doing what you are."

He snorted: "Cripes, you give me a pain, you do! All your ethical hindsight. Where was this moralistic pap when you were so hot to have our enemy wiped out? Look, this friend Moskowitz who knows about these things says these guys are professionals. They don't talk. They have something to worry about too, you know."

"*Mon fils*, listen! This Moskowitz, how can he guarantee this? How can he guarantee they won't need money sometime? Or that they won't drink too much like Emmett did and talk to someone? They are human, these people, not stone. And they have a weapon against you."

"I remind you also that Manfredi has a weapon against us, *ma mère*."

"I think he does not much longer." Her voice had a prophetic quality to it, as if she were gazing into the future at a certainty he could not yet see. She was telling him about Archibald's dying.

"I see."

"Stop them."

"I'll think about it. *Au revoir, maman*."

She hung up then and in another moment he did also. Then, before the impulse left him, he dialed the number of Moskowitz's home in Newton.

The phone rang for an interminable time during which he suspected Moskowitz and his wife might be away and almost changed his mind. But then the receiver was lifted and he heard Mordechi's yawn.

"Listen, galoot, this better not be a wrong number."

"Mordechi, this is James. James Sutherland."

"What's wrong? Why are you calling at this hour, James?"

"We have to stop those guys from East Boston! Something has changed."

"Something changed? The baby? Something happened to the baby?"

"No, my father. He's in a bad way. He's not the candidate for prison any longer we thought he was, so Manfredi doesn't have the ax to beat us with that he thought he did. There's no necessity in sending those gentlemen over to talk with him any longer. How do I get to De Santis?"

"Let me go to the kitchen extension, James."

He heard Moskowitz say something to his wife, presumably,

and waited nearly a minute until he heard the voice again and the click of the bedroom extension being returned to its cradle.

"Do you really want to stop it, James? Be sure. Because there won't be a second act if you haul down the curtain on the first."

He took a long breath, "I'm sure. Can you call those people who set this up?"

"There's no time. You're going to have to go right to the beast himself." Sutherland heard a match being struck, heard Moskowitz puffing on the cigar to light it. Then he exhaled and spoke again. "He hangs out most of the time in a bar in East Boston called Uteri's. It's on Maverick Street. If they tell you he's not there, knock on the door to the back room at the end of the bar. That should impress them. Good luck, James, with that one. He's one crazy guinea. His first name's Joe, by the way."

He hung up and Sutherland did also, quickly dressed, grabbed his parka and keys and ran down to the garage. He started the car, drove out onto Beacon Street and turned onto Storrow Drive moving north. When he reached the end of the Callahan Tunnel, he swung off into East Boston, found Maverick Street and Uteri's Café after about a minute of cruising toward the harbor lights. It was what he expected: An old place with a peeling wood front and half-curtained windows. Above the curtains, blinking lights advertised Schlitz and Narragansett beers. He opened the door and went in. Inside the place was filled and noisy with laughter and men calling out to each other. There were no women anywhere to be seen.

Sutherland walked to the end of the bar and the bartender and a few patrons eyed him curiously. He knew he did not look right.

"Can I help you, sir?" the bartender asked.

"I'm looking for Joe De Santis." Sutherland could hear the sudden lull in the noise.

"Joe ain't here. I ain't seen Joey in over a week."

Sutherland nodded meaningfully toward the door to the back room then strode over and knocked on it.

"Wait a second, sir," the bartender said, picking up a phone beneath the bar and dialing a single number.

"There's some gentleman out here to see Joe De Santis."

A pause, then, "Tedeschi."

Pause, then: "Sir, what's your name, please?"

"Sutherland. James Sutherland. I'm a lawyer."

"He says James Sutherland. He says he's a lawyer."

Pause, then as he prepared to hang up the phone came finally, "Ciao. Okay."

Sutherland watched as he reached under the bar and pressed something. Then the door lock chattered like an apartment-house door and Sutherland pushed on it and went into the back room.

It was small, perhaps fifteen by twenty, with a pool table in the middle where two men resumed playing after eyeing him for a long moment. There was a long fluorescent light over the table and four wall lights near the corners. The place was filled with the smoke of cigars and cigarettes. When his eyes grew accustomed to the dimness, Sutherland made out about eight men in the room. He knew Joe De Santis before the man broke into a great smile and lumbered forward to greet him. He was an enormous, brooding presence who had sat in the courtroom during his daughter's trial. He had the most menacing eyes Sutherland ever remembered seeing. He had not even smiled when his daughter was acquitted.

"Mr. Sutherland. What an honor! What a pleasure, sir!"

Sutherland's hand disappeared in the other's great ham hand. Then his arm went around Sutherland's back and he began guiding him toward a small bar. Two men scurried away at their approach. De Santis' other hand held a tall glass of something that was a deep purple.

"Come on, sir, and we'll mix you a glass of something. What would you like? I'm having a little *grappa*, but I don't think a gentleman like you would like the taste."

Sutherland did not want anything, but he decided to go along: "How about a scotch and soda?"

"Coming right up, sir," De Santis said as he moved behind the bar. Sutherland noticed he spoke in an accentless, even cultivated voice, and that somehow made him even more menacing. He shipped out a bottle and the scotch was Johnnie Walker Black Label. In some ways these guys lived well, Sutherland supposed. De Santis put in lots of scotch and very little soda and passed it over the bar.

"Now, how can we help you, sir?"

"I want you to call off what you're supposed to do tonight."

The smile disappeared and the menace came into the eyes: "Why?"

"Because it's no longer necessary. The threat is no longer there. It's over."

The menancing eyes now showed a taint of mockery.

"I'm afraid, Mr. Sutherland, that you're in almost as bad a bind as the intended victim. The hit man has already been dispatched and I don't know where he is or how to call him off. It's too bad you got cold feet but you bought yourself a hit and a hit is what you're going to get."

"But there has to be a way!" Sutherland pleaded.

"There isn't. And to be truthful, even if there was a way to call him off, I wouldn't do it. Otherwise I'd lose a lot of credibility with certain people to whom a man's word is very important."

Sutherland shook with a terror he had never felt before—not even when Manfredi was stalking them in the days before they got him deported. He looked into the madman's eyes and saw the incredible psychotic strength gleaming out of them. His jaws were clamped fiercely shut and the muscles of his neck quivered and jumped. The voice had become darkly accented and Italianate. I'll go to the police, was the only thing Sutherland could think. He looked down to where he had taken an impassioned grip on the short brass rail of the bar. His knuckles gleamed white even in the scant light. When he staggered a little away from the bar, the rail came away in his hands. When he remembered to release it, it clattered to the floor with a loud, brassy resonance. De Santis laughed and a loud general laughter immediately followed.

De Santis took a long drink of the *grappa*. When he put

down the glass, the psychotic's mien had receded and the great wreath of a smile returned.

"I wouldn't do that, by the way, Mr. Sutherland. I mean what you were thinking."

"What—what do you mean?" Sutherland stammered.

"Go to the police is what I mean. Tsk! Tsk! Tsk! I thought you were supposed to be such a smart barrister, Mr. Sutherland. Can't you see that if you implicate us, you implicate yourself? The only one who gets away scot-free is the victim. We all go to jail. I'd kill you before I'd let that happen."

"But De Santis, he's innocent!"

"No, he's not. If he was once a major threat, he'll be a minor threat to you all your life. You don't think so, but I know. I know about things you couldn't begin to understand."

Sutherland tried the last thing he could think of: "He's Italian."

De Santis shrugged: "So what, Mr. Sutherland? Do you imagine I've never wasted an Italian before? Plenty of them, sir, I assure you. Look, I'm your friend. I want to help you. You helped my daughter, after all."

"She was innocent, too!" Sutherland asserted.

De Santis smiled harshly. "You're a naïve man, Mr. Sutherland. She was guilty as shit and you got her acquitted. She'd been a drug courier for years when the cops busted her. She's a courier again. Go home now. Go to sleep. We'll take care of everything. There's the door."

Sutherland left then, and when he closed the door behind him he heard the explosion of laughter from the back room. In the bar, when he expected more laughter, there was only silence, the silence of men looking downward shamefacedly. The back room intimidated them, too.

As he climbed into the car to return to Back Bay, he resolved to be out on the Esplanade that morning to warn Manfredi. De Santis would not kill his friend.

He began shaking uncontrollably from the cold. When he switched on the ignition, he zipped down his parka. The inside was completely wet from where he had sweated so profusely in his fear.

CHAPTER 28

Good-bye, Manfredi

The snow began falling about 1 A.M. By three-twenty, when Sutherland waited for Manfredi on the Esplanade, the night was a virtual whiteout. So much so that Sutherland did not realize Manfredi had arrived until he stood only ten feet away. When he saw him, Sutherland rushed up to him and grabbed his arm.

"Fredi . . ."

"So you have come to talk, James, even though you said you would not."

"Fredi, come on! You've got to get out of here! There are men coming here to kill you!"

Manfredi shook his arm loose: "I do not to believe you, James. You will not frighten me away with this nonsense."

"Fredi, you've got to believe me! I—I hired them! I tried to stop them, but they wouldn't listen to me! I tell you, they're coming."

"I don't to believe you, James, because I know you would never do a thing such as that to me. We will talk here. I won't to go anywhere else with you."

"Fredi . . ." Then he broke into tears of frustration. "Fredi, I did hire them! You've got to believe me!"

"No, never, James. I cannot. You are bluffing with me."

Sutherland tried one more tug on Manfredi's arm, and Manfredi responded by pushing him off, propelling him backward with a mighty shove so that when his heel hooked on something beneath the snow, Sutherland fell heavily to the ground. His frustration turned instantly to rage.

"All right, stupid! Have it your way! I tried. But sometime just before you experience the final gleam of light tonight, you're going to have to admit to yourself that I wasn't lying. Good-bye, pal of mine . . ."

Then he got up and ran away as fast he could in the snow, lest De Santis and Company suddenly appear and find their client together with their victim. Both would have to die.

He ran all the way back to their building and the elevator rose to the apartment in less than a minute. As he opened the door he could hear the telephone ringing. He ran into the kitchen to the wall extension, praying it would be De Santis who had somehow changed his mind.

"Did you stop them, James?" It was his mother.

"No. They're madmen. They're killers. It's their sport. I couldn't make Manfredi run away either. God knows what they'll do to him."

She hung up swiftly then, with only a single word: "*Merde!*"

Sutherland went into the living room and poured himself a scotch neat, then went to stand at the window. The lights of the Esplanade gave considerable illumination despite the storm, and he could see clearly across the drive and onto the Esplanade to where Manfredi must be standing. There were no cars parked in the breakdown islands, so he presumed that De Santis' men had not yet arrived. Not a single vehicle passed in either direction.

The first vehicle to appear, approaching from the north, was a four-wheel-drive Ford pickup, its body easily identified, suspended high above the wheels like his own. It took thirty seconds more to recognize its color and the New Hampshire plates and to realize it was his truck. He nearly fell down from amazement because he knew it was going to stop in one of the breakdown islands. It did, the lights were doused, the door opened on the driver's side, and Marjorie, his mother, clambered down. When she touched the ground she reached back inside the cab and out came Archibald's old 12-gauge shotgun. She hurried through a break in the fence that ringed the

Esplanade and moved quickly toward the river. She passed through the last circle of light that extended onto the ice and then was swallowed up in the darkness with Manfredi. Sutherland seized the scotch bottle and began swigging on it, gripping the edge of the drapery hard with his free left hand. In less than a minute, he saw the spurt of flame and heard the echo of the shot and knew it was the Luger that had been fired and not the twelve-gauge and wondered with a remote, unfocused terror if his mother had just been shot dead. The drapery came down beside him.

But she had not. She reappeared beneath the light in seconds more and scrambled toward the land again. Halfway across the Esplanade she stopped, hoisted the shotgun in the air in a gesture of defiance, then hurried back to the truck, threw the gun inside, pulled herself in behind it, started up the engine, put on the headlights, moved back out onto the drive and was gone. He swigged more scotch and stared after the pickup as it headed up the off ramp to the Harvard Bridge, crossed to the Cambridge side, turned sharply onto Memorial Drive and in less than a minute disappeared beyond the Longfellow Bridge on its way north to the interstate that would carry it out of Massachusetts and across the line to New Hampshire and safety. It was Manfredi who was dead then, and perhaps she had made certain he was dead by his own hand. Not a single car had passed by all the while. He suddenly grew so curiously calm that he put down the scotch bottle and set about repairing the fallen drapery.

The mob showed up late, ten or so minutes later, three of them in a large black car, a Buick or Oldsmobile perhaps. De Santis' men went through the same break in the fence, took a bearing on the apartment building that Moskowitz had indicated housed the Sutherlands, headed with guns drawn over the Esplanade as his mother had done in search of their victim, then returned in another minute from the darkness to the light, shrugging and gesturing their confusion to each other. De Santis was with them. He clenched his fists in exasperation. They regained the car, ran quickly back onto the drive, also exited at the Harvard Bridge off ramp, made an illegal left turn eastward on Massachusetts Avenue and fled home to East Boston and its own peculiar safety.

Sutherland put away the scotch, turned off the lights and lay down on the couch, where he slept soundly, certain all was safe now.

* * *

In the morning he awoke about eight o'clock remembering that all was safe now. He waited for things to fall into place.

He made his breakfast and watched "The Today Show" and the weatherman concurred that six to eight inches more was on its way and would continue in the Northeast until midday or early afternoon. The two local newscasts that came on during the show made no mention of a suicide being found beside the Charles. Tom Brokaw said good-bye and Sutherland turned off the kitchen portable.

He walked to the window and stared out to the Esplanade. Manfredi was gone and there were no cops around anywhere and the only person was a man in a full-length raccoon coat who walked two enormous Borzois at the end of chain leashes. He expected he would be hearing from Mike Mallory very soon.

The phone rang as he closed the curtain and he knew it had to be Mallory. It was and the detective sounded very tired and depressed.

"Michael, have you got a hangover, perchance?"

"You're ahead of yourself. That's tomorrow morning. This morning I came in bright and lucid, eager for another day of busting the criminal element's ass. Were you, by chance, looking out the window at the river last night?"

"Nope. Missed it. I was here with my old girlfriend, Maureen, getting very stoned on less than an ounce of dope."

"Who gives a fuck about your dope? Listen, your friend showed again last night."

"Aw, Mike! For God's sake, send out a couple of cops and pick that nut up, will you? Otherwise, they'll be hauling me off to the funny farm."

"You have nothing to worry about, James. Those capers

were dress rehearsals. And last night the play opened and closed after one run as sometimes happens in Boston. He's dead. A neat wide hole through one temple and out the other with an old German Luger. Boy, was I stupid! I need a church or a bottle. I don't know where to start."

Sutherland began applying the soothing balm. "Try the church, Mike, and stop blaming yourself. We thought he was just a prankster kid and he did take a couple of nights off, after all."

"Yeah, yeah, I know all that. But if I wasn't so stupid, I would've had the good sense to go nab him the second or third night and get him into psychiatric someplace so they could turn his head around."

"It would probably only have been a holding action, Mike. If a guy wants to kill himself, he's going to kill himself. That's all there is to it. Who was he anyhow?"

"This is the really weird part, James. He was an Italian from Rome named Stiffelio. Manfredi Stiffelio. Why the fuck would he come all the way to Boston to kill himself? It makes absolutely no sense!"

"Stiffelio? Stiffelio?"

"Did you know him? Does the name ring a bell or something?"

"Wait a minute. Just a second, Mike . . ." Sutherland puzzled: the name recalled something, or somebody he had known perhaps. Then it came to him: the name of the Verdi opera. My God, how perfect! How incredibly perfect!

"No. No, it's nothing. I thought I once knew or met somebody by that name, but it's not who I was thinking of. Anything else?"

"The resolution of the plot. A very sad clincher indeed. There's a lady involved, as in all good stories. She shows up from Rome this morning on the four A.M. TWA flight. An American named Marlena Avgerinos. A real looker. A Greek kid from up in Chicopee, New Hampshire, who's been shacked up with this Stiffelio guy over there in Rome."

Sutherland fought to control himself. "What happened then, Mike?"

"Well, the victim of the tragedy is supposed to be staying with some friends here in Boston. But when she calls, they don't know where he is. So she next calls her family up in Chicopee and they've heard from him, but he's not there either. So she calls here at Central to see if we know anything. By this time, some dog walker had spotted him around dawn and phoned us and we have him, complete with ID, since he's carrying his passport, traveler's checks and a permit to carry that Luger, which permit turns out to be phony, by the way. So her call is switched to me and I ask her where she is, and she says at the TWA lounge out at Logan, so I tell her stay put and roar out there to complete my sad, sad duty. I take her to the morgue and there's the lover, dead as a doornail—"

"It's so awful, Mike. I feel like crying—"

"Be my guest, James. Be my guest by all means. I've been a cop for over twenty years, licensed with the privilege to stare up society's asshole, and thought I'd seen it all. But I wiped away a few myself, let me tell you . . . Aw, you should've seen that poor kid. She sat here in my office until about fifteen minutes ago when her brothers came down from Chicopee for her. Jet lag plus shock equals coma just about. I tried to get her to answer a few questions and the answers came out in English, Greek and Italian. I had my secretary running all over the place trying to find a Greek cop and a wop cop who could translate. Anyhow, as soon as the lab boys are finished, we hand him over to an undertaker and she'll take the body back to Rome early next week." He paused a moment, sighing heavily, "We checked out the possibility that he might have been a drug trafficker, but that didn't fly. The place he was staying was clean, the lab boys say he was in first-rate shape and not a user and we did get out of her that he was a prizefighter in Italy . . . Jesus! It doesn't make any sense!"

"No, he doesn't sound like the trafficker type," Sutherland agreed through a layer of phlegm.

"Well, I'm going home, James. The wife's already been down to the liquor store and she'll forgo her wrath about morning drinking for this one. Church always feels better when you're hung over anyhow. See you around town, James."

"Yeah, Mike. See you soon."

He put down the phone and cried bottomlessly on the leather top of his desk.

He was still crying when the next call came in. It was Marjorie.

"Why are you crying, *mon fils?* I thought you would be dancing on the ceiling."

"I would be except Mike Mallory just called with the Marlena chapter. She flew into Boston this morning."

"Ah . . . *mauvaisement, eh?*"

"The worst. Even the cops were crying. Anyhow, they bought the suicide bit."

"What was one to do? He himself was a menace, but more importantly, I didn't want those men to get to him. They might even have taken him away and tortured him first. And mostly"—she paused a moment here—"I didn't want him to know that we had considered doing such a terrible thing."

"I guess I have to thank you. But answer one question. Did you do it?"

"No, of course not. He did it. I gave him the choice. He administers the coup de grâce himself or I blow his head right off his shoulders and he agreed he would not look very good in his coffin with no head. One can live with a single hole, but no head at all?" She paused a few seconds, then went on reflectively: "*Tu sais, mon cher,* I loved Manfredi very much, but he was a very vain man. Always looking in the mirror, fixing his hair or looking at his teeth . . . like a woman would do, *tu sais?* A man should not be like that."

He was even laughing a little now. Marjorie had a very funny streak in her after all.

"Well, *petite maman,* I want you to know I'm very glad you beat three Italian guys from East Boston out of a dinner at Rudolfo's."

"*Alors.* I am sorry. Send them to me when they are not so angry and I will cook them a good French meal. If I can remember how, that is. *Merde!* Thirty-eight years of New England cooking. Boiled this, boiled that, boiled everything.

Thirty-eight years I am dreaming of just once going to Montréal for a decent meal—"

"Well, since you've still got Archibald over a barrel, maybe you can convince him to take you to Quebec for a decent meal."

"Hmmm. Well, it might just happen Saturday night."

"Aha! You did it! Going on a little trip, huh? How's he feeling today, by the way?"

He heard the tears in her voice now, and all of a sudden he knew.

"Yes. I am going on a trip. You had better brace yourself for one last thing because it cannot possibly get any worse for you after this. Your father died very peacefully in his sleep at five-thirty this morning, *mon petit*. I have already told Elaine."

"Oh, my God, I can't stand any more!" he raged. "I think I'm going to lose my mind!"

"Don't be absurd!" she screamed at him. "Take a grip on yourself and behave like a man! He died thinking you were happily married and a brand-new father! He knew nothing of Janie and nothing of Manfredi! The only thing that upset him was the drunk whore you showed up with the night before we left! But that did not kill him!" She stopped and took deep breaths of air to calm herself. "He was old and he was sick, *mon petit*. This had happened before, but we said nothing to you. The doctor told me weeks ago to expect this anytime. Be thankful he lived to see what he thought he saw. *Merci à Dieu*."

"*Merci à Dieu*." Sutherland echoed her. He grew calmer now, awaiting her next words.

"Now dry your eyes, get in your car, and come up here before the storm comes. The service at the Presbyterian church is Saturday morning and he is to be buried in that place he always liked on the hill above the lake. Money was left for a funeral supper for the friends and the neighbors after the burial."

"How?" he asked her.

"How what?"

"How are you going to get a grave dug? There must be five

feet of snow and three or three and a half feet of frost underneath. He'll have to be stored until the spring thaw."

"No he won't. First you shovel the snow away, then you burn the ground the way they have been doing it in Québec for about four centuries now. When the fire is done, the ground is soft and you dig. I leave for Montréal on the Michaud bus at four o'clock Saturday afternoon and my brother Armand picks me up about nine o'clock at the terminal in Montréal. I will be home by Sunday afternoon. I want him under the grass before I leave. Now again, dry your eyes, get in your car and come. There is no need to telephone Janie. She knows everything. She leaves the hospital on Friday. Mrs. Crawford will drive her and the baby to the apartment and stay with the baby and her own children to watch the place until you return. Maggie will drive Janie up on Friday afternoon."

"I don't want her at that funeral, Mother. I'm not ready to talk to her yet."

"I do. Now that your father is dead and until I leave for Québec, I give the orders in this house. Then you give the orders. The only person who is not to come is Otis. And there is no need to tell him. Maggie just left the office, went home and threw his clothes out of the apartment into the street. If he does not understand this, then he understands nothing. *Comprends?*"

"*Oui, ma mère.*"

"*Bon. Je t'attend. Viens toute suite.*"

He grabbed his parka, ski hat and keys and started for the door, when the buzzer sounded from the doorman in the lobby.

"Yes, what is it?"

"There's a Ms. Edith Watkins here to see you, Mr. Sutherland. Shall I send her up?"

"Tell her to wait there, George, and I'll be down. I'm on my way out, unfortunately."

"Yes, Mr. Sutherland."

Edith? What could she want today when she had never once phoned since they had been divorced? He went down in the elevator and when the doors opened she stood alone wearing a fur coat in the center of the lobby. Beyond, through the plate-glass windows, he could see her car idling at the curb with George the driver seated inside.

"Can we talk a moment, James?" she asked as he kissed her cheek.

"Yes, of course. There's a place over here against the wall where we can sit." He indicated across the lobby to a group of chrome and crushed velvet chairs beyond a small fountain.

"I hope this won't take long, Edith. I'm afraid I've got to leave for New Hampshire."

"Yes, I know. I'm sorry about your father, James. Emmett called this morning to tell me."

"Emmett? Why would Emmett call you?"

She looked at him for a long moment, wordless, her eyes wide, trying to tell him something. Then she smiled a sad smile, shrugged a little and said simply: "Emmett and I have been friends for a long time, James."

Oh. Then it came back to him a rush: McGivern's plaintive words, oft repeated, about the terrible man who had done this thing to Edith. The man who had seduced her, deflowered her, given her the clap and the consequent hysterectomy and voided the chance of her ever bearing Sutherland's child. He had an instant vision of them racing toward each other in the summer nights to make love in the fields between the Sutherland farm and the Watkins estate. My, he thought, how little we are occasioned to really understand about life. No wonder the poor bastard drank.

"Congratulations on the birth of your baby girl, James. You must be very happy."

"We are, Edith, thank you. We're quite happy indeed. What was it you wanted to talk about, Edith?"

"Emmett. He wants you to know he's very sorry he gave away the secret about the barn. He's doubly sorry because he understands it got your father in some sort of very bad trouble here in Boston."

"Does he know what the trouble was?"

"No, your mother wouldn't tell him. Only that it was pretty awful."

"If he only knew. Boy, would I like to strangle that guy!"

"James, don't say things like that. He's made amends, after all."

"What amends? What the hell are you talking about, Edith?"

"He—well, he and I—paid back the insurance company all the money they gave your father for the barn."

"You did, Edith? Why? I mean, I thought you always despised my parents." He looked at her incredulously. She was able to meet his eyes with more self-assurance than at any time since he had first met her.

"I never despised them, James. They frightened me, that's all. Your mother especially. It was easy to see she didn't like me."

"Well, that's all water over the dam now. Anything else?"

"Yes, one thing more. Emmett wants to stay on as caretaker after your mother leaves for Quebec."

"No way. He drinks too damn much and he's irresponsible unless there's someone there to keep an eye on him all the time."

"He won't be drinking anymore. And I'll be looking in on him from time to time."

She met his eyes steadily again, and even winked this time. Her face broke into a never-before-seen foxy grin.

"Edith . . . Edith, I confess I never did understand you."

"No, James, I guess you didn't. Think about letting Emmett stay on, won't you?"

"I'll think about it. I'll let you know what I decide."

She rose to leave and came up to kiss his cheek again, then suddenly threw her arm around his head and held him very close, the touch of her fur soft and cool on his face.

"Good-bye, James. Again, I'm sorry about your father."

Then she hurried away like old Edith and he went wonderingly down to the garage for the car.

CHAPTER 29

The Ground-Burning

Sutherland made the farm in two hours. The storm that was fast overwhelming Boston had not yet made it to New Hampshire, so the highways were still dry. There was an assortment of cars and pickups in the farmyard and the old stone sledge was already stacked high with a couple of cords of dry hickory. The sheriff's car was there, too, and Sutherland decided resignedly that the brothers Avgerinos had already taken their vengeance.

Inside the house, Marjorie, Emmett, five of the neighboring men and the sheriff drank glasses of Archibald's cheap moonshine. All the men rose as Sutherland entered, and after kissing his seated mother he shook hands all about, removed his parka and sat down. Someone poured him a glass of the moonshine and they all laughed as he grimaced at his first sip.

"Your father is at the beauty parlor being made to look like a respectable gentleman for the first time in his life," his mother told him.

"Poor Arch," Sutherland joked. "Always marching to the beat of a different drummer."

That brought another laugh, then he grew serious and confronted the sheriff, "I take it, Richard, that this isn't a condolence call."

"No, it ain't, James. There's two Greek fellas from Chicopee called the Laconia courthouse and the judge got me out of bed this mornin' with a warrant for his arrest, so I had to come over."

"Thank the Jesus Lord he's gone to his maker," one of the men said. "Dead men can't stand trial."

"Oh, hell, he wasn't goin' to the pokey anyhow," the sheriff said. "I was goin' to accidently forget to read him a statement of his rights and the judge would chew out my butt and have to throw the case out of court. You'll have to settle up with the insurance company, James, but that's as far as she goes." The lawman pointed an accusing finger at Emmett. "You always was a goddamn stupid drunk, Emmett! Look at all the trouble you caused!"

Emmett was silent for a moment, but not shamed, then his eyes searched out Sutherland's: "Did you get a chance to talk with Edith, James?"

"Yes, Emmett, this morning before I drove up here. She came to the apartment and we had a very interesting chat."

"It's over, James. I don't have reason to drink anymore."

"No, I don't think you do, Emmett."

Then a radiant smile crossed his face, so bursting with happiness and so unexpected, considering that Sutherland could not remember the last time he saw Emmett smile: "James, how did she look?"

"She was beautiful, Emmett. She looked very beautiful as always."

Around them the puzzlement was universal, except for Marjorie, whose face had broken into a predictable scowl on hearing the name Edith.

"What's this all about, James?" the sheriff wanted to know. He stood scratching his neck, the look of his face one of irritation with other people's secrets.

"I learned this morning, Richard, that restitution has already been made to the insurance company. A special friend of Emmett's, Edith Watkins, the girl from the place next door, and to whom I was married up until a few years back, paid the bill. Nice of her, wasn't it?"

"*Mon Dieu,* I always knew she was crazy!" Marjorie judged. "Why would she do this for us?"

"She didn't do it for us, *ma mère*. She did it for Emmett here because he felt so bad about spilling the beans about Archie. Like I say, she's a special friend of Emmett."

Sutherland watched the others in the room thoughtfully reevaluating Emmett, and it was evident that in their minds he was making a speedy transition from pathetic village drunk to an enigmatic kind of man who must be their equal if he was worthy of the love of a beauty like Edith Watkins.

"James, did Edith say anything about me staying on as caretaker?"

"Yes, I've been thinking about that one, too, on the drive up here."

"What if he slips, James?" Marjorie asked. "What if he starts to drink again? Those cows won't be milked or mucked and the S.P.C.A. will have you in court on a cruelty-to-animals charge and—"

"I'll tell you what, *ma mère*, we'll make it easy for him. Sell the herd. What's the point of keeping them? Archibald could never get this place out of the red for all those years, so they're no financial asset. He just liked having lots of friends around. I'll call the lawyer in Laconia and tell him to arrange a sale. How many are there, anyhow?"

"Fifty-one."

"They're five of us here farms. We could each take ten," one of the men said. "You'd be gettin' prize stock if you got Archibald's cows."

There was a mumble of agreement on that and Sutherland could see they were all takers.

"Done. Make me a fair offer after I get back to Boston and choose what you want, then take them away."

"What about the horses?" Marjorie asked.

"How old are they now?"

"Very old. Fifteen, maybe sixteen years. I don't remember exactly."

Sutherland shrugged. "Keep them. Let them die here, then bury them. Otherwise they end up in a dog-food factory."

"James, would you mind if my widow sister Rachel comes to live here?" Emmett asked. "She's havin' a tough time makin' ends meet in Laconia with them two kids of hers. It'd be good for the kids here on the farm 'n' Rachel could keep an eye on me and keep the house clean. We'd take fine care of the place. It'd be fit for a king when you decide to come back here and live."

"Okay, Emmett, we'll try it your way and see how it works. You tell her to phone me down in Boston if I don't see her at the funeral. But I'm not coming back here to live, so you don't have to worry about losing your home. One of my children might decide to throw off the Harvard yoke and head for the School of Agriculture in Durham, but you'll only see me on weekends. I wasn't cut out to be a gentleman farmer."

"Thanks, James. I'll make you proud. You'll see."

"I guess we will," Sutherland agreed. Then he remembered something. "Mother, where's Archibald's viewing?"

"Here. When the beauty parlor is finished they bring him back and we set up in the living room."

"It may not be the best idea, ma mère. If this new storm hits as badly as they predict, not too many might make it. At least they'll be plowing the streets in Laconia."

"They'll come," the sheriff avowed. "If it gets too bad for four-wheelers, there's always snowmobiles. And I never yet did see a storm could stop a horse."

Again the general agreement. Then it had all been said, "Well, gentlemen, shall we to our task?"

They rose ponderously from the table and began pulling on jackets and hats. Sutherland poured his hardly tasted moonshine back into the jug and put in the cork. He scowled at the sheriff. "Why don't you do your duty as a lawman and close down that damn still?"

"Would you run your car in winter without antifreeze? Don't ask such a damn fool question. You was born and raised around here. Did you manage to lose every bit of common sense was bred into you?"

"The revenuers might get there first."

"Never yet heard tell of a man could outrun a phone call."

"Oh, God! What's the use?"

But he was only pretending to be exasperated. He was part of these people. These neighbors and friends who lived their lives by a code so time-honored and immutable that they perceived assembling themselves at a dead man's house to dig his grave as nothing less than duty. He had grown up among them, and though he had changed his life, and consequently the rules that governed it, much of the old law still clung to him. When he was home, among the farmers in the area around Laconia, he understood and abided by the rules.

He tramped outside with his neighbors and friends to prepare the ground for his father's grave.

* * *

The snow began when they went outside.

He assumed they would take the tractor and drag the sledge over the ice of the lake, but Emmett came out of the barn leading the two old Percherons, Ned and Nell, who were already in harness. Despite their age, they were huge and powerful and Archibald had loved them inordinately because they had won him a lot of first-prize sledge-drag medals at county fairs.

"Why no tractor, Emmett? We could go over the lake. The ice has got to be thick enough."

"The bluff's too high, James, gettin' up that hill to the gravesite. We'd waste hours carryin' the wood up there. It's best to go over the fields."

"What about the creek? The banks are pretty steep."

"They've done it before, 'n' with six of us to help, they'll do it again."

They hitched up the horses and one of the men brought two cans of gasoline from the back of his pickup and they started off across the field in the snow that was now driving hard from the southeast: an anomalous burial team in a procession of horses and men that seemed to Sutherland more compatible with another time and maybe even another place. Nineteenth-century Russia perhaps, where a peasant was being laid to rest by his friends. Trudging through the heavy snow, he fell easily into the romance of that earlier time. Russian words, vaguely remembered from long-ago trips to that country, flitted through his mind and even found their way to his tongue until he jolted himself back to the present and its reality. Dead Manfredi, traitorous Jane, Emmett and Edith, his mother who would leave for Quebec, and his dead father, the peasant whom they were about the business of burying. There was no time for romantic ramblings these days.

When they came to the creek, Emmett led the horses over the lip of the bank and the Percherons braced hard against the weight of the load that came over after them, lost their footing near the bottom but ran off the momentum over the ice of the shallow creek which did not break under their weight. Going up the other side was easier. Emmett tugged at their bridles from the front and six men pushed the sledge from behind, the load cleared the lip, and they all got behind the horses again, who were breaking a path through the waist-high snow.

When they reached the site of Archibald's final resting place, they shoveled clear an area that was about twenty feet square and began stacking the wood on the ground in a pile that was approximately eight feet wide by ten feet long. Each time they put down a layer, Emmett doused it with gasoline. When the pile was complete, one of the men blindfolded the horses and turned them about, facing back toward the house. Then Emmett threw a match onto the pile and an instant bonfire erupted. Sutherland, staring absorbedly into the flames, thought it looked like an Indian funeral pyre. One of the others thought so, too. He yanked the cork from the jug of moonshine, took a slug, then opined, "They say in India, when one of them Hindu fellas dies, this is the way they cope with the high cost of dying. Only thing is, sometimes the wife throws herself on the fire and gets fried with the husband."

"That's pretty goddamned stupid, I think," another said, after taking his slug. "If I was her, I'd take the guy's insurance money and raise myself a little hell. That's what I want my old lady to do if I kick off first. I told her, you do down to Miami and find yourself some nice guy who ain't a farmer, then bring him back to New Hampshire and settle down."

"What's Marjorie gonna do when she quits the place, James?" yet another asked.

Sutherland puzzled, "You don't know? She's doing back to Quebec. To the village where she was born."

"Cripes, why's she doin' that? I figured you'd take her in, or Elaine, or she'd get herself a little apartment in Laconia."

"She's going back to liberate the province," Sutherland said dryly after he had taken his slug and passed on the jug. "She thinks she's Joan of Arc or something. God, she's such a dead-eye Dick with a rifle, I hope she doesn't get herself into trouble."

They all laughed at that one and the Sutherlands' nearest neighbor spoke next. "You know, I must know Marjorie forty years now. I knew her when she couldn't hardly speak a word of English. But when you come right down to it, I really didn't know her. Nobody did. She was always polite 'n' always there when you needed her, but she never got tight with anybody. Not even the women. Used to drive my wife crazy. Wouldn't never gossip, always talked about things, but never people, 'cept for you or Elaine."

There was another one of those general rumbles of agreement, then Sutherland, anxious to halt their analysis of his mother's reserved character, told them, "Well, let's end this Druids' party, gentlemen. There's nothing more we can do here until the fire burns down."

"We'll all be back tomorrow at first dawn. With so many of us here, it shouldn't take too long to go down six feet," the neighbor said. "I got a compressor and jackhammmer, James. I can haul it over with the truck 'n' we can use the team to bring it out in case we hit ledge. Cripes, whatever possessed Archibald to choose this spot anyhow, James? Your family's got a couple nice plots in the Presbyterian cemetery in town."

Sutherland shrugged in response: "There were parts of Archibald even Archibald couldn't understand. He and I and Elaine went for a walk one time, and when we got to this spot, he stood here a long time looking around at the lake and the woods and the meadow, then he simply said, 'This is where I want to be buried,' and that was that. He made Elaine and me promise that this would be the place and not the Presbyterian cemetery. There were apparently people buried there that he didn't like, and he said there was no way he was going to be buried anywhere near them. All he wanted was a little peace and quiet in the afterlife."

They roared with laughter at that one.

"Oh, Jesus! Oh, Jesus! Is that ever Archibald Sutherland to a T!" the nearest neighbor howled.

But then it was time to return to the house, and they set off, following the team once more after Emmett took the blindfolds from the horses' eyes.

Behind them, the fire would burn eerily all through the night.

CHAPTER 30

Country People's Mourning

The mortician brought Archibald back about five o'clock that afternoon. The neighbors had left by that time and there were only Marjorie, Emmett and Sutherland in the house when the mortician and his assistant wheeled him in and set up on a draped dais of sawhorses in the living room. From a pickup truck they brought in lots of folding chairs that they set up nearly everywhere there was space. Then the mortician and his assistant left after another warning from Marjorie that there were to be no flowers, and they were alone at last with Archibald.

"He looks kinda like a lawyer, I think," Emmett said after a long moment of silence.

"Archibald has not looked this good since the day he married me," Marjorie sighed. "I cannot ever remember him wearing anything but a work shirt or hunting jacket since then. Both you and Elaine were born during the winter, and I am sure he went to both your christenings in a hunting jacket. Even to church on Sunday . . ."

Sutherland stared in silence for a long time at his father. As yet, he felt no real sorrow, only a kind of wonderment that the waxy, somehow shrunken form that he saw before him was real. That the life had finally gone out of the old man, that the howlings within that vast, irreverent chamber of the winds were silenced forever. How could it be? Especially since Sutherland, for all of his childhood and most of his adult life, had read into the old man's boundless energies a robust touch of immortality that made the idea of death an absurd intrusion.

It was only very recently, in fact, that he had begun to admit to himself for the first time the inevitability of his father's dying. When the memory lapses and the fainting spells began, when it became necessary for Marjorie to interpret for him some of the most apparently simple statements or questions. Sutherland's mother stood beside him now, a faraway look in her eyes as if she were not seeing the reality of her husband's corpse, but through it to the endless memories of the past. Suddenly she reached down and began fingering the earring Otis had given Archibald for Christmas.

"I think under the circumstances we ought to take off that gold earring, Mother," Sutherland said.

"Oh, no, James!" Emmett chimed in. "He was crazy about that earrin'! His friend Otis down in Boston give it to him. You know, the hairdresser fella."

"Shut up, Emmett! Leave us alone!" Sutherland ordered him.

"Marjorie . . . I'll—I'll be out in the barn checkin' on the stock," Emmett told her as he slunk away from the coffin.

"That was not necessary, James," his mother chided him. "Emmett knows nothing about what Otis did. Neither did your father. He died thinking Otis was his friend and he liked Otis very much. What sense does it make to take off the earring? Do you intend to leave a letter in his coffin so he will find out what he did not know about you and Janie when he has a chance to open his mail in heaven? *Alors?*"

He shrugged. "*Non. Evidemment. Pas de tout.*"

"*Puis, laisse tomber.*"

"*Oui, ma mère.*"

In time, they left Archibald looking like a lawyer in his coffin and went into the kitchen, where Marjorie began preparing a light supper. When it was ready, Sutherland went out to the barn for Emmett, interrupted a conversation Emmett was having with two cows, apologized for flying off the handle and brought the hired hand back to the house to eat.

The first mourners began arriving in the storm about seven o'clock. True to the sheriff's prediction they came in every undaunted fashion: by eight o'clock, the floodlit barnyard was a confusion of jeeps and other four-wheel-drive vehicles, sleighs and snowmobiles and tethered horses. The mourners divested themselves of coats or parkas, stood for a few reverential moments before the coffin, gave their condolences to Sutherland and his mother, who were stationed off to one side receiving cards and shaking hands. Then began the traditional separation of the species: the women sat all together in one room, gossiping and talking in hushed tones; the men commandeered one another in the kitchen, where the caterer had set up the liquor and the light buffet and occasional irreverent laughter began echoing out of the kitchen as the "Remember the time Archibald . . ." stories came tumbling forth from memory.

At eight-thirty, approximately, Marlena Occhapenti telephoned from Chicopee.

Emmett took the call in the kitchen, then walked quickly up to Sutherland with a look of puzzlement on his face. "Manfredi's wife's callin' from Chicopee, James. Funny, I thought she was in Italy."

"Talk to her upstairs in our bedroom," Marjorie told him. "Emmett, hang up the kitchen phone when they are speaking."

Emmett nodded and headed back to the kitchen. Sutherland's mother grabbed his arm as he made for the upstairs bedroom. "It would not be"—she searched for the word—"proper, I think, for Marlena to come here either."

"I understand, *ma mère*."

He went up to the bedroom and lifted the receiver.

"Okay, Emmett, I'm on now." The wall phone in the kitchen went off with a dutiful click and Marlena's voice came over the wire. She sounded as if she were speaking from far back in the darkness of a tunnel and he supposed she was heavily sedated still.

"Hello, James. I'm very sorry about your father. He was such a wonderful man. We found out from Otis this afternoon . . ."

He felt like telling her she was lying, that the Avgerinos family had probably found out from the Laconia District Court, but in the end, what did it really matter? The whole world had become a lie, and they had all learned a new language, an Esperanto of deceit and untruth, by which to communicate. One had to play by the rules.

"Yes, but he was an old man and had lived a full life and there was never a dull moment. It's harder to say this to you, but we're more devastated by Manfredi's suicide. We heard from Maggie this afternoon. We didn't even know he was in the country. He never even telephoned. We had no idea you were coming over either—"

"He never phoned? He never tried to contact you?" Her voice had reached the plane of the incredulous despite the sedation.

"Not once. And if he had, I would have rushed to him and gotten down on my knees to beg his forgiveness. The reason they deported him—the burning of the barn here on the farm? . . . Marlena, it wasn't Manfredi like everyone assumed —it was Archibald! My own father did it! He burned it down for the insurance money! He understood he was going to die, so he confessed to it! When Marjorie phoned me to tell me, I almost fainted—"

"Oh, my God, I think I'm going mad! It makes no sense, James! . . . Nothing makes any sense anymore. Why? Why would Manfredi kill himself? He loved life so much. . . . Nobody loved life like Manfredi did. . . . It just makes no sense . . ."

It makes no sense: The constant refrain. It was boring already and he supposed they would be hearing it for years to come.

"James," she began again, "I'd like to come up from Chicopee for Archibald's funeral. My brothers could bring me to Laconia—"

"I'd rather you didn't, Marlena. Some friends and neighbors are here now, but we've decided to make the funeral just a quiet family affair. The sheriff was here this morning with a warrant for Archibald's arrest, and by Saturday morning, when he's to be buried, the word will be all over the county. It would just be too embarrassing to have people come and then have all that explaining to do and listening to everybody's lying assurances that somebody must have framed him. I just don't think Marjorie's up to it all. You should understand better than anyone. As is, she's so ashamed she's leaving for Quebec the afternoon of the burial—"

"Oh, poor Marjorie. . . . Of course I understand, James." She paused a moment, then spoke again. "James, would you and Janie come to Manfredi's funeral on Monday in Boston? I don't think there will be very many people there . . ."

It was Sutherland's turn to be incredulous. "He's being buried here? In America?"

"No. No. In Italy. In Rome. There's just going to be a mass here in the North End. His old confessor, Monsignor Allergucci—you remember, the good-looking priest Manfredi used to play tennis with? . . . Well, he wants to say a mass for him before I take him home. It's at nine-thirty in the morning at St. Theresa's Church. We leave on the late-morning Alitalia flight from the airport after the service. I hope you can come—"

"Of course, Marlena. We'll be there." He felt like sobbing a little himself right then, but he found humor instead. "I take it the main event occurs in Rome, huh?"

She responded in kind, even laughing a little now. "Yes. I've telephoned his brothers. They're arranging everything. You know . . . the bishop, the band, the hearse with the plumed horses, the friends . . . He had a lot of friends waiting for him back in Italy when we got there. It was a little overwhelming at first—all those gifts and parties and big-shot Italians falling all over each other to help us get started again . . . Not like Chicopee, New Hampshire, if you know what I mean."

There were tears rolling down his cheeks now when he had not meant for any to flow. They were on terra firma again. They were out of the swampland of lies.

"I guess I do understand. They do things with style, those people."

"Everything except running a government. The notion seems to offend the Italian sensibility."

"Will you remain in Italy, Marlena?"

"Yes. I prefer the life there. Again, James, give my condolences to Marjorie . . ."

Then there was nothing left to say. So he told her simply, "Yes. Good-bye. We'll see you Monday morning at the church."

When he rang off, he went to the upstairs bathroom, splashed a little water on his face, then went downstairs to greet the last of the still-arriving friends and neighbors of Archibald Sutherland. He had no more thoughts about Marlena Avgerinos. He had thought too much about her already.

CHAPTER 31

The Gathering of the Clan

The storm was spent by six-thirty the next morning, and the radio announced they would have the runways cleared at the airport in Manchester by 9 A.M. At about six-fifty, Elaine phoned from Connecticut to say she and her husband would be arriving shortly before noon. He told her about the gravediggers, who would be there just after first light, and said he meant to help them, but promised that someone would be found to drive the truck to the airport and pick them up.

Dawn came shortly after 7 A.M. and the neighbors showed up as promised with the compressor and jackhammer in tow about five minutes later. Marjorie had coffee ready for them in the kitchen and they all tramped in, took off their coats and sat down around the table.

Sutherland asked if one of them would consider remaining behind and picking up Elaine and her husband. The response was a collective silence and Emmett chose the moment to seize the initiative and suggested it was Sutherland who should go rather than any of the rest of them, because Elaine was family, after all, and Sutherland would probably have a lot of things to say to her. Their instantaneous agreement startled and humbled him at the same time, and the foxy look of his mother's face confirmed his suspicion: that when it came to the grunt and toil of digging a grave through the ledge-infested New Hampshire earth, he was a liability, a kind of voyeur, in their eyes. So it was Sutherland who would go to Manchester.

In time they rose from the table, went out to the barn for the horses, hitched them to the compressor, and disappeared across the fields to the burial site through the snow.

If he remained stung by his exile from the grave diggers, by ten o'clock he was delighted to oblige his sister, Elaine. Anything to get away from the seemingly unending barrage of phone calls that he and Marjorie fielded in shifts. Marjorie got off more easily by far, for the ones who called knew her and spared her all the reminiscences. In the case of most of the calls Sutherland took, after the polite commiseration was given, the historical research began, and the realization of the truth of one of the most commonplace axioms was reinforced time and again: the world of individual lives was a very small and territorially defined place after all. When he had left the reality of Laconia and its schools and churches and sports and friends for the not-so-distant but different reality of Harvard and Cambridge and Boston, he might just as well have gone to the moon. He climbed into the truck and gratefully fled to the reality of Manchester.

The flight was on time and Elaine and her second husband, Hank, were the only two passengers on board to disembark at Manchester.

Sutherland marveled at the condition of his sister. Remarried six years, mother of two children, she looked as if she were ten years younger and children were yet a future consideration. Husband Hank was a doctor and had been her star pupil when she taught skiing at Vail. He had chased her up and down the expert slopes for two long spring-skiing months, then brought her home to Connecticut. Compared to her first marriage, with Hank it looked as if Elaine was intended to live happily ever after. Sutherland kissed his sister and shook hands with his brother-in-law when they came into the arrivals area.

"End of an age?" Elaine said wistfully.

"*Oui*. It sure looks it."

"I thought you were supposed to be digging your father's grave in the finest ritual fashion," Hank said.

"I was humiliated by some true-blue country gentlemen who didn't consider a Boston lawyer up to the task and sent me to fetch you."

Elaine was laughing now. "It's evident they were only thinking of your best interests. You'd have a lot of trouble snowing a jury when the only part of you they could concentrate on was your scarred and bandaged hands."

That brought more laughter, then Hank grew serious. "How's Marjorie taking it?"

"As usual. It was his time. I think she's more concerned with her travel plans. Did you know she leaves tomorrow after the burial for Quebec?"

"We knew. Found out a little before you did though, I think," Elaine said. Then she whistled. "Poor Trudeau. There's no way he could possibly know our little old bomb-chuckin' mother is about to enter his once-happy little country on a Greyhound bus."

That notion, the idea of their timid, slavish mother turning to separatist violence, sent Elaine into a fit of giggles that attracted the curious stares of a lot of people in the airport waiting room. Then their baggage came and they went out to the truck and headed north to the farm.

"Well, I guess congratulations are in order, brother of mine," Elaine said, pecking his cheek with a kiss. "How's Janie doing? You must be absolutely ecstatic! Even if you didn't quite get what you wanted. Isn't it wonderful that Arch lived long enough to see her! Mother said he was more flipped out than you were!"

"Yes, we're very happy," Sutherland answered. Then he heard the echo of his own voice in the cab of the truck and realized he had said it tonelessly and without enthusiasm and he snatched a glimpse of their puzzled faces in the rear-view mirror, so he knew he had to fake it. The way he would have to fake it when Maggie brought Jane to the farm that afternoon.

"Sorry, folks. I was just trying to remember something Archie asked me to do. Are we ecstatic, you ask? We're delirious! The whole thing was so effortless! If Janie were any younger, I'd beg her to have five more. One a year for the next five years!"

It nearly worked: Hank reached over and began clapping his shoulder effusively. But Elaine was not convinced. He caught another glimpse of her in the rear-view mirror and saw that her eyes were narrowed and her lips pursed and that meant that her intuition was hard at work trying to figure out what was wrong. Even now, Sutherland still had a healthy respect for his sister's perceptions. When they were kids, lonely on a farm far from town, she had practiced on him incessantly until there were times he thought she understood what he was going to say before he actually got a chance to say it. He knew she would start digging at his mystery today. He also knew she would be returning to Connecticut with the mystery unsolved.

They reached the farm within an hour and by the time the truck was parked outside the barn, Sutherland had absolutely reinforced his conviction that, as much as he trusted his sister and brother-in-law, there were certain things that they, like many other people he knew, were better off not knowing.

Marjorie rushed out to greet the new arrivals and Sutherland carried their bags into the house. Emmett and the neighbors had finished their task and were seated about the kitchen table warming up on Archibald's moonshine. Sutherland joined them while Marjorie took Elaine and Hank in to see Archibald looking like a lawyer. When they returned to the kitchen, both Hank and Elaine were misty-eyed but smiling, and Elaine, shaking her head, said it all. "God in heaven, I never thought I'd see the day—"

"What, Elaine?" Emmett asked. "That he'd be dead?"

"No, worse yet. That he'd end up looking like the gentleman his overeducated children thought they wanted him to be."

When the howling subsided, Marjorie sat them all down to bowls of the stew she had prepared for the gravediggers. Marjorie and Emmett drank coffee; the neighbors drank the moonshine; Sutherland, Elaine and Hank shared a good bottle of Bordeaux Hank had brought with him.

* * *

Elaine began her digging into his secret moments after lunch was finished and they stood up from the table. Marjorie was seeing the gravedigger-neighbors out and Sutherland and his sister began clearing the table.

"James, why don't you and I take a little walk together when we're finished? I have a feeling there's something you need to talk about. Something that's troubling you."

"There's nothing wrong with me, Lainey."

"There's something wrong between you and Jane, isn't there, brother?"

"Nope. We're quite happy, thank you."

"James, we've always talked to each other when we had a problem."

"Well, I don't need to talk, so it must mean I don't have a problem."

"I know you do, and I'll worry about it if you don't tell me."

"You won't worry. You'll just lie awake at nights full of curiosity to know what I know and you don't until the realization will suddenly hit you that there was nothing to know."

"But you aren't very enthusiastic about the baby."

"I told you I was preoccupied about something. Now leave me alone before we suddenly aren't speaking to each other for the next five years."

"I couldn't have that, James."

"Good. Now, there's nothing. I'm telling you."

"I don't believe you," she smiled sweetly as she stalked away to say good-bye to the neighbors. "I'll find out, too."

* * *

Jane arrived after the neighbors had left and Emmett was sent into Laconia on an errand. With Marjorie, Elaine and Hank, Sutherland had walked off lunch along the road in front of the farm. They were sitting at the kitchen table drinking coffee when Sutherland tensed at the unmistakable sound of a Volkswagen engine gearing down as it entered the farm. He knew it had to be Maggie delivering Jane from Boston. Marjorie knew also, apparently.

"*Mais alors, c'est ta femme, je crois!* Go out and meet her, *mon fils!*"

Dutifully, Sutherland went out to greet his wife as if their marriage, and all the world besides, were in a state of absolute perfection.

Both women emerged from the car and wore the same look of trepidation. He went up to Jane, threw his arms around her and held her tightly.

"James—I—"

"Fake it!" he hissed in her ear. "Hank and Elaine are here. They go back to Connecticut after the funeral tomorrow. Then we talk, woman. Hello, Maggie. We trust your usual enthusiasm cum discretion is operating in high gear?"

"Have I ever let you down, James?"

"No, Maggie, you haven't. I know it's a curious compliment, but you're the sort of woman a man could take on as a law partner."

"Sorry about Otis, James. It came as a shock to me, too."

"I'd like to strangle him, that sweet little elfin ex-lover of yours!"

"I did something better. I threw his ass out into the snow. He was very surprised to come home from work one early evening and find everything he owned being picked over by looters. He's been seen weaving drunk or stoned all over the city ever since."

"Good!" Sutherland spat. "Let's hope he weaves in front of a truck someplace. It wouldn't be punishment enough for this ridiculous chain of events he's set in motion."

He took their bags and they started for the house. Sutherland walked between the two women and Maggie spoke once more. "It was incredible about Manfredi, wasn't it, James? I mean you'd think he'd be the last person in the world ever to do something like that. It's just as Jane keeps saying, he loved life so much. . . . So what if he wasn't going to get what he came for? There must be children in Italy they could have adopted. Maybe there were some things we didn't understand. Maybe things weren't so happy with him and Marlena?"

Sutherland shrugged. "Who knows? We weren't exactly close neighbors after they left for Rome. He leaves again Monday morning on Alitalia, by the way. There's a funeral mass being said for him in the North End before the flight."

"Are you going?" Maggie asked.

"But of course. He was a friend after all, wasn't he?"

Neither woman said anything as they entered the house and he knew they had understood his meaning perfectly.

Maggie and Jane went softly into the room where Archibald lay and made their quiet good-byes before they joined the family at the kitchen table.

* * *

They made their token peace that night, and the ease of it surprised the rage right out of him. When the mourners, who numbered almost four hundred, had finally departed, and Marjorie, Maggie and Emmett were busied in the kitchen trying to find storage space for all the casserole dishes, pies and cakes the women had brought a second time, Sutherland and Jane took a walk in the moonlight that dimmed occasionally as fast-moving clouds scudded across the face of the moon. It was bitterly cold and the snow crunched beneath their feet and their breath smoke was clearly visible in the night. Since they did not choose to speak to anyone who might be driving along the road, they took the path toward Archibald's grave instead. It was well beaten down by now.

"I guess we have to talk, James," Jane said at length. "I asked you a question in the hospital, but you wouldn't answer it, so I have to ask you again. Are you going to divorce me?"

"I don't know."

"How long are you going to answer 'I don't know'? It's one thing to keep up appearances at my father-in-law's funeral and pretend that our marriage is absolutely sacrosanct, but if we try it for the rest of our lives, we're only cheating ourselves. And people aren't so dumb, by the way. Your sister Elaine is onto something."

"Sometimes Elaine is a nosy bitch."

"Elaine's just about the least bitchy female I've ever met. She's only concerned, that's all. But I'm sure if no one told her, she wouldn't guess what the problem was in a million years."

They were nearing the top of the pasture behind the barn. He turned to face her and took a strong grip on both her forearms. "I have no intention of telling her, Marjorie won't, and make damn sure you don't. Understand?"

"James, stop it! You're hurting me. Do you think for a moment I'd consider spilling the beans to your sister just to get the weight off my soul? It's out of the question. She'll never know from me."

He dropped her arms and they started walking again. To their right at the edge of the meadow was a forest of birches, ghostly white in the moonlight and groaning in brittle pain as they moved in the wind. To the left was the lake, dotted here and there with ice fishermen's shacks, the dust devils of powdered snow blowing between them easily seen in the moon's brightness. This winter night reminded Sutherland of all the beautiful things he had ever encountered growing up in New Hampshire. He wished Jane were not there to intrude upon them.

"You blamed everything on Otis today, James. But it's really my stupid indiscretion sometime back that started all this when you come right down to it—"

"Is it? Well, it's academic by now as far as I'm concerned. If Otis hadn't blown the whistle to Manfredi, I'd still be a duped father with somebody else's kid, who never once suspected since I completely bought Marjorie's little Québecois story and never gave it a second thought."

She shook her head depressedly. "That's why I think we can never stay together. You'd hate that child knowing how we came by her. Or if you learned to love her, it might come too late. It might take you years to get over your bitterness and anger. This isn't like it was with Edith. That was contempt and there's a difference. Part contempt for her, but mostly for yourself for having been ludicrous enough to marry her. Now you've got nothing but anger, the righteous kind, and that's dangerous stuff. And you haven't nearly vented enough of it, not even when you had Manfredi killed—" She sighed deeply as he stared at her in amazement. "Surprise you? You might as well know that Vogelmeister told me about those three heavies from East Boston you hired to do it. His conscience got the best of him during the evening after you'd been to the aquarium and he telephoned me to beg me to head you off at the pass. I know you were talking about a contract that day at the hospital, James, but I never really thought you'd go through with it."

They were at the edge of the creek now and he turned to face her, his face a sudden great wreath of a smile, a mock reverence in his voice. "And you didn't do it, Janie? You never once considered phoning the police? You love me that much? Enough to sanction the murder of your own ex-husband?"

"James, I love you. You're my husband now. . . . Do you think I'd be responsible for you going to jail?"

Just then the lip of the creek bank gave way beneath him; Jane stepped back to safety, but he tumbled down the snow-covered slope end over end, howling with laughter all the way. When he reached the bottom he righted himself and stood up, laughing still and brushing the snow from his hair and face. Jane stood peering down from the top, hands on her hips.

"James, are you losing your goddamned mind?"

"Somewhat, darling. But it's nothing to worry about."

• When he clambered up the bank, they walked arm in arm back to the house, smiling and kissing each other. They were still kissing as they walked in the door where the others still sat around the kitchen table and everyone clapped and cheered at the sight. Then the reaction turned to amazement as Sutherland went directly to the pantry, pulled the cork from a jug of Archibald's moonshine and poured himself a glass right to the rim. He told the others he wanted to be alone for a private moment with his dead father, marched into the room that held the coffin and closed the door behind him.

He touched his fingers to the awful liquor in the glass, then to his own lips, then to the cosmetized lips of his father where he held them for a moment of remembrance.

"*Merci, mon père.*"

PART VII

The
Final Things

CHAPTER 32

The Iceboats

They buried Archibald the next morning. It began with a short and simple service at the Presbyterian church in Laconia. Afterward they followed the hearse back to the farm, hitched the horses to the sledge and laid the coffin, contained now in a pine box, on the bed of the sledge. Then began the procession to the place of Archibald's lowering away.

Emmett led the horses first, and the pallbearers, the same men who had dug the grave, walked beside the sledge, holding ropes they meant to use to slow its descent into the creek bed.

Behind came the family on foot. Sutherland walked first with his mother, her arm through the crook of his. There was no evidence of sorrow in her face. Instead it was set and determined, and it came to Sutherland that she was not thinking of the immediate reality of burying her husband but looking far beyond to the promise of her return to Quebec. He knew she carried her euphoria quietly within her. He hoped Quebec would not disappoint her.

Hank and Elaine were next, and after them Jane and Maggie, then a line of about two hundred friends and neighbors, most of whom walked, though a few very old people had been mounted on horses for the passage through the creek. There were few young people anywhere to be seen. Most of the mourners appeared to be in their sixties or seventies, contemporaries of Archibald and Marjorie, the same people for whose names Archibald had searched obsessively through the obituary pages of the newspaper every day. He had that kind of mind. Every old friend or acquaintance that he survived he counted as a personal triumph that made the sun shine brightly for him even when there was no sun. Remembering, Sutherland looked up. The sky overhead was murky and gray.

At the graveside the minister gave a brief eulogy. Through it, Sutherland felt no sorrow. He stared not at the coffin but out on the expanse of the lake where iceboats flashed past, heedless of the burial onshore, their bright-colored sails dulled by the grayness of the sky where clouds whisked away in the wind. He smiled on the scene, mesmerized by its beauty, thinking of its absolute anomaly so close to the place where they were about the task of lowering an old man into the earth. But the pageant of the iceboats at Archibald's burial was Archibald's kind of pageant. Had he come from another culture, and not the scrub-faced rigidity of the one to which he was born, he would have provided for a brass band or clowns or jugglers to distract his family and friends from the hard fact of his coffin and the six-foot hole that waited beneath it. Sutherland understood this about his father: he had always been a crazy bastard within the limits of his rigidity.

Sutherland turned back to the end of the service. A number of the men and many of the women were crying, but Marjorie's and Jane's eyes were dry.

The minister ended his prayers, the lowering of the coffin began, and Marjorie made the announcement that everyone was invited back to the house for a catered buffet. But a good number had to leave, and they came up to her to make their good-byes. As she shook hands with each one, Sutherland saw the truth of what the neighbor had said the day they went out to burn the ground for the digging: she was somehow remote from them, an entity apart from these small-town and country people who blurred into a collective sameness before his eyes. He wondered if it was not because she was his own mother that she assumed this specialness, but in the end he decided that was not the reason: she was different. That's all there was to it.

Now the coffin rested in the bottom of the hole. The family

members each threw the traditional handful of earth onto its lid, then turned to follow the mourners back to the house, the last ones to leave the gravesite except for Emmett and the pall-bearers who were to fill it in. Sutherland walked with his mother and Elaine, and Elaine recalled an Archibald anecdote. They were all laughing until Sutherland stopped abruptly and his heart gave a little leap of fear. On the far side of the creek, standing on a little knoll, surveying and occcasionally nodding to people in the line of mourners that passed before him, was a tall, stocky man in hat and overcoat who puffed on a long cigar.

"I wonder who that can be?" Elaine asked.

"Mallory," Sutherland told her. "His name is Mike Mallory. He's a police detective from Boston."

"And nothing is troubling you, huh?" his sister asked.

CHAPTER 33

Au Canada

When the three reached Mallory, he had removed his hat and thrown away his cigar and was engrossed in conversation with Jane and Maggie. Hank, uncertain what was happening, stood a deferential distance away.

"Welcome to rural New Hampshire, Michael," Sutherland told him. "I'm afraid you're a little late, though. We just finished burying my father."

"My apologies, James, but I got lost. All these country roads look the same to me despite your explicit instructions. I found the Presbyterian church in town and the minister's wife finally steered me in the right direction."

"Well, Mr. Mallory, at least you got here in time to join us for a little buffet lunch," Marjorie invited. "I'm James's mother, by the way. This is my daughter, Elaine."

"I'm sorry, Mother," Sutherland said, "but for some reason I thought you two had met."

"My deepest condolences, Mrs. Sutherland. My very deepest condolences indeed. I never knew your husband, but I understood from James here many times what a fine, upstanding gentleman he was, and . . ."

Sutherland stopped listening to Mallory, whose poetic muse had caught fire and was singing the lilting Irish dirge for death. What the hell was Mallory doing here? And how much did he know? And who had told him? But of course: Otis. Done with treachery, he must now be crazed for vengeance on learning of

Manfredi's death. Not for a moment would Otis believe his friend Manfredi had killed himself.

"This is quite a glorious place, Mrs. Sutherland," Mallory told her. "Serene and lovely and right next to the lake. Swimming in the summer, skating in the winter, nature walks in the spring and fall . . . How many acres do you have, anyhow?"

"About thirteen hundred all together, including the woodlands."

"Will you continue farming it now that your dear husband has passed on to his reward?"

"No, Mr. Mallory, today is my last day after thirty-eight years on this farm." She turned to smile at him radiantly. "In a few hours I return to Québec, to the village where I was born . . ." Small tears gathered in the corners of her eyes, tears Sutherland had not seen for the death of her husband. "It is more than forty years now since I have been home."

Sutherland could see she had gotten to Mallory, set loose an arrow that pierced the thick hide of his euphuistic bullshit and silenced him the rest of the way to the house. They would talk later, Sutherland knew. Mallory had much on his mind.

They entered the house, where the mourners who remained had already formed a line and were moving along the row of tables the caterer's staff had set up. There was a bar also, and after they removed their coats Mallory took Sutherland's elbow and steered him toward it.

"We have to talk, James. We're going to need a drink."

At the bar Mallory ordered a bourbon and water, and Sutherland a scotch and soda. Then the detective joined the food line and put a small sampling of everything there was on his plate while Sutherland settled for a turkey sandwich. When he reached the coffee urn at the end of the line, Mallory inexplicably poured his bourbon and water from its glass into a paper coffee cup.

"Let's go outside, James. We can't talk in here."

They went outside into the twenty-degree cold carrying their food and drinks. Neither had bothered to put on his overcoat. Mallory sipped at his bourbon and surveyed the farmyard with a look just short of wonderment.

"You know something, James? I've never been on a farm before. Neither have my kids. Boy, they'd get a real bang out of seeing this place. Would you mind if I brought them up for a day sometime during the spring?"

"Bring them up for a month if you like. After today there won't be anyone here but the caretaker."

"What's in that barn over there?"

"Cows. About fifty of them."

"Can we see them?" Mallory asked, the deadpan set of his detective's face suddenly transformed to that of a child clamoring to get into a circus. Sutherland frowned in response. He was afraid of this man, of the questions he might ask, and he wondered now if the ineffably shrewd Mallory was not about the process of disarming him.

"I guess you'd better see them now since they've all been sold. I expect tomorrow or the next day their new owners will come and take them away."

The door to the barn was slightly ajar and they slipped inside, where it was many degrees warmer out of the wind and from the animals' heat. The cows were feeding, and when an occasional curious one lifted its head from the trough, Mallory, holding his plate of food against his chest, waved to it and gave it a name. At the end of the line he stood squarely behind the last animal and patted its rump.

"I wouldn't do that if I were you, Michael," Sutherland told him. "Cows are very stupid animals. They do unwitting things like suddenly lifting a leg, and their kick can send you right across the room."

Mallory left off patting the cow's rump and started to eat his food. Sutherland took a bite of his turkey sandwich and found it to be dry as cardboard. He washed it down with a slug of his scotch and threw the rest of the sandwich into an empty bucket.

"What did you want to talk about, Mike?"

"Stiffelio," Mallory answered through a mouthful of food.

"What about him? You told me he was pretty much dead."

"Oh, he's dead all right. Very, very much so. But a few little bitty technicalities have slithered their way under my office door since his, uh, suicide."

"Mike, I'd very much appreciate it if you would talk now and chew your food later. Okay? Now what technicalities are you hinting at?"

"Well, first off his name isn't Stiffelio. It's Occhapenti. Manfredi Occhapenti. He was here with a phony Italian passport reading Stiffelio because as Occhapenti he was persona non grata in these United States."

"I suppose you found all this out from Otis."

"Otis who?"

"Forget it. If you don't know Otis, it's just as well. If you're trying to get to the bottom of something here, it's a sure bet you'll never reach it if you start talking to Otis."

Mallory shoveled a forkful of potato salad into his mouth, chewed, then swallowed before he spoke again.

"So we forget Otis, whoever he is, for the time being. I've got nearly all the parts of the puzzle anyhow, James. I just need a few more and I think you can supply the answers I'm looking for."

"Maybe. Aren't you operating a little outside your jurisdiction, Mike?"

"Don't get lawyerlike with me, James. I may be a cop from Boston who's supposed to be home sick in bed with the flu today, but I bet that if you and I took a little ride into Laconia to the police station, I could prove to you just how chummy and fraternal we cops are. What I mean to say is I could make sure your mother doesn't leave for Quebec this afternoon."

"Mike . . . don't . . . please don't. She just buried her husband not an hour ago. She's been dreaming about returning home to Quebec for forty years."

"Yes, she did seem very excited about going, James. That's the best reason I know right now for you to help me with the missing parts of my puzzle. Okay?"

Mallory took another slug of his drink and Sutherland did the same, choking for a moment on the remnant of an ice cube until he spit it out on the floor.

"What is it you want to know, Mike?"

"Suppose we let me narrate a bit more and any place I make a wrong turn you correct me. Any place I come to a big hole in the road, you fill it in. Agreed?"

"Shoot."

"Okay. Quickly now to the point. This Occhapenti was your lovely wife Jane's ex-husband. This Occhapenti comes back to the States and starts harassing you with phone calls and playacting at suicide out on the Esplanade right in front of your building because he wants to entice you out for a little chat. This I know, James, because I was standing about two hundred yards away from you two on Christmas night, the first time you actually did go out to powwow. And unfortunately, I was standing on the wrong side of Storrow Drive the night that a little old lady with a very lethal-looking shotgun climbed out of a big blue pickup sporting New Hampshire plates and helped convince this Occhapenti that the rehearsals were over and it was time to go onstage. And today, of all things, here in this dreamy little Sutherland kingdom, I find both the little old lady and the pickup truck. Well, what say, James?"

"Jesus . . . oh, Jesus, no . . ."

"Yes, I'm afraid so, James. But let me continue. James, I'm the kind of cop who has a profound sympathy for essentially decent people who are driven to acts of desperation. But my sympathy took a brisk walk away from me when I returned from my car after calling into headquarters and saw none other than Crazy Joe De Santis, the terror of East Boston, looking very pissed off that someone had beaten him to the meat. Now we come to the first big hole in the road, James. What does Crazy Joe De Santis have to do with Manfredi Occhapenti?"

Mallory sat down then atop a bale of hay and started eating again as Sutherland began pacing a slow circle around the detective. His mind was groping desperately for an escape, but he knew there was no escape because Mallory knew too much already, and even if Sutherland kept silence it would be only a matter of time before the cop found his missing pieces.

"James . . . What was De Santis doing there?"

"He was . . . Oh, God, Mike, he was enlisted to eliminate

Occhapenti," Sutherland blurted out. Then he stopped his pacing, put his hands to his face and broke into a flood of tears. Mallory dropped his drink on the floor and furiously flattened the paper cup with his foot.

"Jesus H. Christ! James, how did you arrange for this—this disposal?"

"I went over to East Boston to a bar called Uteri's and struck a deal with our man De Santis. It was as simple as that."

"You're lying, James. You wouldn't know a person like De Santis. You wouldn't know the first damn thing about waltzing with a hit man. Who was the broker? Who set it up for you?"

"I told you, Mike, I did it on my own. I knew De Santis. He owed me a favor. I got his daughter off on a pot rap a couple of years back."

Mallory was eating again. He shook his head in the negative at the same time: "No, James, that's not how it was. Uteri's has a back room and Crazy Joe just about lives in it. If you actually did see him—and I have my doubts—there had to be a middle man involved to get you in there. Who was it, James? You might as well tell me now and save yourself some needless trouble because you know I'll find out sooner or later."

"I did it on my own, Mike."

"Who, James?"

"Me. Only me."

"Goddamn it! Who?"

Sutherland exhaled a long sigh, the breath wheezing out of him like air being forced from a bellows. Then he told Mallory what he wanted to know in a weak, strangled whisper: "Mordechi."

"Jesus, Mary and Joseph," Mallory whispered back as he put the last of his plate of food down on the hay bale beside him. Now there were tears in Mallory's eyes too.

"James, is it fair to ask who the fuck isn't in on this caper?"

Sutherland did not answer, instead held up his hand for quiet. He could hear the sound of footsteps running toward the barn, and when the footsteps hit the first planks of the barn's floor behind him, he knew it was a woman. Then Elaine was standing beside him, closely scrutinizing his and Mallory's tears.

"What's up, James? It isn't every day I chance upon two grown men crying in a barn. You two fall out of love or something?"

"No, we're just—" Sutherland began.

But Mallory took charge: "Forgive me, Elaine, for being such a selfish man on the day your father was buried, but I'm having a marital problem and James here is one of the few people I can trust to load it off on. He knows my wife well, so it's got him a bit upset too. There's a little matter of five kids being involved."

"Oh, I'm so sorry, Mike. Look, why don't I bring you two guys another drink? But after Mike's finished tearing out his hair, James, you ought to come back to the house. People will be leaving soon and they'll want to say good-bye. Let me see now, James is a scotch and soda and Mike, what can I bring you?"

"Bourbon and water, Elaine, thank you."

"Be right back," she said as she turned and headed for the house again.

"Thanks for the uptake on that one, Mike," Sutherland told him. "She's a curious lady and I had no idea what I was going to tell her."

Mallory picked up a piece of shrimp from the plate beside him and shrugged his shoulders as he popped it into his mouth: "Cops are born actors. It helps in our profession. James, let me ask you something else. How did your shotgun-toting mother get involved in this business?"

It was Sutherland's turn to shrug: "Call it a mercy killing for want of something better to call it. She, like a good many other people, was pretty crazy about Manfredi Occhapenti, and doing what she did was her idea of the easy way out for Manfredi. She was afraid of what De Santis might have done to him. She was also afraid that De Santis and his boys might put the squeeze on me every time they needed money for a long time to come." He began pacing again in a slow circle around Mallory. Then he blurted it out, heedless of the fact that he heard the crunch of Elaine's boots on the snow coming toward the barn: "I'm glad she did it, Mike. I did go to East Boston to try to stop De Santis. I never met a man who frightened me so much. They don't call him Crazy Joe for nothing. He might have taken Manfredi somewhere and tortured him for days before he got around to wasting him. That man is a killer!"

"You're right about that at least. If I had to arrest that guy I wouldn't try it with anything less than a platoon of cops. Shh," he suddenly warned as Elaine entered the barn. "Elaine, you're much too refined-looking a lady to ever make it as a cocktail waitress."

"You say the sweetest things, Mike. That must be why I made you guys doubles. Here, drink up, you look like you need them. Don't forget to come back to the house one of these days, James," she reminded as she turned about and went outside again. Mallory waited until he could no longer hear her footsteps before he spoke again.

"Well, James, I guess we've worked our way up to question numero uno. Why did Manfredi Occhapenti have to die? What did he want that you weren't willing to give him?"

"I should think you would have found out already from the Avgerinos family, Mike."

"Nope. That bunch is being very close-mouthed about this whole affair. They aren't looking to create any headlines. Occhapenti came here as Stiffelio and he goes back to Italy as Stiffelio. They don't understand the reason for his—shall we say—suicide, but the fewer people who know, the better, as far as they're concerned. Now what did he want, James?"

"The baby."

"Your new baby?"

"His new baby. He's the father."

Mallory's face registered his astonishment for a long silence, and then he emitted a low whistle: "Are you sure about that, James?"

"Blood types are unerring, Michael, and three doctors who know about this all can't be wrong."

Mallory stood up now and began pacing a circle beside

Sutherland. He took a sip of his drink and rattled an ice cube around his mouth against his teeth before he evidently swallowed it.

"You don't really have to answer this next question, James, because it's being asked by your friend Mike Mallory and not Mike Mallory the detective, but is it fair to ask how this Occhapenti got your wife pregnant? If memory serves, you two were living together a lot longer than nine months ago."

"How, Michael? Vintage wine, soft lights, oodles of sentimentality and all the rest of it. Plus the fact that I was out of town on the two occasions that Jane's—shall we call it insemination—apparently took place. The only thing that really surprised me was the fact that Jane turned out to be as fallible as the rest of us poor humans. I hadn't figured my darling wife to be that way at all, Michael."

Mallory clapped a heavy hand on his shoulder: "I hurt for you, James. I hurt for you very badly. This is Mallory the proud father of five rowdy Charlestown kids talking, not, as I said before, Mallory the cop. But I need to know more now, James."

"Ask away. You know practically everything there is to know already."

"How did Occhapenti find out the kid was his in the first place?"

"You met Maggie Hanson today, I believe, Michael. Up until a few days ago she was living with a guy named Otis who bats both ways in bed. He was the one who wrote Manfredi in Rome and told him he had fathered the baby, a baby Manfredi was desperate to have since his new wife turned out to be barren. Unfortunately, having children was an obsession with Manfredi."

"Yow! The plot, she does thicken. If this story ever makes it to court, the prosecution is going to have to provide road maps for the jury. But let's continue, James. There are some parts I still don't fathom. You were instrumental in getting our man Occhapenti deported and you knew he was persona non grata here, so why didn't you call up Immigration and send his ass packing?"

"He didn't come unarmed, Michael, and I'm not talking about that old Luger he was toting either. See this barn, Michael? It's brand-new because my own father torched its predecessor during the summer to collect the insurance money that put this one up. That, as we both know, is highly illegal and Manfredi found out about it and that knowledge was the ace he was going to use against us if he didn't get what he came for. He was particularly avid about using that ace too, since it would clear his own name. We charged him with burning the old barn down and the charge stuck. It was the main reason Immigration deported him."

"I'd say you overreacted, James. I hate to seem indelicate, but your father is presently asleep in his coffin back up there on that hill. If he's dead now he was dying then, and there isn't much the authorities would do to a dying man except try to get restitution for the insurance company. Your man Occhapenti didn't have to die."

Sutherland sighed wearily, then swilled down the last of his drink: "I guess we know that now, Mike, but we didn't when this business started. First off, I was seething with rage and like many other people, a New England WASP isn't always above the need for vengeance. And secondly, until the day before he died I didn't have an inkling that my father was even sick. I just assumed like a lot of other people that a man with his kind of energy had to be fit as a fiddle and strong enough to serve a jail term. But when I found out he was very sick I did try to stop De Santis. About that I'm telling the truth. I went to Uteri's and tried to reason with him, but he wasn't about to be convinced. He said that the hit man was on his way and there was no way to call it off, and he hinted at worse things for me and my family if I dared go to the police. I don't doubt for a moment that he meant it."

Mallory's eyes had a reflective look to them as if he were dredging up the past and trying to recall how often the name of De Santis had figured into it. He took another sip of his drink before he spoke: "Oh, I'm sure he meant it all right. He might not try anything as drastic as actually wiping you out, but you can bet you'd be quaking in your boots for a long time to come wondering when that guinea monster was going to make his move. Of course, he might never, but you'd never know. Crazy Joe isn't completely crazy. He's a pretty savvy psychologist who understands the uses of intimidation. Boy, would I like to slap his ass into Walpole! I'd like to see him chained to a wall in that place for about the next thirty years!"

"I tried to warn Occhapenti too, Mike. I told him what was supposed to happen and tried to get him to run away with me before De Santis showed up, but he wouldn't believe me." Sutherland shook his head miserably at the memory: "He kept insisting I wasn't capable of doing such a thing."

"I saw that little confrontation too, James. I couldn't figure out what it was all about, but I knew one minute you were pleading with him and the next you were pretty pissed off after he knocked you down. If I had any brains I should have intercepted you coming back across that footbridge over the drive and found out what the hell was going on."

"I wish the hell you had, Michael, I was flat out of options at that stage of the game."

"Except for your mother."

"That wasn't the kind of option I had in mind, friend. Believe me, seeing her down on that Esplanade with a shotgun was the absolute surprise of my life."

"Offhand, as far as Occhapenti is concerned, I'd say your mother's presence beats the shit out of a run-in with Joe De Santis and his pals. Okay, James, one last question. Besides Moskowitz and your mother, who else knows about the De Santis contract?"

"My shrink, a doctor named Vogelmeister, who tried his damnedest to talk me out of it, and, alas, Jane, my wife, who didn't try to talk me out of it."

Mallory, still pacing, had a smile on his face that could only be described as sardonic. He mouthed another ice cube, then swallowed it before he spoke again: "Tsk! Tsk! What a mess! I have never in all my career seen so many innocents bungling around on the inside of one spittoon. A shrink, a wife and her stung husband, a mother and a deli owner. All untutored amateurs who were naïve enough to think that they had a pesky fly of a problem on hand that would go away with one thump of a flyswatter. Cripes, De Santis! In your church don't they ever talk about the incarnation of evil?"

"What are you going to do, Mike?"

"I don't know. I have to think this one through for a while."

Sutherland glanced at his watch: "What about my mother? Her bus for Montreal leaves Laconia in less than an hour."

Mallory grimaced before he spoke: "She can go for now. I can always get her back if I have to. Far be it from me to ruin a friend's mother's euphoria when all it depends upon is getting a look-see at some terrain she left behind so many years before."

Sutherland did not know what else to do, so he threw his arms around Mallory in a bear hug of gratitude: "Thank you, Mike! Bless you for understanding so much!"

"Save it, James," the other told him, backing off and draining the last of his bourbon. "I have a thing about being nice to other people's mothers since it appears I failed my own so bitterly."

"How could you fail her? You're a settled married man with a fine wife and batch of wonderful kids. You've often told me that. She should be proud of you."

Mallory clapped a hand on Sutherland's shoulder again and steered him toward the door to the outside: "My mother wanted a priest. She could give a rat's ass about my fine wife and wonderful kids. Let's go, James. I'll say good-bye to your mother and sister, retrieve my coat and head back to Boston. You know about Stiffelio-Occhapenti's funeral mass in the North End on Monday?"

"Yes, his wife gave me the news."

"Are you going?"

"It seems like the right thing to do. Yes, we're going. And you?"

"Yes, indeed. I wouldn't miss it for anything, James. Afterward we talk. I wouldn't make too many client appointments for the rest of that day. We'll need some time together."

They walked across the farmyard to the house, where Mallory made his good-byes, extended his condolences again and

wished Sutherland's mother a safe return to Quebec. Then
Sutherland saw him outside to his car and watched Mallory
drive away. He had no idea what Mallory might have in store
for him after the funeral mass for Manfredi Occhapenti on
Monday morning. Marjorie could be charged with first-degree
murder.

* * *

Then it was time to drive to the bus station in Laconia and
the Sutherlands' widowed mother made it an easy leave-taking
for everyone.

Emmett brought down from her bedroom her two bags
which had already been packed. Sutherland might have wept
at the sight of them. Old and tired leather pieces, they were the
exact two she had arrived with at the farm thirty-eight years
before. On the side of each were stamped the initials of her father.

She kissed Emmett good-bye and wished him luck, then em-
braced a weeping Maggie and thanked her for all she had
done. Elaine, who was also crying, was next, then Hank, who
was trying not to cry. She admonished them to have more children and invited them to drive up to St. Etienne for a visit
that following summer. They were not going to see her off in
Laconia; she had asked them to stay behind. Sutherland and
Jane were to drive her to the bus station.

She took a last look around, then cracked them all up by saying simply, "*Alors*, at least I did not have to pay rent
here . . ."

Then they went outside, got into the Jaguar and left the
farm for Laconia. On the way, she smiled on familiar sights
along the road and only once broke silence.

"*Dîtes*, everything is fixed now between the two of you?"

"*Oui, ma mère.*"

"*Bon. Restez tranquille.*"

But that was all until they arrived at the bus station in
Laconia. They parked the car and went inside the station to
wait. Jane and Sutherland sat near her luggage while Marjorie
went to buy some magazines. When she returned, they were
predictably in French: two Montreal weeklies, each of them a

variety of political commentary. She sat beside them and began leafing through the pages and Sutherland could think of absolutely nothing to say. In another minute, a woman sat down beside Marjorie, began looking at the pages of the magazine as well, then broke into the unmistakable patois of Quebec. Within minutes they had decided to sit beside each other on the bus for the trip.

In ten minutes more the Michaud bus rounded the corner and rumbled up to the station, its sign indicating it was destined for Montreal. They rose and went outside for the boarding. Sutherland had the baggage ticketed while Marjorie talked briefly with Jane, then quickly kissed her good-bye when the boarding call was given. Sutherland kissed her good-bye as well, then she climbed into the bus with a single backward glance and a wave, and then was gone from sight.

The thought came vaguely to Sutherland that his mother was a variety of lend-lease from Quebec that was finally being returned.

CHAPTER 34

A Society of Friends

Manfredi's funeral mass and send-off to Italy was the last business to be attended to before the grim prospect of the confrontation with Mallory began.

On Monday morning, with Jane and Maggie, Sutherland drove to the North End church for Manfredi's American funeral.

There were few people in attendance. The coffin was wheeled in to soft organ music and Marlena came behind it wearing a black veil, supported between her two brothers. About ten members of the Avgerinos family and the traitor Otis brought up the rear. They took their places on the right side of the church and Sutherland, Jane, Maggie and Moskowitz were the only ones on the left. Vogelmeister had refused to attend.

The two groups scrutinized each other across the aisle. Marlena gave a small wave and the rest of the Avgerinos crowd stared with a kind of thoughtful perplexity, as if they were trying to decide what, if anything, the Sutherlands or Maggie had to do with Manfredi's death. Otis cringed fearfully in their midst. Turning toward the rear of the church, Sutherland saw that there were another ten or so old black-clad Italian ladies in the last pews, and he supposed they showed up like a death chorus at every funeral because it gave them something to do until they reached their own mortality. Mallory sat behind

them in the very last pew and nodded and smiled wanly to
Sutherland.

Bells tinkled and Allergucci the monsignor came onto the
altar and the mass began. Sutherland followed the ritual movement of the priest and his acolytes back and forth across the
altar, but his mind was elsewhere preoccupied—first with
Mallory and what Mallory might do, until he decided this consideration was witless and a waste of time for any halfway intelligent civil-liberties lawyer's mind. The question was not
what Mallory might do, but what he must do and would certainly do because Mallory was an honest cop and a churchgoing Catholic to boot. And if he knew his man the way
Sutherland thought he knew his man, then Mallory was inca-
pable of living with the guilt of keeping silent about what
Marjorie had done. Sutherland turned about again for another
look at the detective. He played the beads of a rosary slowly
through his fingers and did not acknowledge Sutherland this
time. Instead he gazed off to one side of the church where a
weak winter's morning sun streamed through a stained-glass
window of some martyr of the early Church who was being
burned alive at the stake. The set of Mallory's face was pained
and confused at the same time. Before him the black-clad old
women responded in unison to the monsignor's prayers and it
was the first time Sutherland realized the mass was being read
in Italian.

It was all over soon. The cortege marched out, and on the
church steps Sutherland, Jane, Maggie and Moskowitz wished
their final condolences to Marlena while avoiding the other
members of the Avgerinos family and Otis. Then they went to
the car, waited for the hearse to be loaded and followed the
procession out to the airport.

The Alitalia 747 was waiting for boarding. The four and
Mallory went up to the observation deck and met Mrs. Crawford, who had brought Manfredi's daughter to the airport as
Sutherland had asked. Then they went beyond the glass parti-
tion to the outside deck, leaving Crawford behind, and waited
for the jet to depart. Sutherland carried the baby in his arms.
The day was now brilliant with sunlight and a clear and cloud-

less blue sky. The towers of the city rising up over Beacon Hill were perfectly defined across the harbor. It was cold though, and a brisk wind came in from the Atlantic.

The passengers were boarding. They could hear the thump of their feet down the enclosed rampways to the plane, then they were seen moving on the inside through the windows.

Manfredi's coffin came out on a small truck that had a hydraulic platform to raise it to the cargo hatch level. It stopped a moment and Allergucci came out, said a brief prayer, sprinkled it with holy water, then made a sign of the cross over it and the truck moved away as the priest went hurriedly back inside the terminal.

The coffin was the last thing to be loaded; then the enclosed rampways were drawn away and they saw for the first time that the flagship name on the plane's nose was Città di Roma. Maggie and Jane were both crying now and Sutherland could barely restrain himself from joining them.

Mallory was the only one to break their long silence, nearly shouting to be heard above the wind: "That poor bastard! That poor, poor innocent bastard!"

The jet engines started and after a minute the behemoth began moving away from the terminal. It taxied an interminable time to the distant end of a runway, then suddenly began its ascent, a giant roaring along the runway looking as if it would never fly until all of a sudden it lifted off the ground then began rising sharply into the air.

It flew northwestward for a long moment, then turned back toward the city, passing over it, the bright red, green and white of the Italian colors gleaming in the brilliant sun, then reflecting in the mirrored walls of the Hancock tower as it gained its eastward course. Then it rose quickly due east moving out over the Atlantic. Sutherland held up the child to see it off until it was a mere speck over the bright-blue waters and Manfredi Occhapenti was returning home to Rome forever.

"We have to talk now, James," Mallory spoke again. "You and I have a lot to talk about."

PART VIII

Mallory

CHAPTER 35

Brother Tony's Car Wash

They left the International Terminal at Logan in Mallory's unmarked car and were silent on the way back to Boston through the Sumner Tunnel. Mallory was first to speak as they crossed beneath the Fitzgerald Expressway and headed south along Atlantic Avenue.

"What are you going to tell the wife, James, if she asks about our quickie departure after seeing off the recently deceased to Italy?"

Sutherland shrugged, then braced a hand against the roof as the car hit a massive pothole then slammed down hard on the cobbled roadbed beyond: "She's feeling at a bit of a moral disadvantage these days, I wager, so she probably won't ask. But if she does I'll just say you needed some lawyerly advice. . . . Maybe refer to that little fib you palmed off on my snoopy sister Elaine out in the barn about having some sort of marital problem. Maybe that you're thinking about a divorce."

They stopped for a light at India Street across from the wharf and Sutherland reached over to switch on the car's radio for the news. Mallory reached for the same knob seconds later to switch it off as the light changed and they started off again.

"I do, James."

"You do what?"

"I do want a divorce."

"Oh, God, another institution crumbles. Why? You always struck me as one of those in-it-for-life Irish Catholics with the neighborhood, the house, the wife, the kids, the church and the Fraternal Order of Police all sleeping in the same bed. Where are we going, anyway, to talk about the divorce you think you want?"

"To Southie. To my brother Tony's car wash."

"Is it fair to ask why we couldn't go to a nice bar someplace or to my office?"

"Because I always do my best thinking and escaping inside a car in a special bay Tony has down there. He can put the sprayer on automatic and leave me in there for hours if I want. I find the water soothing. That's why."

"You're a complicated guy for a cop, Mike."

"I don't need any condescending from you, pal. You're in a bit of a jam yourself. Or at least your mother is."

"I suppose we're going to talk about that, too."

"Yes."

"What are you going to do to her?"

"We'll talk about it at Tony's place."

Mallory turned off Atlantic Avenue onto Summer Street just before the hulk of South Station. They crossed the bridge over Fort Point Channel where garbage bobbed outward toward the Harbor on the tide. They followed Summer into the heart of South Boston, then turned onto East Broadway, where Tony Mallory's gas station and car wash were only a block away.

Mallory swung the car in front of the single bay whose door was closed and sounded the horn. A man years younger than Mallory with an impish face and slight of build emerged from the station's office and walked quickly toward them. He went around the front of the car and Mallory rolled down the window to speak with him.

"Hi, Tony babe. This is James Sutherland, a friend of mine. This is my brother, Tony, James. Tony, I need some time in the bath."

"It's been waitin' on you for hours, Micko. You forget you called this mornin'?"

"I remember now. Sorry, I had some things on my mind. Open her up, okay?"

Mallory's younger brother fished in his pocket for some keys, unlocked the door and raised it. Then Mallory drove inside and turned off the ignition. Water leaked from the sprinkler system and a mound of ice was forming beneath it against one wall.

"You want the brushes today, Mikey, or just the water?"

"Just the water is all we need."

"Okay. It's all yours. Honk on it when you want out."

Mallory nodded and his brother left, and the door swung down behind them. Then the water came on, spraying in many jets from a wand that circled the car on an overhead rack.

"Soothing, isn't it, James?"

Sutherland shrugged, throwing up his hands: "Whatever turns you on, Michael. What do we talk about first? My mother or your proposed divorce?"

"I like you, James. I like you very much. So I'm going to put us on an equal footing. I'm going to share a little secret with you so it won't seem like I'm holding an ax over your head while your hands are tied behind your back. I'm going to give you an ax to do battle with, too."

"Does this mean I'm going to find out something so awful about you that by using it I could effectively prevent you from bringing charges against my mother?"

"I don't know. Let's put your mother on the back burner for now. I'll have to work that one out later."

The water jets continued around the car and a trickle of water started down the inside of the window beside Sutherland where the rubber molding was evidently loose.

"We're leaking, Michael."

"Fuck it. It's not my car. The taxpayers bought it."

"What's the terrible secret?"

Mallory exhaled a long sigh as of exhaustion and turned to stare at Sutherland. There was the same pain in his face that Sutherland remembered seeing in the church earlier that morning. He found his imagination working overtime: Payoffs? Extortion? Prostitution?

"I have a mistress, James."

Sutherland frowned his disappointment: "That's the terrible secret? What the hell's so terrible about that? Lots of married men have girlfriends on the side. As far as I'm concerned, you haven't given me much of an ax to clobber you back with."

"I'm having a hard time dealing with it."

"From my vantage point it looks like you're just plain wallowing in guilt. Your priest sounds like the better man to talk to about this. Does your wife know about her?"

"Nope. Only Tony, my brother, knows. None of the rest of the family because I'm pretty sure my sisters would blow the whistle to my old lady."

"Well, that's one less problem for the time being. Have you broached the possibility of a divorce to your wife?"

"Yep. Couple of days ago."

"And . . . ?"

"No way. She's a pretty fair old Catholic herself and divorce and abortion are about one and two on her list of many taboos."

"So? Lots of guys' wives won't agree to a divorce. Why not just keep up the façade of the marriage and have the girlfriend too?"

"Because Rita and I—that's the girl's name, by the way—are tired of sneaking around like we've been doing for the last three years, and last week I got an ultimatum from the lady."

"Oh. Oh. Marry me or else, huh?"

"I can barely stand to be away from her, and I couldn't stand to lose her James. I think the pain would be more than I could handle. James . . . James, I'll tell you what. I'll make a deal with you. Your mother goes free to live out her days up there in Quebec if you can convince my wife to give me a divorce so I can marry Rita."

Sutherland stared at the other, dumbfounded. "Jesus Christ, Mike, are you losing your marbles? That's no deal. That's out-and-out blackmail if I ever heard of it. If you couldn't convince your wife to give you a divorce, how do you think I'd be able to?"

"You're a lawyer, aren't you? You're supposed to be an arbitrator, a go-between for people. You handled lots of divorces in your time."

"Yeah, but always between basically consenting parties.

Cripes, talk about a John Alden in reverse gear. Instead of asking for the lady's hand in marriage for another guy, I have to ask her to unshackle her husband. I'm warning you right now, Mike. I might have to tell her about your Rita. And if somehow, by the grace of God, I'm able to convince her, then you'd better not welch on your promise about my mother."

"You have my word of honor, James."

He extended his hand and they shook on it. Mallory's hand was clammy and cold. Then he started the engine, turned on the wipers and sounded the horn for his brother. In less than a minute the water stopped and the garage door clanked upward behind them. Mallory backed the car outside. Brother Tony came up beside the driver's window and Mallory rolled it down.

"How'd it go?" Tony asked.

"He bought it."

"Let's hope to Jesus she buys it now. He's never met Catherine, has he?"

"Not yet, though I've spoken to her on the phone a few times."

"Well, then, luck to you, Sutherland," Tony said as he extended a grease-stained hand past his brother. "You're goin' to need it, too. She can be a real tough bird, that sister-in-law of mine. One time she slugged me right in the puss for drinkin' too much."

"Nice meeting you, Tony," Sutherland said. "Thanks for the free car wash. Where are we off to now, Michael?"

"To Trader Vic's for lunch with Rita. She's a real cultivated lady. She's a college teacher. I want her to know I have at least one cultivated friend in the world."

"Oh, God, Sutherland," Sutherland moaned. "How has so much luck managed to find you lately?"

"You're farther ahead than you think, pal. Tony doesn't know anything about what happened to Signor Occhapenti. He never will either. Nor does any other cop in Boston. And if you win my case, you'll never have to worry about that one either."

CHAPTER 36

Miss Malone

She was an exceedingly plain woman, Rita Malone. Overweight and devoid of makeup with intense, darting eyes that served to underscore the certainty in Sutherland's mind that she had begun her final assault on the heart of Mallory. Even the near-darkness of Trader Vic's at midday did nothing to hide the scrubbed asceticism of a spinster who taught French at the Newton College of the Sacred Heart. Sutherland found her sincerity embarrassing and her nervousness irritating. She munched daintily on greasy spareribs, then bolted three Mai Tais in quick succession before she began her interrogation. Mallory, himself an educated man, seemed stupefied in her presence. His face was childishly aglow and proud when she invoked a few throwaway phrases in French as if to prove his assertion that she was truly a cultivated woman.

"I suppose you'd like to know how Michael and I became" —she searched for her kind of word and when Sutherland was about to say "lovers," whispered—"paramours."

"It may not be that important, Rita," Sutherland told her. "I think what we've really got to discuss is how to approach the problem at hand. That is, how to deal with Mike's wife's intransigence, shall we say?"

"I'm not a homewrecker. I don't want you to think of me that way."

"Of course not. People's lives change. Their needs and affections change. Everyone understands this."

"I was just coming out of Filene's down on Washington Street one Saturday morning when a young man snatched my purse right from my arm. Michael apprehended him. He was off duty and shopping with Catherine and two of their daughters that day. Afterward we all had lunch together. At the Parker House."

Sutherland wanted to hear no more of the reminiscence filled with the breathlessness of middle-aged lovers. Across the table from him they held hands tightly now, giddy with the recall of Mallory's heroics, of the lunch with Mallory's wife and two daughters when their first timid gropings toward one another had begun.

"Then nothing happened for a month afterward," Mallory supplied, "until we had to decide on a school for my oldest girl and I suggested to the wife that we look into that college where Rita taught. It was a ploy. You understand, James. Just to get near her again. Anyhow, my daughter goes there now."

"She does exceedingly well in French, as you can imagine," Rita said. She said it with unexpected wickedness, like a lewd woman obsessed with her sexuality, Sutherland thought for a moment until he changed his mind: No, she said it like a starved middle-aged spinster who had suddenly awakened to the wonder of her sexuality in her fifties. To finding out that it actually existed. To Sutherland's mind, for the first time ever, it made her consort Mallory seem somehow a little pathetic. It was as if he were abandoning his wife to run off with one of the aunts from Joyce's *Dubliners*.

"When will you speak with Catherine, uh, James?" she asked.

"No time like the present, I guess. I'll just go back to the office and give her a call and ask her to come in for a little talk. Call me at home tonight, Mike."

"This means everything to us, uh, James," she said, suddenly clamping a chilled hand over his. "She's got to give him his freedom. We can't go on like this, meeting in places where we hope nobody recognizes us, making love in the back of a station wagon in Michael's brother's car wash, and—"

"That's where you make love?" he asked incredulously. "In Tony's car wash?"

They nodded their heads in unison like two embarrassed teenagers caught by parents returning home early. Sutherland knew he had to leave them then. The world as he knew it was teetering on the edge of insanity. He himself felt on the verge of hysterical laughter that was partly for them and partly the need for relief from everything that had overwhelmed him since the few days before Christmas when the mad scenario of the past week's events began. He stood up and shook hands with both of them, saying good-bye and inviting them to pray for him. To join their hands in fervent prayer over Mai Tais in Trader Vic's.

Then he hurried outside and leaned against the tiki in front of the building and laughed and laughed until his sides literally ached from the laughter. People stopped to watch and apparently wondered at his madness.

"Jesus! This Boston can be a crazy town at times!" he bellowed at a man who sauntered past.

"You don't know the half of it, buddy," the man answered. "You don't know the fuckin' half of it."

CHAPTER 37

Mallory's Wife

He phoned Mallory's wife from the office. She lifted the receiver after a long moment and he heard the sound of a baby crying close by. "Shh. Shh. Quiet, love. Hello? Who is it?"

"Mrs. Mallory, this is James Sutherland."

"Oh, hello, Mr. Sutherland, how are you? I'm afraid Mike isn't here right now."

"Well, actually, it isn't Mike I wanted to talk with. It's you. I wonder if it would be possible for you to come into my office this afternoon?"

"I'm afraid it's not. As you can hear from the shrieks, I'm babysitting a neighbor's child until this evening."

There was a silence while he thought of proposing going over to Charlestown to see her. He could hear her patting the baby's back and trying to quiet it and then she spoke again: "What is it you want to talk with me about, Mr. Sutherland?"

"Well, it would be better if we spoke face to face, Mrs. Mallory. I could hop in a cab and come right over to Charlestown."

"So you can try to persuade me to give Mike that divorce he thinks he wants so he can marry that middle-aged chippie of a French teacher he's been screwing in Tony's car wash down there in Southie? The one he thinks I don't know about? Bullshit, James! Save yourself a trip. You can't be much of a man to let a fat-assed turkey like Mike talk you into running interference for him, even if you two are friends!"

The voice he knew as soft and deferential and incessantly curious from previous telephone conversations was now rasping with anger. The child she held started screaming anew with fright and she raged at it—"Shut up, you little bastard!"—and Sutherland had a terrible vision of her heaving the child against a wall in a blind fury.

"Mrs. Mallory . . . please! Please calm yourself!"

"The rotten bastard! All these years of marriage and getting myself knocked up every two years so he can finally have that fucking linebacker he spent so many hours on his knees praying for, and now he wants out, huh? Well, there is no out. He married me in our parish church two doors from this house and that's the same church he'll be buried from when his time comes! Rita Malone can go teach French in hell! The only reason I haven't blown the whistle on her out at the college is because my own daughter's a student there and I wouldn't want the word floating around that her old man was having an affair with that lace-curtain whore of a faculty member! Imagine the sniggers that would set loose?"

Sutherland sighed at his own impotence. He stared out the windows and across the harbor toward the airport, where another plane was lifting off the runway in the brilliant sunlight and dreamed about running away from it all on one of them. Then he remembered Manfredi and wondered where over the Atlantic the Alitalia jet bearing his body home was now.

"Mrs. Mallory—Catherine—is it fair to ask how you found out about Mike and Rita?"

"Everybody knows, James, I assure you. The only one who doesn't know anything is one hot-shot Boston sleuth named Michael Mallory. You see James, I'm a Southie girl and down there people don't usually miss a trick. The word got here to Charlestown after about his second trip to the car wash and his own sisters were the bearers of the news. They'd like to gouge his eyes out. I had to swear them to secrecy so the children wouldn't find out. Anyhow, do we have anything else to talk about, James? This baby I'm holding just shat his diapers. They need changing and you must pretty much get the drift of my answer by now."

"It'll hurt him terribly, Catherine, that answer of yours. She's going to leave him if they can't marry."

"What a misery! What an awful, awful misery! Boy, that's a pretty dumb argument from somebody who's supposed to be such a bright State Street lawyer. Do I have to paint you a picture to make you see that that's exactly what I want to happen? One, I want to hurt him the way he hurt me, and two, I want her to go away so I can keep up the façade of my marriage and my neighbors' respect into the bargain. Now, why don't you just get in touch with your friend and pass along the word, dummy?"

"He's got something on me, Catherine. On my mother, actually. He'll use it on me too if I don't come back with the right answer from you."

"I'm sorry for your mother, then. Very sorry indeed. Goodbye, James."

She put down the phone with a gentle clicking sound. Sutherland put his head down on the beautiful leather-top desk Jane had given him and grieved with the hopeless despair of it all.

CHAPTER 38

The Greatest Anger Yet Seen

He returned to the apartment just after first darkness, feeling foolish over his desperation in having spent the remainder of the afternoon since his talk with Catherine Mallory compiling a list of the countries that did not have criminal extradition treaties with the United States. In the end he could not imagine shipping his mother off to any of them to live out her days as a fugitive who could never return to Canada. El Salvador? Ecuador? What unfit places for a dream-filled old lady whose passion was to help found a new French-speaking nation in North America.

He plodded wearily through the apartment doorway and found Mallory already there, talking with Jane and sipping nervously on a drink. Mallory's eyebrows arched immediately in a question, and before Sutherland had even removed his overcoat, he supposed the detective had deduced his wife's answer.

"Where's the baby, Jane?"

"Upstairs in the bedroom. Maggie's there with her now."

"Why don't you go up and look in on them? I want to talk to Mike alone."

"All right. See you later, Mike."

" 'Bye, Jane. Thanks for the drink."

They watched as she mounted the stairs, then disappeared through the bedroom door, closing it behind her.

"No go, huh?" Mallory asked.

"I wish we weren't such desperate men, Michael, because women spot vulnerability like hawks spot field mice and they know how to use it. You sent me on a fool's errand, Michael. Her answer was an unequivocal no, and she knows everything, by the way, as does a good part of South Boston, evidently, including your sisters, who blew the whistle on you to your wife. About Rita, about the car wash and I guess about whatever else there is to know."

"Oh, Jesus, no. How could I have been so stupid? Do my children know?"

"She says no. That's why she never said anything about it to you, apparently. She didn't want to drop any hints around the house."

Mallory stood slowly, leaving his drink balanced on the arm of the sofa, and walked to stand at the window. He stared across the frozen Charles in the direction of Cambridge, but Sutherland guessed he was not really seeing the neighboring city. His eyes were glazed and his face plainly showed the pain of his forthcoming loss.

"I'm going to lose her, James. Rita will leave me now. There'll be no way to make her stay."

"I'm sorry for you, Mike. I could see you cared for her very much. I know this is probably an off-the-wall suggestion, but you and Rita could run away. You could—"

He turned and smiled ruefully at Sutherland. "And leave a wife and five kids with no support in Charlestown? Plus a bigamy charge, an arrest warrant and sure-fire excommunication from my church? Sorry, pal, it's just not in the blood. Mine or Rita's, for that matter."

"What about my mother, Mike?"

"One thing at a time, James. First I break the news to Rita and we have our last cry in Tony's car wash together. Then I go back to Charlestown to face the Iron Mistress and take my lashings there. Then we get around to the business of your mother, who forced a man to kill himself. A man whose coffin is probably being unloaded in Rome right at this very time."

"Mike . . . please, I tried. I tried to do what you wanted me to do. Didn't I?"

"But you didn't succeed, did you, Jamie boy?" Mallory told him in a voice whose unmistakable rage was fast approaching the threshold of his wife's own earlier that afternoon. "And because you didn't we're both very miserable men right now, wouldn't you agree?"

Sutherland stared now toward Cambridge also, not seeing it either. They were both silent except for Mallory's heavy breathing that quickened as his anger grew. Then it exploded. "I've made up my mind. If I have to suffer, then you're going to suffer too. And suffer plenty!" he screamed as he shoved Sutherland savagely aside and headed for the door, the bitter tears already bolting from his eyes. "All I care about is my Rita, Goddamn you!"

He opened the door and then slammed it furiously aside. In the hallway Sutherland could hear him repeatedly punching the elevator call button as if it could cause the damn thing to rise up and take him away any faster.

CHAPTER 39

St. Mary's Parish, Charlestown, Massachusetts

It was late February when the first real thaw began and the ice started breaking up on the Charles. Mallory had still not made his move and Sutherland could not sleep at night from wondering when it would happen. He lost weight and grew haggard and several times overheard his office staff whispering about how terrible he looked. He was distracted in conferences with his clients and realized one afternoon with a sudden shock that he was spending hours of every day watching the jets rise off the runways at Logan. Rita Malone phoned him every night through January and into early February to sob out her brokenhearted sorrow and deplore her loneliness until he told her finally there was nothing he could do for her and she was never to phone him again. He had no use for Jane or her baby. He slept in the guest bedroom to be away from them and when she came to him many nights to beg him to let her at least lie beside him in bed, he told her to go away, once even physically shoving her out the door. In early February he finally decided that his mother had to be warned about the danger he felt was very imminent. But when he got through to

St. Etienne de la Neige and heard the lilt of her perfect joy and the boisterous greetings of his Oncle Armand and Tante Thérèse, whom he had never met, he found he had not enough courage to do it. They ended the conversation in English, his mother clucking her tongue over how rusty his once-perfect French was becoming. He stayed up practically all night running the tenses of French verbs through his mind and realized with near-panic that she was right. The ice of the Charles was breaking up right on time, but there was no hint of thaw in the icy terror in Sutherland's heart.

Then on the last day of February the news came. The phone rang at about 8 A.M. as Sutherland prepared to leave for the office and it was Mallory's brother Tony, crying so bottomlessly that he was nearly incomprehensible.

"James . . . this here's Tony, you know, Micko's brother . . . ?"

"Yes . . . yes, Tony, I remember . . . the car wash. What is it? What's wrong?"

"James . . . they're both dead . . . the both of them!"

"Who? Who?"

"Micko 'n' Rita . . . James, they killed themselves! They drove into the special bay last night 'n' turned on the water 'n' left the motor runnin'! I come here this mornin' to open up 'n' found them naked as jays 'n' blue from the monoxide . . ."

He sobbed again for minutes before he could bring himself under control. Tears ran down Sutherland's cheeks and his own body was wracked with sobbing too, because of his certainty that the thaw had just begun.

"You knew he went to college, didn't you James? That he had a degree in philosophy?"

"Yes, I knew, Tony. It was easy to tell he was an educated man."

The car wash brother grew enraged: "Well, he was too fuckin' educated, if you ask me! If he had to go to school why couldn't he go to the Jesuits? No, he has to go to B.U. 'n' picks up a lotta weird ideas from all them lefties that was there durin' the time he went! He was supposed to go to seminary 'n' become a priest! A philosophy priest! Cripes Almighty! Suicide! That's against our church, did you know that?"

"No, I didn't, Tony. I'm very sorry . . ."

Then he heard the brother taking deep breaths to calm himself and in another minute he was able to speak again.

"James . . . there's this here letter . . . it tells why they did it . . . you know about being in love 'n' all that stuff, but there's a part for you too . . ."

"What does it say? Read it to me, Tony."

"It says . . . it says tell James Sutherland that he was the friend that meant the most to me 'n' that nobody knows nothin'—"

"Tony?"

"Yeah?"

"Burn that letter. Don't show it to the police whatever you do. Understand me? Burn it or it will be in all the papers and your family won't want that."

"I—I understand, James. . . . I wasn't gonna give it to the cops· anyhow. . . . Even if I did, it wouldn't be in the papers. . . . You know how them cops are. They take care of their own family first before anybody, you know? Only what did he mean? Was you two guys queer together or somethin' like that?"

"Of course not. We were very good friends, that's all. That's all Mike could have meant."

"Thank the Jesus God! If that was it—if the word ever got out here in Southie—well, that kinda shit don't fly too good down here, know what I mean?"

"Yeah. I know what you mean, Tony. Have you phoned the cops yet?"

"Yeah. I gotta hang up now. They just come. They're out front now."

"Don't forget the letter, Tony. Don't give it to them. It was an accident, remember? They turned on the motor to warm up the car and the fumes got to them. Right?"

"Yeah, right . . . I got it straight now. Uh, Sutherland, one last thing . . ."

"What, Tony?"

"The wife . . . Would you tell her, uh, the news? I don't think I know how to do somethin' like that. . . . I never done it before, you know?"

"I don't think it's my place, Tony. Ask one of your sisters to do it. They seem to have a pretty fair track record when it comes to bearing bad tidings over to Charlestown."

"Huh?"

"Nothing. Phone one of your sisters. They'll know how to tell her. I'm afraid I've got to say good-bye now. Again, I'm very sorry . . ."

"Yeah . . . I know how you feel. . . . I know how you liked Micko so much. . . . I gotta hang up now, they're comin' in. Thanks for the good legal advice, you know?"

Sutherland returned the phone gently to its cradle, took a handkerchief from his pocket and put it to his eyes. He cried softly now, no longer shuddering, the monster tension ebbing out of him already meeting the flood tide of relief that was on its way in. He did not notice that Jane had come into the room until he lowered the handkerchief one time and saw that she stood in stocking feet not far from where he sat on the edge of his bed. Then he felt the soft touch of her hands on both sides of his head before she spoke.

"James, what is it? Is it Marjorie?"

"No, friend, it's Mike Mallory. He's dead. He and his girlfriend gassed themselves last night by leaving their car engine running on the inside of a closed car wash. Lovers' suicide, I think they call it."

"Oh, my God, how tragic, James! I know how you must feel, too. He was your friend. You always said you liked him quite a bit—"

He reached up and removed her caressing hands from the sides of his head before he stood.

"It would surprise you to know, Janie my dear, how friends sometimes have ways of becoming dangerous liabilities. But then again, maybe you don't need to be reminded. Think of your ex-husband Manfredi, after all."

Then he walked past her out of the room, needing to wash his eyes before he left for the office. He did not bother to tell her that Marjorie was safe now. She had never known that Marjorie had been unsafe during those two long, agonizing months.

* * *

He anticipated Catherine Mallory's phone call all that day at the office, but it never came. She did not call that night either when he returned home, nor the next morning at the office again. But at a few minutes past noon, just when he meant to leave for lunch, the intercom on his desk sounded and his secretary told him there was a Mrs. Mallory waiting who would like to see him privately. He asked the secretary to show her in and stood to greet her, expecting the tear-stained, splotchy face, the broken heart that would have to be consoled, the ruined future that would need to be recharted. But there was none of that when she entered. Only the resolute set of a very determined woman's face with narrowed, dark eyes that looked as if they had not even bothered to cry over her husband's dying. What struck him, too, was that despite her incessant house toil and the bearing of five children, she was still a far prettier woman than the lover, Rita Malone. He motioned her to a chair beside the desk before he took his own seat again.

"I guess Mike's sisters brought you the bad news, Mrs. Mallory. His brother Tony phoned and told me he didn't think he could do it, so I suggested your sisters-in-law might be the best ones since you indicated you were rather close to them—"

"How thoughtful of you, James. No, it wasn't those two old statue-worshiping flagellants from Southie who brought the news. It was the Fraternal Order of Police. Two very embarrassed flatfeet who couldn't meet my eyes and stood there shuffling nervously in the carpeting until they finally stammered out the word."

"What did they tell you?" He heard the echo of his own words and realized the caution in his voice.

"A bunch of shit. The lies cops always tell to protect other cops. They told me that Mike had driven in there and turned on the water to think the way he often did and must have turned on the engine to warm the car and fallen asleep while it was still on. It was a good story. And I relayed it just so to the children, who swallowed it whole because they always got such a kick out of the idea of their old man who sat inside a running car wash to solve crimes. I guess only you and Tony and I know the real truth, huh?"

He threw up his hands: "How did you find out, Mrs. Mallory—Catherine?"

"The hard way. Not through any brilliant deductive reasoning, let me assure you. Even before those cops left the house I figured out that the dummy had driven into that car wash to commit suicide since he spent most of his free time moping around the house pining for his lost love, Rita. But it never dawned on me for a second that he didn't die alone. Not until I decided to ring up La Malone and tell her the tragic news. . . . Oh, don't get me wrong, James. Part of it was the spurned wife rubbing salt in the wound for sure. But part of it was also dutiful, because I didn't think anybody would let her know unless she happened on that phony obituary the cops are getting ready for the *Globe*. So I phone her apartment and no Malone. And before I even got a chance to phone the school, my daughter comes home all freaked out over her daddy's accidental death and just happens to mention offhand that her favorite teacher, Miss Malone, died yesterday also. Oh, boy! Oh, boy! Same time, same station. My, my, what a fucking coincidence! Absolute verification of the fact was wrung out of my creepy brother-in-law, Tony!"

She lit a cigarette and stood up and began rapidly pacing the length of the room, expelling her pent-up hurt and anger in the exhaling of cigarette smoke with a noise more audible to him than a hissing steam pipe. Sutherland looked hopefully through the window toward Logan. There, perfect timing, a jet lifted off the runway just when he needed most to wish he was aboard and getting away.

"Do you know where she died, by the way, James?"

"Not in the car wash, I guess."

"Nope. Certainly not bare-assed naked in a car wash with a

much-decorated Boston cop. She died at home from an over-
dose of pills. People at the college—faculty and students—did
seem to remember under prompting that she was rather depressed and not herself lately." She started to laugh now: "You
know something, James? I laugh when I hear people talking
about the Mafia brotherhood. Because it doesn't equal a fucking fart in a hurricane compared to the brotherhood of cops.
And I know what I'm talking about. I was married to one of
those mothers for twenty-some-odd years—"

He stood, knowing this had to end soon: "Is there anything
you want me to do, Catherine?"

She stopped her rapid pacing and moved slowly toward the
door now. When she reached it, she stood a moment with her
hand on the doorknob: "Yes, James, there is. We bury him in
two more days from St. Mary's in Charlestown. I want you to
be a pallbearer at his funeral. Since you two were such good
friends, I want you to participate in this sham right to the bitter end. By our rules."

Then she opened the door and walked out, closing it softly
behind her.

* * *

So: they waked Mallory after a nearly extinct tradition in
some mortician's palazzo that was too small for the large numbers who came to pay their condolences. They read a mass over
the suicide's remains in St. Mary's Church, where he had been
christened, received first communion, married and then worshiped nearly every Sunday of his life. Finally they planted
him in the parish cemetery.

Mallory was a heavy man. With five other pallbearers,
Sutherland struggled up the long flight of steps that led from
the hearse into the church. Inside, in addition to members of
Mallory's and his wife's families, were platoons of police,
greater numbers still of neighbors and friends, a generous scat-
tering of city and county dignitaries and people from the district attorney's office, representatives from the American Le-
gion and Knights of Columbus and even a troop of Boy Scouts
who had come in uniform to say farewell to their scoutmaster.

During the mass, Sutherland realized the truth of something he had always suspected about Mike Mallory. The man had been truly an enigma who must have balanced on a greased tightrope for most of his life. For this he had needed special graces, special powers to make others see him as he chose to be seen. Witness the full house of mourners here now who thought he had died unfairly for one reason when only three people in the entire church knew that he had arrived near the end of his days feeling trapped and opted for his own death as the only way out. Joiner and loner. Aspiring philosopher-priest who had become instead a cop with a reputation for terrible swift retribution. To all appearances a long-married, stable family man who was willing to throw it over in a trice for the beauty he saw or thought he saw in a homely spinster's mind. Perhaps, after all, there had been too much of Mallory. Mallory had not run confused and aggrieved to his death. He had doubtless intellectualized the need for it, then gone ahead and done it. Sutherland knew he would not ever stop thinking about the man for the rest of his life. The priest who spun out a eulogy now from the altar could not possibly fathom a tenth of what Mallory had been all about.

The ceremony at the cemetery was brief. When it was ended Mallory's brother-in-law approached him and said: "My sister would like you to escort her to the limousine."

He was not surprised. He expected she would have something more to say to him. She had arrived at the church with her widow's face transformed into a sardonic mask of a smile that never left her all the way through the mass and the graveside ceremony. Halfway through the ceremony he could tell from the frownings and whisperings that her smile was making some people visibly uncomfortable.

She walked beside him slowly toward the waiting car, silent until she opened her purse and took out a small newspaper clipping. It was from the *Globe*'s obituary column of the day before.

"They buried Rita Malone yesterday from the college chapel. I found out there were barely ten people at that service, James."

"Make you happy, does it?"

"Yes, it does," she assured him as she scanned the hundreds who walked across the graves to waiting cars. Then she lifted the veil and reached up to peck a kiss on his cheek: "I was a part of the reason all these people are here. Not Rita Malone. Good-bye, James. Take care."

"Take care yourself, Catherine," he told her. But he did not kiss her back as he escorted her the last few yards to the car and saw her inside. Then he walked the brief distance to the limousine that waited for the pallbearers, reading the few lines as he went. There was little to say about her. She had evidently not bothered much with cloaking herself in the raiments of a larger life. At the car he crumpled the clipping and dropped it onto the frozen grass. God knows where they had buried her. She was not from Boston and he knew he would never care enough to try finding out.

* * *

At home that night he made love to Jane for the first time in four months. He found it took a long time. He had grown used to his celibacy and the passion he evoked now was altogether different from the effortless passion of their many days together before the baby's birth. He was saddened that it was so, and when they were done and she lay beside him crying softly, he understood what it was. A wariness about her had entered him and by now, he was certain, entered her about him as well. He could see it in her eyes as they worked to bring themselves to climax. He knew it would always remain in him, too, for as long as they were still called man and wife. And ever afterward if another woman somehow came into his life. He knew also that she was crying for what they had lost, that absolute completeness of their love for each other that could never return.

Across the room, Manfredi's baby began howling in her crib. Sutherland got out of bed before Jane began to stir and lifted the child into his arms, holding her against his naked chest and patting her back gently, the way he had seen others do it.

Annabella, liking it apparently, stopped crying in moments more.

He moved slowly toward the window and, when he reached it, stood staring out at the Charles. The moon was bright and he could see that the ice flocs were creeping downstream. He supposed that the tide must be going out and that the locks to the harbor were open to let the ice out with it. They were into March now; the river would not freeze again.

He suddenly thought of his age and what it meant. He would be thirty-eight soon. A genuine middle-aged artifact, a necessary respecter of the omnipresent signs in life that called for caution. But he smiled to himself when he recalled the past. He had done that right too, been everything he was supposed to have been: smug and proud and overly confident, but never nearly cautious enough.

He turned away from the window and carried the baby to their bed, where Jane sat upright against the headboard now, watching him steadily and puffing on a cigarette. He slid into bed without waking Manfredi's daughter and sat very close to his wife. She put out the cigarette and kissed him softly on the lips.

"Been a hell of a winter, huh, friend?"

"Yep. You can say that again."

"But things worked out, the way things always do, I think."

"Yes," he agreed again, thinking of the litter of bodies in the wake of the winter's happenings.

Dear God, what an incredible price had been exacted.